P9-AFI-753

also by J. R. Salamanca

The Lost Country
Lilith
A Sea Change

EMBARKATION

EMBARKATION

J. R. Salamanca

Alfred A. Knopf
New York
1973

THIS IS A BORZOI BOOK
PUBLISHED BY ALFRED A. KNOPF, INC.

Published in the United States by Alfred A. Knopf, Inc., New York, and simultaneously in Canada by Random House of Canada Limited, Toronto. Distributed by Random House, Inc., New York.

Library of Congress Cataloging in Publication Data

Salamanca, J. R. Embarkation.

I. Title.

PZ4.S158Em [PS3569.A458] 813'.5'4 73-7292

ISBN 0-394-46028-6

Manufactured in the United States of America

First Edition

To the memory of
my grandparents,

Joseph and Annie Nuttall

NOAH was the first tiller of the soil. He planted a vineyard; and he drank of the wine, and became drunk, and lay uncovered in his tent. And Ham, the father of Canaan, saw the nakedness of his father, and told his two brothers outside. Then Shem and Japheth took a garment, laid it upon both their shoulders, and walked backward and covered the nakedness of their father; their faces were turned away, and they did not see their father's nakedness. When Noah awoke from his wine and knew what his youngest son had done to him, he said,
"Cursed be Canaan . . ."

GENESIS 9: 20–25

In what torne ship soever I embarke,
That ship shall be my embleme of thy Arke;
What sea soever swallow mee, that flood
Shall be to mee an embleme of thy blood;
Though thou with clouds of anger do disguise
Thy face; yet through that maske I know those eyes,
Which, though they turne away sometimes,
They never will despise.

from John Donne's
"A HYMNE TO CHRIST, AT THE AUTHOR'S LAST GOING INTO GERMANY."

EMBARKATION

"JUST WHAT IN GOD'S NAME DO YOU MEAN TO IMPLY BY *that*?" Sylvie said. "Do you mean to suggest by any chance that we killed *him*, for the love of God? That monster? Is there any one of us that doesn't have the scars of his teeth and claws all over us?"

She was speaking of our father, who was dead by assumption and probably by assumption only, if the drowned *are* dead, his medal glinting on his dirty chest and his yellow dog's eyes staring through fathoms of Chesapeake Bay water, amiable but questing, and undeterrable, like those of a beagle trotting through frosty grass on a winter morning toward some doomed, delicate thing betrayed to him by the perfume of its blood and its legendary wings. She turned her head impatiently and looked out through the darkness of the front porch toward the wild persimmon tree under whose mooncast shadow I had crouched twenty years ago and stared down the cliff to watch that man stand spraddle-legged in the surf and shout Shakespeare at the stars in a voice like a shattered gong. My God, what a voice he had, the bugling of a frenzied, ravening, wounded, inspired hound with a rattlesnake very likely hanging onto the tip of his tail, a fox trap clanking from one paw and just ahead of him in that icy, chiming bush, the Dove of All Doves, The White Dove of the World. What I always wished I had gotten was that voice which would have made me the greatest actor since Kean, but what I got were those great ragged ears, a taste for Jack Daniel's, and a slightly shipwrecked look. Oh, a little more, maybe, maybe the beat of iambs in my blood that made me want, like him, to stand on some floodlit beach and trouble deaf heaven with my bootless cries, but along with that dangerous meter in my pulses I should have inherited a beagle's voice to bellow in, dog's eyes to pierce the dark, and a blue hound's nose to smell out milky-feathered treasure. I didn't, though, bushes were always bears to me, not dovecotes, he was the one who should have been the actor, my God yes, he could have played Falstaff without makeup because there he was already with his gnawed ears and lightning-scattered hair and blue nose and something the matter with his feet that made the toes of his shoes curl up like barrel staves within a week of purchase. I myself, when I was in my prime, ran more to Second Citizens, Attendant Lords or if I was very lucky, Wounded Sergeants, I say when I was in my prime because nowadays almost anybody who watches T.V. would recognize me instantly as the guy with the excruciating headache that starts all the way back at his coccyx or who changes his destiny by buying a can of Command or who opens his medicine cabinet and is confronted by a boob whose only possible contribution to the human race is that he smells good, which could possibly have been one of the reasons why my father was dead before his time. A thought which after a good many years of consideration I had just proposed to Sylvie.

"I wish for God's sake you wouldn't be so *urbane*," she

said. "People seem to think the most sophisticated thing in the world, these days, is candor. I mean *absolute candor.* It's become just one Goddamned confessional, the whole world. Everybody shouting, 'No, *I* did it! *I'm* the guilty one! *Me!*' Talk about sick. Talk about flagellation."

Her boy friend, the Professor, murmured and made a little convulsive movement of dismay or possibly of congratulation and touched her hand with which she was now indignantly plucking a shred of cigarette paper from her lip.

"Anyway," she said, spitting, "do you think Poppa gave a damn about what either one of us was doing? Not since the day we pulled out of here, boy, you know that as well as me. He didn't even come up to College Park for graduation. Not even when I got my M.A. He couldn't have cared less."

"I guess you're right," I said, it was the best thing to say to Sylvie when she got going. Behind us, inside the house, Momma had lit the kerosene lamp (because although we had a refrigerator and a television set Poppa had refused all his life to install electric lighting), and I could see her leaning toward Jamed at the table, trying to get a spoonful of lima beans into his mouth. He was flapping his hands and grunting rapidly as he did when he was tired or excited, and she would pause occasionally to brush back the brown curls from the good side of his forehead. The other side, the side that was caved in above his right eye, was left unillumined by the yellow light, and the deep irregular-edged depression was like a black hole in his gilded, beatific, twenty-five-year-old child's brow. That was one of the scars Sylvie was talking about, that pool of shadow in his brain.

"Poor old Jamed," I said. "You think he knows? He seems to, somehow."

"I don't know why the hell she didn't just tell him," Sylvie said. "She's got to, sooner or later. Or one of us does. Me, most likely." There were June bugs bumping against the door screen: pitter-patter, pitter-patter, that gentle, blundering, insect passion for light. "Oh, listen to that sound," Sylvie said. "God, every time I hear that sound—God, listen, Aaron."

"June bugs," I said.

We all stood listening for a while and the Professor for some reason started nodding in a sort of poetic way, he seemed to feel that there was a perpetual demand for his approval for any phenomenon that happened to be developing in his presence, I don't know from whom, God maybe. Inside the screen door Jamed was snorting and batting at the spoon and getting pretty excited, he started yelling, "I want to see Sylvie! I want to see Sylvie!"

"I'm right here, Jamie," Sylvie said, raising her voice for him. "I'm right out here on the porch. Now you eat your beans like a good guy, and then we'll play some dominoes. I'm not going anywhere." She turned back to the bay, which lay black below us in the moonless night, like a maw, making merciless digestive noises along the shore. It had swallowed my father and it was softly, awfully, digesting him. "I don't know what the hell she's going to do," she said, lowering her voice. "Just what in the hell is she going to do?"

"Well, maybe we can get her to have Mrs. Cryer come up and stay with her, for a while anyway. They'd get along fine. She won't have to worry about money, or anything. I mean even if she doesn't sell the shop. I think he had plenty of insurance."

"Oh, don't you know he did," Sylvie said. "Don't we all just know he had plenty of insurance."

I knew what she was talking about and I thought it was a good bit short of charity but I didn't say anything because her face had a wracked look as if she might be undergoing something like rape, which is what it was, in a way. I knew what she was feeling, that grief inside her like a pain in her womb, I knew because I was feeling something very similar, we were discovering together that this is the only real initiation there is in life, the first real violation, this kind of grief, and that what our father was doing to us was what he had done to God knows how many black girls under the persimmon trees along the shore and God knows how many others of all colors, what his intention had been, probably, toward every living thing he ever met, he was ravishing us, he was taking our virginity, at last. Sylvie's and mine, anyway, Jamed's he had already, or maybe Jamed had lost his senses trying to preserve it, I never knew which.

"My God, there's so many things to think about," she said. "Just getting this porch painted, for example. None of them can even drive, for God's sake. What are they going to do in an emergency? They couldn't even get up to Offutt's if there was a northeaster and the roof blew off or something. You can't trust Jamie to cut a little firewood, even."

"Well, hell, you know Mr. Offutt would come down if there was a storm or anything. They *have* got a telephone. Listen, Sylvie, you're trying to think of too many things at once. It'll work out."

The Professor nodded his approval and put his hand on Sylvie's shoulder.

"Aaron's right," he said. "You're upset, that's all, Syl. You're all boiling over inside. It's a mistake to try and cope with anything right now. You'll feel a hell of a sight steadier in the morning."

"Oh, I know, I know," Sylvie said. "Don't you think I know that? Let me blow off a little steam, for God's sake."

The three of us stood and looked out over the black water below us and we saw far out and fainter than the Pleiades a pair of low stars twinkling in the fragrant murk that comes off the sea on summer nights but they were not stars because they were red and green and were matched with too mortal a precision and they were moving up the coast with that almost imperceptible and thrilling stealth of distant boats. Then we saw that there was a third light riding with them, a thirty-two-point white stern light from an ensign staff, the three of them making what we recognized now as the sweet trinity of a ketch with her riding lights afire, alone on the midnight sea. Sylvie and I did, anyway, and well we might because our father had spent a lifetime prowling those waters, lighting the bay skies with that very constellation, and the nights the four of us had spent on that front porch, Momma and Sylvie and Jamed and me, watching for that jewel ablaze in my father's rigging while he sat roaring drunk at the helm somewhere between Port Federation and Baltimore had seemed as long as a lifetime each. So now Sylvie said, "Oh," in an undone way and put out her hand and touched me. I took her hand and clenched her fingers lightly and we stood there almost not breathing, watching. As a natural thing, as any kind of credible, earthly, spectacular, it was impossible, of course, because it was six days since he had vanished somewhere south of Cambridge in a Force Nine gale, and as a miracle, I thought, as a resurrection or something, it would have been a particularly outrageous, a particularly sleazy one, but anyway we stood there watching with our breath held to see if those lights would make for Port Federation because, after all, the sleazier it was the more likely Poppa was to be involved in it. But they moved on up the bay, of course, as slow as frost forming on your heart, toward Baltimore.

"Now stop that fuss, Jamed," we heard Momma say inside the house, "you just stop that fuss and eat your beans, and then Sister Syl will play some dominoes with you, like she said. Won't that be grand?" She warbled to him like a young wife to her baby, I had forgotten what it was like, I didn't know how I could have stood it for so long, him sitting there twenty-five years old with a pouty face and drivel on his chin and his eyes gone shallow as a sparrow's. On the wall above the sofa there was a big framed picture of the *Anabel Ellis* with her foresails set full, lifting to a violet sea, he used to stand there sometimes and lay the palm of his hand flat on the glass pane, staring with that wide, sweet, blasted stare, and I would wonder if he remembered anything. I didn't think he did, I prayed not, I wished I could remember as little.

WE ALL GOT IN BED TOGETHER, SYLVIE AND JAMED AND ME, because the storm was making so much noise we knew Momma wouldn't hear and even if she did she was too worried to carry on much. So I shook Jamed and said, "Let's go get Sylvie and make a tent."

He was scared, Jamed always was scared in storms, he was very delicate. He had little bitty hands and the purplest eyes. Outside we could hear the wind in the wire fence and the apple trees groaning and every now and then a twig or branch would rattle against the siding or crash against the shutters or go skittering across the shingles. "Wow-ee, it's a-blowing," Jamed said, big-eyed.

"Come on, let's go get Sylvie," I said.

"Uh uh, I'm staying here," Jamed said, so I sneaked out the door and into Sylvie's room myself. She wasn't asleep, she was up on her knees in bed with her cheek pressed down flat against the windowsill, trying to see up between the slits of the shutters. I poked her in the rear and she said, "You crumb, Aaron, you better not do that."

"Come on and get in bed with us," I said. "We're going to have a tent."

"O.K.," she said. "But if we get caught I'll say you made me." So we sneaked back around the corner and got in bed with Jamed and made a tent. I left the door open a crack so we could see Momma where she was sitting at the table with her shark's-tooth collection. We let Jamed be the tent pole because we figured it would keep his mind off things. We got stuff off the bureau, a hand mirror and a comb and brush and a jar of Vaseline, those were our utensils, we couldn't ever think of much else to do but cook. It was always the same game, we were lost in the North Woods in a terrible blizzard and running out of food and ammunition.

"What would you like to have for dinner?" Sylvie said.

"Moose," I said. I always said that, Sylvie whacked me.

"You crazy," she said. "You know there ain't no moose. Now you get out there and catch us some fish."

"O.K.," I said. So I opened up the blanket to make a door and threw my line down off the edge of the bed into a river that was down there and fished.

"Hey, Jamie, Aaron's going to catch a octopus," Sylvie said, giggling, but he wouldn't talk, he just sat there being a tent pole with his head holding up the blanket in the middle, he was worried. I fished for a while and Sylvie fussed around with her pots and pans, humming.

"You reckon Poppa's dead?" Jamed said.

"How in the hell could Poppa be dead?" Sylvie said, quick, she was waiting for it. "You are crazy as a bat. There ain't no northeaster can kill Poppa, don't you even know anything?"

"I heard some men up at Offutt's say it could," Jamed said. "I taken some Coke bottles up there yesterday evening and these men was talking. One of them said, 'He's going to get it next time, you just wait and see.' I heard him."

"Don't you know there ain't nothing but crazy people up there at Offutt's?" Sylvie said, her voice rising. "I think you are the dumbest thing in Port Federation. In the whole state of Maryland, even."

"They said Poppa was crazy," Jamed said. "This guy did.

They said he had more luck than any one man, and he'd done run out."

"You children hush, in there," Momma called. "Now you go to sleep, I'm not going to tell you again."

We looked out the crack of the door and saw that she had raised her head to look toward the bedroom, scowling, not so much because we were carrying on as because we had interrupted her worrying, almost as if she had been listening to music and we had started stomping or shouting or something and broken her attention. She had these shark's teeth, ancient ones, petrified ones, black and shiny as coal, with sawtoothed edges, some of them, that she kept in an old Roi Tan cigar box and whenever she was waiting up for Poppa which was about five nights a week she would get them out and spread them around on the oilcloth, sorting them out in the proper sizes and shapes to make a necklace out of. I didn't know if it was going to be for Poppa but if it was it was a beautiful idea, he would have looked great with a necklace made out of shark's teeth. We hushed up and watched her for a while through the crack until she settled down and started pushing around the shark's teeth again, not really paying a whole lot of attention to what she was doing but just sort of keeping her hands busy, and her eyes. Then we went on with the camping game again, but it wasn't much of a success, Jamed was not really playing, none of us was. After a while we gave up and just lay there looking up at the ceiling, listening to the wind. There was a long golden line slanted across it where the light from the lamp came through the crack of the door, and when a heavy gust would hit the walls the door would swing a little in the draft that swept through the house and the line would widen and then thin slightly, like a nerve beating slowly in your head.

"I sure wished Poppa wasn't out there," Jamed said. Jamed loved Poppa better than any of us, we all knew that. And it was funny, because he couldn't do hardly anything to suit Poppa, not like we could. He was the youngest and littlest and most delicate, more delicate even than Sylvie, with his little hands and brown curls and squirrel eyes. He couldn't throw a ball right, he hated guns, he turned blue in about five minutes when he went swimming, he got lost every time we went to the Calvert County Fair, he was always getting stung by jellyfish and would stand there screaming, once he painted himself green all over with Magic Marker, he had colitis, and, worst of all, he couldn't sail. I think Poppa would have forgiven him anything but that and maybe even forgiven him that if Jamed would have tried, but he wouldn't even try. He was scared of boats, you could see that, he started shivering the minute he got on one and didn't stop till he got off, even if it was August. He didn't do anything right, he got lines fouled just by looking at them, he dropped heavy things like the anchor on the deck and made dents in it, he broke a compass once, he spilled Karo syrup in the chart drawer. He was sure he was going to get drowned, he told me once, "I'm going to get drowned sometime, I just know it, Aaron, and fishes are going to eat my brains." Poppa would roar at him when he did those things and sometimes cuff him up alongside of his head and Jamed would stand there with his face all screwed up like a prune, crying as quiet as a mouse. If Momma saw it she'd freeze her fingers into claws and tell Poppa in a shrill whisper that he was a devil and to let her boy alone. "That boy is useless!" Poppa would yell. "He's shiftless. He don't want to learn. He's got soup in his head." It was terrible, the way he'd light on Jamed sometimes, like there was some red devil in him sure enough, that Jamed drew out with his fumbling. It hurt him, though, it hurt him worse than anything in the world to hurt Jamed, I thought maybe it was the only thing that did. He'd always go out by himself after something like that happened and walk on the beach, for hours sometimes, and when he came back he was shamed and sad, he'd go around the house real quiet and try to do little things for all of us, maybe he'd bring Jamed back a hatful of wineberries from his walk, or a specially fine shark's tooth, or take us to the movies in Marlboro that night. He would look little in his clothes, and shriveled up, like a rotten walnut in its shell. There was something terrible between them that none of the rest of us ever understood, but it scared us, we didn't even talk about it. And yet the funny thing was that Jamed loved him best of any of us, in a kind of dumb-dog way that no amount of whacking around could undo, but only made stronger, as if even though he couldn't tie bowlines or haul sheets or chop kindling or spell, there was, by God, one thing in this world he could do for Poppa that nobody else could, ever, and he wasn't quitting. It seemed to me like there was some question that Poppa was always asking everybody, all his life, that only Jamed knew the answer to. Sometimes when Poppa would whack him in the head like that you could almost hear Jamed's ears ringing, his eyes would go blank for a second before he got his senses good and then his face would screw up and he'd stand there trying not to cry, trying not to make too much of a fuss, and Poppa would stare at him like a crazy man, scared at what he'd done and sick about it, but excited too, sort of enchanted-looking, like a man about to step off a cliff, as if he was asking, "Well, Jamed. Now?" And Jamed might flinch some, sure, he'd almost got his head knocked off, but he wouldn't run or cave in or give up. He'd stand there starting to cry with his face screwed up and a welt like a doorknob coming out on the side of his head, but still not giving up, as if he was standing ground for both of them, as if he was saying, "No, Poppa, not yet. Not never." It was hair-raising.

After a while we fell asleep and we slept for half an hour or maybe an hour, it was hard to tell, until we heard Momma's chair scraping on the floor and we woke up, startled, and looked out through the crack and saw her get up from the table and go over to the coat tree by the door. She took down a black oilskin that was hanging there still wet from her last trip outside and put it on and wrapped her head up in a wool scarf and went out on the front porch with the screen door swinging and banging in the wind. We could hear the surf roaring in that minute the door was open. She stayed out there for maybe fifteen–twenty minutes and I could imagine her standing pressed against the porch rail with the wind whipping her scarf, staring down at the black wild sea. We lay there waiting, not hardly blinking, until she came back in the house and took off the scarf and oilskin and hung them up again and came back to the table. She took a handful of the shark's teeth out of the box and held them in her hand and sat there staring at them, her face clean and pure as a snowdrift, as if she was listening to music. Once in a while a green apple would come flying off the trees and bang up against the side of the house and she would jerk her head up like a deer's to a gunshot and hold it that way for a moment, high and thrilled, more beautiful than when she was cutting roses or cuddling us or anything else I could remember. Then she would look back down again at those black teeth and dip her fingertips into them.

That happened four or five times, all night, we would keep falling asleep and then waking up when the door banged and then we'd watch her for a while through the crack and then drift off to sleep again until the door slammed and there she'd be coming in out of the rain, shining in her wet black cape, all draped in glittering folds around her.

One time when the door went to banging and we woke up it wasn't Momma coming back inside but Cap'n Weems standing there in a wet sou'wester and oilskins and rubber boots, making a puddle on the linoleum and whooping, "Whoo-ee!," he was being very hearty for Momma's sake. She was staring at him with her face gone pale because of course she hadn't known who it was banging at the door out there in the storm, she had thought it might be Poppa, you could see that, she put out her hand and touched the table to steady herself and then said, "You get out of that slicker, Cap'n Weems, and come sit down here at the table and let me get you a cup of coffee. I've got some hot."

He said, "No, thank you, Miss Anabel, I'm not going to stay but a minute. I just thought I'd see if they was anything you might be needing. I don't reckon you've heard anything?"

"No, I haven't," Momma said. "Not since I called Cap'n Parks. He said Joel left Cambridge about six thirty, so God knows where he is now. I don't guess he's going to try to make port in this kind of a sea. He *can* sail."

"Well, don't you *know* he can," Cap'n Weems said. "Why, Miss Anabel, I'll tell you what that man is doing: he's sitting out there hove to, right this minute, just as pretty as a picture, just waiting for her to blow out. Now that's just about what he's doing."

"Not in that boat, he's not," Momma said. "You know that *Windsong* won't heave to kindly, Cap'n Weems. He always did pride himself he made boats to move, not to sit still. More likely he's running under bare poles, right down the bay. But if this keeps up, he'll be clear to Norfolk in the morning. I just hope to God he's got leeway."

"Why, ma'am, you know that man is not going to get himself caught on a lee shore," Cap'n Weems said. "When did he ever do any such of a thing as that? Now Miss Anabel, what you've got to do is try and get some rest. First thing you know them children is going to be yelling for their breakfast."

"They'll have their breakfast when they want it," Momma said. "They always did and always will. That's one thing they can count on." I could see she still had a handful of the shark's teeth clenched in her hand, and she laid the edge of her palm on the table and opened her fingers to spill them out slowly onto the oilcloth, making a whispery rattle like a burst of hail on a windowpane. "Will you tell me why a man with a wife and three children would set out on a night like this?" she asked softly, not Cap'n Weems especially, but just everybody. "Why? When there's been small-craft warnings up for almost twenty hours?"

"Well, I'll tell you a fact, Miss Anabel," Cap'n Weems said. "That man has worried himself near crazy on that boat, and he's been more than anxious to find out how she would do in a seaway. He's told me that himself. He thinks she needs more iron in her keel."

"Yes, that's what I need, too," Momma said, nodding her head. "That's what any woman needs, has got anything to do with that man."

Cap'n Weems took a big blue handkerchief out of his oilskins and dried his face with it, dabbing at his eyebrows, they were dripping. "Now Miss Anabel, what I want to ask you," he said, "is, how would you like for Amy to come up and set with you a spell? That's what she sent me up here to say. I know for a fact she's more than willing."

"I just wouldn't hear of any such foolishness," Momma said. "You give her my thanks, Cap'n Weems, but you tell her that if she dares to set foot outside on a night like this, I won't let her in my door. Now I mean that. I'm perfectly all right here."

"Miss Anabel, you're a hard woman to do business with," Cap'n Weems said. "But if you say you're all right, I reckon you are. Still, I don't want you worrying no more than you've a right to. They're going to get the Coast Guard cutter out from Solomons just as soon as they can, and I'll let you know the minute I hear anything."

"I'd appreciate that very much," Momma said. "It's very kind of you to come up here in this weather. The phone would have done."

"Well, you need to see a face," Cap'n Weems said. "I reckon there's times a person needs to see a face. I don't know if it's any help to see one like mine, but it's the only one I got." He let out a roar of laughter and Momma put her finger on her lips and looked toward the bedroom. So he left then, backing out the door and letting in a far-below boom of surf, saying he would call her as soon as he heard from the Coast Guard.

We didn't any of us say anything but just lay there looking up at the ceiling and I thought about Poppa when he was lofting plans for the *Windsong* that he was in out there right now, down on his knees with a big pair of dividers, transcribing the sheer lines of her hull onto a big sheet of brown paper that covered the whole floor of the loft, or after he had got her planked, sitting there in the shop at night with a candle lit on the end of a box and a bottle of Jack Daniel's between his feet, his eyes pickled with lust as he looked up at that great softly lighted hull breasting the seas of darkness that she sailed on.

It was about eight o'clock in the morning when they called up Momma and told her that the Coast Guard had him in tow and were hauling him in to Solomons with his rudder post gone and his foremast split. So Cap'n Weems came up and drove us down there in his pickup and we went out on the pier to wait. The sun had come out bright, the way it does after a northeaster, and it was hot and quiet with steam coming up in clouds from the wet woods and the honeysuckle bushes along the fences. We were so happy we were goofy with excitement, pounding each other with our fists and hollering and carrying on, Sylvie and me were, anyway, Momma was sort of stern and thin-lipped and Jamed just smiled mostly, like it was Christmas. The sky and the water were blue as bedspreads and pretty soon we saw them, still miles off, coming up from the south between the channel buoys, getting bigger and bigger in the slow beautiful way ships do when they are bearing for you, bringing back the part of you that has been in danger for a while, seaborne out there. And when they came alongside there was Poppa standing on the foredeck and throwing lines to us, bigger than any mountain, with his shirt unbuttoned and his big hairy belly bulging out above his belt buckle, and his blue nose, and his eyes bright as honey in the sun, roaring down to us and calling us his doves, his fancy flock of pigeons, and making out like he was surprised as hell that we'd bothered to come down there at all, why my God, what was all the excitement about, he'd ridden out half a hundred gales worse than that, and why weren't we up home making a batch of griddle cakes and sausage for a hungry man? When we'd made her fast he jumped down on the dock and swooped up Sylvie, who was screeching like a jaybird, and held her under one arm while he gave Momma a hug and a couple of pats on the behind, winking down at me and saying, "Well, Aaron old mate, you keep 'em all in line while I was gone? You done real good." Jamed stood there with his face going to pieces, trying not to make too much of a fuss, and all the time Poppa was kidding and kissing the rest of us and whacking us on the behind he'd take an occasional quick peek at Jamed, secret and sort of shy. Then finally when Jamed couldn't hold it in any longer, he ran up to Poppa and hugged him by the leg, hugging that big thick leg up tight against him like a tree trunk with his shoulders heaving, and Poppa put his hand down and laid it on Jamed's head, stroking his hair down to the nape of his neck and then pressing Jamed's head against his thigh as gentle as if he was calming one of his doves that had broken its wing or got its beak split or something.

Momma had softened up by the time we got home but she was still sort of thin-lipped and quiet, cooking breakfast, you could see she was saving up to give Poppa hell after we'd got in bed that night. But he ran on like he didn't notice anything, and it wasn't all put on, he was happy. There wasn't a lot of damage to the *Windsong* and I guess he'd found out what he wanted to know: she was the kind of boat he'd thought she was, maybe a little bit tender but that was a good thing in a seaway, nothing a couple of hundred pounds of iron couldn't fix, and the sweetest little weather helm you ever did see, and by God she could run.

"Eat those cakes," Momma said. "They're getting cold."

WE COULD HEAR THE CLATTER OF CUTLERY INSIDE THE SCREEN door coming from the kitchen, Sylvie turned her head and called, "Momma, I'll come in and do those dishes in just a minute. Now just leave them, will you? Will you just lie down for a while?"

"No, Baby, I've got to keep busy," Momma said. "You children enjoy yourselves, there's nothing to fuss about. Would you like some more coffee out there?"

"No, thank you," Sylvie said, and then to the Professor and me, "Would you?" We shook our heads and Sylvie resumed her gaze through the wire screen into the yellow resinous interior of the house where we had grown up, where we had finished growing up anyway if such a thing could be said of any of us, because it wasn't the original house, the one that we were born in, there wasn't anything left of that but a chunk of blackened brick or a piece of rusted pipe that you would turn up with a pitchfork now and again when you were digging in the vegetable garden, it was the one where we had learned the most, you might say. In there were the dusty volumes of the *Encyclopedia of Ships*, the moose's head that he had bought at an auction sale in Wye, the string of hand-blown glass seine buoys like enormous

Christmas tree balls, the rack of meerschaum pipes on the mantelpiece, their bowls gone brown as cinnamon, the bronze statue of a wounded stag, the gigantic board-bound volume of Shakespeare's *Collected Works* with gold fore edges and murky illustrations of humpbacked kings, demented queens, gravediggers, minstrels, whoremongers, raving princes, all his boon companions, and the framed painting of the *Anabel Ellis*, the most beautiful boat he had ever built, the one he loved best and had never sold, you could see she was the model for the *Windsong*, in whose embrace he lay now in the last bed that he would ever visit, where she had borne him with his fingers clutched tight in her streaming shrouds of hair, and where they would lie together till they were undressed to their very bones, rocking slowly back and forth forever in their endless ecstasy. And out behind the house was the apple orchard where sometimes he would sit with Sylvie and Jamed and me up in the branches with all the bay spread out below us, singing chanteys, telling us we were in the rigging of a clipper ship bound for Ceylon, and we had better watch out for pirates. And back there was the wooden shed he built to store the cider press and the great copper kettle and wooden paddles he used for making apple butter in the fall. In there was a jumble of crab pots and long-handled nets and sea-bleached buoys and oars and canvas life preservers bulging with cork blocks, hanging stiff and untouched for years from their row of rusty nails with our names stenciled on them in fading letters: JAMED, AARON, and SCREECH, for Sylvie. And next to that shed was the pigeon loft standing silent in the darkness, where I knew that now his white doves would be sleeping, milk-pure and cool and delicate as dreams. I could not get hold of the thought that he would never again cup their warm breasts in his huge hands or hold them up against our throats while we giggled and shivered at the suavity and fragrance and the gentle, pink, indignant eyes, or that we would never again stop hurling rotten apples at each other in the orchard to watch with astonishment while he came out of the loft door into the Sunday morning sunlight with all those white wings whirring madly about his scattered hair, holding mounds of cracked corn in his outstretched palms as he marched up toward us in a storm of doves.

Momma had put the dominoes on the table in front of Jamed and he was using them for building blocks, piling them up to make monuments or cenotaphs or maybe his castle that he had never finished building out of brown sand.

"I'd better go play some dominoes with him," Sylvie said, "so we can get him to bed and then have a walk. I need a long walk on the beach."

"You want us?" the Professor said. "Four-handed, it'll go quicker."

"I'm going down to the shop," I said. "Somebody ought to look around in there, see what needs straightening up. I'll come back and sit with Momma while you're gone."

"O.K., thanks," Sylvie said. So I went down the hill along the path by the edge of the cliff in the dark, remembering by some imperishable topological wisdom to lift my feet high at exactly the place where the roots of the catalpa tree bulged up in the path, so I wouldn't stumble. The old hotel at the bottom of the hill was abandoned and falling to ruin, a heap of shapeless shadows in the dark, and the pipe in front, where the spring water used to gush out ceaselessly, hour after hour and summer after summer, had run dry or been capped because there was now no sound of icy water splashing on the mossy bricks under the silver maple tree, water so cold that when you held your feet under it on the way back from Offutt's with a brown paper bag full of groceries hugged against your chest it made the bones of your toes ache, or when you held your head under it, gasping and breathless with agonized delight, it made your chest heave like a bellows and your heart vault like a deer over a rail fence, and if you leaned over and turned your face up with your mouth open it would bulge your cheeks full of that tooth-chilling, luscious, Arctic-flavored essence of the earth. I went over and felt the mouth of the pipe and it was dry, it wasn't capped, the dead cavity crusted with rust or lime and from the feel of it infested with spiders. But down at the bottom of the hill there was still a smell of mint in the air from the wild herbs that had escaped from Mrs. Cryer's kitchen garden and gone frolicking down through the meadow to the shop buildings of my father's boatyard, the creek shore and the slips where the dark sloops stood pointing their fingers at somethiing among the stars. I unlatched the white wooden gate and went in onto the planked walk that ran along the shore with the slipways joining it at right angles, in almost every berth a sailboat rocking softly in the suck and slurp of tidal flow among the pilings, their halyards tap-tapping against the spars in an ardent, clandestine way, like the fingertips of a lover against a windowpane. I walked down to the end of the boardwalk, my heels ringing hollow on the wooden planks above the water, to the vast, high-gabled bulk of the main shop. The great barnlike doors were slid closed and in front of them on the railway that sloped down to the water the twin tall frames of the boat hoist stood empty with their wheels chocked still on the slanting rails and the empty canvas slings drooping between them like hammocks. All over the yard there was a jumble of vacant cradles, winches, coiled cable, and all the junky fabulous litter with which a boatyard teems. There were boats in two of the cradles, a twenty-seven- and a thirty-two-foot ketch, standing there with that slightly scandalous look that a sailboat has when she is totally exposed, the tender and intimate profiles of their naked keels gave me a sudden unfathomable sense of trespass as if I had stumbled upon a pair of naked maidens that my father was holding captive for some unholy purpose in a stock, I had abdicated the right of ever really knowing what went on in that place. Over the office door there was a weathered white sign hanging under a lightbulb and I could read the letters that my grandfather had painted on it in 1898: J. LINTHICUM & SON, BOATWRIGHTS.

I took out of my pocket the huge old skeleton key that I had carried for ten years and slid it in the keyhole and turned the lock. Then after waiting for a minute in a kind of humble trepidation I opened the door and went in and switched on the light and stood there once again embraced as if by my father's arms in the reek of clean redwood and pitch and hemp and oakum, shellac and creosote, the litter of sawdust and tendrils of shaved mahogany, tarry buckets and casting ladles and ladders and sawhorses and jumbled paint lockers and drill benches and lumber racks of fragrant teak and spruce and afromosia and white pine, and beyond, in the shadowy vault of the shop, tall and royal as a harp, the skeleton of a ship that he was building. The lightbulb I had switched on hung in a metal shade over his rolltop desk, which was open, its pigeonholes bulging with communications from clients, lawyers, chandlers, naval architects, seed salesmen, and no doubt undone widows as far away as Old Point Comfort, all of them regardless of their tidings jammed into the recesses with what appeared to be an unvarying fury that had ruptured many of the envelopes and permitted to escape here and there a business card, a pocket calendar for 1958, a snapshot of a buxom lady in slacks holding up a string of mackerel, or a handful of marigold seeds. In a little enclave that had been raked clear of all this rubbish there lay on the desk an overall plan for the boat he was building, a thirty-foot sloop with unmistakable log-canoe ancestry that had all over it the stamp of his style: the steeply raked transom, the breathtaking sweep of sheer, the drawn-out length of bow and counter, that combination of lyricism and robustness that to my eyes and many others, some of them more or less grudgingly confessed, nobody on the bay had ever equaled and maybe nobody in the world. I picked up the plan and held it closer to the light and studied it for a while with that slight sense of indignation that something truly beautiful creates in you because after all it is an assault upon you in a way, a sort of seduction. Well, I thought, you never got anything but better, all those years your genius ripening in you like wine in a battered cask, everything finer, cleaner, more spontaneous, stronger, and, most surprisingly, more joyful. Yes, you made joyful boats, and never lost anything until you lost it all, which after all is the way to go, and I suppose we all ought to be rejoicing, really. I laid the plan back on the desk and went out into the shop and looked up at the part of it that had so far been born. She was all ready for planking, the keel laid and the stem and transom in place, the sweeping ribs of her frames bound in by ribbands so that you saw the shape of her body emerging out of my father's dreams by some strange incantatory process that involved blows and blessings, curses and caresses, whisky and Shakespeare and the breasts of doves and women, just as mine had. I looked up through the shadows of her ribs and saw her beating into a blue wind with her sails blown full, and thought, Well, Sister, you got the best part of him, the part I always wanted. I had said it before.

After standing there for quite a while I went across the floor to his tool locker and opened it and looked inside with the same sense of awe I had felt when he first stood me up on a crate and took them out one by one and told me their names, what they did, how you held them, and what you had to do to keep them clean and keen and faultlessly functioning. It was the only part of his shop that was ever in any visible kind of order, I had always been smitten by the austerity of those rows of perfectly graded, fine, cold, darkly gleaming tools, chisels, spokeshaves, gouges, bits and augers, adzes, their blades carefully, devoutly honed on oilstone to bitterly twinkling edges, their handles worn smooth as ivory and burnished by half a century of his grasp. I took down a chisel and held the blade across my cheek, cringing from the cold brand of it, my flesh twitching as if after all those years reawakened by its elegance. I slid the chisel back into the rack and closed the door and went back across the floor to the office and began disgorging and sorting out the contents of the pigeonholes in his desk. The correspondence went back twenty or more years and had, as I say, no discernible order or significance. A lot of it, like the letter containing the photograph of the lady with the mackerel and some sinister-looking plain brown envelopes, was pretty clearly personal which in my father's case meant intimate and probably scandalous, and this I threw into a wicker basket, moved by a compunction that only his death could have produced, to carry out and burn later. There was something so careless and almost aggressively innocent about the way it was jammed into his desk for anyone in the world with a dirty, mean, or vindictive mind to ferret into that it made me feel ashamed. I had spent enough of my life digging into or stumbling upon the evidence of his perfidies, all of us had, we didn't need any more evidence of that kind, especially not my mother, his tools would make a better memorial. So I saved only the legal-looking envelopes, bills, invoices, blueprints, business documents, a couple of issues of the *Pigeon Breeder's Journal* and the packet of marigold seeds. One of the business letters was a fat-looking envelope with an insurance company's crest so I sat down and opened it up and sure enough it was a life insurance policy for twenty-five thousand dollars. It had been taken out in 1952 and named my mother as beneficiary, but whether or not it was in order and paid up was another matter. But there was nothing I could do about it now, I would have to find out by a telephone call in the morning, right now I wasn't particularly interested in brooding about it. If there wasn't any insurance, then the yard could be sold off at what ought to be a pretty substantial profit, maybe it ought to be anyway, who the hell was going to run it, not me, boy, and my mother would be all right. So I stuck the envelope in my jacket pocket and decided to carry out the stuff in the waste basket and burn it, but my father's mysteries were not so easily disposed of as by dropping them in an oil drum and tossing a lighted match on them as I ought to know having already tried the much more elaborate measure of running halfway across the world to escape from them.

WE HAD THE CAVE WIDE ENOUGH NOW FOR TWO PEOPLE TO sit side by side in the mouth of it and look out at the bay, it was getting deep, too, as deep as all three of us stretched out end to end. Sylvie was the digger right now, we took turns at that job because it was the hardest. She had the garden trowel and we could hear it thudding into the clay and then grinding through the soft white fossil shells and Sylvie grunting while she worked. She would fill up the hat and then pass it back over her shoulder to Jamed and Jamed would pass it to me and I would dump it out from the mouth of the cave and watch the lumps of moist fresh-dug gray clay and the scraps of crushed fossils go raining down the cliff face to the beach, eighty or ninety feet below. It was cool in there, cool and dim out of the sun glare beating all around us on the sea and air, and you could lie and watch the freighters coming up from the southeast as tiny and slow as little brown snails on the horizon, crawling into the white haze toward Baltimore. We had hauled some boards up there and some old asbestos shingles for a floor because the clay was damp enough to wet your pants if you sat on it very long, and we had a box in there with our stuff in it, some candles for nighttime and a bottle of shark's teeth and some fishing rigs and a mirror for sending semaphore. It was our fortress, nobody knew about it, not even John Michael Offutt, and there wasn't much danger that they would ever find out about it because we had chosen a place where the cliffs were scarred and ravined by a landslide and a clump of sumac grew in a clutch of sandy soil, hiding the cave mouth from anybody on the beach. Sylvie quit digging, she stuck the trowel into the clay and turned around and crawled out beside us and sat down bang on her rump with her elbows hooked around her knees and said, "Boy, I'm bushed."

"You didn't do but half a hour," Jamed said. "I had to do a whole hour."

"That's a bunch of crud," Sylvie said. "I dug twice as *far*. What does it matter how much times it takes, if you go twice as *far?*"

"You didn't either," Jamed said. "Lookit there what I done. I done ever bit as much."

"Why don't you guys shut up?" I said. "You guys are always bellyaching. Let's eat that other sandwich."

"Yeah, if we *can*," Sylvie said. "That dumb Jamed got sand all over it, like he always does."

"It was not either me," Jamed said. "You did it yourself with your own big fat fanny, knocking all that dirt all over everything."

"Boy, you are the world's champion liar," Sylvie said, sticking out her jaw and craning her face toward him. "You are a real champion *liar*, Jamed, you know that?"

"Come on, shut up, you guys," I said. "You better eat this thing or I'll throw it out there for the gulls."

I wiped my hand off on my shirt and broke the sandwich into three pieces and handed them around. There was sand on it all right and it was peanut butter and jelly, so you couldn't do too much about it. Sylvie nibbled at the bread with the sand grating between her teeth and then shuddered and spread her lips away from her teeth in a horrible snarl and said, "Yug, this is cruddy. It's just like biting on sandpaper. Nobody can eat this stuff." She threw her piece of sandwich out of the cave mouth down the cliff, and a gull swooping down from above us like a stone falling caught it in midair, swallowed it in a gulp, and veered away from the cliff face, his flight slowing again as he floated out over his shadow on the sand.

"Wowee, did you see that?" Jamed said. "That guy is something. Watch here, I'm going to try it again."

He threw out his piece of sandwich and then I threw mine and a gull caught them every time. All of a sudden there was a flock of them soaring around the cliff face in big tilting circles, their heads twitching back and forth between their shoulders, sailing and watching. Sylvie threw out some chunks of clay to see if she could fool them but she couldn't, they would make a little dip toward the falling chunk of clay and then veer away sort of proud, that stuff bored them. We sat and watched them for a while, throwing chunks of clay.

"Come on, I'm hungry," Sylvie said. "Let's go down to the shop and get Poppa to buy us some cones."

So we climbed down the cliff toward the beach and Jamed got stuck as usual. We had cut footholes in the clay but some of them were pretty far apart for him, he had short legs, he would stand there ass-out, pressed up flat against the cliff with his knees beginning to tremble and a terrible tense look coming into his face and his eyes getting big, he wouldn't yell for help or anything but you could see he was too scared to move, so Sylvie or me would work our way back up and get ahold of his foot and lower it down and set it in the next hole giving him some upward pressure with our hand to steady him and then get ahold of his belt or something and guide him on down, going slow, hole to hole. He could make it all right if there was just somebody near him, touching him.

We walked up the beach toward the creek, stepping on our shadows in the low afternoon light, we tried to step on our heads but we couldn't ever make it, they always just slipped out from under our feet. The sand was gold-colored and speckled with little white chips of broken shells and here and there little tiny periwinkle clams with wide-open pink or blue or yellow wings hinged together like butterflies. We always watched for shark's teeth, you saw them mostly in the rubble of broken shells along the tidal rim, black triangles, some as tiny as your little fingernail, some as big as your hand, always with that sparkling dangerous shape you could spot from ten yards away, it made your nerves ring like the shape of an arrowhead does, or the shadow of a hawk or the way the grass tops shiver when a snake is sliding through underneath. I walked along in front and then Sylvie and then Jamed, way back, all of us staring at the sand. Sylvie was the best at spotting them, she must have found a bushel every summer, it made me mad the way I would walk right past one sometimes and then she would yell, "Hey, Aaron, you missed another one!" The tide had come in, it was clear up to the base of the cliffs, we had to roll up our pants legs to get by. There was a foundered tree there, half buried in the sand and white as bone. I climbed up on the smooth branches and then Sylvie did too and we sat there waiting for Jamed to catch up, yelling at him now and then. Sylvie rested her chin on her knee and started winding a piece of seaweed around her toes.

"You know who I'm going to have next year, for fourth grade?" she said. "Mr. Hazelgrove."

"He's awful," I said. "Carter Simmons had him last year. He says all he ever does is yell at people. He's supposed to be really awful."

"I don't think so," Sylvie said. "I think he looks famous. I bet he is famous."

"What do you mean, he looks famous?" I said. "How

could he be famous? He's a schoolteacher."

"Well, what's the matter with that?"

"Well, how can you be famous by being a schoolteacher? You've got to *do* something to be famous, like invent something, or be the first guy to climb a mountain or something. There aren't any famous schoolteachers, for crumb's sake."

"Well, I think that's just the trouble," Sylvie said. "I don't know why you've always got to do something to be famous. Why can't you just be a famous *person?* I think there ought to be. I know a lot of people that ought to be famous."

"Like who?"

"Well, like Turk Diamond, or that guy that works in Blood's, with the pink eyes, or Mr. Hazelgrove. They've all got a sort of look, like these real famous people you see in magazines and everything. Poppa does, too."

"You're crazy," I said. "I never saw anybody in any magazine that looked anything like Poppa. Or anywhere else, either."

"Well, he ought to be famous for that, then," Sylvie said. "For not looking like anybody else in the whole world. I think that's a pretty big deal."

"You're crazy," I said. "That's what you're famous for, being crazy. The famous crazy woman of Port Federation."

"I'd rather be crazy than a crumb, which is what you are," Sylvie said. She raised her head and yelled at Jamed, who was sitting down again, digging in the sand. "Come on, you stupid slowpoke! We won't get any ice cream if you don't come on, it's going to be dinnertime."

"Jamed Linthicum, the famous slowpoke," I said. Sylvie giggled and then started hiccoughing, giggling always made her hiccough for some reason, her breathing system was all mixed up, sometimes she would start hiccoughing when she was supposed to cry, or in the middle of a yawn or while she was sneezing or something, almost anytime. Jamed got up and started coming toward us, not coming any too fast, he had a way of rocking forward onto the front of his feet when he walked, in a sort of stagger that wasn't a very great system for walking in the sand, or anywhere else for that matter. He had to stop every couple of yards and lift up one of his feet, hopping around on the other one while he dug out a piece of shell or something that had got stuck in it, he was always getting stuff stuck in his feet.

"Why don't we go on?" I said. "It'll be so close to dinnertime Poppa won't get us any. Just let him stay there if he wants."

"We can't," Sylvie said. "If we want some ice cream we better have Jamed with us. You know that."

So we waited while he got up to the tree, he held out his hand and showed us a cat's-eye he'd found. "I found a cat's-eye," he said.

"Yeah, well, come on," Sylvie said. We got him in front of us and kept poking him in the back to keep him going while we went across the stretch of hot dry sand where the beach widened out at the bottom of the cliff below the house. We looked up and saw Momma sweeping the front steps so we kept in close against the bank so she couldn't see us, it wasn't a good idea to let her see us going down to the yard that time of day, it always meant we were after bubble gum or ice cream or something. We crossed the road and went in through the white gate and then ran along the hot planks of the pier to the shop, there was sap oozing out of them in the sun, it made us dance. Inside the office we sat down on the pine bench along the wall and scrubbed the soles of our feet on the sandy floor, trying to get the sap off them, coming out of the shop door we could hear the shriek of saws and the whine of drills and the booming of mauls and the hollow shouts of workmen under the high vault of the galvanized iron roof. There was a gigantic floor fan on a metal stand in the corner with red ribbons tied to the wire cage that the blades spun in, the ribbons fluttering out straight in the cool gale from the fan and the stand shivering and the leaves of the calendar on the opposite wall shifting all the time like tree leaves in a breeze. Sylvie went and stood in front of it, she always did that, holding out her arms, her eyes closed in the wind, her hair streaming and her shirttail fluttering like a flag. She was starting to get bosoms, you could see the little points on them sticking out where her shirt was flattened against her chest in the fan breeze. I whispered to Jamed, "She'll get them blowed flat if she don't look out," and he blushed and said, "Shut up, Aaron."

In a minute Poppa came into the office from the shop with sawdust all in his beard and along his arms like cinnamon sugar, he had that spicy wood smell on him all his life, when he leaned over us in bed at night to give us a tickle and hug or carried us on his shoulders at the fair you could smell that resiny, foresty smell that came out of his skin and hair, and whisky, a kind of wild, golden perfume that all his words and kisses smelled of. Sylvie didn't see him come out, she was still standing there being windblown, so he snatched her up by the armpits and held her straight out, wriggling and yelping.

"Hey, Screech," he yelled, "what you doing using up all my good cold air?"

"I ain't!" Sylvie yelled. "I'm hot! Hey, we want some ice cream, Poppa."

He grabbed her against him and bit her on the neck and started munching on her ear, saying, "Aw, that's good. That's better than any ice cream. That's real crab meat."

"I ain't no crab!" Sylvie screeched.

"Well, now I would of swore you was a crab," Poppa said. "You talk just like one. And looky here, what's these here? Ain't these claws?"

"No, they ain't claws!" Sylvie yelled. "They's *hands!* And I'm a girl, and you know it, you old dumb goon. You set me down, Poppa, we want some ice cream."

He slung her over his shoulder and turned around to look at Jamed and me, puzzled, his head cocked and his ears sort of pricking up like a hound's. "This girl says she wants some ice cream. You reckon she's telling the truth?"

"Yeah, she is," I said, I giggled, it always tickled me when he played dumb. "So do me and Jamed. Come on and take us up to Offutt's, Poppa."

"Boy wants to go up to Offutt's," Poppa said. "Well, you get out there in that pickup before I count to five and I'll see what I can do."

Jamed and me tore out the door and across the yard to where the pickup was parked and had got into the cab and had the door slammed shut before he was halfway there, still carrying Sylvie across his shoulder, she'd gone all limp and was playing dead, her arms hanging down his back and swinging while he walked. He shoved her up on the cab seat like a sack of meal and climbed in beside us, saying, "This girl has done died. Died from lack of ice cream. Ain't that a terrible thing?" She was all collapsed, flopping all over me with her eyes shut, so I gave her a poke and said, "Come on, get off me or I'll kill you sure enough."

We drove up the clay road with yellow clouds billowing up behind us and turned in beside the gas pump at Offutt's and climbed down and went up the wood steps into the store. The screen door banged behind us and we went across the sandy floor and stood there beside the freezer, breathing in the cold smell of frost while Bud Offutt dug out scoops of velvety, tongue-numbing ice cream and jammed them in the sweet brown papery cones, strawberry for Sylvie and vanilla for Jamed and chocolate for Poppa and me. We got double scoops and the top scoop was just about gone by the time we got back to the shop. Poppa drove one-handed, licking at his cone and at his fist and fingers where it was dribbling down, it was melting fast. He did the steering and worked the clutch pedal and Sylvie did the shifting, she wasn't much of a shifter, every time she yanked on the shift stick you could hear the gears grinding and Poppa would say, "Oh my God, oh my God." Sylvie would giggle and screech.

There was a pale blue Cadillac with D.C. tags on it parked outside the shop when we got back. We went inside and here was this rich guy from Washington, D.C., wearing cufflinks and a waistcoat with brass buttons. He was sitting on the pine bench with one of those cardboard tubes that you carry blueprints in laid across his thighs, tapping on it with his fingertips. He got up quick when we came in, very happy to see Poppa, and held his hand out. Poppa said, "Well, howdy, Mr. Clapperton," very hearty, and shifted the cone into his left hand and shook hands. The guy's smile got a little weak when he got hold of Poppa's hand, which was all stuck up with chocolate ice cream, but he was very gentlemanly, he didn't let on. Sylvie and Jamed and me went out into the shop to finish our cones and watched them planking up the hull of a work boat they were building, walking careful not to step on the nails and junk that were all over the floor. Earl Gibson was up there on a scaffold, he looked down and said, "Howdy, Sylvie, Jamed, Aaron." We said howdy and stood around licking our cones, watching him drill and plug, I let on like I was watching anyway, but the fact was I wanted to get back and stake myself out by the office door, I had a powerful feeling Poppa was about to get himself in trouble.

The thing was, he wasn't supposed to build pleasure boats. There was this guy named Vernon T. Allnut, he worked for the Calvert County National Bank in Marlboro, who used to come out to the shop every now and then and unload his briefcase on Poppa, that man would spread papers around like he was setting up for a picnic but it wasn't any picnic as far as Poppa was concerned, you could see that. He'd sit there sort of bewildered, picking up one of them every now and then and peering at it for a minute and then he'd put it down and pick up another one and give it a looking-over, scratching his beard and saying stuff like, "Um hm, oh yeah," he didn't know what the hell was going on. Vernon T. Allnut would sit there tapping on the papers with his fingertips, trying to set Poppa straight about how things were going and what he had to do and what he couldn't do, I didn't know what gave him the right to tell Poppa how to run his business but what I finally figured out was that he'd lent Poppa the money to run it with and he was going to make damn sure that he ran it right. He told Poppa to stick to storage and repairs and building work boats, tonguers and buy boats and that sort of stuff, that was where he made his money, there wasn't any profit in pleasure craft, they took too long to turn out and there was too much custom work involved and not enough volume. But of course that's what Poppa was interested in, he wanted to design boats, real boats, made to first-class scantlings that only rich men could afford, boats built to make a Bermuda crossing or a South Pacific passage with a bone between their teeth, boats built to sail, he wasn't interested in repairing some old scow or turning out these barrel-bilged clunkers that you threw together out of cheap pine for drudging oysters in the bay, there wasn't any design to that kind of work, you built them from stock plans that you knew by heart, he'd made a thousand of them. But that's what he had to go on doing, Vernon T. Allnut told him, at least until this Recession or whatever they called it was over, or the yard would most likely go down the drain, and the Calvert County National Bank along with it, from the way he talked. And now here came Mr. Clapperton with his cufflinks and his fancy waistcoat and what looked like a set of custom blueprints under his arm, a man like that was sure as hell not interested in drudging oysters, what he wanted was a yacht, a luxury boat, and if I knew anything about Poppa there would be snow in August before he'd let an opportunity like that slip by.

Usually anybody that had the money for that kind of a boat went over to Annapolis to somebody like Trumpy, who had about a million dollars' worth of equipment and a whole army of master boatwrights and a worldwide reputation for luxury yachts. The ones who came to Poppa were ones who had a mighty special taste in boats, or had asked a hell of a lot of questions around the bay, or else had a real eye for a hull and had maybe seen one or two of Poppa's on the water, but there hadn't been many of them show up for a long time, there wasn't that kind of money around. This guy didn't seem to fit into any of those classes particularly, but you couldn't tell. A man buying a boat gets sort of crazy, like a man chasing after a woman, I had learned that already. He gets kind of wild and feverish and his eyes get this funny spooked-out look in them, you can't tell a whole lot about what he would be like in his normal state, so maybe this guy really knew something about boats, but I wouldn't have bet on it, that waistcoat he had on for one thing.

I wanted to find out what was going on, though, so I eased over to the office door and slid down with my back against the jamb, I had one ear practically inside the office so I could hear fine, and if I worked my head around a little I had a pretty good view of the desk. They were boat plans all right, I could see them spread out flat on the desk and Poppa sitting there studying them, still working on his ice cream cone, taking a lick at it once in a while and then holding it up in one hand like a torch. Mr. Clapperton was standing behind him bending over to point at something now and then and answering questions very quick, his eyes sort of seething, a sick man.

"Pickering makes a right nice plan," Poppa said.

"Yes, he does," Mr. Clapperton said. "He just finished them Tuesday night. I think she's just beautiful."

"Yes, sir," Poppa said. "Now, what is that displacement? I don't see too good."

"Twenty thousand, four hundred pounds," Mr. Clapperton said. "I wonder if you'd kind of watch it with that ice cream cone, Mr. Linthicum?"

"Oh, I'm watching her," Poppa said. "I tell you, Mr. Clapperton, I'm just a little bit surprised. That ain't a whole lot of weight, is it, on a thirty-one-foot waterline?"

"Oh, it's adequate," Mr. Clapperton said. "It's more than adequate. He assured me of that. You see, I don't intend to do a lot of deep-water sailing. I'm going to have to stick to weekending, pretty much, I'm afraid, right here on the bay."

"Yeah, I know how it is," Poppa said. "That's about all I get to do any more, myself. Still, I'll tell you something, Mr. Clapperton. A boat that don't give a man big ideas ain't no kind of a boat to live with. I figure after a man been sailing his boat for a while he ought to start thinking about taking her down to Florida and cutting out across the Gulf Stream for the islands. A boat ought to make a man think about doing something big once in a while, something dangerous, you know what I mean?" He had opened the bottom drawer of his desk and was fishing around in all the papers and junk in there and in a minute he came up with a bottle of Jack Daniel's. All the time he was waving around his ice cream cone in his free hand, it was getting pretty soggy by now and Mr. Clapperton never took his eyes off it.

"Something dangerous," he said, smiling a little and nodding his head as if he didn't want to be disagreeable, you could see he was worried sick about Poppa getting ice cream on those plans.

"That's right," Poppa said. He shoved the rest of the cone in his mouth and crunched it up and gulped it down, then he gave his hands a couple of wipes across his thighs and started ferreting around in the drawer again. "Now a boat like this here is fine for gunk-holing around the bay here and I reckon she'll cozy along real well in light air, but I tell you she's going to have one hell of a motion in a seaway. If you don't have a real good stomach you're going to spend most of your time hanging on the rail." He found a couple of beat-up Dixie cups that were all crumpled and dusty and brought them up and started straightening them out with his fingers.

"Of course, light displacement is all the thing now, I understand," Mr. Clapperton said. "Mr. Pickering tells me there are light-displacement yachts making Atlantic crossings regularly these days." A little bit of zip had come back into his voice since Poppa had got rid of the ice cream cone, but it was just about canceled out by watching him get those Dixie cups straightened out, you could see he felt there were fresh dangers ahead. "And of course, they're a lot easier to handle, with so much less sail. If you're getting that for me, Mr. Linthicum, I don't believe I'll have any."

"Oh, why hell, a man can't make a big decision like this without a little bit of fire down below," Poppa said. "This here is Jack Daniel's Black Label, it can't do you nothing but good."

"Well, just a finger, I guess," Mr. Clapperton said.

"Oh, yeah," Poppa said. He rapped the bottoms of the cups on the desk top a couple of times and then held them up and blew the dust out of them, shutting his eyes tight because there was a good bit of dust in there and also what looked like a dried-up spider, in one of them. Then he poured out a couple of good slugs from the bottle and pushed one of the cups across the desk to Mr. Clapperton. Mr. Clapperton picked it up and took a quick peek inside to make sure there weren't any more spiders or anything floating around in there and then saluted Poppa with it, smiling kind of faintly, and took a tiny sip just off the rim with his lips.

"Hey," he said, lifting his eyebrows. "I think maybe I'll have just a splash of water in that, Mr. Linthicum, if there's any around."

"Oh, we got water," Poppa said. "We got a whole bay full

of it, right outside the window." He let out a big roar of laughter, Poppa's laugh sounded like somebody had dropped a couple of cinder blocks into a threshing machine or something, it sort of jolted Mr. Clapperton. He picked up the cup and carried it over to the water cooler and held it under the spigot. "Yeah, they right easy to handle," he said, "but you got to pay for it, with all that motion. Them things bobble around like a toy duck in a bathtub, you seen 'em do it." He let a couple of glugs of water into the cup and carried it back to the desk, setting it down in front of Mr. Clapperton and raising his eyebrows at him, serious. "And ugly? Oh my Lord. Little old skinny short-ended things with a piece of rag stuck up there on a stick, not no bigger than a pocket handkerchief. Yeah, you can handle 'em, but by God they *need* handling, every minute. A real light boat is too sensitive for my taste. You got to trim 'em and fiddle with 'em every minute. You can't relax. Me, I like to set back and enjoy myself." He sat down to show Mr. Clapperton what he meant, heaving back in his swivel chair till it tipped him almost out of sight. "Now, in a good heavy boat, that's dug in right, you can set back like this and enjoy yourself. You don't have to worry about a gust or a little bit of sea."

Mr. Clapperton smiled again and nodded and then leaned forward and tapped the plan with his fingertip.

"Of course, in my opinion," he said, "this is a very handsome boat. A beautiful boat. I think she has very elegant lines. Very."

"Oh, she ain't a bad-looking boat," Poppa said, nodding, agreeable as hell. He hitched himself forward and had a better look. "No, she ain't bad at all, considering her displacement. I don't say they ain't light-boat men that can't turn out a fine design, fellows like Cy Hamlin, they turn out a real pretty boat. Yeah." He lifted his cup, nodded at Mr. Clapperton, drank off about half of it and then lowered his chin, squinched his eyes shut tight, doubled up his fists and went into a terrible convulsion, a look of plain-out agony twisting up his face, as if maybe his appendix had just busted. "Hoo-*oo!*" he said, coming out of it with a shake of his head that made his cheeks flap. "Don't that coddle your balls, though. You better have a sip of that, Mr. Clapperton, and then we can get down to business." Mr. Clapperton took a good-sized sip, shivered a little bit and then smiled to show his appreciation, he was a pretty nice guy, really, I felt kind of sorry for him.

"Now, I reckon this here is your first boat," Poppa said. "Am I right on that?"

"That's right," Mr. Clapperton said. "But I've done a good deal of investigating."

"Oh, sure you have," Poppa said. "I can see that. And I'd say judging from this accommodation plan you got here, you're a cruising man, ain't that right? I mean you ain't interested in no stripped-down racing machine just yet."

"No, I want to do some cruising," Mr. Clapperton said. "Of course, I want a boat that will step along pretty lively, too. I don't want any clunker."

"Naw, they don't nobody want any clunker," Poppa said. "No, sir. Well, now, I reckon you know about the displacement rule."

"Well, something," Mr. Clapperton said. He looked a little uneasy, but eager, he wanted to find out about it but he didn't want to let on there was much he hadn't heard already. "Of course I know there's moderate, and light, and heavy. And so on."

"Yeah, well they's a sort of formula that's a right good guide for displacement," Poppa said. "I'll just write her down here, so's we can see what we're doing." He pulled an envelope out of a pigeonhole and then scrabbled around until he found a piece of pencil and started writing while he talked. "Now most stock boats you see will come within ten percent of this here formula. Eight tenths of the waterline length, plus four, to the third power. You see that?" Mr. Clapperton studied the equation and nodded. He looked happy, he was getting into the mystery of the thing. "You got a LWL of thirty feet, that'll give you right close to twenty-two thousand pounds." He did the arithmetic fast, he'd done it a million times, and shoved the envelope toward Mr. Clapperton, who nodded again and started mumbling while he checked the sums. "Now, like I say, most designers, they don't want to get in no trouble. They'll stick to within ten percent of them figures, every time. Oh, once in a while you'll find a guy that's got a lot of guts and a ding-dong idea and knows what he's doing, he'll spread out to maybe twenty-five percent lighter or heavier, but it ain't regular. It ain't regular because if you go to one of them naval architect schools, they'll tell you that's how it's *got* to be. They *tell* you that, but now what would you say if I told you that many a boat I've built had over twice the displacement that there formula calls for? My daddy built boats by rack of eye all his life, he couldn't add up the grocery bill, and that man put fifty-five tons of displacement on a forty-one-foot waterline, regular, and them boats sailed to New Zealand and back, and won Bay regattas like picking cherries. They was one of them won the Norfolk race every damn time she entered. Now if you was to pay any mind to that formula, they'd ought still to be coming up on the starting mark."

"That's amazing," Mr. Clapperton said. "That's really amazing. I didn't have any idea a boat could get that far off the norm and still perform."

"No, they ain't many people that do," Poppa said. "They ain't many people that do because their brains is all constipated. Too much book-learning. It's like eating too much cheese. It binds a man up." He poured out another slug of whisky into his cup and then a quick one into Mr. Clapperton's, Mr. Clapperton waved his hand a little bit to stop him but Poppa didn't pay him any mind, he slipped it in quick.

Then he heaved back in his chair again and pointed his finger at Mr. Clapperton and said, "No, sir, they tell you a boat that heavy won't move, but I'm here to tell you she will, as long as you know what you're doing with hull shape. That there is the whole thing: hull design." Mr. Clapperton nodded and had another pull at his Jack Daniel's, he was getting warmed up now.

"Wave making, that's what you got to watch out for," Poppa said. "You know what wave making is, I reckon." Mr. Clapperton tossed his hand up as if he'd heard about it, sure, but he wanted to get Poppa's ideas on the subject. You could see he didn't know any more about wave making than he did about cotton picking, but he wanted to learn, that man had boat fever.

"Well, let me just run over it with you, real quick," Poppa said. "A man can't know too much about boats, if he's fixing to buy him one. You know, in them old days they used to have fellas called marriage brokers, would fix a man up with a wife. Well now that's a serious business, and you got to go over things real careful. But I figure fixing a man up with a boat is ever bit as serious, maybe more. You got to know all you can find out about her, or you get in trouble. You can't know too much."

"I appreciate that," Mr. Clapperton said. "A craft like yours is an old and honorable one, Mr. Linthicum, and ought to be conducted that way. There are too few things in this world that are, any more." He nodded again, his nod was getting a little bit loose by this time, more like a wobble, and had another pull at his cup, he was getting her down pretty close to the bottom. Poppa heaved himself forward and went to work on the envelope again.

"Now if you take the speed of a boat and divide it by the square root of her waterline length," he said, "you get what's called the speed–length ratio. Now if that figure is one, or less, there ain't no serious resistance from wave making. Let's say she's traveling six knots and got a LWL of thirty-six feet: well, that works out to one, don't it?" Mr. Clapperton nodded agreement. "All right, then, that boat is moving right well. She ain't making waves yet that amounts to nothing. But you get that figure up to one point two, then you got the second bow wave back at her aft end and you're climbing up the first one. Going uphill, so to speak. Of course you got resistance from skin friction, too, but that goes up slow, it's wave-making resistance goes up fast when you start to move. Well, you get her up to one point four and you just about reached your limit. Your wave resistance is just about equal to the power you're getting out of the wind. That there is what we call hull speed. You can't go no faster, unless you start surfing or something. You see what I mean?" Mr. Clapperton nodded, his face very serious, he was concentrating like hell. He peeked inside his cup and tossed her down and smacked his lips, frowning, thinking it over, he was pretty near a professional by now.

It looked like Poppa was going to give him a whole course in naval architecture, but I knew what he was up to, really. I had him figured out by now: he was going to sell Mr. Clapperton the *Ariel*. What I mean is, he was going to get Mr. Clapperton to put up the money to build her, because the *Ariel* hadn't even been built yet. She wasn't anything but plans. Poppa had spent years designing that boat, three years at least. He'd sit there at night with a kerosene lantern and a bottle of liquor, all night sometimes, till he fell asleep anyway, figuring and drawing plans and once in a while sitting back and singing a couple of verses of *The Leaving of Liverpool*, all the time dreaming up this boat. Sometimes me and Sylvie would see him when we sneaked down at night to go crab fishing on the pier, we'd see the light burning and look in through the office window and there he'd be, with his shirt off if it was hot, scratching the hair on his chest and squinting through his spectacles, bent over those plans like a jeweler over a watch, working away with a pair of calipers and a slide rule and his eyes gone cold as amber. And then sometimes in the morning we'd have to go down to fetch him up to breakfast and there he'd be, still, with his cheek resting on the desk and the bottle empty more than likely, sound asleep and snoring like a diesel engine. He spent the next two years trying to sell that boat to somebody. He couldn't build her himself, of course, on speculation, because she would have cost too damn much, fifteen thousand anyway, cost price, there wasn't that kind of money in the whole of Port Federation, maybe not in the whole state of Maryland. I heard him say that six or eight years ago, when there was money around, men would have beat each other to death to buy those plans, but not with this Recession going on or whatever it was. I think he was kidding himself, I don't think he could have given her away, any time, she was too strange. And too beautiful, you don't trust a boat that beautiful. He'd designed her off those log canoes that he loved so much, and his plans called for building her just the way they used to build them around Tilghman Island in Civil War days, with a bottom of solid logs all the way up to the turn of the bilge. Only he'd drawn out the ends so fine they near whistled, and he'd put a cutwater on her like an eagle beak. My God, what a boat. She had a flair to her topsides like a battleship and he'd rigged her with these funny old-fashioned leg-of-mutton sails with sprits instead of booms. And he'd put a ballast keel on her, that was another thing. No regular log canoe ever had a ballast keel, especially not reinforced concrete, but that man was crazy for weight. Reuben Bingham, the shop foreman, would stop and look down at those plans sometimes when he was going through the office, and he'd say, "Judas Priest, you really cooked one up this time, Joel. That thing is half swan and half spiny lobster. You reckon she'll sail?" "Oh, she'll sail," Poppa would say, "she'll sail like a bitch." He believed it, too, he *knew* it. That was the one thing he was living for right then, to see her sail. But it was no wonder he couldn't get anybody to put up money for a boat like that, for something they'd never seen the likes of. He tried like hell, though. Anybody that came around, even if they were looking for a dinghy or maybe a pair of water skis, he'd try and sell them the *Ariel*. It was a good thing they didn't take him up, because of course he wasn't supposed to build pleasure craft at all, not till times got better, he would have caught hell from Momma, let alone Vernon T. Allnut. She used to live in fear and dread that he'd talk somebody into a contract for that boat someday, and have the shop tied up for six months and go bankrupt. And now here he was trying to sell her to Mr. Clapperton, I could see that, and the way things were going it looked like he had a pretty good chance, because Mr. Clapperton didn't know his ass from a hole in the ground.

I'd finished my ice cream cone and I was getting pretty discouraged, I figured it was just a matter of time, he'd hang himself before the day was up, so I went on over to where Sylvie and Jamed were climbing around in the timber racks and said, "Come on, you guys, we got to get on back and weed some, before dinner."

"What for?" Sylvie said. "Why do we have to go already? It's not but about four o'clock." She always said it was four o'clock no matter what the hell time it was, her clock had got stuck when she was about three years old.

"It's not either, it's after five," I said. "Come on, you guys, or I'll catch hell. I'm the one that's supposed to get you guys back there."

So we went out through the shed door and back up the hill to the house. Mrs. Peabody was sitting in her rocking chair on the veranda when we went past the hotel, flapping at herself with a straw fan, she was always there, I think she was born there, fan and all. She said, "Afternoon, chil'ren," and we said, "Afternoon, ma'am." Sylvie started giggling and snorting and Jamed poked her in the ribs and said, "Hush." She giggled all the way up the hill, she thought Mrs. Peabody was a riot. We went out back of the house and got the garden trowels and forks and a peach basket out of the shed and went in through the gate of the kitchen garden, Poppa had it fenced off from the rabbits, and sat down in the hot ground between the lettuce rows and started rooting out the weeds. I didn't really mind weeding all that much, once you got down to it, it was sort of nice. It was hot and quiet and you could feel the sun on the back of your neck and on your hair and hear the doves cooing in the loft and smell the cabbage and mint and carrot greens and after a while you fell into a sort of trance.

The only trouble was, you had to keep an eye on Sylvie and Jamed because they got sidetracked pretty easy, with Sylvie it was bugs and with Jamed it was castles. Sylvie would run into an ant or a caterpillar or something and start fiddling around with it, experimenting, like pulling its feelers off or burying it and seeing if it could dig itself out of the sand, and Jamed, whenever he got near dirt he would start building these castles. It was his big specialty in life. One time when he was about three Poppa showed him how you could pick up a handful of wet sand and let it dribble out of your fist and it would dry instantly in little gray droplets, like cement, that would pile up in stalagmites and spires and all sorts of gingerbready stuff, and from then on Jamed was set, he'd found his calling. He would sit there for hours, all afternoon, day after day, summer after summer, with his baseball cap on his head and his eyes in the shadow of its peak as dreamy as a cat's, talking to himself while he built those castles. Whenever you couldn't find him you'd know where he was, down there on the beach at the bottom of the cliff with his shadow growing longer and longer on the sand and those walls getting higher and higher all around him.

We dug a whole peach basket full of weeds, plantain and

fennel, with their leaves gone limp and dark, and by that time the shadow of the house had crept halfway across the lettuce beds and you could smell supper. Momma came out on the kitchen steps and called, "Oh, Aaron. You run down and tell Poppa to stop at Offutt's before he comes up. We need a pound of butter."

"I reckon he's going to be late, Momma," I said. "He's got a man down there in the office he's talking with."

"What sort of a man?" Momma said.

"Well, he looks right rich. He's got rings on his fingers, and cufflinks and all. They're talking about a boat."

"What sort of a boat?" Momma said. "A yacht, I guess, that sort of a man."

"Well, I reckon so, yes ma'am, it sounded like it."

"Oh, yes," she said to herself, "Oh, yes." Then, loud, to me, "Well, you'll have to go up to Offutt's yourself, then, Aaron. Come on in here, I'll give you the money. Now you hustle."

I LOCKED THE OFFICE DOOR, I DON'T KNOW WHY I BOTHERED, A child of six could have opened it with a hairpin, and dropped the key in my pocket and walked across to the trash drum and dropped in the armload of rubbish I had cleared out of Poppa's desk. Then I struck a match and dropped it on top of all the papers, hearing the soft puff of the flames bursting into instant blossom and watching the lady with the mackerel writhe very fetchingly as the flames consumed her, whoopsing out her belly in a last surprising fling as she vanished smilingly into eternity. Poppa will be surprised to see you, I thought. I waited until the papers had all curled and blackened into ash and the flames fallen suddenly and then went back up the hill under the stars toward the house.

Sylvie and the Professor had gone on down to the beach and Momma was sitting by herself in a rocker on the front porch in the dark, I could see her dimly through the screen and hear the creak of the rockers on the floor. She said, "Hello, Aaron. You have a nice walk?"

"Yes, ma'am," I said. "I've been down at the shop, Momma."

"It's warm."

"Yes, it is." I came in on the porch and shut the door quietly, I figured Jamed was asleep, and sat down on the end of the glider next to her and reached across and took her hand. She patted my hand and then covered it with hers and sighed.

"It's nice to have you children home. If only it was some other occasion."

"I know, Momma."

"I've been sitting here thinking how he used to get you all up in that apple tree on Sunday morning, giggling and carrying on."

"I have, too," I said. She rocked slowly, looking out at the stars over the sea. It was a dark night. "Sylvie looks good," I said.

"She's thin. She doesn't eat."

"Well, she never did," I said. "Nothing but bubble gum and ice cream." Momma clicked her tongue. "Jamie get to sleep?" I asked.

"I hope so. He's been so excited, that poor child. I wonder if you'd just go and check on him, Aaron."

"Yes, ma'am." I went inside and across the living room to Jamed's door and opened it quietly. He wasn't asleep, I could hear him murmuring to himself softly, the way he used to do when he was building his sand castles. I went across to his bed and leaned down and brushed his hair back. His brow was moist, like a child's. He said, "Aaron?"

"Hey, fellah. You too hot?"

"Uh uh, not real much." He reached up and grabbed my hand and pulled it down and hugged it under his chin. "I sure am glad you-all came home, Aaron," he said. "Boy, I been missing you-all."

"I missed you, too, Buddy."

"Can we do something in the morning, me and you and Sylvie?"

"Sure, I guess so. What do you want to do?"

"Can we go crabbing or something? Up there where we went last time? You know, where that old scow is stuck in the mud? Can we, Aaron?"

"Yeah, as long as you get to sleep," I said. "It's late, now."

"Can we sure enough? Oh boy, sure enough, Aaron?"

"Yeah, we'll go up there," I said. "Now you get to sleep, Jamie."

"I will," he said. "I'm real tired." He lay there with my hand clutched under his chin, breathing easily and deeply. After a minute he said, "Aaron, is Poppa out there in a boat?"

"Yeah, he is, Jamie."

"You reckon he's all right? It ain't no storm or nothing, is it?"

"No, it's real calm now," I said. "He's all right, Jamie."

"I sure hope so," he said. "Boy, I sure am glad you're home, Aaron."

"Me too," I said. "You want a glass of water?"

"Uh uh, I had one. Momma give me one."

"All right. Good night, then, fellah."

I closed his door and went out into the kitchen and found a pitcher of iced tea in the refrigerator where it always sat, with a saucer on top of it. I poured out a glass and carried it back onto the front porch.

"Well, I see you found it," Momma said.

"Yep. I know where to look by now."

"He get to sleep?"

"He's going off now. He's all right. He's real happy we're home."

"That's a fact," Momma said. "He's real good, mostly, I don't have any trouble with him. He's happy, anyway. Thank the Lord."

"This is the world's greatest iced tea," I said. "I always thought those English people knew how to make tea, but they can't come anywhere near it."

"Well, it's little enough to do well."

"Oh, yes. As if that was all."

We sat quiet for a long time in the darkness while I sipped the iced tea. The lights of a freighter went by, far out in the channel.

"We saw you several times last winter on the television," Momma said. "It was that razor blade business, I believe. My, didn't Jamed get excited."

"He did?"

"Oh, he just carried on. 'That's Aaron! Yonder's Aaron on the television!' You must enjoy doing that."

"Well, not so much, Momma."

"You don't? Well, I imagine it pays very well."

"Yes, it pays pretty well."

She loosened her collar about her neck and laid her head back against the rocker. I saw her sitting in her quilted blue bathrobe humming softly to herself while she unfastened the high soft tiers of her pompadour, dropping the hairpins one by one into a little glass tray:

> "*Black and bay*
> *Dapple and gray*
> *All the pretty little horses*"

And the pitter of hairpins in the tray. Then she would brush it for half an hour at least, every night, with an amber-handled brush that had belonged to my great-great-grandmother in England. It was her one extravagance, that evening ceremony, gravely, luxuriously feminine. That was her secret life.

"Well, then, there wasn't any news today, either?" she said finally.

"No, ma'am. Reuben said they worked down around Solomons all day, but there wasn't a sign. Of course it may take months. It may take forever."

"I'd just as soon it did," Momma said.

I would, too. I hoped to God it did, I hoped they never found him, I hoped she had to wait forever: Those were the two sovereign examples of beauty, the two truths between which I had lived my life: Poppa's boats and Momma's vigils, and I didn't want either one of them to be revoked, ever. He had his boats still, in a way, he was out there with them now, and it seemed to me that in order to preserve some grave congruity of things Momma should be allowed to keep this last vigil of hers forever, you couldn't take that away from her or you would take away her soul, she would crumble into dust.

"I don't know what good it would do him, or me either, to bring him up and bury him over there at the church. He wouldn't rest near as easy. He's better off out there."

"I think so, too, Momma."

Her rockers milled the silence, June bugs pattered against the screens, the persimmon leaves were rinsed softly in the night breeze.

"I suppose," she said after a considerable time, "there'll have to be some decision made soon, about the yard."

"Yes. You could keep Reuben on as manager, maybe. Of course there'll be some loss of business, with Poppa gone, but it'll bring you in something. On the other hand if you sold it you'd have a nice little nest egg. I don't know just how much, there'll have to be an estimate made."

"Yes," she said. And then in a minute, "Of course, I'd hate to see that sign come down. I paid for that sign."

I WAS HAVING A LOT OF TROUBLE WITH THE BUBBLE GUM machine and had just started kicking the Goddamned thing when I heard this car pull up outside the office. I figured it was Mr. Clapperton because he showed up almost every day now since they had got the keel laid and she was beginning to take shape so I didn't pay any particular attention, I was getting kind of bored with Mr. Clapperton. I gave her a couple more cracks with my heel but that didn't do any good so then I picked up a butt of timber and gave her a real ding-dong whack with that, right up near the top of the pedestal, which looked for a minute like it might produce some genuine results because there was all this uproar inside the glass globe, all those bright-colored gumballs rattling around like mad, but nothing came out of the chute. So I decided I'd go in and talk Poppa out of a penny to replace the one that had just gone down the drain and walk up to Offutt's and buy a chunk of Fleer's, which wasn't half as much fun to chew but stood up better under heavy blowing. So I went over to the office door but I never stepped inside because I saw that it wasn't Mr. Clapperton in there but Vernon T. Allnut, and you didn't bust in on his conversations with Poppa without thinking it over. I didn't know what the hell was going to happen now that Poppa had signed that contract with Mr. Clapperton but I had a pretty good idea Vernon T. Allnut was going to blow a gasket. It was a good chance to find out so I slid down and sat with my back against the wall right next to the office door in my famous eavesdropping position, where I could hear them and by edging one eyeball right up to the door-jamb see them, too.

Well there was Vernon T. Allnut with his trusty brief-case opened up and about ten million papers all over the desk and I could see things weren't going too well because he looked like he had just swallowed a toad. Poppa didn't look a whole lot happier himself.

"Now, these items here," Vernon T. Allnut said. "A Black and Decker thirty-six-inch tilting-frame saw, one power auger, a number three Jiffy portable winch, and what is this here, a bolt-threading kit." He lowered the sheet of paper he was reading and gave Poppa a very unhappy look over the top of his glasses. "There are expenditures right there of over five hundred dollars, Mr. Linthicum. It's very difficult to understand."

"This here is a yacht I'm building," Poppa said. "It's impossible to do yacht quality work without the proper tools. My shop has got run down."

"That is exactly the point," Mr. Allnut said, "which I have tried to bring home to you so many times that they can't be counted. The only way in the world you can make this yard self-sustaining in times like these is by sticking to repair and storage and doing commercial work on the side. You know as well as I do that yacht work will run you in the poor-house, there is just too little margin for profit. There is too much special ordering, too much high-priced equipment, too much custom fitting, too much delay in delivery, too many man hours lost in details." He shook his head, weary, and lifted the sheet of paper and gave it a kind of sad, hopeless shake. "I don't know why I go on telling you all this. You just don't seem able to comprehend. Anyway, it's too late, I'm afraid."

Poppa looked pretty uneasy, he stirred his feet and raised his hand to scratch his head, he eyes wandering around the floor. "You see, my shop has got run down," he said. "I figured if I could get ahold of these few tools I'd be in shape again. Ready to turn out quality work with anybody, Trumpy even. All I need is a little time."

"There isn't any time left," Vernon T. Allnut said. "Will you explain to me how you are going to meet these invoices? It is six weeks now since your last mortgage payment was due. It is only by the grace of God that I've managed to get you an extension on that. That being the case, how in the name of heaven can you justify an investment like this, in brand-new machinery, to build a yacht that's going to yield you precious little profit, even if you finish her in six months, which I doubt? There's only one thing I can call that, Mr. Linthicum, and that's irresponsible. I might say wantonly irresponsible."

"Well now, look here," Poppa said, raising his hand to calm down Vernon T. Allnut a little. "How about this here: I was figuring I might get me a little personal loan to pay them bills."

"From who? There isn't a bank in this county, not in this state, nor *country* either, would lend you another penny on this business. Man, you're mortgaged right up to those rafters." He poked his finger up toward the ceiling, raising his eyebrows at Poppa like a fierce little ruffled-up owl that the dogs had got at. Poppa frowned with his face sort of twitching and wincing as if he had a toothache.

"You see, I been working on this hull design for a long time," he said, "and I know she's going to work. She's going to be a beauty. I figure I might even work out a stock run on her. There's going to be a big demand for this type of cruising boat in a year or two. Times is getting better, and I'll be right in on the ground floor with a popular design. It's a little bit of a gamble, sure, but you got to gamble if you want to do anything worthwhile."

"You don't gamble with our money, Mr. Linthicum," Vernon T. Allnut said. "Calvert County National is not in the gambling business. We are in the business of good sound investments." He sighed and took off his glasses and held them in his fingertips, staring at them sadly for a minute, trying to pull himself together. Poppa leaned over and started rummaging around in the bottom drawer, for a bottle most likely, but then he seemed to think better of it. He pushed the drawer shut and leaned back and just sat scratching his beard for a minute, waiting to see what Vernon T. Allnut was going to come up with, you could see he was getting wound up for a real oration.

"I want you to understand that we do not like the idea of forced sales or receiverships or foreclosures or bankruptcies of any kind," Vernon T. Allnut said, he'd quieted down now, his voice sounded calm and cool, almost friendly. "What we are interested in is a stable business community, conservative management, reasonable rates of interest, a slow growth upward out of this mess we are in right now. We want to see private enterprise *flourish*, not flounder, that's what we lend our money *for*. That's why we lent it to you, Mr. Linthicum, although I might say with considerable reservations. And when you indulge in reckless expenditures like this, without any advice or consent from us whatsoever, why, those reservations are all too well justified. I can pride myself that I don't make too many mistakes of this kind, but I can see that I've made one this time. I made it out of a desire to see one of our oldest and most picturesque local enterprises preserved. Your father was running this boatyard when I was a little boy. People have talked about Linthicum boats in this end of the county all of my lifetime. Well, I don't have to tell you that. We hate to see the name go. But I don't know what more to do. Now that's the truth of it, Mr. Linthicum. There is just nothing more to do."

"Nothing more to do," Poppa said. "How do you mean, Mr. Allnut?"

"I mean you have exhausted your resources," Vernon T.

Allnut said. "You have no more capital, no more collateral, and very little in the way of prospects. As far as I can see, you have come to the end of the road, Mr. Linthicum." He put his glasses back on and peered forward at one of the sheets of paper on the desk. "As far as I can see, these expenditures for timber, hardware, fittings, tools, etc., will just about entirely absorb your advance from Mr. Clapperton on laying the keel. That leaves you with a payroll to meet in ten days, all these invoices from Wexler Brothers, and your note, which is already six weeks overdue. It's just beyond any remedy. I can't see anything for you to do but file bankruptcy papers. I can't see anything else for you to do."

Poppa hunched forward in his chair and clasped his hands together and dropped them between his thighs. "Naw, naw," he said. "I can't do that. You see, I got to build that boat." He looked so big and healthy it seemed silly to talk about him being at the end of his road. He looked like a man who hadn't even got started good, it didn't make sense. I couldn't understand how a man who could do as many things as he could and do them better than anybody else in the world couldn't learn how to keep his records straight. It didn't seem important, it was a little old fiddly thing that anybody with a pair of Sears Roebuck glasses and a ledger book could do, but the way Vernon T. Allnut talked it seemed like it was the most important part of the whole business. It wasn't enough to know how to make the best boats in the world, you had to know how to do all that fiddly business with the ledgers, too. I felt mad, I wanted to cuss somebody. If people wanted boats why didn't they leave him to hell alone and let him make them? Poppa got up and took a walk over to the electric fan and yanked on the string that was hanging down from the switch, snapping it on and off a couple of times, and then turned around and said to Vernon T. Allnut across the room, "All right, I'll tell you what I'm going to do. What is the absolute most time you can let me have, Mr. Allnut?"

"Time for what?" Vernon T. Allnut said. He was sitting there at the desk watching Poppa, worried but kind of curious. "You have no more resources, man. What good is a couple more weeks going to do you? What you need is money. Mr. Linthicum. What you need is about five thousand dollars."

"Yeah, I know," Poppa said. "And I know where I can get it. I don't need but a week or ten days." He started fumbling around in his pockets for his pipe and got it out and gave it a whack on his palm. "You see, I got a brother lives out in Cleveland, Ohio, has got a good bit of property. That's Abner, I reckon you remember him, he never taken to boats. He moved out yonder about Twenty-three and set himself up in the used car business. He's done real well, too. Now we ain't been real close over the years, but Abner, I know I could count on him to tide me over with four or five thousand. He's got it."

Vernon T. Allnut sat there doing eye exercises. He crossed his legs a couple of times and started swinging his glasses around by the stems. "How certain do you feel of this?" he said finally.

"Oh, hell, I'm more than certain," Poppa said. "I know Abner. He's quiet, but he's right there. You just give me a few days, Mr. Allnut, I guarantee you I'll make that payment, and a couple more in advance."

Well, I didn't feel a bit better when I heard that, as a matter of fact it seemed to me that things were going from bad to worse because as far as I knew the only property that Uncle Abner owned was a 1929 Reo, which I suppose you could say put him in the used car business in a way, but it certainly didn't make him any merchant prince. As a matter of fact we used to get letters from him two or three times a year asking if Poppa had any old clothes he didn't have any more use for and if so could we send them out there to Cleveland and maybe stick a couple of packs of Bull Durham in the pockets.

"You understand you cannot offer him any interest in this yard whatever as collateral?" Vernon T. Allnut said. "It will not support any more liens of any kind."

"Oh, I know that," Poppa said. "He won't want no collateral. No, it's just a matter of pride with him, keeping the family name up on that sign."

Vernon T. Allnut gave his glasses another twiddle or two and them put them back on and gave a big sigh. "Well," he said, "I'll see what I can do. I'll try and get you another two weeks. I don't promise, now, but I'll try. I hope you realize I'm going to have to fight tooth and nail with my Board of Directors."

"Well, I appreciate that more than I can tell you," Poppa said. He got back across the room in about three steps and clapped Mr. Allnut on the shoulder, his face breaking into a gigantic smile that spread his beard all over the place like a mop going to pieces. "This'll carry me right through to September," he said. "Then I'll be collecting the balance from Mr. Clapperton, and I got those contracts for three tonguers I can work on all through the winter. I'll be in the clear for good."

"I hope so," Mr. Allnut said. "For your sake, I hope so, Mr. Linthicum, because this is absolutely as far as I can go."

"Oh, I realize that," Poppa said. "Yes, sir, I realize that. There won't be no trouble, Mr. Allnut, you can bet on it. I wonder if I could offer you a little snort of Jack Daniel's?"

"No, thank you," Mr. Allnut said. He started gathering his papers together and sliding them into his briefcase, still looking pretty grim, as if maybe he'd just stepped in the cat box, but bearing up. "I'll have to call you Tuesday morning to confirm this," he said. "I suppose you'll be in the office around ten o'clock?"

"Yeah, I'll be here," Poppa said. "I'll be sitting right by that phone waiting for the good word. You're doing the right thing, Mr. Allnut."

"I sincerely hope so," Mr. Allnut said. He snapped his briefcase shut and picked his straw hat off the pine bench where he had set it and shook hands with Poppa very fast as if he had got hold of a bear trap or something by mistake. Poppa laid his hand in the middle of Mr. Allnut's back and sort of guided him across to the door as if he was showing a little boy the way to the bathroom and then followed him outside and walked him across the yard to his car. I got up off the floor and went in the office to get myself a drink of water out of the cooler, there was a tin cup hanging there on a string, and while I was gulping it down I heard the car door slam and then in a minute Poppa came back in the office.

"Hey, looky here, here's old Aaron!" he yelled. "You going to outchin me today, boy?"

There wasn't any ceiling in the office, there were just these two-by-six beams laid across the top for a ceiling to be nailed onto if Poppa ever wanted one, which it didn't look like he did because he used those beams all the time for these chinning contests he had with me and Sylvie and the workmen. He was the chinning champion of Calvert County and maybe the whole state of Maryland, because there were guys that came clear over from the Eastern Shore and even as far away as Baltimore and Frederick counties to see if they could beat him, but mighty few of them ever came close, although there was this steamfitter some guys brought over one time from Oxford who gave Poppa a pretty good run, fifty-six to eighty-three. Whenever me and Sylvie and Jamed came in there he'd grab us and hoist us up to those ceiling beams and make us see how many times we could chin. I could do about eight or ten and Sylvie could do five or six, but Jamed, of course, he couldn't do anything. He'd hang on and puff and groan a little bit and maybe haul himself up once or twice and then start twittering in his arms and turning red as a lobster and Poppa would get madder than hell, shouting at Jamed to chin, damn it, and not hang there like a wet rag. Jamed would get scared and start blubbering, I can't, Poppa, honest, I really can't, Poppa. Grab me, please, Poppa, I'm going to fall. Poppa would get so mad he wouldn't even haul Jamed down sometimes, he'd just let him drop clear to the floor, which was a pretty good fall for Jamed, him not being much taller than a turkey cock. One time he twisted his ankle pretty bad and lay there clutching at it and grunting while Poppa stared down at him, so mad he'd turned white, and all Jamed did was sort of whisper, he was hurting so bad he couldn't talk loud. "I'm sorry, Poppa. It just don't seem like I'm ever going to be much of a chinner, somehow."

So anyhow, Poppa came on back in the office and grabbed ahold of me and hoisted me up there to the ceiling so I could catch ahold of one of those beams and said, "All right now, let's see you break ten one time." I gave it a good try but I couldn't do more than eight, to tell the truth I couldn't concentrate too well, I was sort of worried about that business with Vernon T. Allnut. It didn't seem to bother Poppa any, though, he was cheering me on and whacking me on the ass and carrying on generally as if he'd just got money from home, which in a way I suppose you could say he had, although I figured it would be a long time coming. I gave out pretty quick and dropped down, so then Poppa jumped up and caught ahold himself and said, "Hey, looky here, Aaron, I got a new one. Watch this, now." Then he started swinging clear across the room from one of those beams to the next like we did on the parallel bars at school, those great big long legs of his hanging down not more than a couple of feet off the floor, he was so tall he had to hike them up to clear the desk when he got over in that corner. Then he turned around and started back toward the water cooler, hand over hand, all the time yelling, "Tarzan! Me Tarzan! Hey, looky here at old Tarzan!" He made four complete trips across that ceiling, which was pretty good considering there were about fifteen of those beams and they had sharp edges that were mighty hard on your hands.

AFTER MOMMA WENT IN TO BED I SAT THERE BY MYSELF ON the front porch listening to the hot bugs in the trees and the wash of the bay at the bottom of the cliff, I was making a list in my head of things to do, it had got to be a habit of mine, I've found that as long as you're working on a list of things to do you can keep in pretty good shape. What I had to do was call up in the morning and find out if Poppa's life insurance was still active, I had to check with the Coast Guard and see if the *Windsong* had been recovered yet, and along with it, his body, and if they had I had to make arrangements about salvage and burial respectively, although neither word seemed to apply properly to either of them, I had to persuade Momma to arrive at some decision about selling the shop or keeping it, I had to make some permanent provision either for a companion for her or somebody to run her errands and take her shopping and keep the house in repair, I had to call New York and postpone or cancel a Tuesday morning engagement to make a commercial for Tally-Ho Toilet Bowl Tablets because I was beginning to realize that all this was going to take more than another two days, and not least of all, I had to telephone a cross-eyed model named India Jones who right about now would be going into her usual Friday night decline over Civil Rights, her Electra complex, the Vietnam mess, and the scarcity of demand for cross-eyed models, I had plenty to think about. There was a kind of deathroom sweetness in the air from the honeysuckle that seemed to be swallowing up everything in sight, the ruins of the summer hotel, the pump, the garden fences, the stumps in the cliff sides, there was a voracious, fragrant predator moving in, devouring the whole damn place. Where did all that honeysuckle come from? I wondered, there didn't used to be all that honeysuckle when Poppa was around, and he's only been gone a week. It smelled just like Tally-Ho Toilet Bowl Tablets, I hated the stuff.

I could hear Jamed stirring around and murmuring in his sleep, he was happy as a clam in the daytime but sometimes at night something in his dreams would make him whimper and tremble, so I went in and pulled up the sheet to cover him, he had kicked it off in the heat but it was getting cooler now and I was afraid he'd catch cold, he woke up for a minute when I tucked the sheet in, and murmured, "Night, Aaron," just as if it was a night fifteen or twenty years ago, as if I'd never left the place. I laid my hand on his wrist and said, "Night, buddy," and then went back out and sat down in the glider and started working on my list again. Pretty soon I ran out of things to do in the next couple of days so I started working on my Lifetime List, there was always plenty of stuff to add to that one, like Join a Party of My Own Choice, Learn to Play a Musical Instrument (Probably the Recorder), Read *Oblomov* by Goncharov or *Goncharov* by Oblomov or whatever the hell it is, Find Out What Ethical Egoism means, Plant a Tree, Write a Nasty Letter to Ronald Reagan, Make Decision About Toupé, etc., etc. After a while I got pretty depressed because the Goddamned thing was so long already that I knew a lifetime would never be time enough to get it all done, it was what always happened, so I added my usual final item, the one I always capped it off with: Have a Drink, and went in and started digging around for the Jack Daniel's. It didn't take me long to find it, I knew it would be in a half-pint bottle, laid down flat under something where nobody else in the world would have suspected, but I was my father's son, boy, I knew a thing or two about where the goods are hidden, so after a couple of minutes of searching I flipped over a tin pie plate in the pots-and-pans compartment of the oven and there it was, right under Momma's innocent eyes. I took it back out on the porch and sat down in the glider and got to work, and with the smell and taste of the stuff my father came swarming back, he filled up the front porch, he was storming around in the summer darkness, he was everywhere, whisky-breathed and golden, with his dog's teeth and his plum-colored nose and beautiful broken hands, singer and sorcerer and master builder in a world of little pale men with rapid pulses and twitching lips, men whose only virtue was prudence and whose only God, for all their praying, was property, he came flooding in through every crevice of the night, driving away the death scent of the honeysuckle and filling the world with his good smell of sawdust and turpentine and fresh-woven cordage, whisky and dove flesh and the salt of the eternal sea. Oh my dark father, I said, come back to me, abide with me, you who have wounded us with these strange wounds, come back to heal them with the light of your golden eyes, the touch of your terrible great hands, you never said *I love you, Aaron,* you cannot be dead yet.

I was drunk as a skunk by the time I heard the murmur of Sylvie's and the Professor's voices and looked out through the screen and saw their figures moving up the hill, black against the starlight. They came up the steps and through the screen door onto the porch and when she saw me lolling there in the glider with the bottle between my knees, Sylvie said, "Well, just like old times. For God's sake, where did you get *that?* Or did you bring it?"

"You've got to know where to look," I said. "You want a snort?"

"We don't touch the stuff," Sylvie said. "You don't happen to have a joint, do you?"

"I've got ten thousand of them," I said. "And I'm stiff in every one." I gave a big happy giggle.

"Oh, boy," Sylvie said. She sat down in one of the rockers and put her feet up on the rail. "Has Momma gone to bed?"

"Yep," I said. "You have a good walk?"

"I don't know," she said. "We walked. What happened to the old tree trunk, anyway? Where we used to crab?"

"I don't know. I guess it got washed away, or rotted or something."

The Professor lit a cigarette and Sylvie said, "Ron, for God's sake, that's the tenth one tonight. What are you going to do, kill yourself for the American Tobacco Company?"

"Eighth," the Professor said. "We're only human, you know."

"Oh, Jesus," Sylvie said. "How can you tell?"

The Professor smiled luxuriously in the flame of his match and then stretched out his hand and quoted in a treacly voice: " 'Let me kiss your hand.' 'Let me wipe it first. It smells of mortality.' " He really wasn't too bad, I'd heard worse at the Greater London Academy of Drama.

"Oh, Jesus," Sylvie said. She leaned forward and peeled off her shoes and then settled back in the rocker and looked out at the stars over the bay. "Did you talk to Momma about selling the shop?"

"Yes," I said. "She doesn't know what she wants to do yet."

"Well, listen, Aaron, I've been thinking. Do you think she really ought to? I mean, it would be an income for her, wouldn't it?"

"I don't know," I said. "No more than the dividends on municipal bonds or something, I don't think."

"Oh. And I guess you wouldn't have any interest in coming back and running the place, would you?"

"What the hell is *this?*" I said. "Who the hell is *this* talking? Didn't you spend half your life telling me to clear out of here?"

"Well, I know. It's a nutty question, I guess. But after all."

"What we need is the light of day," the Professor said. "Questions now, answers later."

"How about shoving it up your ass?" Sylvie said.

"I'm giving you good advice, Syl," the Professor said, he made a point of sounding imperturbable.

"I don't want advice," Sylvie said. "I want—I want my life back. I want—" She started to hiccough, pretty violently. You could see the Professor was burning with suggestions about holding the breath, sipping cold water, putting the head between the knees, everything in the book, but he kept it all in, you had to give him credit. "Oh, Jesus CHRIST!" Sylvie said. "Now *this*."

We sat there for a while, the Professor puffing away, Sylvie hiccoughing, me taking a slug of Jack Daniel's every couple of minutes. After a while I said, "I couldn't, Sylvie. Not any more. Not even if I wanted to."

"I know," Sylvie said. She reached out and laid her hand on mine, turning her head to look at me through the darkness. "You're losing your hair, good-looking, you know that?"

"Yeah, I know."

"God, you had such beautiful hair."

The Professor crushed out his cigarette into one of Poppa's ashtrays that Momma had resurrected for our use, then he stood up and said, "Well, I don't know about you two, but I'm going to hit the sack. I've had it for one day."

"Momma put a pillow and a blanket on the sofa for you," I said. "You might have a little trouble with those springs."

"Hot bricks wouldn't bother me tonight," the Professor said. He came over and leaned down behind Sylvie and kissed her on the cheek. "What about you, Syl?"

"I'm going to sleep out here on the glider," Sylvie said. "Don't worry about it."

"O.K. Good night. Good night, Aaron."

"Good night," I said. He went inside the house and into the bathroom, we could see a little light coming out from the crack under the door.

"You love this guy, Syl?" I said.

"Love. Now what the hell does that mean, love?"

"I don't know. I thought you might know, by this time."

"Oh, sure. Anything you want to know about love, just ask your sister Syl." She raised her hand and shoveled it around restlessly under her hair. "Oh, we get along. He's a very nice guy, really. He leaves me alone, he's thoughtful, he's *polite* as hell. What do I expect? A bullfighter?"

"Well, I mean are you going to marry him, or what?"

"*Marry* him?" Sylvie said. "Sure, we're going to get married and have twelve children and name them after the Apostles. Didn't I write you about that?"

I took a couple more slugs of whisky and Sylvie started humming *The Isle of Capri*, I had to laugh out loud, I hadn't heard that corny song in twenty years, not since I heard her shrieking it out in six different keys from the catwalk of the *Susan Stapleton*.

"Hey, you still know all those great tunes," I said.

"Listen," Sylvie said, "they don't write them like that any more." She started giggling, we both did, we sat there giggling like kids. After we'd calmed down a little she said, "What about *you*, Buster? I haven't heard anything about you getting married."

"Not me," I said. "One thing I finally got figured out about me, I'm not the husband type. I'm pretty good at first aid, and that's about it."

"What does that mean?" Sylvie said.

"I just go scurrying around the battlefield with my box of Band-Aids and my bottle of iodine, but don't ask me to do anything with a diaper. It's a different instinct."

"You mean all those years you spent in London and New York, all those actress chicks you've been playing around with, and you never got bit, not even once? Come on, what are you trying to give me?"

"Oh, I've been bit. Did you mean have I ever been in love? Oh sure, too damn much. I'd say about ten times a day, on the average. But that doesn't mean I could ever get married. I'm just not a long-distance runner, that's all. It took me awhile to figure that out."

"That sounds sadder than hell, when somebody *else* says it," Sylvie said.

"Well, some people are, and some people aren't. You do the best you can." I started popping my thumb out of the bottle top the way Poppa used to do, we sat there listening to the sound, a sort of festive sound, New Year's Eve, boy, I wonder what he was celebrating all his life? I thought.

"What did you do over there all that time, anyhow?" Sylvie said. "I never did know. You know how many letters you've written me in the last ten years? Four. Just exactly *four*. I call that crummy, Aaron, I really do."

"I'm sorry, Sylvie," I said. I really was. "I just can't write letters, somehow, I don't know why. It's just a hangup of some kind." The truth was I'd always been waiting to write her *the* letter, the one about how I'd been given the lead in a play that had become the rage of the West End, not a lot of hokum, boy, Sylvie was not a noted consumer of hokum, just a couple of quiet little lines that said, "Dear Sylvie: Thought you'd like to see this," with a clipping attached of a review from the *Observer* by Ken Tynan that said: "To the names of Burbage, Garrick, Kean, Forbes-Robertson and Gielgud, we must now add that of Aaron Linthicum," she deserved it, if anybody in this world deserved anything from me. Right now she hiked her heels up onto the porch banister and slumped down in the rocker, letting her arms drop from the elbows so that they hung like a pair of pale oars drifting in the darkness, she looked strengthless and derelict there for a minute like a drifting skiff and I was so moved by the fact of her disappointment in me and by what were for Sylvie a phenomenal patience and silence in the face of it that I wanted to do some old-fashioned consolatory thing, ask her to sing *Deep Purple*, buy her an ice cream cone, any damn thing.

"Actually, I had a pretty good time over there," I said. "For a while, I had this really great place to live, up on Camden Hill in Kensington. Did I tell you about that?"

"You didn't tell me about a damn thing," Sylvie said. "Two of those letters were postcards, and one of *them* you couldn't read because it had coffee all over it or something."

"It was a great place," I said. "Right up on top of the tallest hill in Kensington, in one of those old Victorian town mansions. I guess it used to be the servants' quarters or something, because it was right under the roof. There was this sloping studio ceiling and a dormer window you could stand in front of and look down over the whole city of London. God, I loved that place."

I could see it while I told her about it, that huge, twilight-purple city smoking with mystery and passion, the lavender slate roofs, the chimney pots, the dome of St. Paul's, Big Ben, the stacks of freighters in the Thames, the towers of Westminster and Waterloo Bridge, and far away on the south shore of the river a kind of ghostly radiance above the Embankment where the Globe had stood, where all of Poppa's friends had roared and strutted and sung their sad songs and downed their cakes and ale, I loved to come home to it through the winter evenings and drop a shilling in the meter and light the gas grate and stand at the window with a cup of tea dreaming of Keats wandering through the mist down there on Hampstead Heath, that was where I had been going to take my stand, right up there between the stars and that sea of fragrant, fecund murk teeming with so many noble ghosts, I used to run through a litany of them while I stood there smiling like a fool: Marlowe, Shelley,

Shakespeare, Johnson, Dickens, Linthicum, that was *Aaron* Linthicum, boy, there were better things to do in this world than build boats.

"It sounds like a great little love nest," Sylvie said. "Is that where you used to make all those chicks?"

"All what chicks?" I said. "There was only one."

"I thought it was ten a day."

"Oh, those weren't chicks. Those were just people I fell in love with."

"What sort of people?" Sylvie said.

"Well, there was this guy I saw in the hall one day at GLAD, a great big skinny guy from Birmingham. Somebody had spilled some raisins on the stairs and he was squatting there picking them off the floor and cramming them into his mouth. Then there was this sad-looking sack that used to prowl around Hampstead Heath with a pair of binoculars, spying on lovers. And a guy I saw coming out of Finchley Hospital one day with absolutely devastated eyes. And a bunch of little eighteen-year-old tarts that used to hang around Bayswater in the evening with monkey-fur coats and Cuban heels. All kinds of people. One-legged veterans that drew pictures of Windsor Castle or portraits of Prince Philip on the sidewalk with colored chalk, guys at Hyde Park Corner that would stand there shouting about free love or Rosicrucianism or some damn thing while everybody jeered and whooped. People with home haircuts, especially, that really bothers me. And not just people. Dogs, cats, even this stuffed polar bear, for God's sake, that used to stand outside a furniture store at Goodge Street Station. I tell you that bear had a look of absolute anguish in his eyes, you never saw anything like it. I think they were the wrong kind of eyes, in the first place, they must have been made for a moose or something."

I was getting pretty drunk by this time, I took another slug out of the bottle and it seemed to be just about empty,

I gave it a couple of shakes and there was a very modest slurping going on in there, not more than a thimbleful, so I set it down carefully on the floor to save for a nightcap. Sylvie didn't say anything, she sat there with her arms adrift staring out at the bay.

"That was the saddest-looking Goddamned bear I ever saw," I said. "I don't know how anybody could bear to shoot him, he must have just stood there and sobbed and sobbed, all the time they were aiming at him. Of course, you stand around on a London street corner for fifteen or twenty years, you've got a right to look sad. He was standing there sort of holding out his paws as if he was begging you for God's sake to stop and do something to alleviate his agony, give him a quick shot of cyanide or something. Only of course he was already dead, so there wasn't a whole lot you could do, except maybe to bury him."

Sylvie raised her hands and held her face between them. After she'd sat there like that for quite a while, she said, "That's what you call love? Jesus."

"Well, love, pity, necrophilia maybe, who the hell knows? You give it the fanciest name you can."

JAMED STUCK HIS HAND OUT IN THE LIGHT AND WIGGLED HIS fingers slow, he had a red hand, purple-red, it looked as if it was stained in raspberry juice. The rest of his arm was blue as bay water all the way down to his wrist and his face was blue, bewitched, he was long gone when he got in church. He never seemed to be listening especially to what was going on but somehow he soaked it all up, all that organ music and gladiola smell and the light from the stained glass windows, he was like a sponge. I thought if you squeezed him good when you got him home all that red and blue dye and organ music and flower smell would come squishing out of him and make a puddle on the floor, he soaked up things like that. Sylvie was sitting next to him but she was out of the light, she had on her white church dress and white socks and black patent leather shoes and a white bow in her hair, she was bewitched too, but not with Jesus Christ, with Sylvie Linthicum, boy. Jamed moved his bloody hand and laid it on Sylvie's skirt and when he did it changed color, it was bleached white. She whispered, "Quit that, Jamed," so he moved his hand back and it turned red again and then blue, it was a real magic act, he was a walking piece of litmus paper.

Dr. Duryea was talking about the difference between obligation and responsibility, obligation was something you *had* to do, like paying taxes, and responsibility was something you *ought* to do, like sending your children to the dentist regular, and I could see it was going over big with Momma but not so big with Poppa, who was having a lot of trouble with a hangnail. It was the only time I ever saw Poppa in a suit and tie, on Sunday, and I couldn't say I liked the look of him too much. He looked sort of humiliated and foolish and dangerous, like one of those animals you see dressed up for a gag, a goat with a hat and coat and pair of pants on and somebody hanging onto him pretty carefully while he gets his picture taken. He didn't come to church because he believed in it, you could see that, but as a favor to Momma. You could see he wanted to sort of make up to her for all the stuff he did that she didn't like. He didn't fuss about going and she didn't have to nag at him, he got up every Sunday morning and trimmed his beard and got dressed and drove us all up to Poole and then sat there all through the sermon fiddling with his fingernails and every now and then stealing a quick look at any pretty woman who happened to be around. I did quite a bit of fiddling and looking around myself, so every now and then our eyes would meet and he'd grin at me and wink and then look quick at Momma to see if she'd caught him winking and then get back to his fingernails again. I didn't believe in it all that much either but I liked the atmosphere, the smell of waxed wood and flowers and the music and Momma in her blue hat, smelling of talcum powder, with her hands clasped in her lap and her eyes at peace for a little while, not wondering where the hell Poppa was or whether Jamed had got drowned or something. I liked Jesus, too, I thought he was great, and I liked the pictures on the fans showing all the stuff he did like walking on the water and multiplying the loaves and fishes, but somehow I didn't have too much faith that those things had really happened. It always seemed like a fairy story to me, maybe I got that idea from Poppa, I don't know, but I could see that Momma set a lot of store by it, so I never let on.

Dr. Duryea said he hoped that by the time we came back next Sunday we would all have assumed one additional responsibility of our own free will, something that involved giving up one of our many pleasures so that we could contribute to somebody else's welfare. Momma pressed her lips together and pinched her nostrils in, you could see she was hoping Poppa had taken that in good. Then we all got up and said the Lord's Prayer and then Mrs. Weems played the organ and we opened our hymnbooks and sang *Jesus, Savior of My Soul.* Jamed wouldn't sing, he never would, he just stood there looking sort of stunned, but Sylvie sang like crazy. I didn't sing either, I just moved my lips and pretended I was singing, I couldn't carry a tune. Then they opened the doors at the back and we went out, shuffling along slowly with everybody turning around to smile and chat with each other, I liked that. Dr. Duryea was standing out on the front steps shaking hands with everybody when they came out, he always put his hand on my head and said, "Well, young man, you've grown another inch, I see," or if it was Sylvie,

"Well, young lady, etc." Jamed seemed to think that Dr. Duryea had some special private connections with God, maybe that he had personal conferences with Him every week or something, he would stand there staring up at Dr. Duryea with his mouth hanging open until Momma pushed him on by. We came down the steps and walked back behind the church to the graveyard, we always did that after services, to look at Granma and Granpa Linthicum's graves. They were in a nice spot under a little group of cedar trees beside a low stone wall that looked out across a meadow that in summer was usually yellow with hops blossoms and buzzing with bees. We stood there looking down at the graves and Momma shut her eyes and whispered a prayer to herself clutching her pocketbook against her stomach. Poppa took his hat off and pulled at his beard and shifted his feet around and then in a minute he said, "Well, dove, I reckon we better get on back," he didn't like anything to do with death. It was kind of odd because after all they were his parents, Momma's folks were buried way across the state at Thurmont and we only went there on Decoration Day or Easter. Sylvie crouched down and picked a buttercup off of Granma's grave and stuck it in the buttonhole of her dress, she always did love Granma. That was too much for Jamed, his face went all to pieces and his shoulders started heaving, and Poppa said, "Now let's go, Anabel, the children is getting all upset."

So we walked back down the path to the gravel parking lot at the side of the church and climbed in the pickup, Momma and Poppa in the cab and all of us kids in the back end on some peach baskets that Poppa set in there on Sundays so we wouldn't get our clothes dirty. It was smooth enough on the highway but when we turned off Route 49 and hit the dirt road down to Port Federation we bounced around on those baskets till our teeth nearly shook loose. Poppa always turned in there fast on purpose to give us a thrill, but this time when he hit a patch of corduroy that had got worked up in the wet weather he gunned the pickup so we sailed up off those baskets like rockets, I thought we'd take off. You could hear him whooping up front and Momma laying him out, saying wouldn't it be fine if he had our deaths on his conscience just for the sake of a stupid joke, and it was heathen anyway, that kind of boisterousness on a Sunday. It scared Jamed nearly to death and it made Sylvie mad, they both gritted their teeth and hung on like crazy, but I thought it was great.

We went in and changed our clothes when we got back and Momma started fixing lunch. Poppa went out to feed his doves, he always did that when we got back from church, you could hear him back there in the loft crooning and talking to them: "Coo, Babe, coo. Now you settle down, Babe. Come here give your Daddy some loving. Now ain't that a sweet dove." Momma had got the soup hot, it was bean-and-ham, and we were going crazy from the smell. She went over to the back door and called through the screen, "*Oh*, Joel! Come, now. Lunch," and in a minute Poppa came up the back steps with his coat over one arm, rolling up his sleeves.

"Now don't that smell like heaven!" he said. "I tell you, if they don't have ham and bean soup up there, I ain't going." He hung his coat on the back of his chair and went over to the sink to wash his hands, giving Momma a pat on the bottom when he went by, she gave him a look like what they served for lunch in heaven was the last thing he had to worry about. He splashed around and hummed and then dried his hands and came over to the table, we were all sitting there waiting by this time, and sat down and unfolded his napkin very slow to tease Jamed and Sylvie and me, and then bowed his head and clasped his hands together on the edge of the table and said Grace: "Lord, thank You for this food." I think he'd set the world's record for saying Grace, he got it out in about one fourth of a second. It was

Momma's idea for him to say it, she made him do it every meal of his lifetime, but she left the blessing up to him so of course she didn't get much fireworks, I guess Poppa figured we got enough fireworks for one day from Dr. Duryea.

He ladled out the soup and we got to it. Nobody had much to say for a while, there was just the sound of spoons clicking and crackers being crumbled up, Jamed was the world's champion cracker crumbler, and everybody trying hard not to slurp, and outside the doves chuckling in the hot morning silence like voices coming up from deep under the sea. After a while Momma said, "You going down to the shop today, Joel? I reckon that Mr. Clapperton'll be back around wanting to see his boat."

"No, he ain't coming around," Poppa said. "He's tied up somewheres." He raised his eyebrows to look up at Momma. "Did you want me to do something, dove?"

"I wanted some canning jars left up to Mrs. French's, if you got the time," Momma said. "I promised her a dozen."

"Yeah, I can do that," Poppa said. "I ain't planning on doing a lick of work all day." He nodded his head at Momma. "You ought to do the same thing, dove. You been working too hard."

"Oh, yes, wouldn't that just be fine," Momma said. "What would you do for dinner, I wonder?"

Poppa smiled and nodded again. "Well now, I might just have the answer to that," he said. He reached over to dish himself out another ladleful of soup, he was being mysterious as hell. "Yes, sir, I got a right good idea on that."

"What are you hinting at, Poppa?" Sylvie said. "He's hinting at something, Momma."

"You hush up, Screech," Poppa said. "Let your Momma ask the questions."

"I'm not asking anything," Momma said. "I've got better sense."

"All right," Poppa said, ducking his chin down like if she

wanted to stay ignorant he didn't give a hoot. "You know what the Book says. 'Ask and it shall be given.' "

"Well now, just listen who's quoting scripture," Momma said. She reached over and gave Jamed a rap on the wrist, he was going wild with the crackers. "How many crackers you going to put in that soup?"

"It's not but twelve," Jamed said.

"Twelve is too many. You got to cut it with a knife already."

Poppa leaned back in his chair and brushed his beard with his napkin. "What I had in mind for supper was oysters," he said, spreading his hands on his belly. "Big fat Chincoteague oysters. About a dozen on the half shell, and then a big plateful of fried ones, and then a nice hot bowl of chowder. We got any oysters in the house, dove?"

"What we've got is meat loaf," Momma said.

"Well, that's a pity," Poppa said, "because what I heard, they having a oyster roast down at Drum Point this evening, all you can eat for a dollar and a half, with cole slaw and potato salad and cold beer throwed in. And no dishwashing afterward. Now I call that a bargain."

"It's a bargain for anybody that's got a dollar and a half they don't need," Momma said. She looked surprised though, pleased, and her voice was milder.

"Momma, let's go!" Sylvie yelled. "Come on, let's go, Momma! Me and Jamed loves oysters, don't we, Jamed?"

"I don't know," Jamed said. He'd got a cracker ground up in his hand till it was practically powder and was blowing it in his bowl.

"You do so!" Sylvie yelled. "You know you do. He does, Momma."

Poppa folded up his napkin and laid it on the table and gave it a little pat, then he said, "Well, thank the Lord for that little bit. Many a man would of made a meal off that." He said that every time he finished eating, that was his own idea of Grace-saying. Then he heeled over on his chair and reached into his pocket and took out a wad of money that he unpeeled slowly until there were six ragged-looking one-dollar bills lying there in a heap in the middle of the table. "There's more than enough right there," he said. "Children is half price. Now what do you say, Momma? You been working too hard, beauty. You look tired."

"I don't know what to make of you," Momma said, shaking her head. "I just never do know."

"There's pony rides for the kids, and a horseshoe pitching match," Poppa said. "And I reckon the Weems and Offutts will be down there, so you'll have somebody to jaw with. You got it coming, dove." He leaned across the table and laid his hand on hers.

"Well, the Lord knows I'd be grateful for a day out of this kitchen," Momma said. She moved her hand out from under his and raised it up to her face and laid her fingers flat against her cheek, thinking, she looked pretty. "It *is* a nice day. Well, all right. I'm grateful for it, Joel."

"Hey, yay!" Sylvie yelled. "We're going to have pony rides, Jamed! We're going to eat oysters!"

"Hey, wowee," Jamed said. It was just getting through to him.

"Well, I guess I'd better get this mess cleaned up, then," Momma said. "And go get myself dressed up again." She smiled at Poppa, a nice young smile, I couldn't hardly remember one like it on her face. "Good land, if I have to change my clothes one more time today, I'm going to get dizzy."

"No, you don't do no cleaning up," Poppa said. "You go in there and get yourself fixed up. Me and the children will do the dishes." He got up from the table and flapped his hand at her, shooing her out. "This here is going to be your day off, dove. Right from now on."

"No, you're not either going to wash my Sunday china," Momma said. "You shoo, yourself."

"We'll be careful," Poppa said.

"Oh, yes, I know. That was Grandmother Parker's china, that she brought from England. If you broke a piece of that china I'd lose my mind." She got up from her chair and folded her napkin on the table. "Now you men just run on. Sylvie and I will do the dishes. There's plenty of time to get ready."

Sylvie looked disgusted so I grinned at her and said, "Boy, you get all the fun, Sylvie," and she said, "You shut up, Aaron, you crumb."

Momma said, "You stop that, deviling your sister, Aaron. Now you get out of here, all three of you."

"O.K.," Poppa said. "Come on, men. They don't have no use for us, I guess." He stooped down with his back to Jamed and said, "Hop up here, Jamie." Jamed giggled and hopped up onto Poppa's back, hugging him around the neck, and Poppa carried him out the screen door and down the back steps to the orchard. I came along behind banging Jamed on the ass and saying, "Get up there, mule," he was giggling like crazy. Poppa climbed up into our tree with Jamed hanging right there on his back, he was strong. He reached down for me and hauled me up beside them and we climbed on up to the big branch where we always sat and looked out over the top of the cliffs and the blue water sprinkled with diamonds in the sun.

"This here is a pretty spot," Poppa said. He grunted suddenly and put his hand on top of his head, squinching his face up and clenching his eyes shut tight as if he had a headache. "Oh, Jesus Christ."

"You got a pain, Poppa?" I said.

"Yeah." He moved his hand down and opened his eyes slowly, staring down wide-eyed at the potted geraniums Momma had set on her kitchen window sill, they seemed to dazzle him. "Aaron, how old is Jamie?" he said in a minute.

"Five," I said. "Don't you know that?"

"I forget them things."

"I ain't either," Jamed said. "I'm four hundred and sixty-five million." He giggled.

"You're four hundred and sixty-five million kinds of crazy, that's what you are," Poppa said. He reached over and tickled Jamed in the ribs. Jamed squealed and hollered and hung on, kicking at Poppa with his feet. I heard Momma yell out the kitchen window, "Now Joel, you be careful up there with those boys. Now stop that nonsense, up in that tree."

"You hear your Momma?" Poppa said. "You stop all that ruckus." He went on tickling Jamed and Jamed went on hollering and kicking. Then Poppa gave him a final pinch on the belly and settled back against the tree trunk and looked up through the branches at the sky and started singing, he cut loose, boy, roaring out loud:

"In the year of our Lord Eighteen Hundred and Six
We set sail from the cold quay of Cork.
We were sailing away with a cargo of bricks
For the grand city all in New York."

He went all the way through to the end. Jamed loved that song, he giggled all the way through it. Then Poppa sang *The Leaving of Liverpool*, that was the one I liked, it was sad. He sang it soft, down in his throat, with his eyes shut. I didn't even know where Liverpool was but that song made me homesick for it. Sylvie came down the kitchen steps and over to the tree and stood underneath listening till he'd finished.

"Momma's near ready," she said. "She wants you to put the canning jars in the pickup."

"Yeah, O.K.," Poppa said. "Come on, fellas, let's go get them oysters." He took Jamed by one hand and lowered him down to the ground and then jumped down himself and reached up for me. We ran over and climbed in the back end of the pickup and Poppa went over to the shed. There was a lot of clinking and clanking in there and in a minute he came out with a peach basket full of canning jars all sparkling between his arms like ice in the sun. He brought it over to the truck and heaved it up onto the edge of the sidewall and Sylvie and me lowered it down into the truck bed.

"Jamed, you go get your bear," Poppa said. "You might want him."

"Uh uh, I don't want him," Jamed said.

"Yeah, well we might get back late and you'll want to go to sleep up front, and then you'll want him."

"Uh uh, I won't want him."

Poppa stood there staring up at Jamed, he looked sad, like all the boats in the world had just sunk. Then all of a sudden he got mad, you could see his face change, I thought he was going to reach up and swat Jamed. He probably would have if Momma hadn't come down the steps right then carrying a wicker basket that she kept her crochet work in and a couple of blankets folded across her arms. Poppa heard her feet on the steps, he turned around and said, "I'll get them, dove." He went over and took the blankets from Momma and carried them to the pickup and tossed them up on the front seat. "You get in," he said. "I got to get my tobacco." He went back across the yard to the house and up the kitchen steps. Momma got in the cab and slammed the door. "Now you children sit still back there," she said. "I don't want anybody falling out. Did Poppa put the canning jars in?"

"Yes, ma'am," Sylvie said. She picked one of the jars out of the basket and held it against her throat.

"Why you doing that?" Jamed said.

"Because it feels good," Sylvie said. She was nuts about cold stuff. She had an icicle in the refrigerator she'd broke off the porch roof two winters ago and kept in there frozen ever since. Every once in a while in the middle of summer she'd get it out and hold it against her throat for just a second and then stick it back in the freezer. We couldn't none of us touch it. She was going to try and make it last till she was fifty years old or more, and then one day when she was an old lady she'd get it out and feel the cold from a winter when she was nine years old. "Won't that be great?" she said. "I'll be able to hold the very same icicle I broke off the eaves when I was a little girl." She was always getting fancy ideas like that, about losing things, especially. She was scared of something.

"I don't know what is keeping that man," Momma said. "In such a terrible rush, till everybody else is ready."

Sylvie started banging on the cab roof and hollering, "Come on, Poppa, we want to ride them ponies."

"You stop that nonsense," Momma said, "or the only thing you'll ride is a hickory stick."

Poppa came out of the house and down the kitchen steps tucking his tobacco pouch in his shirt pocket.

"What's all this hollering about?" he said. "You just hold your horses."

"That's what we *want* to do!" Sylvie shouted. "That's what we're waiting to do, is get over there and hold our horses! Hey, Aaron, he said, 'Hold your horses,' and I told him, 'That's what we want to do!' "

"Yeah, I heard you," I said.

Poppa climbed up into the cab and started the motor. "How about we stop at the Frenchs' on the way back, dove?" he said. "We don't want to miss out on that dinner."

"Well, that'll do, I guess," Momma said. "She's not going to use them tonight, I don't reckon."

"O.K., here we go," Poppa said. "Next stop is Drum Point. Anybody wants to go to the bathroom has got to use one of them jars."

"Now there's no call for that kind of talk," Momma said. Sylvie giggled and Jamed stared at his feet and pretended he hadn't heard it.

Poppa drove slow up the dirt road this time, he wasn't going to rile Momma up again. It was beautiful, going slow, looking at the trees. I always did love September. It was the time when everything was supposed to be dying or going to sleep, but not me, I was just waking up. It was the first Sunday in September so it was still plenty hot, as a matter of fact we got some of the hottest weather of the year in September, but the mornings and evenings had a smell of frost in them and the light was different, it soaked right into you and made your heart fizz and tingle like a strawberry dropped into soda water. I sat there and watched the woods going by full of deer prints and ripe wineberries and humming with quail. I wouldn't of cared if we'd never got there, it would have been fine with me if we'd spent the rest of our lives right there in that pickup, all five of us driving along to an oyster roast on a Sunday afternoon.

This place at Drum Point was a Methodist campground. They had picnic tables set around under the trees and stone fireplaces for barbecues and horseshoe pits and a sandy pony ring with a rail fence around it. There was a big banner stretched across the road between two oak trees where you drove in, it said:

CALVERT COUNTY ANNUAL METHODIST OYSTER ROAST
$1.50—All You Can Eat
Everybody Welcome

There was a booth there with a lady in a pink dress selling meal tickets. Poppa handed her his money through the car window and she gave him a strip of tickets and said, "Now you folks enjoy yourselves, you hear?"

"We're going to do that very thing," Poppa said.

We parked in a place that was roped off for cars and Sylvie and Jamed and me climbed down and ran over to the pony ring. They were pretty rugged-looking ponies, shaggy sleepy-eyed things. Jamed said, "Them things is mean." He was right about that. It took a lot of persuasion to get him up on one. He sat there scared to death, hanging onto the saddle horn while a man led the pony around the ring by the bridle, after he'd been around a couple of times he wanted to get down. I thought Poppa would get mad, I thought he'd make Jamed stay on till he got over it, but he didn't. He just said, "O.K., son," and lifted Jamed down and gave him a hug before he set him on the ground, it wasn't natural. Sylvie and me rode by ourselves. She wanted to gallop but the pony wouldn't do it, he just plodded along with his ears laid back looking fed up with the whole thing and every now and then reaching back and trying to bite her on the leg. She kept kicking him in the ribs and hollering, "Get up, you dumb horse. You bite me, I'll tear your ears off," till the man made her quit. Poppa laughed and said, "That girl is a ring-tailed snorter," and Momma said yes and we knew where she got it from.

They had swings, too. Sylvie and me got on one together, standing on the seat facing each other so we could pump both ways. We got her up so high we were nearly lying out straight on the chains. There was a sensational moment when we would pause just for a second at the top of the arc, hanging up there stone-still in the air, everything seemed frozen, Sylvie's hair scattered in the blue sky, Jamed underneath looking up with his mouth wide open, Momma looking up too, holding her hat on her head with her fingertips so it wouldn't fall off, and Poppa with his bright yellow eyes and teeth to match grinning up through his beard, his arm drawn back to fling an acorn at us. Every now and then he'd let fly with one, those things stung, he popped Sylvie on the ass one time and she screamed, "You better cut that out,

Poppa. You're going to be sorry." Momma said, "Joel, stop deviling that child."

After a while Momma spotted the Floyds and we went over to visit with them. They said why didn't we eat with them so we hauled another table over and set it endwise to theirs. They had R. B. and Donna with them, they were just about Jamed's and Sylvie's ages, so right away they all ran off to hunt frogs, R. B. said he knew where there was a good creek for frogs. I didn't go, Poppa and Mr. Floyd were going to pitch horseshoes and I wanted to watch. We went over there to the pits and they made up a team and played a couple of guys from Deale. They lost, Poppa wasn't much good, he didn't play much. He had a whale of a time, though. What he would have won at was a contest for how *far* you could throw the things. They let me try but I couldn't even pitch it clear to the other pit, those shoes were heavy. Poppa said, "What you need is oysters, boy. Come on, let's go get some."

So we went back to the table to get Momma and Mrs. Floyd, the kids were back by this time, they had a couple of bullfrogs in a Mason jar, then we went and got in the chow line. There was half a dozen men in spattered aprons standing back of a row of tables shucking oysters as fast as they could, they'd skinned their knuckles raw. They'd haul up a gunny sack and pour out a heap of them onto the table and then pry open the shells and set them on a paper plate. Right next to that they had fried ones, a couple of ladies would roll them in batter and meal and dump them in a big vat full of boiling grease and then fish them out in wire baskets and pile them on a serving tray so you could help yourself. Then they had a chowder table with a ladle in a big steel drum and paper cups you could pour it in, steaming and peppery. Next to that there was a roasting pit, where you raked the lumpy gray shells off a sheet of hot tin over a birchwood fire, I never smelled anything as good. I got some of each kind, I didn't know if I was going to get through it all but I was going to try. Then when we got over to the table a man came along and set down a pitcher of beer and a pitcher of lemonade and a minute later a lady brought over two whole hot apple pies, that was some meal. Momma said, "Land, it's a good thing we don't come here every day, I'd gain twenty pounds a week." She was happy, it was a real treat for her. She and Mrs. Floyd got on fine, they were having a great time together. Poppa and Mr. Floyd were too. They got in an argument about who could eat the most raw oysters, so they decided to have a contest, they put up a dollar each. Well, my God, Poppa ate five dozen, I couldn't believe it. He kept me going back and forth to the serving table for half an hour there, bringing him supplies. I'd set down a fresh plateful and he'd get to work on them, not too fast, slow and businesslike, real professional, and then smack his lips and take a big swig of beer and say, "O.K., Aaron, I need stoking up, boy," and push his plate over to me again. Sylvie and Jamed and me would cheer every time he finished a plateful and R.B. and Donna would cheer every time Mr. Floyd finished one. Momma and Mrs. Floyd didn't cheer any but they couldn't help smiling. Momma said they were both crazy and they'd suffer for it plenty tonight. Poppa winked at Mr. Floyd and said, "We ain't the only ones going to suffer tonight, are we, Ben?" and Momma and Mrs. Floyd clucked their tongues and grinned at each other and shook their heads. Poppa won easy, Mr. Floyd gave up halfway through his fourth dozen, he pushed his plate away and said, "Well, Joel, I give. I just barely got room left to pick my teeth." So Poppa picked up the two dollars and folded it up and stuck it in his shirt pocket, he said, "I can use that. We'll stop on the way home, dove, and get a couple dozen oysters for breakfast." Momma whacked him on the shoulder.

We were all full, we were ready to bust. Sylvie pulled her shirt out of her pants and stuck her belly out like a watermelon and smacked it with her hand and said, "Hey, looky here, I'm 'bout to have a baby."

"Now, looky *here!*" Momma said. "You stop that right this very *minute!* That's a fine way for a lady to act."

"That ain't no lady, that's my daughter," Poppa said. Sylvie jumped on him and grabbed ahold of his beard and tugged it good, and he howled like a bear and said, "I give! I give! O.K., you're a lady!"

"You-all stop that roughhousing," Momma said. "You want some exercise, you help me get this table cleared off."

We all went to work on the table and when we had it cleared off Momma spread one of the blankets over it and opened up her crochet basket and started showing Mrs. Floyd some kind of special stitches. She had a piece of stuff she was working on, about the size of a bath towel, it was very fine work, a lot of knobbly octagons sewed together. Poppa sat drinking beer and smoking his pipe, watching the women's hands while they crocheted, he seemed to have gone off in some kind of a trance.

"What is that you're making, dove?" he said after a while.

"It's going to be a bedspread," Momma said. "That's a very old pattern that Granma Parker taught me. Won't that look pretty on the bed?" She spread out the piece of work in her lap and smoothed it with her hand, her head tilted to one side, admiring.

"Yeah, that'll be real pretty," Poppa said, he didn't much more than whisper it. He drank down the last of his beer and then whacked his pipe bowl on the sole of his shoe and said to Mr. Floyd, "Hey, Ben, how about a little more horseshoe pitching, sort of ease them oysters down?"

"Yeah, that'd be fine," Mr. Floyd said. They got up and started down toward the horseshoe pits, but they never got there, I was watching. Where they went was down through a strip of woods into the field where the cars were parked. They were down there a good while, I kept watching, and when they came out I could see they were feeling pretty good. Poppa was sort of stumbling over rocks and every now and then he'd put out his hand to touch a tree trunk and steady himself. I figured one of them had a bottle down there, Poppa most likely, and it got me worried, Momma was having such a good time, I didn't want any trouble. I went over and sat on one of the swings so I could keep an eye on them. They were standing there by the edge of the woods, laughing and snorting, looking over toward the pony ring. Every now and then Mr. Floyd would smack himself on the thigh and bend over double laughing. I heard Poppa say, "Well, put up or shut up, Ben. I say I can do it, and I got two dollars here in my shirt pocket says I can do it."

"O.K, I'll take that," Mr. Floyd said. Poppa looked around the campground and spotted me sitting there in the swing.

"Hey, Aaron, come here a minute," he yelled. I went over and stood in front of him and he took a swing at my chin with his fist and said, "Hey, boy, want you to do me a favor."

"O.K., what, Poppa?" I said.

"You see that boy over yonder at the pony ring?" I looked over and saw a boy in a pair of overalls, not much older than me, rubbing down one of the ponies with a gunny sack. The ring was closed now, everybody had drifted up from that end of the campground to the picnic tables. The ponies had been unsaddled, they were standing there with their heads down, nibbling at fresh hay, tethered by their halters to the fence rail. They were dark with sweat across their backs where the saddle pads had pressed.

"Yeah, I see him," I said.

"Well, you go over there and tell him Mr. Jensen wants to see him. Tell him you'll watch the place till he gets back. Mr. Jensen's up there getting his dinner, if he wants to know."

"What are you going to do, Poppa?" I said.

"You go over there and do what I told you, and you'll find out. Go on, now."

I went on over there, I wasn't feeling any too happy about it, and stuck my head over the rail fence and said to the boy, "Hey, Mr. Jensen wants to see you. He told me to watch the ponies till you got back."

"What's he want?" the boy said.

"I don't know. He just said for you to get right on up there. You want me to rub that pony down while you're gone?"

"Yeah, O.K.," the boy said. "Just get him dried up a little. I ain't going to be long, I don't reckon." He tossed me the gunny sack and climbed through the fence and went up toward the picnic tables. He hadn't hardly got started before Poppa and Mr. Floyd were up there at the ring and climbing through the fence.

"Now Aaron, I want you to watch this," Poppa said. "You're going to see something you don't see every day." He unfastened the pony's halter from the fence rail and handed it to Mr. Floyd. "Let him eat till I get set," he said. "Then hang on tight and keep his head up. I don't want that little bastard biting me." He spit on his hands and then rubbed them on his thighs, grinning like a fool.

"You ain't going to get in trouble, are you, Poppa?" I said.

"Trouble? No, no, when was I ever in trouble?" He crouched down beside the pony and worked his feet in close between its legs. The pony lifted his head and looked around, a little bit uneasy about what was going on, but Mr. Floyd patted him on the neck and said, "Easy, boy, that's all right, that's all right. Just go on and eat your hay." So in a minute the pony lowered his head down again and started to eat and the minute he did Poppa put out his arms and circled his front legs with one arm and his hind legs with the other and shoved his head in between them, bracing his shoulders up under the pony's belly, then he heaved up, slow, his face turning red and the cords standing out on each side of his neck like ramrods, his knees unbending slow and shivering with strain, the pony starting to kick and struggle and his eyes getting wild, Mr. Floyd hanging onto the halter and whooping like a fool, Poppa coming up slow and steady till he was standing straight up, well my God, he lifted that pony clear off the ground, I wouldn't have believed it could be done. The pony didn't believe it neither, that was one surprised-looking animal. There he was six feet off the ground with his ears laid back flat and his eyes rolling around like golf balls and Poppa standing there bowed over and a little bit wobbly in the knees, peeking up through his eyebrows with this Goddamned horse on his back, it was one funny sight. I laughed so hard I got weak and fell down.

"My God, you done it!" Mr. Floyd yelled. "Give him a ride, Joel, while you got him up there!"

So by God if Poppa didn't start up the track with him, not really running of course, just sort of staggering along in the sand with Mr. Floyd trotting along beside him hanging onto the halter and the pony whinnying and pawing like he was having a bad dream. Poppa only got a few yards before he was done in, that wasn't surprising of course, what was surprising was that he ever got him up off the ground in the first place, then he sort of sank down onto his knees and dumped that pony off the back of his neck like a sack of grain. The pony hit the ground *whump* like a watermelon falling off a truck and started working his legs like crazy trying to get onto his feet and finally made it and took off around that ring like he was coming off a hot stove. Poppa took a great big breath and said, "Whoo!," he was beat. He got up and started rubbing the back of his neck, grinning at me like he'd made a million bucks, not just two. "Well now, boy," he said, "You seen a horse take a man-ride. That there is news, like they say."

"*News!*" Mr. Floyd said. "*News!* Oh, Lordy! I never

seen nothing to beat it!" He raised his head up and howled and then collapsed against the fence again, beating at it, sort of helpless, with one hand.

I don't think another single person in that whole campground had seen what happened, it happened so fast, and I was just as glad because if Momma had got wind of it, it would have been bad.

"You hurt any, Poppa?" I said.

"Hurt?" he said. "Why hell no. I never felt better. If a man was to do that every morning before breakfast he'd live to be a hundred." He slapped the dust out of his pants and said, "O.K., Ben, I'll take that two bucks."

"Oh Lordy, yes," Mr. Floyd said. "It was worth twice that to see you toting that horse around. That's better than a circus, Joel." He dug a wad of bills out of his pocket and peeled off two of them and handed them to Poppa, still chuckling and snorting. Poppa tucked them in his shirt pocket along with the other two and winked at me and said, "Oysters, that's what done it, ain't that right, Aaron?"

"Yes, sir," I said.

"We best go fetch that pony back here," Poppa said. "See can you get him, Aaron."

"O.K.," I said. I got up off the ground and went and brought the horse back; he was pretty damn skittish by this time, and we climbed through the fence and walked back up to the tables, all three of us giggling and snorting and stamping our feet. We didn't tell any of the rest of them anything about it, naturally, but Momma knew we'd been up to something the way Mr. Floyd kept on grinning and chuckling; she kept her eye on Poppa but he had as straight a face as I ever saw on a preacher.

It was getting to be evening and dusky in the oak grove and a sunset breeze came stealing in through the trees and rustled them with a soft rush like the sound of the tide turning. We sang some hymns, *Shall We Gather at the River* and

Rock of Ages and *Nearer My God to Thee*, watching the sky grow red between the trees and the pit fires flare a little in the stir of breeze. Jamed was tired, he leaned up against Momma and she put her arm around him and cuddled him while she sang. He just lay there and stared at me with those moony eyes, and every now and then when an acorn would fall down and hit the ground with a little soft thump they'd wander around for a minute, listening, like he'd heard a footfall he'd been expecting for a long time.

It was getting close to dark when we said goodbye to the Floyds and folded up the blankets and piled into the pickup to go home. Jamed got up front so he could sleep, he was out on his feet, he didn't fuss about not having his bear though, he didn't dare. Sylvie and me got in the back end and lay down on a blanket with another one on top of us for a cover and looked up at the twilight sky with stars beginning to prickle out like fireflies and every now and then tree branches swooshing by above us as if they were blown in the same cool wind that showered our faces with the smell of woods and stone and evening dew and cowy fields, quick sweet smells like pipesmoke blowing past. Sylvie said, "You know what? R. B. Floyd is in love with me, he tried to kiss me twice." But I didn't feel like talking, I was going to sleep, sliding into a warm dark sea that crept up over me until it touched my chin and then my lips and then my eyes and then put out my brain like a lamp. I woke up when we stopped at the Frenchs', half woke up, I could hear Poppa rooting around for the basket of glass jars and then lifting them down and the glass clinking as he carried them away through the darkness, it was all faint and faraway like a dream, I heard Mrs. French calling out to Momma from her front steps, "Thank you kindly, Anabel. You sure you won't come in?" and Momma calling back from up front, "No indeed, Dorothy, we've got to get these children to bed, they're worn out." Then Poppa climbed up into the cab and the door slammed and the pickup started moving again and I slid back into the black sea.

About two seconds later I came out of that dream fast, the pickup was bumping and slamming over that corduroy road down to Port Federation about a hundred miles an hour and I could hear Jamed sobbing and Sylvie pounding on the cab roof and screaming, "Oh Poppa, hurry, hurry, Poppa please!" I thought for a minute it must be another dream, they couldn't all have gone crazy like that at once, but then the truck lurched hard and threw me against the sidewall so I cracked my head fierce, that wasn't any dream, boy. I scrambled out of those blankets fast and grabbed ahold of the sidewall to haul myself up and see what was going on, just then I heard Momma say in a terrible gray voice, "Oh my God, it can't be the hotel, Joel, it's too far up the hill. Oh my God." By that time I had reared my head up above the top of the cab and I looked out over the dark of the tree tops and saw what she was talking about, the whole sky up there above the cliffs one clambering scarlet flame, one great wild rose of fire blowing in the darkness with a horrible kind of beauty, it hypnotized me, I couldn't take my eyes off it, it lit up the low clouds with a scarlet flush the way they blaze at sunset and sent up boiling billows of black smoke marbled with orange like terrible black and orange silk flags gone mad in a gale, roiling above the wreckage of our house up there like some kind of an awful celebration in the sky. I was cold everywhere, I had ice bones, I couldn't stop shuddering. I hung on for my life, I thought I'd get thrown clear out of that truckbed. When we came around the long bend that led down to the water I saw there were showers of sparks falling everywhere, long thin red pencil streaks of fire raining down like meteors as if all the stars in heaven had broken loose and fallen all at once or like Fourth of July fireworks, like the biggest Independence Day bustout of all time. I looked over at Sylvie to see if she was all right, she wasn't standing up any more, she had sunk down in the truckbed and was sitting there hugging her head in her arms banging and bouncing against the sidewalls without even trying to brace herself, sobbing and hiccoughing. I could hear Jamed up front howling like a wolf, I hadn't ever heard him make that much noise in his whole life, it was weird. We came on down the bend toward the shop and I could see there were cars everywhere, all their glass and chromework glittering with crimson light, and people standing like chess pieces, with rosy faces and long shadows behind them, looking up toward the cliff. Lined up in the road between the hotel and the boatyard there were four fire trucks, the two from Poole and a pumper each from Marlboro and Solomons, I could read the names on the big red doors, and the whole road was a tangle of white hose like a gigantic plateful of spaghetti. We didn't have any hydrant at Port Federation, I just that minute realized it, it had never occurred to me before, or that we didn't need one, they had run their feeder hoses down into the bay and were pumping up from there. I thought, now that's smart, build your house beside the ocean and you don't need no fire hydrant when it burns down, I was going sort of crazy.

Poppa swung the pickup around back of the hotel and started up the hill to the house and right then we got our first look at it or what was left of it. The roof was gone already, sunk in like the top of a fallen cake, there was just a few feet of wall all around, eaten away from the top as if it had been gnawed by rats, and a few stud posts and the chimney standing up, black as charcoal in that bath of scarlet and yellow flame, and all of a sudden a hot roar as if somebody had opened the door to hell. We couldn't get any further, there was another truck up there blocking the road and a line of firemen in slickers and helmets standing in pairs, braced back against the pressure of the big brass nozzles, playing slick bright streams of water into all that flame and smoke, it ate them up like icicles. Poppa slammed the pickup to a stop and was out of the door almost before it stopped moving, running up the hill against the firelight. I was down out of the back end almost as fast, running along behind him, I don't know where we were going, either one of us, it was a funny thing, I wished I was ten thousand miles away, anywhere else, but still I couldn't stop watching, I had to *be* there, I had to see it happen with my own eyes.

Somebody in a black slicker and helmet with a pair of rubber boots slogging around his thighs came down the hill waving at us, it was Mr. Whetzel, he was the Chief, he yelled, "Joel, don't bring that boy no closer, he'll get burnt." But Poppa wasn't about to be stopped, he said, "I got to see did them doves get out," he kept right on going. Mr. Whetzel grabbed him by the arm and said, "I done checked. They ain't a one in there." So Poppa stopped then, he couldn't have got any further anyway, the heat blast down that hill nearly withered my eyeballs, my face felt scorched, I thought my hair would start to crackle. It seemed to wither Poppa too, all of a sudden. He stood there looking stooped, shriveled up, older than hell, just for one second he seemed damn near to die in his shoes, like he'd just come back from one of his walks after he'd hit Jamed. He put his hand up and rubbed his eyes. Mr. Whetzel said, "This is a sorry sight, Buddy. It just makes me sick."

"You get anything out?" Poppa said.

"We got out one chair and a moose head and a statue of some kind, and one of the fellas got a handful of Anabel's clothes, it looked like. They're scorched right bad."

"That's all you got."

"Yeah, we couldn't get near nothing else. She was just a-roaring by the time we got here." He spit out a little gob of dry white froth and rubbed his lips with the back of his hand. "You got them old Georgia-pine studs in that house, them things burn like kerosene."

"Yeah, I know," Poppa said. "They'd of stood for two hundred years."

"That's the truth. Them things is pure pitch." Mr. Whetzel put his hand on my head and said, "I'm sorry, sonny boy." I didn't say anything, I couldn't talk. He looked back at Poppa and said, "Dorsey White's here looking for you, I reckon you got insurance with him. Here he comes now."

Mr. White was coming up the hill past the pickup holding his hat in front of his face to keep the heat off. He was a little fat guy with a bald head that was shining in the firelight like an apple. He got up to where we were and said, "Hey, Joel," solemn.

Poppa said, "Hey, Dorsey." Mr. White stood there puffing for a minute and shook his head.

"This is a son of a bitch," he said.

"Yeah," Poppa said.

"Where was you-all?"

"We was down at Drum Point to a oyster roast. We never even heard the sirens."

"No you wouldn't of heard them down there. We was just sitting down to dinner when they went off. I called the station and they told me where it was. I got up here as fast as I could."

"I appreciate it," Poppa said.

"Well, you won't have no trouble, South Atlantic is the very best. Of course they'll have to send an adjuster down. He won't be able to do much till she cools down, three–four days, but you better stop in at the office tomorrow, Joel, get your claim in. They's a lot to go over."

"Yeah, I'll do that," Poppa said. Just then the kitchen wall fell in with a terrible roar and a sheet of flame like blazing gelatin went soaring up into the sky, lighting everything brighter than high noon, I thought it would blind me. I looked at Poppa and it was as if I was seeing his face for the first time in that terrible light of our burning house, all those hundreds of tortured lines around his eyes and mouth, running through his lips like scars, riving his jaws and neck in dry leathery wrinkles like a turtle's and the hugeness of his teeth that I'd never really seen before, big worn-down yellow dog's teeth bulging out of his lips like a hound's, with cracks running down them lined with brown stain like old dirty chinaware and worst of all those yellow dog's eyes shining like jelly, fearsome, proud, wild, he'd pulled himself back together by this time, boy, those were wolf's eyes. I could see the flames reflected in them fluttering like little red flags, it looked like that fire was inside of him, not outside, some roaring holocaust in there that burned and destroyed so it could build, I was scared of that man. I turned around and ran down the hill to the pickup, the doors were open and there were a bunch of ladies standing around, Mabel Offutt and Mrs. Younkins and some others, trying to give Momma some comfort I guess, whatever they could. She was still sitting there in the cab, she hadn't moved an inch, staring through the windshield with frozen-looking eyes as if she was watching the last judgment. She had Jamed's head in her lap, he was still sort of moaning and twitching, and she was stroking his hair with one hand. She had the other one reached up to pet Sylvie, who had her head shoved through the rear window against Momma's and was sniveling in her hair. I sat down on the running board, the ladies made room for me, and leaned my head against Momma's hip and she took her hand from Jamed's head and put her arm around me. I felt like I was going to cry, which was pretty strange for me because crying was something I hadn't hardly done a speck of in my whole life. I never did like to cry, it just didn't feel right, but I tell you I was close to it right then. Mabel Offutt patted me on the head and said, "Aaron, you-all are going to come up and stay with us for a while till you get straightened out, and you and John Michael can have a big old time, ain't that nice?"

I said, "Yes, ma'am," I was glad to hear it, I hadn't had any idea what we could do, I guess I was figuring we'd have to sleep in the boats or something and I don't think I would have done it, the way I felt right then. You couldn't have got me in one of those boats, I'd have slept in a field first.

Poppa was up there a while longer talking with the Chief and Mr. White and Bud Offutt and some others, then he came back down to the pickup, looking at the ground all the time, with a bunch of Momma's clothes laid over his arm. Mabel Offutt said, "Joel, we want you-all to come up and stay with us, just as long as it takes for you to get settled. Now they ain't no two ways about it. Bud tell you?"

"Yeah, he did," Poppa said. "I'm mighty obliged, Mabel. We just ain't in no position to say no."

"Well, I reckon not. Now I'm going on up and fix a pot of coffee and some sandwiches. You-all come right on up and have a bite to eat and get to bed. These kids must be dead, and you too."

"Yeah, we'll do that," Poppa said. "Thank you kindly, Mabel."

The ladies all patted Momma's hand and fussed around her a little bit and then said good night and went on down the hill. Poppa handed the clothes up to Momma through the cab window, he said, "They got these out, beauty. Anyways, you'll have a clean dress to put on in the morning." Momma took the clothes and folded them over her lap, there was a scorched spot on one of the collars, she plucked at it with her fingertips, trying to get it clean. Poppa climbed up into the cab and sat there with his hands on the wheel. He reached over and laid his hand on Momma's knee and said, "It ain't too bad, dove, we got insurance. We'll come back." Jamed started sobbing again, "Andy got burnt. Andy got all burnt up. Andy got burnt." Poppa moved his hand over and put it on Jamed's head and said, "Yeah, I know, boy, but we'll get you another bear. There's lots of bears." What

I figured right then was that I'd run away from home that night. Then I thought, what home? I aint got no home, and I started to laugh inside. That's what I did pretty much right from then on was laugh.

"Andy got all burnt up," Jamed said. "He's all burnt up."

"Yeah, and my icicle, too," Sylvie said, they were both sobbing away. "My icicle got all melted."

MY STORY ABOUT THE POLAR BEAR SEEMED TO UPSET SYLVIE pretty badly, she sat there brooding about it for a while, then she yanked her feet down off the porch rail and said, "Listen, how's that Jack Daniel's holding out? I think I'm going to make a big exception and have a shot of it. Maybe a double. Is there any left?"

"Yeah, there's a couple of good snorts in there yet," I said. "Help yourself. As a matter of fact, I was thinking about running up to Bud's and replenishing the supply. I've got a feeling it's going to be a bad night for sleeping."

I handed her the bottle and she tilted herself back in the rocker and poured down a couple of fingers with no trouble at all, for a girl who didn't touch the stuff she showed an amazing natural capacity for putting it where it did the most good, you could see there was Linthicum blood there, boy. She shuddered and pushed her fist into her chest and said, "Oh, my God, that stuff is pure poison." I started to say that it was the best there was, that Poppa never bought anything but the very best, but I could see it leading to all sorts of sardonic remarks about the quality of the poison around the place, a general perversion of value, etc., etc., so I figured, what the hell, let's try and have a little peace for once in our lives, maybe it's the one thing we all deserve by this time. I leaned back in the glider and looked out at the stars over the bay, it was building up a little cloudy around Antares, there was a milky swath in the sky that meant maybe a gray morning and a day of soft southeast drizzle with the diesel clam boats thumping through it like ghosts with great sad remonstrating hearts.

"So tell me about this *one* chick," Sylvie said. "I mean if it isn't too sacred or something. What was her name?"

"Cynthia," I said. "Cindy. Actually, she was a very strange-looking girl. I mean she wasn't any raving beauty or anything."

That was the truth, Cindy was the only girl I ever saw over the age of eighteen who had absolutely no breastworks of any kind, she went straight down from clavicle to hip in a flat vertical plane like a large tongue depressor, then there was a rickety-looking bony arrangement around her pelvis like something made out of a Meccano set, then after a negligible addition at the rear she went on down to the floor in a pair of totally uncontoured legs as straight and thin as broom handles, she was in my Movement class at GLAD, and even in a black leotard against a white plaster wall she was practically invisible, which was no particular detriment as far as I was concerned, since in my case, to put it very charitably, The Body was not All, as a matter of fact up to that point in my life it was next to nothing. It was her face that turned me on like nothing ever had before or since, all that ragged yellow hair that smelled elementally of fern or warm stone, and eyes, if you could imagine such a thing, like a blue-eyed seal, and a sweet mouth with a crick in it, in the left corner of her upper lip, just a nice tiny touch of irony, like salt on a melon. There was a kind of old-fashioned romanticism about her clothes that I liked too, she wore a black beret a lot of the time and a black silk raincoat, like the heroines of old Jean Gabin movies about the agony of love, and she had a lot of odd but memorable habits such as falling into a sort of trance in the tube train and rubbing her nipples through her sweater with the tips of her fingers, sitting there with a look of stupefied contentment all the way home, or taking out a clockwork mouse made of white fur that she carried around in the pocket of her raincoat and nuzzling it at unexpected moments. The first time she came up there to my dormer room in Clifton Terrace she took it out of her pocket and wound it up and set it down on the carpet and we sat there in front of the murmuring scarlet gas fire and watched it hop around in widening circles until finally it hopped up into her lap and lay there kicking spasmodically in her slackly spread skirt while we giggled at each other, happy as clams. Then we suddenly went quiet and she looked straight into my eyes and gave me her rickety smile and said, 'Look, I've just got the most wonderful idea, love. You know what you ought to do? Seduce me.'

'Well, I don't know whether I ought to do that or not,' I said.

'Why not? Everyone else does.'

'Well, I know, but that's just the trouble,' I said.

'What do you mean, love, trouble?'

So then I came up with my Moralspiel, as I called it, I had it memorized by this time because over the years I had been presented with the opportunity, or maybe necessity would be the proper word, of reeling it off to a very modest assortment of girls with whom my relationships had run well past the point where a man's concern about whether or not a girl is eating properly, or getting the right amount of rest, or is provided with carfare is beginning to wear a bit thin and she demands more robust evidence of his affection. Not being able to come up with any such evidence, I had composed my Moralspiel as an alternative, a pretty poor one as it turned out, because most of the ladies in question were off and gone within a week of its delivery.

I don't mean that I was absolutely impotent but I was so damned fastidious about the circumstances under which I went to bed with anybody that it came to pretty much the same thing. I mean everything had to be absolutely perfect, in the first place I had to know the girl a certain amount of time, I had to be convinced of the purity of her heart, the singleness of my own devotion, and the sympathy of our natures, and after all this spiritual stuff had been gotten out of the way there were still a certain number of simple mechanical conditions that had to be satisfied, most of them relating to hygiene in one way or another, for example I could never make the grade in absolute darkness, there had to be a light of some kind burning somewhere on the premises, there also had to be at least one window open in the room, the dishes had to be washed, the bedsheets freshly laundered, no spiderwebs anywhere, all dirty socks and underwear out of sight and ideally there ought to be a strong smell of Lysol around the place. Even with all this going for me, the smallest, most ridiculous thing would turn me off, like a run in her stocking, the sight of a bit of loose wax in her ear, a whiff of garlic on her breath, a caraway seed lodged between her teeth, any damned thing at all that hinted at earthly imperfection of almost any kind. Well with a list of prerequisites like that of course a man can't count on spending too much of his time in bed with people, as a matter of fact it can lead to some pretty satirical observations on the part of his female acquaintances, even on his own part as far as that goes, it can play holy hell with his self-esteem. I mean if you're making out pretty well and then all of a sudden discover a pimple between the girl's shoulder blades and immediately find yourself just about as functional as a wet noodle, you've got to do a lot of talking to yourself before you feel like marching in any parades. Naturally the list of my sexual achievements was a very limited one, to be perfectly candid about it, it consisted of just two names. One of these was Becky

Stirnweiss, a girl in my European Lit class at the University of Maryland, and the other was Lt. Elizabeth Maxwell, a nurse in the army hospital at the U.S. base in Ruislip where I was laid up with mononucleosis. The list would probably have been limited to just Becky's name alone if it weren't for the fact that about the time I came down with mononucleosis I got a Dear John letter from her in the hospital advising me that as a consequence of driving her car into a telephone pole she had met a perfectly wonderful claims adjuster named Harold Oglethorpe to whom she had decided to entrust the balance of her life. News like that in combination with a case of mononucleosis can make a man very discouraged but Lt. Maxwell, having had placed in her hands the responsibility for my well-being, did one hell of a job of cheering me up. In fact she was so thorough about it that I misunderstood completely, I got the idea that This Was It and that our love would last as long as the immortal stars but as it turned out she was just a very conscientious nurse who was every bit as scrupulous in attending to the needs of her other patients as she was about my own, a fact that it took me some time and a good bit of agony to digest. Experiences like this had added even further to my circumspection in sexual matters, so by the time Cindy showed up it was practically prohibitive, which was regrettable because I liked the girl, I wanted to keep her around for a while. She had a lot of the same effect on me as stuffed polar bear or a shabby old voyeur or a three-legged dog or something, maybe I needed her in a way, something like the way Lt. Maxwell needed me.

"You know what I mean?" I said to Sylvie. "Don't you ever need people like that sometimes?"

"No," Sylvie said. "I need healthy people around me. But I'll take your word for it."

. . .

So anyway, after Cindy sprang this proposition on me like that I was pretty flabbergasted, I mean I'd never had to drag out the old Moralspiel that early in my acquaintance with anybody I'd ever met before, so naturally I got it pretty bolluxed up, I had to more or less depend on the inspiration of the moment.

'Listen, Cindy,' I said to her, 'that's all *anybody* ever does. My God, that's what's the matter with this Goddamned world, can't you see that? Nobody loves *anybody*. Everybody just wants to jump in bed the minute they see each other. It's just like that damn joke where the guy meets the girl on the train and asks her where she's going and she says, "Pittsburgh," and he says, "O.K., enough of this lovemaking. Take off your clothes and lie down." I mean that's a *dirty joke*. I mean when even somebody as nice as you—'

'Oh, love, don't,' she whispered, she looked sort of scared, I don't think she'd ever run into that sort of a reaction before. 'It doesn't matter, honestly. It's just that—well, everyone seems to expect it of you, I suppose. You know? But it doesn't matter tuppence to me, love, one way or the other.' Then all of a sudden she swung her legs around and got up onto her knees, shattering one of my Woolworth teacups on the hearth God bless her and clapped her hands over my ears and started kissing me all over the face, eyes, nose, mouth, everything, as if she were trying to put out a fire or something, murmuring to me a mile a minute, 'I'm sorry, love, I don't know why I said a stupid thing like that. I should have seen that wasn't what you wanted. Stupid sort, I am. Now don't go on about it, love. I didn't really mean it, honestly.'

"You see what she was like?" I said to Sylvie. "She understood my problem right away. And she *cared* about it, you know? Believe me, a lot of girls don't."

Sylvie didn't say anything, she looked as if she *wanted* to, a sort of restlessness, a sort of indignation, rippled over her, she looked for a minute like someone twitching with fever in a sickbed, but then she closed her eyes and folded her fingers over the Jack Daniel's bottle which was still lying in her lap and went slack in the rocking chair as she used to do when she was a little girl playing dead. I thought she might have passed out, that was a pretty healthy slug of whisky she had taken, so I reached over and touched her on the wrist and said, "You all right?" She nodded without opening her eyes and said in a minute, "You remember how I got you smoking cigarettes? You remember Oma Pearl used to give me some at school once in a while, and we'd smoke them up there in the woods on the way home?"

"Yeah," I said. "Our secret vice."

"Yeah, and I didn't even care for that too much," Sylvie said. "You know, that's been the biggest disappointment of my whole life, vice." She dropped her hand again from the elbow and started flopping it around in the air inviting me to take it, which I did, we sat there holding hands like a couple of schoolkids.

"As far as being fastidious goes," Sylvie said, "that's what distinguishes an artist from an athlete. You take it from a little girl who knows."

"No, it doesn't, Syl," I said. "It's just being tidy, that's all. It's what Dylan Thomas called 'putting your socks in the drawer marked "socks," and your pajamas in the drawer marked "pajamas." ' It just means you don't like crumbs in your bed, it doesn't mean you have any passion for moral order."

"Honest to God, you make me sick when you talk like that," Sylvie said. "You've got some kind of a crazy guilt complex or something, which is just about the dirtiest joke that ever came out of this Goddamned place. And that's saying something. Even in high school you were one of the best actors I ever saw. You're an *artist*, Aaron."

"Oh, sure," I said. "Be sure to catch my Tally-Ho Toilet

Bowl spot next month on Channel Nine. It'll knock you out."

"Oh, for Christ's sake. Sure, you've got to do some crap, to make a living, who doesn't? But you stick with it, and you'll be recognized yet. It's got to happen. Just remember your little sister said so. You're an artist to your fingertips."

"No, I'm not, Syl," I said. "And anyway, I don't want to be, any more. One of them is enough for any family."

THE INSURANCE ADJUSTER CAME OUT ABOUT THREE DAYS after the fire and poked around in the ashes for a while with Poppa, all fitted out with a pair of knee boots and a scratch pad and a metal tape measure that he kept measuring things with, like the dimensions of the hearth or what was left of it and the distance of the shed where the propane tank was to the kitchen stove, which was now a big lump of melted metal. He was a great big red-headed guy who looked like he'd just discovered there was too much vinegar on his salad and had a pretty strong suspicion that Poppa was responsible for it. He kept asking questions about the condition of the flues and what the roofing material was and how long since the electric wiring had been done and was he sure the stove had been turned off when we left for the oyster roast, things like that. Poppa would answer him very slowly and thoughtful, his forehead wrinkled up, searching back in his mind to get all the details just exactly right, sort of puzzled and hurt, like he'd be damned if *he* could figure it out, wasn't it a terrible thing to happen to a hardworking man who had plenty of problems to handle without getting his Goddamned house burned down. The guy made a lot of notes and did considerable muttering to himself and then gave Poppa a lot of forms to fill out and climbed into his car and drove off.

I don't know why I went along, I guess I just had to know what was going on up there, I had to be sure. I didn't really like going up there any more at all, it looked so Goddamned lonesome or unnatural or something, this big empty space up there on top of the cliff between the apple trees and the pigeon loft with just the chimney standing up black and crumbling in the middle of this ash heap where Sylvie and Jamed and me used to lie and listen to leaves skittering on the shingles at night and look out at the moonlight on the bay. Some of the apple trees died, the ones nearest the house, they were all heat-blasted and their leaves turned black and curled up like fingers. The stuff in the kitchen garden died too, all the carrot tops were singed off and the pea vines withered up and rattled in the wind like rattlesnakes. The tool shed was still there because it was made out of corrugated iron, it just had a few smoke stains on it, but the funny thing was the pigeon loft didn't burn down. You'd have thought it would have caught fire from the heat, it wasn't more than twenty yards from the kitchen steps, but the only thing that happened to it was the paint got blistered on the front wall and cracked off in places and there was a film of ash all over it like dirty snow. The doves didn't seem to mind that any because they moved right back in, as a matter of fact they were back the very next morning. Poppa was worried about them, he was up there about six o'clock with a sack of meal and sure enough there they were, all milling and cooing around and lighting on his shoulders waiting to be fed and maybe to have the whole thing explained to them, anyway he did a lot of talking to them in that burbling dove talk of his, I'd come to hate it.

Sylvie and Jamed and me didn't like going near the place. We were staying up at Offutt's and we'd just play around the yard with John Michael and Paisley or spend the whole day in our cave on the cliff. It was a long time before we ever went down to the shop again, it just seemed too different, everything was changed. I don't know whether Jamed suspected anything but I sure as hell did, I had plenty of reason for it, and so did Sylvie, I think. She didn't know anything about Vernon T. Allnut of course, like I did, but somehow you couldn't fool Sylvie about that kind of thing, she could smell stuff out. She didn't say a whole lot, she just got meaner than hell. You wouldn't have thought Sylvie could get a whole lot meaner but by God she did, she got so she didn't like *anything*. She wouldn't kid around with Poppa any more, she got mad when he called her Screech or tried to munch on her ear or something the way he used to, she'd sort of wriggle herself away and screw her nose up and say, "Cut it out, Poppa, *will* you? You're getting me all *wet*, for God's sake." Jamed didn't get any meaner of course, nothing would have made him mean I don't think, he just got quieter and further away and took to doing a lot of staring. You'd see him standing in the back yard sucking on the tip of his thumb and just staring. You didn't even notice he was there half the time, he got sort of invisible.

The thing I hated most was the way Momma used to go up there and poke around in those ashes for hours sometimes. It got to be a sort of ritual she had. She'd finish helping Mabel Offutt with the luncheon dishes, all the time getting quieter and more inside herself, biting her lip maybe and not answering things Mabel said to her, you could see her mind was on that damned ash heap up there, and then after a while she'd take off her apron and say, "Mabel, I'm going to take a little walk. I need to get outside the house for a while." I knew where she was headed for, I'd seen her up there many a time. She'd go into the tool shed and get out a little half-peck basket and one of those long-handled cultivators and wander around in the ashes, raking them over with the cultivator and every now and then bending down and sifting a handful between her fingers. She didn't find much, of course, once in a while a little chip of her Sunday china with the glaze all melted into brown bubbles or maybe one of her old brass beehive candlesticks, wilted and run together like a lump of caramel, or a little gnarled glob of metal that might have been her silver locket with the picture of Jamed in it. But one time she found Granma's wedding ring, I remember Mabel Offutt had sent me out to find her because a guy had come with a special delivery letter and about the time I got up there she was bending over blowing on this little piece of stuff she had found and wiping it clean with her fingertips, her face gone all soft and trembly as pudding. Of course it didn't look anything like a ring any more, it was just a little rough nugget, but you could tell what it was because there was one little part that wasn't hurt at all and you could still read the word *John.* That was Granpa's name, it used to say *Ellen and John, 1878* on the inside, I remembered that. When I called her she stood there for a minute looking at me, sort of getting her face straightened out, and then she came wading over through the ashes leaving clouds of soft black dust behind her, holding this thing clenched in her hand. I said, "What did you find, Momma?" She said, "I'm not sure," and then opened her hand up and showed it to me and said, "Aaron, read that for me, will you? Isn't there something written there? I can't see a thing without my glasses." That was another thing she'd lost in the fire, her glasses. She'd ordered another pair from Mr. Turnbull, who was the optometrist up at Marlboro, but they weren't ready yet so I took the ring and squinted at it and said, "Yes, it says, *John,* Momma. Wow, look at that. That's Granma's ring, isn't it?"

"Yes, it is," she said. "Oh, thank the Lord. I've just been praying to God I'd find that ring. You know, Aaron, I've always counted on giving it to you when you got married, so you could give it to your bride. I've wanted that ring to be worn by Linthicum women forever, right through the centuries."

"That's a real nice idea, Momma," I said.

"Of course they can't wear it like that, but maybe we can have it made over. I'd say most of the gold was still there." She took the ring back and held it in front of her for a minute with her hand clenched tight around it and her eyes closed as if she might be praying. "There's a special providence in that," she said, very soft. "I just know there is."

"Yes, ma'am, it sure does look like it," I said. She put the ring in the pocket of her skirt and pressed it against her hip and then looked up at me as if she was coming out of a trance. "What was it you wanted? What did you call me about?"

"There's a man up there at Offutt's with a special delivery letter. He says you have to sign for it."

"Oh. All right, I'm coming right along," Momma said. She reached down and flapped at the hem of her skirt with her hand to beat the ash dust out of it and we went on down the hill and up the road to Offutt's. She signed for the letter, the man was sitting on the front steps waiting for us, and then broke open the envelope and squinted at it but she couldn't make anything out so she handed it to me and said, "Aaron, will you read that to me? I'm just going to go crazy if I don't get those glasses soon."

So I took the letter and read it off to her, everything, right from the top, having a little trouble with some of the long words but not too much, God help me, I was a pretty good reader. It said, "With regard to property known as J. Linthicum and Sons, Boatwrights, located at Port Federation, Calvert County, Maryland, I should like to advise you that pursuant to your personal petition of the 17th of this month to Mr. Vernon T. Allnut, the Board of Directors of the Calvert County First National Bank has granted an extension of twenty-one days' time for payment of debts outstanding on first mortgage note held by this institution, and hereby further advise you that should payment of such debts not be made in full by the 8th of October, 1953, together with all such debts as shall thereafter have accrued, a public sale of the aforesaid property will be held within fifteen days of such default, on the premises and at the risk of yourself as present titleholder. Yours faithfully, Wilfred Hooks, Chairman."

Well of course by the time I was halfway through it I could see I'd made a terrible mistake, or somebody had, not me especially, but there wasn't anything I could do, I had to keep right on plowing through it, feeling my heart sink down about an inch with every word I read so by the time I got through it was down around my navel somewhere and I felt like heaving. For a minute there, while I was reading, I had a wild idea that maybe I could make up something different from what it actually said in the letter, any kind of crazy thing, like "regret to inform you that the sunflower seeds you ordered are not in stock," but of course once I got through all that business about Vernon T. Allnut I couldn't very well start ringing in sunflower seeds, so I just read it off faster than hell and hoped to God that Momma wouldn't put two and two together and come up with the same answer that I had. As a matter of fact it took her quite awhile to make any sense at all out of it, she just wrinkled up her forehead and looked sort of puzzled as if maybe the people at the bank had made a mistake of some kind in their books or sent the letter off to the wrong person or something but after a minute it began to get through to her, I could see her eyes get sleepy with pain and then she lifted her hand and laid it against the side of her head and stood there staring off at the trees as if she was watching somebody drown or something. But she still hadn't got it straight or at least not the way I'd got it because what she said was, "Oh, my Lord. That poor man. All that on his mind, and then to lose his home." She shook her head slowly and bit her lip. "First his business and then his home. I just don't know how any man can stand so much."

"You mean he's going to lose the business, Momma?" I said, very innocent.

"I just don't know. Maybe with this extra time he'll be able to do something. What I do know is that we've got to try and help Poppa all we can. Do you understand that?"

"Yes, ma'am," I said.

"Now I'm going to take this letter down to the shop and give it to him, because I think he'll want to see it right away."

"Can I do it for you, Momma?" I said.

"No, I want to talk to Poppa myself. You can come with me if you want, keep me company, you know about it already."

So we walked down the road to the shop and went into Poppa's office and sat there waiting for him to come in from the yard. He looked pretty surprised when he came in and saw Momma sitting there, I don't think she'd been inside that office in five years, but he came over and gave her a peck on the forehead and said, "Well, lookie here now, ain't that a prime sight, pretty girl sitting right there in my chair!" Momma smiled real nice, she was trying to help him along, and then laid her hand on his arm and said, "Joel, there's this letter came for you just now at Offutt's, and I opened it by mistake because it was special delivery and I didn't have my glasses." She handed him the letter and he sat down right away and took it out of the envelope and started unfolding it. "I brought it down here because it's important, and I didn't think you'd want to talk about it in front of Bud and Mabel this evening."

"Uh huh," Poppa said. He never turned a hair. He got his glasses out and read that letter through, maybe a couple of times, it took him quite awhile, and then just nodded and laid it on the desk in front of him and reached over and patted Momma on the knee.

"Well, dove, I didn't want you worrying," he said. "That's why I didn't say nothing about it."

"It was a terrible burden to bear by yourself," Momma said. "You ought to have shared it with me."

"Well, I had it pretty well worked out," Poppa said. "I was going to wait until it was all cleared up, you see. You had enough on your mind."

"What were you going to do, Joel?" Momma said.

"Well, I'll tell you what I *was* going to do," Poppa said. "I had it worked out with this fellow up at Dundalk, Mr. Fitzgibbons, where he'd pay off the bank notes and the creditors and then take over possession of the title. Of course he'd own the yard then, but he was going to keep the name and keep me on as shop foreman. That way, we'd 've lost the business, maybe, but I'd still've had a job and there'd still be Linthicum boats on the bay. It wasn't perfect by a long ways, but it was the best I could do. We'd still've eat regular."

Momma nodded, frowning a little bit, it took her awhile to soak it all in. It did me, too. My God, he never stopped to draw a breath, he reeled that story off like it was gospel. You'd've thought he'd been working on that plan for the last six months. And of course the terrible thing, the thing you never could be certain about in a million years, was that he *might* have been. It might have been a real plan, sure enough, that he'd been working on like a crazy man for weeks, trying to save the yard, and everything I'd imagined a bunch of nasty, dirty suspicions. After all, I didn't know *everything* about his business. Just enough to keep me wondering, practically all night long, every night, for the rest of my life.

"You say that's what you *were* going to do," Momma said. She seemed to have it straight by this time, maybe a little bit too straight because you could see just the faintest shadow of a doubt begin to cloud up her eyes.

"Yeah, that's what I *was* going to do," Poppa said. "But I got a different idea now, Momma. Something I think is a whole lot better. Something that might even be a special message from God. Anyways, I want you to tell me what you think about it."

"I'll be glad to, Joel," she said.

"Well, when we drove down this road the other night and seen that house burning up there on the hill, I thought to myself, 'My God, what did I do to deserve this? Why is the Lord punishing me this way?' It just seemed to me too much to bear, for a man to lose his house and his business both at the same time. But you know, the more I thought about it, the more it seemed to me I could see the hand of Providence in that fire. Now that's the truth, dove. You know, it tells in the Bible how the Lord spoke to his people out of a pillar of flame, and I been asking myself if maybe that ain't what He done in our case. How do we know it wasn't a bolt of lightning come right down out of heaven and set fire to that house? How do we know that wasn't His way of providing for us?"

"I don't understand you, Joel," Momma said. But her face was drawn up just a tiny bit tight, as if maybe she was beginning to, all too damn well. "How do you mean, providing for us?"

"Why, the *insurance!*" Poppa said, leaning forward and rapping her on the knee with his fingertips. "The *insurance*, woman! Don't you see that? Don't you see that's the way He decided to answer our need?"

"Answer our need?" Momma said. "Burning our house down? Burning up my wedding dress? Burning up the children's baby pictures? Burning up Momma's Spode china? Everything that meant anything to me in this world?"

"The Lord giveth and the Lord taketh away," Poppa said, dropping his eyes down to the floor, very solemn. "We can't understand it all, beauty, you know that. But I'm more than sure that's how He meant us to use that money."

"That money would buy us another house, Joel," Momma said. "It wouldn't ever buy me back my wedding dress, but it *would* buy us another house. Will you just tell me where we're going to live?"

"Well, dove, we could rent, till we got straightened out good," Poppa said. "I know Quigley'd let us have his place up there at Persimmon Creek real cheap, knowing what kind of trouble we've had. Then, two–three years, when the yard started making good money again, we could build. Right on the same spot. These bad times ain't going to last forever. You can feel things getting better every day."

"I can't," Momma said. "I can't feel them getting any better, ever." Her face and eyes had gone dead still now, she looked just like putty.

Poppa got up and went over to her chair and put his hand on her shoulder. "We're going to be fine, dove," he said. "We had a bad blow, but the Lord is going to see us through. We can't question His ways, Momma." She just sat there with her nostrils pinched white and her lips sucked in between her teeth and her eyes gone cold, I wasn't sure whether she was grieving over the house or whether she was beginning to wonder if it was sure enough the hand of the Lord that had set fire to it, or one a good bit more familiar. She wouldn't ever be certain of course, maybe that's what gave her the most grief, knowing that. Even if she suspected anything she was at a considerable disadvantage, the way Poppa had put it, because if there was one thing Momma believed in it was the will of the Lord, and she would just as soon have given up her place in heaven as to question it, if there was one chance in ten million that that's what she was doing. Maybe she didn't really want to know, maybe she couldn't have stood knowing anything that terrible about Poppa, if it was him that did it. Maybe that's what she decided, sitting right there in that chair. Anyway, she sat there for a minute with a look like plain death in her eyes and then said, "Come, Aaron. We'd best get back to the house. I want you to chop some kindling before dinner."

I wasn't too sure about it myself any more to tell the truth, the way Poppa was going on about the Lord Almighty, and his big plan to turn the yard over to Mr. Fitzgibbons, whoever the hell he was, up in Dundalk, I tell you Poppa was a real spellbinder. He had me pretty much believing him too, even though I had a lot more information on the subject than Momma did. Until I got up to go, he did, because right then I happened to look across the office to where he had all this junk shoved into an old glass-paned bookcase under the window, and sitting right up there on the top shelf was the big leather-bound copy of Shakespeare's *Complete Works* and the pipe rack with all his favorite meerschaum pipes in it, both of which had been sitting on the mantelpiece in our front room for the whole eleven years of my life. So I hustled Momma out of there as fast as I could, saying, "O.K. Hey, come on, Momma, isn't that Jamie yelling?" and thinking to myself, Oh boy, Poppa, you are one son of a bitch.

Of course that could have been a coincidence too, I guess, he *could* have just happened to take that stuff down to his office a day or two before the fire but it sure as hell didn't seem very likely. I thought about it plenty, I thought about it too damn much, but of course I couldn't remember just how long those things had been missing off the mantelpiece, it might have been a couple of months for all I could remember. I hoped it had, I even tried to *pretend* it had, I tried to convince myself that I'd seen the stuff down there in the office way last summer one time when I was fooling around in the bookcase, but I've always had this real finicky kind of mind, I'm hard to convince. Anyway, it's pretty funny that those were the only things that got saved from the fire, Poppa's pipes and his book of Shakespeare. Momma's wedding dress or her family Bible or any of that other stuff she talked about sure as hell didn't get saved and neither did Jamed's bear.

I will say Poppa was pretty decent about that bear though,

you could see it bothered him, Jamed losing that bear. He even got another one for Jamed but Jamed wasn't having any of it. We were sitting on the back steps up at Offutt's one day, me and Jamed and Sylvie, stringing horse chestnuts, when Poppa came back from Marlboro in the pickup. He parked up by the fence and came across the yard with this great big package wrapped up in blue paper from Murchison's Dry Goods. We didn't any of us say anything. Jamie had got so he didn't notice too much of what was going on any more and Sylvie and me were both sort of embarrassed. It was embarrassing, it made you feel sort of bad, Poppa standing there with that great big package in his hand and a kind of silly, shamed, second-hand smile on his face, making out like it was Christmas or something, we had a pretty good idea what was going on. He said, "Hey, you guys, how you doing with them things?" Sylvie looked up at him and said, "We're doing all right," cold as a fish.

What we were doing was stringing these horse chestnuts on fishline to make a bead curtain for the cave. Sylvie had seen this movie up in Marlboro about the South Seas, where they had these bead curtains on all the doorways or something, and she thought it was just cooler than hell. She couldn't wait to make one for the cave.

"We're making a bead door," Jamed said. "Sylvie seen it in a movie."

"You shut up," Sylvie said. "It's supposed to be a secret."

"That looks real pretty," Poppa said. "That's going to be fine." He put the box down on the step in front of Jamed and nudged it with his toe. "Hey, Jamie, looky there," he said. "What do you reckon is in that box?"

"I don't know," Jamed said. "Wowee, it's big. Can we open it, Poppa?"

"Well, I reckon that's the only way to find out," Poppa said.

"Hey, wow," Jamed said. He started tearing off the paper

and then he held the box between his knees and pried the top off and reached in and pulled out this great big yellow bear. It must have been twice as big as Andy, his old bear, and had a fancy leather collar with little bells on it but it didn't do much for Jamed. He held it up by the paw for a minute and sort of nodded at it and said, "Uh huh, that's real nice, Poppa," and then just dropped it back in the box. You could see Poppa was upset, he flinched a little bit and his smile faded for a second but then he reached in the box and pulled the bear out again and said, "Looky here, Jamie. If you turn him over, he talks." He turned the bear over on his back and this weird little mechanical voice said, "I'm hungry, I want some honey." I thought it was pretty amazing, myself, but Jamed wasn't having any. He listened and nodded again, polite, but he didn't do any handsprings or anything. The only bear he was interested in was that old chewed-up Andy that had got burned up in the fire, he wasn't having just any bear. Poppa stood there for a minute looking bad, looking beat up and lonely as hell, then he picked up the box and put the bear back inside and said, "Well, I'll take him on in the house for you, Jamed."

Jamed said, "O.K., Poppa," he didn't even look up, and started working on a chestnut again, shoving a needle through it.

That slowed Poppa down a little, he got sort of quiet and broody for a day or two and took to watching Jamed a lot. He'd sit at the dinner table not listening to what Momma or Bud or Mabel Offutt said, just chomping on his food sort of broody and every now and then letting his eyes wander over and settle on Jamed to see how he was making out with his turnips, sort of shamed and worried, like he was pleading with Jamed to eat hearty and be happy. Sometimes he'd go over to the window and look out where Jamed was standing in the middle of the yard with his thumb tip in his mouth just staring. The two of them would stand there for a while like they were hypnotized, Poppa staring at Jamed through the window and Jamed out there staring at nothing you could see, you would have thought they were both listening to some kind of music or a sermon or something that nobody else could hear.

Poppa didn't stay slowed down though, nothing could slow that man down long. I think his check must have come through from the insurance company about that time because he came back from the shop one day just full of piss and vinegar again like always and picked me up and slung me over the fence into a pile of leaves yelling for everybody to look out because here came a wild curmudgeon broke loose from the zoo. A couple of days after that Vernon T. Allnut showed up again, I saw him driving his car down the road from the highway one afternoon when I was sitting out on the back steps at Offutt's scouring the oven racks for Momma. I set the racks down and started running down the road to the shop, I had to find out what was going on, I wanted to get things straight once and for all. But of course it was a hell of a long ways from Offutt's and by the time I got down there it was just about over. Vernon T. Allnut was coming out of the office with his briefcase under his arm nodding very agreeably at something Poppa was saying and generally looking a hell of a sight easier in his mind than the last time I'd seen him. He walked over to his car with Poppa and then stopped for a minute and looked up the hill where the chimney was standing in all that mess of ashes and charred studs and he shook his head and sucked the air in the corner of his mouth with a little chirping sound and said, "That's a sorry sight, Mr. Linthicum. We're all mighty grieved about it, I don't suppose I need to tell you."

"Yeah, I know," Poppa said. "Well, it's the Lord's will, I reckon. He giveth and He taketh away." He'd figured out that was a pretty good line, I guess.

"You've had your share of misfortunes this year," Mr.

Allnut said. "Let's hope the next will be better."

"Aw, it will," Poppa said. "It can't be no worse. I figure I'm back on my feet again now. I'm going to make out."

"Yes, I think so," Vernon T. Allnut said. "The situation looks much better. Much better. With judicious planning, of course. That's the big thing. Watching those figures, keeping tight books, watching that margin every minute." He nodded his head with each one of these suggestions, keeping a stern but friendly eye on Poppa, they were big buddies now.

"Yeah, you're right about that," Poppa said. "I been too free and easy. Well, I'm going to make use of that accountant fellow, like you told me. Things is going to be different."

"A very small investment to make, for all the security it'll give you," Mr. Allnut said, very solemn, nodding his head deeper than ever, it was scripture. "Well, good afternoon, Mr. Linthicum. And I suppose I ought to say, congratulations. You're back in the saddle again, or maybe I ought to say back at the helm." He got off a cute little smile, just about enough to uncover the tip of one tooth, and bobbed his head at Poppa again like a friendly rooster and climbed into his car. Poppa stood there watching the dust blow back while the car drove up the dirt road, not smiling at all, but not sad either, stony-faced, old, like the Calvert Cliffs, ocean-worn, high and mighty. Then he looked over where I was standing at the gate and said, "Aaron, come in here, boy. We got to have a little celebration."

I went over beside him and he put his arm around my shoulder and walked me to the office. We went up the steps and in through the screen door and Poppa sat me down in his swivel chair at the desk and turned me around till I was looking out through the office door into the shop. It was Saturday afternoon and the workmen had all gone home, it was still and sort of spooky in there. I looked up through the rafters and saw the afternoon light up under the high steel roof, dusty soft burning light like in a church, with one long shaft splitting down through it from a vent in the western gable. The *Ariel* was sitting there in her frames in that dusty beam of light, wild-looking, all her timbers lit with fire along the edges like she was ready to burst into flames, she looked like some kind of a sunlit wooden ghost.

"You see that boat?" Poppa said.

"Yes, sir."

"You know I damn near had to give up building her, Aaron. I damn near did."

"You did, Poppa?" I said.

"That's right. Nobody wouldn't never have seen that boat. But now I got it worked out where I can go ahead and finish her. Wouldn't you say that was worth celebrating?"

"Yes, sir," I said.

"O.K., now what I want you to do is have a little drink with me, to celebrate." He stood there with his hands on his hips looking down at me and winked. "Just you and me, Aaron. Now what do you say? You ever drunk any liquor?"

"No, sir. I don't want none, either," I said.

"Now how do you know that? How do you know till you tried it?" He leaned over and pulled open the bottom drawer and fished out a bottle of Jack Daniel's and a couple of paper cups and started filling them up.

"Poppa, I don't want none," I said.

"Now look here, boy," he said. "Somebody is going to drink with me on this thing. I'm going to drink on this thing, with one of my sons, or know why." His voice had got calm and hard, like his face. He filled up the cups and set one of them down in front of me and said, "Now you hold your tongue. And your nose, too, if you have to, and drink that down." So we both picked up our cups and Poppa turned around and saluted the *Ariel* through the door with his and drank it down, the whole thing, in one long swallow. I took a big breath and brought the cup up to my lips and swallowed a little sip of the stuff and just about blew into ten million pieces. My God, it was horrible. It burned me all the way down into my belly like hot lead, I thought I was going to die. I sputtered and coughed and rolled around in that chair like a crazy man. Poppa clapped me on the back and said, "Come on, boy, drink her down. I made the grade, and you got to, too."

I couldn't do it, though. I knew I couldn't, he could beat me till I was bloody. I set the cup down and said, "Poppa, I can't drink no more. That stuff is horrible." I looked up at him, I felt scared in that place. Way up there in the loft a bee or a big bluebottle fly was buzzing against the roof, banging against the corrugated iron with a little regular tapping sound that made me cringe, it sounded like it would go on forever. And this crazy father of mine beating me on the back telling me to drink whisky.

"I can't drink no more, Poppa," I said.

"You'll drink it," he said. "You'll drink with me, boy, or I'll beat the piss out of you."

So I picked up my cup again and gulped down another mouthful, I like to died. I bent my head down and sat there feeling sicker than a dog, my guts were roiling up toward my mouth.

"Now that's more like it," Poppa said. "That's what I want to see." He made me finish it up, standing there watching me with those yellow eyes, then we walked back up to the house. I *tried* to walk, is more like the truth, I was so drunk I could hardly stand up. Halfway up the road I got sick and leaned over in the bushes and puked. I think that scared Poppa, seeing me sick. He came over and held me by the head and talked gentle then. "Never mind, boy," he said. "You done real good." He stood there patting me on the head, staring around sort of abstracted at the sky as if he was expecting fresh word from the Almighty or something. "You see, Aaron, you git what you git. Ain't that right? You git me for a daddy, and I git what I got. So it's a good thing to know how to hold your liquor, now ain't that right?" I didn't know what the hell he was talking about, I just stood there and puked.

He might have felt some kind of genuine remorse about Jamed losing his bear but he sure as hell didn't seem to care how Momma or the rest of us felt. It seemed to me he could have done something for Momma, anyway. Maybe he figured she wouldn't have taken it too well if he'd tried to hand her a box of chocolates or a new nightie or something, to make up for everything she'd owned in the world. I guess he was right about it, but it sure seemed to me like he could have done something. About the best he ever did was to come out on the front porch when she was sitting out there in the rocking chair after dinner and pat her on the hand a couple of times before he took off for the shop. He just about lived down there now, night and day, working on that *Ariel*. There wasn't anything in the world he thought about any more but that boat, not till he got her finished. He didn't only do the paperwork and supervise the whole job, he did hand work on her too. You'd see him up there in the keel lying on his back with a welding mask on his face and a torch in his hand or a spokeshave or an auger or a sanding block, singing away like an opera star or quoting off whole long battle speeches from *Henry V*. There wasn't anything about boats he didn't know how to do and there wasn't an inch of that hull that he didn't set his own hand to. He'd fit pipe and lay sole and do cabinetry and varnish, all the time singing these chanteys or roaring out this Shakespeare or once in a while when he got to a piece of real fine work quieting down very concentrated and careful, fiddling at something with his fingers like a brain surgeon. He was down there from dawn till dinnertime and half the night too. When he wasn't working on that boat he was just sitting there looking at her. You'd see the light on in the shop till two or three in the morning and if you went down there, which Sylvie and I did sometimes because we liked to sneak out of bed and prowl around at night, you'd see him sitting in there on a keg underneath that hull with a bottle between his feet staring up at her with that wicked soft look like he had his hand up underneath somebody's dress. He didn't care if Momma had lost everything that mattered to her in the world, because he had what he wanted now. He was going to finish that Goddamned boat.

ALONG ABOUT MIDNIGHT SYLVIE AND I DECIDED WE MIGHT AS well make a night of it, the Jack Daniel's was long gone by now and we both had a pretty good thirst going so it seemed like the thing to do was to head up the road to Offutt's and see if we couldn't get Bud to fix us up with a bottle through the kitchen door. He and Mabel usually sat back there having a cup of coffee and adding up the till after they'd closed the store, and he was generally agreeable to "lending" you a bottle, just as a friend and neighbor, if you'd run into an emergency of some kind, which Poppa did just about every night of his life as near as I knew, Bud was used to it. We took a peek through the screen door to check on the Professor, he was out of this world by now in spite of those sofa springs, then we sneaked down the front steps and around back of the house and down the hill toward the clay road.

It was great, it was just like sneaking down that hill together at midnight to go crabbing, I hadn't had so much fun in ten years. We were both barefoot, creeping along over the cool wet grass back of the hotel with the same old feeling of secret high adventure, as if we expected Mrs. Cryer to come pouncing out of the shrubbery any minute, only of course we didn't have that to worry about now because the place was boarded up and silent and the Virginia creeper was working away at the veranda in the darkness, you could almost feel it, gently gathering and binding together the porch banisters into dark fragrant sheaves. We stood under the willow tree for a minute and Sylvie said, "I wonder what happened to Mrs. Peabody?"

"I don't know," I said. "I guess she's sitting in a rocking chair up there in front of the Pearly Gates." But I had an idea she was still out there on the front porch, or her skeleton anyway, with the handle of the old palmetto fan clenched between its finger bones and moths fluttering in and out of her ribcage with a whispery sound.

"I hope so," Sylvie said. "Because if she went the other way they're going to hear one hell of a tune from her, about the heat. Boy, she's going to wear that fan out, down there."

I had a great picture of Mrs. Peabody sitting there in the midst of sulphur fumes and flames, fanning herself like mad and saying to me when I arrived, straight off the ferry, "Evenin', Aaron. Mighty hot today." We giggled ourselves on down the hill, we were both pretty well stoned and feeling sillier than hell.

It was a cool night with a little misty moonlight coming through the thin clouds, enough to make the road look pale between the trees and the beech branches glow like bone in the forest. The little flint pebbles in the clay road pricked at the soles of our feet in a ghostly way and we walked cringing, like someone treading over middens.

"Hey, right over there was our log," Sylvie said. "You know, where we used to have all those talks, when we got off the school bus?" I looked between the pines and I could see its dark bulk through the chokecherry. "What do you say we go over there and sit down for a while?" Sylvie said.

"O.K., but let's get the bottle first."

"Posolutely," Sylvie said, she was feeling pretty good. We walked on up the road through the misty light and when we got around the bend we could see that the lights were off over the gas pumps but there was still light coming out through the kitchen blinds at the back of the store.

"They're still up," I said. "We got it made."

"Ring-a-ding-ding," Sylvie said.

Mabel had gone to bed but Bud was still fussing around in the kitchen, he was glad to see us, when he opened the door he said, "Well, my golly, looky here. If this ain't something. When did you two get down?"

"Just a couple of days ago," I said. "How are you, Bud?"

"Real good. I figured I'd be seeing you-all right soon. I tell you, Aaron, I was real sorry to hear about your daddy. I don't guess I have to tell you."

"No," I said. "Well, we came down to do what we could. Not much, it doesn't look like."

"No, I reckon not. They still lookin', are they?"

"Yeah. They haven't found anything, though, and I'm not sure they're going to. It's hard on Momma."

"I know it is. Mabel was up a couple nights ago and took her some stew. She said she was bearin' up real good, though."

"Yeah. Listen, Bud, we're not going to stay. We'll be down in a day or so, to visit. Right now we were wondering if you could fix us up with a bottle of J.D. We've had a rough day and there's nothing in the house."

"Why sure could, just as sure as hell. Green or Black?"

"Black," I said. "No sense rocking the boat."

"Oh, you know it. My God, I'm going to miss sellin' that man Black Label."

He gave us the whisky in a brown paper bag and walked us out to the pumps. It pained me to see that since the last time I had talked to him, which was about four years ago, something very unpleasant had happened to his ears, they looked like big dried apricots and the skin in front of them on each side of his face had pleated into a set of vertical wrinkles like concertina folds, as if his skull were shrinking slowly within. I started to mention it to Sylvie but then I decided that we could get along just fine without any more references to decay at the moment, so I peeled the foil off the neck of the Jack Daniel's bottle and then unscrewed the cap and handed it to her. She took a pretty good whack at it, without any comment this time, and then handed it back to me, we exchanged possession three or four times, going down the clay road toward the great pale luminous basin at the end of the trees that had been lapping at our souls for a quarter of a century or more. By the time we got down to where our old tree trunk lay in the darkness at the edge of the road we had our hands linked and were hopping around in the sand trying to remember the steps of a schottische we used to do when they had the square dances in the firehouse up at Poole on Saturday nights. We went staggering and panting through the strip of woods at the side of the road and banged our tails down on the log, it had gotten as soft as sponge by this time and had probably become host to an exuberant new generation of chiggers and poison ivy, which we would find out about in the morning.

"Oh boy," Sylvie said. "This is getting to be a real old-fashioned wake."

"Don't you know it," I said. "I'll bet it makes Poppa happy as a clam." I could see him up there in the clouds somewhere, grinning like a fool and slapping his thigh while he watched Sylvie and me dancing in the moonlight, I wished he could have lived to see it.

"Last year down in Mexico I got stoned one night and fell into an arroyo in some little town down in Morelos," Sylvie said. "It took Ron about three hours to get me out of there."

"It sounds like you lead a pretty gay life," I said.

"We have our moments," Sylvie said. "I just wish it wasn't such a Goddamned *effort*. I mean, Ron's got this sense of *duty* about keeping the Dionysian flame alive. You'd think he was earning a merit badge or something." She took a swill in a thoughtful way and set the bottle down between her thighs. "I mean it's not really fun, like this is. Listen, Aaron, why don't you stick around for a few days, no kidding? It's nice, being home together like this."

"I wish I could," I said. "But I've got so damn much to do, Sylvie. I ought to be in New York, right this minute. I've got a commercial to do on Tuesday morning, and I'm supposed to be helping this girl with an audition she's got coming up."

"You mean the one from London?"

"Oh. No, this is another one. No, she didn't come over."

"Old switched-on Linthicum. You don't sound like you had so many problems to me, boy. So what happened to the other one? The London one?"

"Well, she had a pretty bad time, all around," I said. "She got kicked out of GLAD at the end of her first year."

"Oh. Then you just sort of lost track of her, I guess," Sylvie said.

"No, I didn't lose track of her. As a matter of fact, that's when we first started making it together, in a big way, I mean. Which isn't too surprising, I guess, considering this fascination I seem to have with incompetence. That was really one incompetent girl. You have no idea of the number of things she couldn't do right. It was sort of heroic, actually."

I guess that's what turned me on about Cindy in the first place, the fact that she was such an incredibly terrible actress and that without any question whatever she was headed for early and total disaster in her chosen profession. All the time she was studying for her Finals performance at the end of her first year you could see that born-for-tragedy aura about her ripening like a melon in the sun, we used to take the tube up to Hampstead in the fine days at the end of October and wander on the heath with a basket of salami sandwiches and a bottle of cheap wine if we could afford it and lie there in the grass in the soft cool light when she recited "The Duchess of Malfi" in a voice like a tea-shop waitress's, which is what she was, always. There was a little vale down there in a hollow below Jack Straws Hill that the autumn light fell into, a tawny, drowsy place with a carrousel and a sugar-candy booth and you could lie there in the grass and hear the carrousel music come tinkling up the slopes through the gorse. We always saved a couple of shillings for the carrousel, which is where we would wind up, mildly stoned, sitting on a pair of painted ponies with terrible wooden teeth and wild eyes, trying to keep hold of each other's hands while we sailed tranquilly up and down and around and around through the yellow light and the shadows of elms to a tootling steam-pipe version of *I Believe in Yesterday*. I would watch her with a peculiar harrowed anxiety and lift her down carefully from her wooden pony the way a young husband lifts down his pregnant sweetheart, knowing Cindy to be pregnant with her about-to-be-born misfortune, the first of a numberless brood, I had no doubt, swollen and languid and milky and fascinating.

So when it finally happened, when she had failed in her Finals performance and I had taken her home shivering through the murk and drizzle of a dismal London afternoon, after she had gone through the ordeal of sitting in Dame Demeter's, the Principal's, office and listening to that lady deliver her famous and dreaded Little Talk complete with apothegms about the dignity of honest labor and a valedictory glass of wine, after I got her home under the dormer roof in Clifton Terrace and between sobs got her stuffed with hot tea and bread-and-marmite sandwiches, I made the discovery that a certain amount of misery and a gas fire in a cozy room on an autumn afternoon go together like gin and bitters, or sweet and sour pork, or even conceivably heaven and hell, what you get is a certain mysterious harmony such as you get in Donne or Thomas Hardy or the letters of Héloïse and Abelard after their misfortune, or a winter twilight in any of the dying cities of this world. My own particular method of expressing the phenomenon was to gather together my poor little Meccano-set girl friend and nibble her and nuzzle her and kiss her and cosset her and smooth out her draggled hair and tell her that all was well and that we would live there together in our gas-heated bower until the mains succumbed to moles or hemlock roots and, eventually, to take off her lilac-colored panties and defy the abyss. I didn't even have to wash the cups and saucers, I never paused to rake the cobwebs off the ceiling with a broom or shove my dirty socks into the closet or sprinkle the place with Lysol or even open a window, I just gathered her up like a stack of shattered cornstalks and lowered my nose into her raggedy hair and all of a sudden there I was with my arms full of Cindy and my heart full of pinwheels and rockets, red, green, yellow, purple, banners and trumpets, Decoration Day.

'Golly, love,' she said, nuzzling down into my clavicle, 'you make it worth waiting for, I must say.'

"Well, whatever turns you on, I guess," Sylvie said. "I think if I were a man I'd rather have something like one of Renoir's babes. They look like they've got a little blood in them."

"Well, Cindy had a little blood in her. *Very* little, though, of course. I guess as a matter of fact it was mostly Coca-Cola, she lived on the stuff."

"I think you ought to try a flesh and blood girl once in a while," Sylvie said. "It would be good for you. You know the kind I mean."

"Yeah, I know the kind you mean," I said. "You mean the kind Poppa liked."

"I didn't say that."

"No, I know. I said it."

"What is this, anyway?" Sylvie said. "Sock-it-to-me night or something? I don't need it from *you*, for God's sake."

"Who else do you get it from?" I said. "Ron? It sure doesn't sound like it; stumbling around Mexico stoned to the teeth and falling into ditches. You don't sound like you're having such a rough time."

"Well, what about you? Sitting up there in your Madison Avenue pad charming all the housewives of America with your golden voice. What the hell call do you have to get snooty with *me?*"

"I don't know," I said. "Listen, why don't we take it easy, Syl? We don't either one of us need it, I guess. My God, you'd think we'd learn something *once* in a while."

"You don't learn anything," Sylvie said. "Your *bones* learn. It doesn't have anything to do with thinking." She tore off a chunk of the tree trunk and crumbled it between her fingers. I got fascinated, watching her. She was making earth. Well, *she* wasn't, exactly, but she was helping out the bacteria who had already digested the damn thing or whatever it was they did to it. That's what we mostly did on earth, I decided: make earth. It was one of those dime-store revelations you get sometimes when you're pretty well oiled.

"Hey, I just thought of something," I said. "You know what we do, Syl? I mean what we *make?* You know what our *profession* is? We're earthmakers. That's what we do, the whole damn pack of us. Make earth."

"No, we don't," Sylvie said. "Not all of us." She had started to cry, I looked at her and saw the tears running down her cheeks in the moonlight. "Some of us make shapes," she said. "All kinds of wonderful shapes that were never here before we came. That nobody ever thought of before. I mean not even God."

I sat there for a minute trying to figure out what it was she was trying to get across, I didn't know whether she was talking about Poppa, or me, or herself, either way it was pretty damn sad. I leaned over and kissed her on the cheek.

"Thanks, big brother," she said. "I needed to be kissed right about then."

"Well, I needed to kiss somebody right about then," I said. "So it worked out fine. Let's have a pull at that thing." I took the bottle out of her fingers and had one, a very solid one, and then eased it down onto the log. "You know what Poppa said to me one time? 'You get what you get in this world, so it's a good thing to know how to hold your liquor.' I never forgot that, although it's one of the things I never figured out until just recently."

She leaned against me and laid her head on my shoulder, giving a huge dog sigh, like a hound settling himself down to sleep, and then peeked up through her eyelashes at the sky for a minute and said, "I didn't really like it, down in Mexico. You know the stars are all different down there, Aaron? I don't know why it is, but if I get more than fifty miles away from this place I start feeling creepy, like I was cutting school or something. All my life I've felt like I was waiting to get arrested. What the hell did I *do?*"

I WOKE UP AND THOUGHT IT WAS RAINING BUT THEN I LIStened good and realized it wasn't rain but a raccoon. There was a raccoon that used to walk around on the roof at night and his toenails would patter on the tarpaper just like raindrops, if you were still half asleep you could have sworn that's what it was. I didn't know what he was doing up there but he sure seemed to like it, he'd be up there two–three nights a week, just checking things over I guess or maybe enjoying the view of the bay in the moonlight. He'd walk around up there for a while and then he'd climb down the firethorn bush to the back porch and start eating the stuff we'd put out for him. Me and Sylvie had taken to putting a bowl of water and some cat food outside the kitchen door and he'd come almost every night and gobble it up. What got us started on it was this stray cat we used to see prowling around the woods one summer, we set stuff out for the cat one time and in the middle of the night I heard all this scraping and shuffling around out on the back porch so I got out of bed and went out to the kitchen and looked through the screen door and it wasn't the cat, it was this son-of-a-gun of a raccoon out there shoving the dishes around and having himself a feed. After that we took to setting stuff out regular and he got so he'd expect it. If we forgot one time or set out something he didn't like he'd raise hell. He was a real freak about cat food, if we tried dog biscuits on him or cereal or something he'd scratch on the screen with his fingernails and snuffle and squeak till he woke us up. He got real tame, you could even shine a flashlight on him and it wouldn't faze him a bit, he'd sit there and go right on eating, just as happy as a clam. We got to be crazy about that raccoon, we called him Burglar because of the black mask he had on his face and the way he sneaked around at night and stole stuff.

I could hear him out there now so I got up and went into Sylvie's room and shook her awake and said, "Hey, old Burglar's out there. You want to watch?"

"Yeah, O.K.," Sylvie said. She got out of bed and we went out to the kitchen and sat down by the screen door and watched. Old Burglar could hear us in there, he turned his head around and gave us a sort of screw-you-kids look and went right on gobbling up his cat food, that raccoon had class. We sat there watching him pick up a pawful of cat food and then dip it in the water to rinse it off, he was a real fancy eater, and then flick the water off it and nibble away very dainty with his whiskers twitching, it made us giggle. After a while he cleaned up the bowl and took a long drink of water and then ambled away across the porch floor and down the back steps and off into the woods.

"That old bastard was hungry tonight," Sylvie said. "He ate every last bit."

"I never seen him when he wasn't," I said.

"If I could be anything I wanted, I might even be a raccoon," Sylvie said. "Raccoons are cool. What would you be?"

"I wouldn't be any raccoon," I said. I thought about it for a while and then said, "I reckon I'd be an apple tree."

"Sure enough?" Sylvie said. She looked out through the screen door at the apple trees in the moonlight. "Heck, they can't even move. That's crummy."

"They move when the wind blows," I said. "Anyway, what's such a big deal about moving around all the time?"

"Well, I wouldn't want to be stuck in the ground for the rest of my life," Sylvie said. "Judas Priest."

"Yeah, but they break all out in flowers in the springtime," I said. "Boy, that must be a great feeling. Just imagine what it must feel like to break all out in flowers. And then apples. Imagine if you could have apples all over you."

"*Apples* all over me?" Sylvie said. "Holy Judas Priest. Boy, wouldn't you just look great with apples popping out all over you? Oh, wow." She started giggling and snorting and then hiccoughing so I had to bang her on the leg with my fist.

"Shut up," I said. "You'll wake them up."

"Apples all over him," she said. "Oh boy, old Lumpy Aaron."

"Yeah, well just shut up."

"Old Lumpy Aaron with the big red nose. And the big red knockers."

"You're going to get a big red nose if you don't shut up," I said.

She sat there snorting and gurgling with her hands over her mouth, she made me sick.

"You wake up Poppa and he'll give us hell," I said.

"I'm not going to wake up Poppa, because he's not here. He went out a half hour ago."

"Sure enough?" I said. I knew damn well he'd gone out, I just wanted to find out if she did. "I reckon he's gone down to the shop," I said.

"Yeah, what makes you think so?" Sylvie said. She wriggled across the floor on her butt and leaned back against the refrigerator. "Boy, this is nice and cool," she said, it was a hot night. "You know what I'm going to do when I get rich? I'm going to lay in a bathtub full of cold lemonade every afternoon and just sip at it with a straw. That is my idea of living." She leaned her head back against the refrigerator and looked around the dark kitchen. "This is a putrid place," she said. I didn't know why she said that because it was almost exactly like the old kitchen. But of course there were little differences, the ceiling was a little bit lower for one thing and the distances weren't quite the same. But the big difference was that all the marks and scars and stuff that used to be in the old kitchen were missing, like the tracks in the linoleum where Sylvie had rollerskated one time and the dent in the doorsill where she had flung a potato masher at Jamed. Also, everything was brand new, like the refrigerator. The chair legs were all smooth and shiny, not scuffed and dull like the old ones, and everything smelled different, new and painty and slick. It was a pretty good imitation though, you had to say that, especially considering that the plans for the old house weren't around any more and Poppa had had to make new ones, just from memory, out of his head. That came from boatbuilding, he had a dead-true eye for lines, he could build a boat by rack of eye like Granpa did. He said just give him half an hour to look over a boat and he could go home and turn out one you couldn't tell from her sister ship. You had to believe him, too, because that's what he'd done with the house, he'd brought a bulldozer up there and cleaned out all the ash and bricks and rubbish and built a new one right on the same spot. If you hadn't lived in the old house I don't guess you could have told the difference between them but of course we could, we'd lived there.

"It's not all that bad," I said. "It'll get beat up pretty quick."

"Not quick enough for me," Sylvie said. "I hate all this new crap."

"You don't seem to hate that refrigerator none," I said.

"The refrigerator's O.K.," Sylvie said. "In the summertime, anyway." She flattened her back against it and pulled her knees up and hugged them with her arms. "You know something about the old house that I bet you never did know?"

"What?" I said.

"There was an oak tree growing in it. Right in the wood."

"What do you mean there was an oak tree growing in it?"

"There was. Right in an old soft board under my windowsill. An acorn got stuck in there somehow and started to grow, right in the wood. That thing was three or four inches high."

"Sure enough?" I said. "How come you didn't ever tell me?"

"You think I tell you everything I know? You'd be as smart as me, if I did that."

I said, "Shoot."

" 'Shoot a polecat, go to hell,' " Sylvie said. "Hey, let's go out and crab."

"O.K.," I said. "But the batteries are getting pretty weak."

"Well, they'll last a while, won't they? Why don't you buy some new ones, for crumb's sake?"

"Because I don't have any money, that's why. You're the one that's got all the money. You must have ten million dollars in that damn Mason jar."

"You been in my Mason jar?" Sylvie said. "You better stay the hell out of my Mason jar, or I'll kill you. I'm not kidding, Aaron."

"I haven't been in your Goddamned Mason jar," I said. "But you're always sitting in there cuddling the thing like it was a baby or something. You know what you are, Sylvie? You're a miser. You haven't bought one damn set of flashlight batteries in six months. I'm the one that has to buy them, every damn time."

"O.K., O.K., I'll buy them next time," Sylvie said. "Why don't you cut out the bitching and let's go crabbing."

We unlatched the screen door and went down the back steps and across the yard to the tool shed. Sylvie looked like a fairy in her white nightgown in the moonlight. The grass was cool and wet under our bare feet, I felt like rolling in it. We opened the tool shed and took down a pair of long-handled crab nets off the wall and got the flashlight off a joist where it was standing on end.

"We don't have no bait," Sylvie said.

"Yeah, we do," I said. "There's still a chunk of bacon in the bucket." I shined the flashlight into the bucket and saw the bait line coiled up on the bottom and a knife and a couple of strips of bacon.

"O.K., that's good enough," Sylvie said. "We're not going to be but a while, anyway."

We walked down the hill the back way, behind the hotel, because there was a light on in the parlor, we didn't want old lady Peabody to see us. There was a lot of low cloud in the sky and it kept drifting over the moon. Our shadows would fade away and then get sharp and dark like ink spilling out on the ground. It was steep and slippery on the wet grass, I skidded once and landed on my ass and dropped the bucket, it clanked like a dinner gong.

"Judas Priest, don't make such a racket," Sylvie said. "We'll get our tails hauled."

The willow tree out in back of the hotel looked like a big blue fountain. We went and stood under it for a minute and felt it weeping on us, a faint cool sprinkle of sap falling on our skin like mist.

"That is the softest thing in the world," Sylvie said. "That is like angels breathing on you."

I couldn't get her out of there. "Come on," I said, "Are you going to stand here and get weeped on or are you going to crab?"

We went on down the hill to the road and looked across at the shop. The windows were dark, Poppa wasn't in there. I figured he'd gone off roaring around the county somewhere because the pickup was gone, he usually left it parked right there by the shop at night. I didn't say anything about it and neither did Sylvie, we went on down to the beach. The pier lights were on and there was a guy out there crabbing. We could see the circle of his light on the water and the handle of his crab net slanting down, glittering wet.

"Hell's bells," Sylvie said. "We can't go out there, that's liable to be old Boofy Sperling or somebody. He'll tell Poppa."

"Let's go down to the log," I said. "That's just as good."

We walked on down the beach to where the big sycamore log was stranded in the sand. The sand was cool as glass, I dug my toes in deep and let it sift over my feet, it felt great. There wasn't any surf, just a little lapping, like a lakeshore, and the slick wet sand at the water's edge was like a black mirror. There were periwinkles bubbling in it like bubbles in hot glass. Whenever the moon came out there would be a sudden blow of silver on the water, like a wind. Sylvie walked along in her nightgown with the handle of her crab net over her shoulder, like a fairy with a super-duper wand she'd got ahold of by mistake.

The sycamore was beached root end first in the sand with the top branches reaching out maybe thirty feet into the water. Sylvie climbed out first and settled herself in a crotch and then I handed her the crab nets and climbed out after her and straddled a branch where I could lean my back up against the main trunk, we were real comfortable. I tied a piece of bacon onto the end of the bait line and dropped it down into the water under us and then shined the flashlight down through the water so we could see the bait hanging, a little ragged white blob, over the sand. It wasn't more than two–three minutes before the crabs started swarming around in the lighted water, dipping and darting and coming up out of the darkness like wobbly pale monsters. We lowered our nets down and held them ready so we could swoop up the first one we saw that was legal-sized which meant the first one that looked as big as a dinosaur because they all looked about ten times as big as they really were when you saw them down under lighted water at night. There weren't a lot of legal ones though, we knew that already, they'd been crabbed out all summer. We sat and waited, jiggling the bait away when one of the little tiny bastards got too close to it, we didn't have a lot of bait to waste, and listened to the water lapping on the shore and a whippoorwill moaning somewhere up in the cliffs.

"Aaron, you ever been in love with anybody?" Sylvie said.

"Me? Heck, no," I said.

"I wish somebody would fall in love with *me*. I want some guy to be absolutely screaming crazy about me. I mean so he'd let me *whip* him and everything."

"*Whip* him?" I said. "What the hell do you want to whip somebody for? How do you figure that's being in love, when you want to whip somebody?"

"I didn't say *I'd* be in love," Sylvie said. "I just said *he'd* be in love. With *me*. I wouldn't have anything to do with the bastard."

That sort of stopped me cold, I didn't say anything for a while. I jiggled the bait and watched the crabs swarm around and every now and then took a look at the sky, which was really something. It was all curdled and milky and sort of hellish looking, like the picture in Poppa's Shakespeare book that was called *Lear on the Heath*. The flashlight was getting dimmer and dimmer, it wasn't going to last a lot longer.

"We're going to run out of light," I said.

"Yeah, well, tell me some news," Sylvie said.

Right then a gigantic old grandaddy crab came swimming up into the light, he looked about a yard wide.

"My God, look at that one!" I said.

"Hey, wow, that is a sure-enough crab," Sylvie said. "Hey, I get finnies on netting him, Aaron. Let me do it, O.K.?"

"O.K.," I said. "But you better not miss."

I held the bait steady so he'd take it and Sylvie lowered her net down under it and then worked it up slow waiting for him to catch hold. He came in real close to the bacon, scurrying around it sideways, quick and scary, and after a minute he put out his claw and grabbed it. Sylvie brought her net up quick, standing up on the log as she heaved up the handle, and we saw the steel rim break clear of the water, dripping silver on the surface, and here was this big spiny monster tussling around in the mesh, he was two hands wide.

"Hey, whoopy-doo, whoopy-doo!" Sylvie yelled, holding out the net and jiggling him up and down like French fries in a basket. "I reckon we hauled your tail, Mr. Crab."

"You're going to fall off of there, you nut," I said. "Dump him in the bucket."

I held the bucket while she brought the net in and turned it upside down over the rim and then jiggled the mesh until the crab plopped out. He hit the tin bottom with a wicked crunch, I bet he weighed a pound. We crouched down and watched him scrabble around in there for a while, his eyes were roaming around on their little jointed stalks and he was bubbling out of the cracks of his shell with a faint hissing sound, that was one ugly-looking devil.

"I wonder who in the hell was the first man to eat one of them things," Sylvie said.

"I don't know," I said. "But he sure must have been a hungry son-of-a-gun."

We dipped a little water into the bucket and wedged it tight into a crotch and then settled down to do some more crabbing, but the light was too dim by now, you couldn't see a thing down there.

"We're going to have to settle for just that one," I said. "We haven't got any more juice in this thing."

"Hell, we might as well let him go," Sylvie said. "Just one crab isn't going to make a meal."

"O.K.," I said. I didn't care too much anyway, I wasn't all that crazy about crabs, just catching them was the most fun. So Sylvie turned the bucket over and he hit the water with a splash and was gone.

"So long, Granpa," she said. "You got a break, boy."

We crawled back down the log to the shore and walked up the beach toward the house. It was heavy going in the sand with those big crab nets on our shoulders. There wasn't a bit of breeze, even in just my pajamas I was hot as a fox. We didn't talk any. When we got up by the shop I looked across the road and saw the windows were still dark, Sylvie looked too, but we didn't say anything. We went up the road and started walking through the hotel yard toward the house. Just then we saw headlights coming down the road, shining around the bend up at Offutt's and then swinging around and pointing straight down the road toward us like big cat's eyes. Then in a minute we could hear the pickup bumping down over the ruts toward the shop, we knew it was Poppa, there wasn't another car in the county made that kind of racket. We squeezed up back of the catalpa tree in the hotel yard, we sure as hell didn't want him to see us because if there was one thing that riled that man up it was catching us sneaking around down there at night. He pulled up in front of the office and switched off the lights and climbed down out of the cab with a package under his arm, you could make him out pretty good in the light over the office door. He was singing away under his breath, sort of mumbling the words, I could tell he'd had a few because he was having trouble staying on key. He didn't go in the office, he went looping across the yard to the boardwalk and then along the slips, you could hear his boots thonking on the planks, down to one of the big sloops that was tied up there. It was *The City of Oxford*, Poppa had just brought her back across the bay from the Eastern Shore that afternoon. She had her cabin lights on so I figured he'd been in there working on her before we came down.

"That fool is going to fall in the water," Sylvie said, you couldn't tell whether she was afraid he *would* or afraid he *wouldn't*, she was just about fed up with Poppa.

"Well, he never has yet," I said.

We could hear him clamber down into the cockpit, we couldn't see much because it was all dark and shadowy out there under the spars and rigging, but then he opened the cabin hatch and the light flooded out and he looked all wild and gigantic with his beard bristling and his eyes shining, like one of those saints in the Sunday school missal. He went down the companionway and closed the hatch and then the cockpit went dark again.

"I wonder what he's doing out there?" Sylvie said.

"He's probably working on her," I said. "He just brought her in this evening, he must have had some trouble."

Sylvie laid her crab net down in the grass and said, "Let's go see."

"You know what he'll do if he catches us," I said. "Come on, I'm going to bed."

"You're chicken," Sylvie said. "He's not going to hear us, we got bare feet."

"We'll have bare asses, too, if he catches us," I said.

"You're chicken," Sylvie said. She stood there staring at the cabin lights, she looked sort of hypnotized.

"What do you want to go over there for, anyway?" I said. "Why don't you just go on back to bed?"

She put her hand up and raked her hair back out of her face. She was dead set, I could see that.

"You going or not?" she said.

"O.K.," I said. I set down the bucket and the crab net and crawled through the fence rails. I started across the grass toward the slips but Sylvie didn't move, she was still standing out there on the other side of the fence. I turned around and whispered at her as loud as I dared, "Well, what the hell you doing? I thought you wanted to go so bad."

"You go on," she said. "I'm going to wait here."

"Oh, boy, who's chicken?" I said.

"Well, it ain't no need for both of us to go," she said. "But if you don't, I will."

I stood there for a minute and figured out that she meant it, so I went on. I got to the slipway and walked along it quiet, just on my toes. I could hear the water slurping around the pilings, it was black as oil and the moonlight was sliding all over it like hot solder. *The City of Oxford* was riding in close to her slipway, crunching her fenderboards against the pilings. They made a creaking sound, like a barn door swinging in the wind. I started tiptoeing out along the slipway and right then I noticed something that didn't make any sense at all, there was smoke coming out of the Charley Noble, you could see the glow from the top of the stack and a lot of little red sparks shooting up in the draft. Now why in the hell would he have a fire burning in there on a night like this, I wondered, it must be eighty-five degrees on the water. I could see he had the portholes open but with that Shipmate stove burning in there it must have been hotter than the main street of hell. That man has gone pure crazy, I thought.

I was figuring out whether or not to drop down onto the deck when all of a sudden I heard voices. I heard Poppa first, he said, "That bastard charged me three fifty for a six-pack. Now you know that's exorbitant." Then I heard a woman's voice, one of these cream-gone-a-little-bit-sour voices, say, "Now that is tough. Three fifty for a six-pack. And you was going to take me in to the Edgewater Room and dance me around all night. Oh my Lord."

"It ain't the price," Poppa said. "It's the principle. Just because it's one thirty in the morning and he's got to sell it out the back door, he slaps a extra two dollars and a quarter on it. There is people in this world that makes a living off of disaster."

"Well, I would say this is their big night," the woman's voice said. "They better make it while they can. They ain't going to get another opportunity like this for ten years."

"Now, don't let it get to you, Sugarfoot," Poppa said. "The good times ain't over yet, just 'cause we had a little trouble here tonight. You got to take any kind of comfort you can find, that's my philosophy."

"Well, there ain't a whole lot of comfort you can find in a six-pack of Schlitz," the woman's voice said. "You might of made it a bottle of Cold Duck. My sweet God."

"Honey, these boys don't keep that kind of fancy stuff on the shelf. How many calls you going to get for Cold Duck, out here in the County?"

"Well, you got one tonight," Sugarfoot said. "Loud and clear. It'd take a crate of it to give me any comfort. How in the hell much hotter you going to make that thing?"

"Baby doll, if you want them clothes of yours to dry out, we got to have a fire," Poppa said. "Now they ain't no two ways about it. They sure as hell ain't going to dry out in that night air."

I could hear some clanking and squeaking, like a hinge, and then the rattle of charcoal in a bucket, I figured Poppa was throwing some more fuel in the Shipmate, they were going to get boiled like lobsters down there.

"I'd just as soon go home in this blanket as go through this," the woman's voice said. "Don't you put no more coke on that fire, Joel, now I ain't kidding."

"All right, baby," Poppa said. "But you going to look funny as hell in the morning, walking down the street in that blanket."

"I'm going to look funny as hell in the morning no matter

what I got on," Sugarfoot said. "Just look at my hair. I spent an hour and a half setting that hair before I got on this God-damn boat."

"Well, baby, I told you to be careful," Poppa said. "You got to be all kinds of careful when you get on a boat."

"That is one thing you can say again," Sugarfoot said. "I tell you I'm going to be careful as hell before I get on the next one."

"Three fifty for a six-pack," Poppa said. "Goddamn, I can't get over that."

"You can't get over it," Sugarfoot said. "Oh my sweet Jesus. That is the only thing in this world you're worried about, ain't it? I tell you, Joel Linthicum, you take the *prize*."

They didn't say anything else for a while, so I laid down flat on the slip and lowered the side of my face right down on the wood, peeking through the porthole to see what I could make out, I was mighty curious to know what old Sugarfoot looked like. She was sitting across on the starboard berth with the table set up in front of her and all I could see was from about the middle of her neck to the tabletop. She had a blanket wrapped around her under her armpits like one of those sarongs the native girls wore in those South Sea Island pictures but that was about the only resemblance she had to a native girl because that blanket was bulged out like she had a couple of watermelons under it. I figured she weighed about two hundred pounds, just the part I could see would have come to around a hundred pounds by itself. She picked up a can of beer off the table and tilted it back out of sight, you could see the sweat running down her neck in rivers. I couldn't see Poppa at all, I figured he was sitting in the port berth across from her because there was another can of beer on the near side of the table. Old Sugarfoot banged her can down empty on the table and then raised up her arm and wiped off her forehead and said, "Jesus, my eyeballs is boiling right inside my head. My God, you could bake a cake right there on that table."

"Yeah, it's hot," Poppa said. "I'll give you that."

"Yeah, that's about the only thing you'll give me, too. I tell you this is the sorriest night of my life. And just to think I put on my brand new dress and my pretty silver shoes and figured I was going to dance all night in the Edgewater Room. Them shoes is just ruined, I know it. Joel, hand me one of them shoes, let me see what it looks like."

I saw Poppa get up and move across the porthole and then in a minute his hand set down a silver-colored sandal on the table. Sugarfoot picked it up and had a good look at it and those bosoms started heaving, she was going to pieces.

"Oh, my God," she said. "Look at that. Just look at that pretty little shoe. It is purely ruined."

I could understand how she felt because from what I could make out, that shoe was in pretty sorry shape. Poppa took it out of her hand and had a look at it himself and he seemed to agree because he said, "Yeah, that's pretty bad. I tell you, I think we might of got her a little too close to that fire. You see how she's blistering up along here? All that silver stuff is peeling right off. What is that stuff?"

"How in the hell do I know what it is?" Sugarfoot said. "All I know is, it's ruined. And you was the one that told me to wear them shoes. You said, 'Put on them silver shoes, Charlene.' Yeah, *you*."

"Well, honey, I always did think they looked good on you. I didn't know what was going to happen."

"No, I didn't neither," Sugarfoot said. "If I'd of knowed what was going to happen, I'd of wore hip boots. You know them shoes cost me six ninety-eight? And they've not been wore but about three times."

"Well, baby, I'll get you a new pair of shoes," Poppa said. "You ain't got to worry about that."

"I got to worry about everything," Sugarfoot said. "I got

to worry about my new dress. I got to worry about my hair. I got to worry about getting off this Goddamn boat and walking down the street in a blanket. Don't tell me I ain't got to worry." She broke down and started crying again, really all-out this time. Poppa got out his handkerchief and tried to wipe away the tears but she started batting at his hands, shooing him away.

"Don't you come near me," she said. "Don't you touch me, Joel Linthicum. Not never again in your life."

"Well now, come on, baby," Poppa said. "You got to pull yourself together. It ain't all that bad. I mean, what is it happened that can't be fixed up?"

"What is it *happened?*" Sugarfoot said. "I'll tell you what it is happened. What happened is that I get hauled clear across the bay on this tub so's you'll have some place to bed me down without putting out no money for a motel room. Then you leave me sitting here while you go up and have dinner with your old lady. Then I got to get off this thing in the pitch dark, so of course I fall in the Goddamned bay, and not only in the bay but right smack in the middle of a batch of jellyfish. I tell you I got nettle stings all over me would kill a horse. Just look how my legs is swollen."

"Well now, that ain't none of my fault, is it, baby?" Poppa said. "That could happen to anybody."

"Yeah, well why does it happen to me, that's what I want to know. I could be dead ten different kinds of ways, right this minute. Drowned or stung to death or boiled alive or pneumonia or heart attack, just about any Goddamn thing in the book, you name it. And what do I get for it, is what I want to know. A six-pack of Schlitz. And then you got to fuss about the price. Oh my God."

"Well, baby, you're still alive," Poppa said. "That's the big thing, now ain't it? It's going to work out all right. I tell you, I got a plan."

"Well, just don't tell me one word about it," Sugarfoot

said. "I don't want to hear no more of your plans as long as I live. When are you planning on dying? That's the only thing I'm interested in."

"Now look, baby, I'm just as sorry as you are we didn't get to go up there and go dancing," Poppa said. "But that ain't no reason why we got to give up on the whole night. I figure we can still have us a good time down here. I got some Jack Daniel's up there at the shop I can break out, I just remembered. And I got a radio right here in this boat. Why, hell, we can go out there in the *cockpit* and dance, baby. I ain't about to give up on this thing."

"Go out there in the cockpit," Sugarfoot said, she sounded like he'd just told her he was going to run for president or something. "Out there in the cockpit. I'm going to go out there in that little bitty cockpit, about as big as a postage stamp, and dance around stark naked in the moonlight. You know what you are, Joel Linthicum? You are crazy as a Goddamned coot, that's what you are. You know, women been telling me all my life to stay away from you. I remember last summer, first time I was ever going to go out with you, Hester Davis said to me, 'Don't do it, Charlene. That man won't give you nothing but grief.' Well, I figured I'd take a chance. I ought to of got down on my knees and thanked that woman, that's what I ought to of done."

"Now, honey, we've had some real good times," Poppa said. "Now you know that. It ain't all been like tonight."

"No, thank God for that," Sugarfoot said. "They ain't nothing ever happened could make up for tonight. Not if you was to drudge me up every pearl out there in that bay. Open that Goddamn hatch, Joel, I'm going to suffocate if I don't get some fresh air."

I was getting kind of worried right about then because I figured Sylvie might be showing up any minute, I sure as hell didn't want that to happen. I figured she had a pretty good idea of what was going on already, but it wouldn't help to let her know for sure. *I* wasn't going to let her know anyway, stuff like that was bad for Sylvie's disposition. She was mean enough already since that fire, all she had to do was barge into something like this and she'd be finished, boy, I didn't know but what she'd run off or something. Just about all she did any more was to brood about Poppa, she was getting real screwed up about it.

I looked back down the slip to where she was standing but I couldn't see a whole lot, the moon was down again and it was pretty dark. But I could make out a glimmer of white back there by the fence which I figured was her nightgown, so she was probably still standing there. I got up and tiptoed down the slip and jumped off onto the grass and went across the yard to where she was. I climbed through the fence and picked up the crab nets.

"What's he doing in there?" she said.

"I reckon he's working on the engine," I said. "I could hear a lot of clanking and stuff."

"How come he's got the stove going?"

"I don't know," I said. "Maybe that's what he's working on. I couldn't make out too good."

"You are a liar, Aaron," she said. "I'm going to go see."

"Why don't you come on to bed?" I said.

"Because I want to know what he's doing."

"Well, if you want to know, you go on and look," I said. "I'm going to bed."

"I'm going over there," Sylvie said.

"O.K. I'm going on up to the house."

She crawled in through the fence and started across the grass to the slip. I reached down and picked up the bucket, then I let it drop against the fence rails. It made one hell of a racket. Sylvie stopped there in the middle of the grass like she'd been hit with an arrow. She looked across at me and shrieked out in an ice-cold whisper, "You son of a *bitch*, Aaron!" About two seconds later the hatch opened and the light flooded into the cockpit again and I could see Poppa's head and shoulders coming up the ladder. He looked out across the cabin top and yelled, "Now what the hell is going on out here?" He jumped up onto the slip and you could hear his boots hitting down hollow on the planks, he was coming right for us, you could see his black shape moving against the spars, coming across the yard. Sylvie didn't move, she stood right there waiting for him. When he got up to her I could hear her fists thudding against his chest, she started screaming and beating at him like a crazy woman. I heard Poppa say, "What in the hell is the matter with you?," then Sylvie turned around and ran, she came through that fence like a hound after a rabbit and went right on past me up the hill. I wasn't far behind her.

When I got up to the house I shoved the bucket and crab nets into the tool shed and skiddled up the back steps and through the kitchen to me and Jamed's room and jumped into bed beside him, it woke him up. He grunted and fussed and said, "What are you doing, anyway, Aaron, for gosh sakes? You got all the covers."

I said, "Shut up, Jamed. Go on to sleep."

"I bet you and Sylvie was running around outside," he said. "Boy, you're going to get it, Aaron."

"I bet you better shut up," I said. I lay there listening but I didn't hear a thing, it looked like Poppa wasn't coming after us. I figured he wasn't sure whether we knew what was going on out there or not and anyway he was too damn busy at the moment to do anything about it, he wasn't going to bust in there and wake up Momma right now, that was for sure. He'd give us hell in the morning though, I was pretty certain of that. I lay there for a long time listening, I was afraid we might have woke up Momma ourselves. I thought Jamed had gone back to sleep, he hadn't though, he said, "Aaron, was Poppa out there? Did you see Poppa?"

"What do you mean, was Poppa out there?" I said. "What the hell are you talking about?"

He lay still for a while and then he said, "Aaron, you know

what? I been counting my toes and it seems to me like I got twelve of them. Would you count them for me and see? I don't know what I'm going to do if I wake up in the morning and find out I got twelve toes." One of his big problems was that he couldn't count right.

"Oh for God's sake," I said. "What are you talking about? How the hell are you going to get extra toes?"

"I could have growed them," he said. "People do. I read in *Believe It or Not* where this guy had twelve toes. Would you just count them and see?"

So I counted his toes and they came out to ten but he didn't seem too convinced. He said, "Thanks, Aaron. You sure?"

I said, "Sure I'm sure. Now go on to sleep." We couldn't either one of us sleep, though, we lay there looking up at the ceiling and after a while I said, "Hey, Jamed, how would it be if you and me went off and lived by ourselves somewhere? I don't mean right now or anything, but just some day?"

"You mean not Sylvie nor Momma and Poppa nor nobody?" he said.

"That's right. Just you and me. We could have a real great time, you know that?"

"Yeah, I know," Jamed said. "That would be good, Aaron. But I don't really reckon I could. You see, I got to stay with Poppa."

"Yeah, O.K.," I said. "I was just talking, anyway."

I lay there listening to him breathe and I thought, Oh boy, I don't care what Sylvie says, I wish we could *all* be apple trees. Just standing there looking out at the bay for a million years, two big ones and three little ones, every springtime breaking all out in those pretty white flowers, and Poppa could have the doves come and fly through his branches and sit there and coo, and Sylvie could hum away in the wind and flirt with all the other trees and not have to worry about them getting close enough to touch her, and Momma would have a great time because if there was two things she loved in the world it was to wash her hair in rainwater and then to let it dry out in the sun, she could go on doing that forever, and Jamed could just stand there and study his shadow for a million years, I didn't see how you could beat it.

WHEN SYLVIE SAID THAT ABOUT WAITING ALL HER LIFE TO GET arrested I had a sudden wildly missionary impulse to bear witness to the fact that it is possible at least once even in the course of the most inconceivably undistinguished life and on such an improbable site as West Fifty-ninth Street to behold a certain jubilation in the sky, to hear for just a moment above the snarl of traffic a burst of feathery applause pealing in the blue air like a cannonade, a celebration if not of triumph at least of festival, of something that still deserves the rejoicing of doves in the bad-ass world, I wanted to tell Sylvie about that. But it is pretty hard to be convincing about it if you have no evangelical talents of any sort whatever and if you happen to have a bottle of whisky wedged between your thighs at the moment and the generally unpersuasive air of an abandoned sheepdog, so I decided to shake off the impulse before it led me into all sorts of embarrassments. I fished around for a cigarette and found one finally, but no matches, there's always something missing, some form of ignition usually, at least in my case. I put the cigarette in my mouth anyway and sat there puffing away at it, blowing out my imaginary smoke, just like the big guys, I thought. Sylvie leaned against me with a growing heaviness and after a while she started snoring softly, she seemed to have gone into a state of hibernation. Pretty soon my shoulder got cramped from the weight of her head, I had to shift around to get myself unkinked, which woke her up.

"What's the matter?" she mumbled.

"I'm getting a Charley horse," I said. "It looked like you'd passed out for the rest of the summer. Is there such a thing as hibernating in the summertime?"

"Yes," she said. "Some kinds of snails do it. Also some kinds of Linthicums. It's called estivation."

"What do you know about that," I said. "It's a great thing to have a Doctor of Philosophy in the family."

"It's evidence of a stubborn perversity throughout the animal world," Sylvie said. I decided you could look at it that way or you could just say it takes all kinds to make a world. "Just wait till the glaciers come back," she said. "I'll be raring to go, then. I'll be in my element, boy." She sounded pretty well stewed, I thought I'd better get her back up to the house.

"Hey, how about hitting the sack?" I said.

"Not on your life. We've got half a bottle to go. I was just taking a little breather, that's all."

She struggled back up to a sitting position on the log and raked at her hair for a minute with her fingernails and then had another drink and shuddered. "You haven't finished telling me about London, anyway. About what happened to Cindy and all. Where is she now?"

"Back in Stratford, I guess, handing out tea and scones in the family buttery. Her mother had a teashop up there. I hope she is, anyway."

"So she went home," Sylvie said. "How is that your fault?"

"Well, she didn't go right away. She decided to stay in London and take a job, so we could be together. She took quite a few jobs, actually, about one a week. It was miraculous, the way she could screw things up, you wouldn't believe it."

In breathtaking succession she was a dentist's receptionist, a waitress, the girl who sits on the elephant holding a parasol in the Bertram Mills Circus, a clerk in a travel agency, a dispenser of sample cups of coffee in a grocery store, and an apprentice stenotypist. She also filled in between jobs as a part-time blood donor, which must have resulted in some of the most terrible reversals in medical history. I was never really sure if all that was evidence of a hopeless unadaptability to life or a sort of dazzling virtuosity, you had to say this for Cindy: time could not wither nor custom stale her infinite variety. As a dental assistant she got appointments hopelessly mixed up, people would arrive on Friday to get a tooth filled that had been extracted last Tuesday, she sent bills to the wrong patients, she bolluxed up the National Health forms so badly the place nearly broke down, the dentist who hired her finally had to go to Deauville for a week to pull himself together. When she got the circus job at White City Stadium it turned out she didn't have much of a seat on an elephant, she kept falling off the damn thing so they transferred her to a camel but then it turned out that she was allergic to camels, she kept sneezing all the time they were parading around the ring which sort of destroyed the splendor of the spectacle because there was Cindy up there plucking Kleenex out of her brassiere and honking her nose like a goose. When she got the job in the grocery store she kept mixing the coffee wrong, she always put in too much chicory or something so people would take one sip of the stuff and their eyes would bulge out and they'd run up and down the aisles looking for some place to spit, she only lasted there about two days. Then she moved on to the travel agency where she had all kinds of trouble with itineraries and tickets, people who were supposed to go to Blackpool for the weekend would find themselves being whisked off in a limousine for a two-week tour of the château country, we finally had to put up ten pounds in reparations for some guy who was supposed to have first-class hotel reservations in Rome but instead got bedded down with a bunch of student hostelers in a basement that had two inches of water on the floor, that was one mad man. I thought for a while she might make it as a stenotypist, it cost us fifteen pounds for her tuition fees plus a deposit on the stenotype machine that she was learning to operate, a little black gadget with a keyboard that she carried around in a case, she seemed to have a genuine aptitude for stenotyping and by that time she was pretty well determined to succeed at something, she would practice every night after I'd gone to bed, sitting there huddled up with a blanket around her shoulders and the gas fire going, pecking away at that keyboard until one or two in the morning, but then one night when I was walking her home from the Balaclava School of Commercial Arts we stopped by the Chelsea Embankment to look at the moonlight in the river and she got so carried away by the beauty of the scene that she dropped her stenotyper in the Thames, so that was the end of her career as a court reporter, we couldn't afford to buy another one. As a matter of fact we couldn't afford to buy anything any more, with just my G.I. Bill to support us we could barely make the rent every week let alone get out of hock, it was pretty Goddamned ironic, here we were living on spaghetti and cat food half the time and turning over most of our income to the Balaclava School for the thing we didn't need most in the world, a defunct stenotype machine at the bottom of the Thames.

We had to give up our eyrie up there among the clouds and take a bed-sitter in Notting Hill Gate, a mangy back-basement room with a view of an areaway which seemed to be the place where all the cats in London came to die, you could see three of their corpses through the cellar window. Maybe they didn't actually *plan* on dying there, but once they got there and had a look around they just gave up and rolled over, I felt much the same way. I'll tell you a funny thing, that place scared the hell out of me but it was also sort of reassuring in a crazy way, maybe not reassuring but comforting or something, elemental, I mean when you get to the basement floor of 23 Stanley Crescent there's not a hell of a lot farther down you can get, not until they bury you anyway, you figure, well this is the bottom, boy, the ultimate reality, and maybe a tight close-up, really, of that same scene we used to get from the dormer window. The truth is that after we'd been living there for a couple of months I found myself getting sort of adjusted to the place, you could see the holes in people's soles and you had a very nice view of dogs' bellies and babies' asses, not very exalted sights maybe, but interesting in their own way, basic, it was something you missed from up above. I would stand there watching some stray mutt working on a chicken bone and try to run through my pantheon, my catalogue of gods and prophets: Blake, Keats, Byron, Shelley, but it never seemed to work, it didn't have the old zing to it, about the best I could come up with was: John Doe, Kilroy, Joe Doakes, Resident, Aaron Linthicum. Somehow Linthicum didn't sound quite so funny in a list like that, it was more my style.

Finally, though, Cindy got herself installed in the lingerie department of Swan and Edgar's, a sort of middlebrow department store in Piccadilly, on what seemed to be a permanent basis. She worked harder than hell there, I think she actually liked the place, it may have been the *ambiance*, the racks of rustling new dresses and the smell of perfumed soap and the glitter of costume jewelry, that was life's blood to Cindy, that and *Screen Gems* and Coca-Cola. At any rate she took to working overtime, as often as not she would still not be home when I came trudging up Stanley Crescent from the tube station after a day at the academy, I would have the spaghetti cooking and the rainwater mopped up from under the open windowsill and the bed made and the panty hose harvested from the backs of chairs and doorknobs by the time she arrived, sweetly flushed from the furor of the market-place, or so I imagined, and full of fervent plans for becoming the most ravishing fashion model of the century, the Queen of Carnaby Street. For anybody with an attention span and a circulatory system like Cindy's her devotion to the place was really mysterious, it was practically metaphysical. She took to staying later and later, to do inventories and file stock reports, she explained, until finally one night when I had to stay late at GLAD for a dress rehearsal we got home at exactly the same time and a lot of the mystery was cleared up. I came around the corner from Kimberly Place at the very moment she was getting out of a tangerine-colored Rover that was pulled up in front of Number 10 and inside of which a guy with about a bushel of curly auburn hair was flapping a pair of pigskin gloves at her in farewell.

'Who the hell was that?' I asked.

'Derek. He's in Fashion, on the third floor. He gave me a lift, because of the rain. Hasn't he got a smashing car?'

She explained to me inside, over the fish and chips I had brought home from the corner shop, that this guy was grooming her for a job in his department, they needed another model in High Fashion, he said.

'Don't you think it's marvelous, love? And I'd be a natural for it, Derek says.' He was right, I thought. All bones, no boobs, no brain. I sprinkled some vinegar on my fish.

'How long have you known this guy?' I said.

'Oh, I d'know. A couple of weeks. God, I'd love that sort of thing. And I don't know why I couldn't do it. I mean, all you've got to do is stand about with your hips shoved out, looking sort of windblown. I don't think I photograph too badly, you know.'

She was right about that, I had a drawerful of snapshots to prove it: Cindy feeding ducks, feeding squirrels, feeding a carrousel pony cotton candy, and another one, a sort of murky-looking negative that had been floating in the back of my brain for some time, developing very slowly: Cindy walking away from me in a Mary Quant afternoon suit down a long aisle of splendiferous scented trees that bore twinkling shiny fruit like Christmas tree balls, turning to wave to me with her rickety farewell smile as she stepped into the jaws of a waiting tangerine-colored crocodile with solid alabaster teeth. It was very damned painful.

So one night about a week later she didn't come home at all, I walked into the room dripping wet from my evening hike up Stanley Crescent in the rain and as soon as I opened the door I saw this wine bottle sitting in the middle of the table with a note stuck onto the neck of it with a piece of Scotch tape like a little flag. I knew I'd been shafted the minute I saw it, anything that comes wrapped up in a flag is bad news, but I had to admit she put it with unexpected delicacy: *Have been asked up to Herts for the weekend by an old school chum whose just got married. She's having a bit of trouble and wants someone to natter with. I'll go straight in to work on Monday and see you in the evening. Hope you like the wine. I had a sip and it's smashing. Love, C.*

An old school chum with a tangerine-colored Rover, I thought, O.K., my little bitcheroo. I sat down and drank the bottle of wine, which she was right about, it was smashing, by the time I finished it up I was pretty well smashed, and considering that I didn't have a shilling for the gas meter and had been sitting there for about two hours in soaking wet clothes I didn't feel too bad. I decided if I was going to get any work done on my lines the next day I'd better get some sleep so I took off my clothes which I had to remove like orange peel and hung them around on the backs of chairs and after brushing out the cracker crumbs and comic books and hairpins I crawled into that bed which without Cindy in it had all the allure of an albatross's nest. I didn't get much sleeping done though because I started worrying about that brainless eighty-five-pound Lorelei loose somewhere between Land's End and Caithness. The funny thing was, I couldn't hate her, that's always been my big trouble, I can only hate people I don't know. Oh, there might have been a minute or two when I hoped to hell she would get her comeuppance in the form of crabs or pregnancy or maybe a flat tire somewhere on a lonely road, but after I had lain there for a couple of hours watching the windowpanes gradually become visible in the cold morning light and cooking up visions of my little half-witted girl friend getting her ears methodically chopped off and run through a meat grinder by a demented fashion supervisor with testicles tossing between his thighs like coconuts any feelings of jealousy or indignation I might have had had pretty well dissolved into thin air and what I was left with was just plain worry, it was a development I didn't appreciate too much. I was tired of worrying about that girl, it seemed to me I had spent half my life worrying about people, I was getting pretty sick of people. Let him chop her God-damned ears off, I thought, and then coat her with honey and tie her down to an ant hill or whatever it is he has in mind, it'll be a damned good lesson for her.

He was just the type who would do it, too, that was the trouble, any guy who devotes his whole life to ladies' lingerie must have some pretty terrible kinks of some kind. Well, it's her problem, I thought, let her have it, don't try to take it away from her, don't try to be Cindy for Christ's sake, you've tried to be too many people in your life, be yourself for a change. Or Bosola, think about that, boy, Monday morning you've got to get up on a stage and pretend to be Bosola, you'd better get some practice.

It seemed to work. Right away, a voice way down inside of me that I'd never heard before in my whole life said, *Let go*. I'd never heard it before. It was fascinating. I listened and it said it again, *Let go, boy*. So I did, for a minute. For just a minute, I let go. It's astonishing how easy it was. And for a minute there, it was all peace, a very strange damned kind of peace, nothing like I ever expected. It was sort of like leaving the helm untended on a day of blue-water sailing, I didn't know where I was going and I didn't care, I was stretched out on my back on a warm deck under the bluest sky I ever saw, I mean really infernally blue, I was just lying there soaking it up, with the tiller banging away behind me, smiling and smiling.

Then I gave a big sigh and said, O.K., boy, that was great, but it's not for you. What you've got to do is get out of this sack and make yourself a good strong cup of tea and get to work, you've got a lot of worrying to do. So that's what I did, finally.

"I think you like it," Sylvie said. "I think it's the only thing that really turns you on."

"Maybe," I said. "But I didn't like it very much at the time, I can tell you that for *sure*."

I worried the whole damn day, I couldn't learn Bosola for beans, I was thinking about that skinny, blue-eyed nit-wit. I would lie down in front of the gas fire and try to study my lines but every few minutes I'd look up into the blue flames and there she'd be, crouched back against a bed-stead biting her knuckles in agony while this auburn-haired monster lashed her flesh to ribbons with a brass-buckled belt. Or she was being shoved out of his tangerine-colored Rover, stumbling and sobbing through the rain and darkness on the Great North Road until she was smashed to pulp by a speed-ing lorry. It was one hell of a day, I hope I never go through another one like it. The thing that got me most was the silence, Jesus God, you never realize how much silence there is in the world until you're waiting to hear whether somebody is all right or not. The stuff seemed to leak through the walls like fog, the whole universe was one great big bowlful of silence. Any kind of sounds at all, the mur-muring of the gas jets, the lisp of the pages as I turned them, the honking of a horn somewhere out in Stanley Crescent, were blessed, they were like blossoms, like white flowers floating in a dark pool. We had this nutty landlady named O'Gorman who used to pee every six minutes right around the clock and even the sound of her out there clumping up and down the hall to the john had a kind of brave pilgrim quality about it, when she pulled the chain of the watercloset it was like a distant silver cascade, pure rhapsody, I was in bad shape, boy.

After a while I decided I'd better get where the noise was so I put on my mac and went out to a coffe bar on Bayswater Road and nursed a cappuccino for a couple of hours, soaking in the hum of conversation and the tinkle of teaspoons and china like balm. Then after a while I got to worrying that maybe Cindy was trying to get in touch with me, that there might be a phone call or a telegram that I'd miss, so I went back to the flat and got the kettle going and sat there swilling tea for the rest of the day trying my damnedest to be a thin-lipped Jacobean desperado while I listened for the telephone outside in the hall.

I slept about an hour all told that night and by the time I got to GLAD in the morning I was a wreck. I made one holy mishmash out of that part. After a while it got to be kind of funny, the rest of the cast would stare at me with a sort of horrified fascination wondering what I was going to do or say next while I wandered around out there like a soul in purgatory trying to ad lib in iambic pentameter. When it was all over and we went into Dame Demeter's office for our crits she said to me, 'Now Linthicum, that was to say the least an extraordinary performance. You dried up—let me see—eighteen times. I believe that's a record.'

'I know,' I said. 'I'm sorry, Dame Demeter. I've been having this personal problem.'

'It must be a very grave one,' she said. 'I do hope you've got it solved by Finals time, or there's a very great risk, you know, of your being sent down.'

Well, there goes my career, I thought, or halfway gone. Maybe it isn't any very great loss at that, maybe it isn't my real profession anyway, I'd already been having some pretty heavy doubts about it to tell you the truth. I was reaching that point in my life in art where the dreams of glory are beginning to wear a little bit thin and the business of training yourself to be a faultless instrument for the conveyance of the Divine presents itself to you in very unromantic terms. It's one thing to dream about your name at the top of a theater program and another thing to realize after a year and a half of grinding your way through some place like GLAD that there's an awful lot of horse manure around and maybe it isn't the best idea in the world to build yourself a throne right on top of it. Well what the hell is my real profession, then, I wondered, I ought to be getting a clue of some sort by this time. Maybe I could set up as a Professional Pitier or something. Commiseration, Consolation, Lamentation Provided for All Occasions. Call Upon Our Trained Staff for Expert Hand-Holding. Bereavement, Betrayal, Broken Bones, Financial Reverses, Impeachment in Office, Loss of Pets, of Hair, of Potency, No Affliction Too Small to Win Our Heartfelt Sympathy. Victims of Their Own Passions a Specialty. I'd never make a nickel, I thought, the priests and poets and psychiatrists have got the field sewed up, what I am is a Goddamned lifelong amateur.

"You said it," Sylvie said. "Oh boy, you said it, Aaron. And that's not all you are, you're a *fool*, too. You know that? You're the biggest Goddamned fool I ever met in my life. I mean *ever*." She sounded madder than hell. She sat there staring off into the forest with her jaw stuck out, then she shuffled her hair around a little bit and said. "Well, it's what we mostly turn out, in this family. All kinds and sizes, from driveling idiots to Ph.D.'s. God Almighty, maybe the best thing to do is to bed down in suburbia with a poodle and string of credit cards, like the rest of them. Your *teeth*'ll be straight, anyway."

WE HAD TO GET UP EARLY, BEFORE GOOD LIGHT, BECAUSE POPPA always waited for an early morning tide when he took us out for a day's sailing. There was a lot of shoaling around the mouth of Persimmon Creek, and that way you could be sure of having plenty of water under you when you went out, and what was more important, plenty under you when you came back in the dark, the tides being twelve hours apart. So we had to get up at five o'clock but we were awake a hell of a lot before that, listening for wind. Especially Jamed, I think he was awake almost the whole damn night. He never could sleep when we were going to sail in the morning, he was scared to death. I woke up a couple of times in the night and felt him lying there beside me stiff as a poker, too stiff to be asleep, and I'd say, "Jamed, you awake?" and he'd say, "Uh huh. Hey, Aaron, you hear any wind? I thought I just now heard that wind a-coming up." I'd listen for a minute and then say, "No, there ain't any wind, it's still as can be. Go back to sleep, for God's sake." He didn't sleep much though, that was one nervous boy.

Poppa came in at five o'clock and grabbed us by the hair and shook our heads around, yelling, "Hey, sailors, hit the deck! Mess call! Git 'em while they're hot!" He was full of vinegar, there didn't nothing stir that man up like the idea of a day out there on the water, especially when he had a new boat he'd just finished that he wanted to show off to us kids. He wasn't a bragging man, it was just that not being much of a talker it was his way of showing us who he was, what he done. Momma was already up and cooking breakfast,

I could smell hotcakes and bacon. I liked that, the breakfast smell and the stir in the house with the kerosene lamps lit and it still dark outside, with just a faint before-dawn light spilling out over the bay and the water spread out there all the way to the sky, steel-colored and heaving slow in the morning swells like something breathing. To tell the truth, I loved sailing, I guess I felt pretty much the way Poppa did about it. I would 've had a hell of a time if it hadn't been for Jamed, but seeing him sit there scared out of his pants and trying to make his hotcakes go down took all the fun out of it. He wouldn't look at anybody but me and I hated it. I tried not to look at him but every now and then he'd catch my eye and stare at me sort of pleading like he was saying, "Aaron, get me out of this somehow, please. I don't want to go out there." You would have thought that somebody who had spent the whole ten years of his life sitting right on top of the Chesapeake Bay would have learned to get along with it somehow by that time, but not Jamed. I don't know how he could even bear to *drink* a glass of water, he was so scared of the stuff. Sylvie acted like she didn't have any use for him, she stared at him with a sort of disgusted look and then turned her head away, closing her eyes and letting out a little hiss of air over the top of her tongue like he was dirt. She didn't have much use for anybody any more. It was really Poppa she meant all that stuff for, but she took it out on anybody that happened to be around.

Momma was wrapping up sandwiches in waxed paper for our lunch. She did it careful and broody, her mind away off somewhere. She wasn't happy about Jamed going out there but she didn't know what to say, she'd said it all before, lots of times, when he was even littler, and it hadn't done any good: Some children are naturally delicate, Joel, you don't allow for it. He can learn other ways, God has laid down plenty of roads for His children to follow. Whether she was sarcastic or religious or whatever, it was all the same to Poppa, his eyebrows would come down, he would look at the tip of his thumb and lift it up and suck at it for a minute and then say, "Yeah, I know he's scared. Let me tell you something, I get scared too, end of every Goddamn month when them bills start coming in, but that don't pay none of them. That don't buy a can of beans, being scared."

I said to Jamed, "You got syrup all over your nose, for crumb's sake. Why don't you wipe your nose?"

He said, "O.K., Aaron, I didn't go to do it." He was making me sick.

Poppa was licking his fingers and then wiping them with his napkin, one after another. "What is that?" he said. "Buttermilk batter?" He winked at me. "I like that buckwheat, myself."

"I suppose you do," Momma said. She was wrapping the sandwiches. "I say anybody doesn't like buttermilk batter has got something wrong with them."

"There's something wrong with everybody in this house, as far as I'm concerned," Sylvie said, sort of under her breath but not quite.

"Now just what do you mean by that smart remark, young lady?" Momma said, turning sharp from the sink board. "We don't need any remarks of that kind from any smart young ladies. Just you show a little respect."

"I didn't know a person wasn't even allowed to talk, even in their own house," Sylvie said.

"You can talk just as soon as you have something pleasant to say," Momma said. "And not a minute sooner. Now you go and make them beds, if you're through eating."

"And you do it fast," Poppa said. "We going to miss that tide."

Sylvie kicked her chair back and went stamping into the bedroom. I could hear her in there muttering and bumping around.

"And you do it quiet," Momma said. "Without all that ruckus."

"I am *praying*," Sylvie shouted, in the bedroom. "I didn't know a person wasn't even supposed to *pray*."

"I'll give you something to pray *about*, in a minute," Momma said. She turned back to the sink board and put the sandwiches in a bag and set it on the table with a thermos bottle. "Jamed, you eat those hotcakes," she said. "You need something hot in your stomach, if your father's determined to take you out on that water."

"I don't want 'em," Jamed said. "I don't feel good."

"Yeah, well, you'll feel better after you eat 'em," Poppa said. "And I mean right now, boy." He folded his napkin and put it on the table and gave it a pat and said, "Well, thank the Lord for that little bit. Many a man would of made a meal off of that." Then he got up and took his jacket off the back of the chair and put his arms into it, listening with his head cocked to some sparrows cheeping in the chimney. "Listen at them little buggers," he said. He came around behind Momma and put his hands on her hips and smacked them with his palms. "That buttermilk batter is prime," he said. "I was kidding you, dove."

"You never mind the kidding," Momma said. "Joel, I want them children back in this house by six o'clock. You get back here one minute later than that and you're going to have trouble."

"I know that, beauty," Poppa said. "We'll be here. And we'll be something like hungry." He kissed Momma on the back of the neck. "I'm going to feed my doves now. You children come on and get your gear out of the shed."

He was standing in front of the loft when we came out, there were doves perched all along his arm feeding out of his hand. They hammered at his palm with their beaks, sprinkling yellow grains of cracked corn that bounced off the toes of his boots like hail. We went in the tool shed and took down our life vests and foul-weather gear and then came out and stood waiting for Poppa to close the loft. I jammed Jamed's hat down over his ears but he didn't smile, he was looking out over the bay at the low morning clouds, sorry-eyed as a hound. Momma stood in the kitchen door and watched us go down the hill, I could feel her watching.

"You got the lunch, Screech?" Poppa said.

"My name is Sylvia," Sylvie said. "I don't know any person here that is named Screech."

"Oh, my *Lord*," Poppa said, prissy-voiced. "Well, Miss *Syl*via, do you have our *re*-past with you? As Shakespeare would say."

"Anybody with eyes could *see* that," Sylvie said. She liked sailing just as much as me and she was one hell of a sailor, but she wasn't giving Poppa the satisfaction of thinking she wanted to go with *him*.

We went down past the hotel and Mrs. Peabody was out there on the front porch already, flapping her fan and creaking away.

"Morning, Mr. Linthicum," she said. "Morning, children."

"Morning, ma'am," Poppa said. "You up kind of early."

"So hot I couldn't sleep. I had to come out here to cool off. You-all look like you're going out on the water."

"Yes, ma'am, we are."

"Lordy, Lordy," Mrs. Peabody said. I didn't know what she meant by that, nothing she said ever made any sense to me.

"I don't feel good," Jamed said.

"Well, you take some paregoric," Mrs. Peabody said. She went on flapping her fan.

By the time we got down to the dock the sun had come up as sudden as if somebody had raised a curtain. The sky colors had all gone from charcoal and purple to blue and silver and persimmon and everything was wrapped up in cool morning shadows, like blue ribbons. The *Susan Stapleton* was standing up tall as a church steeple in her slip, she didn't budge an inch, there was no wind and it was a full steady tide, swollen up almost to the dock floor. That is a still minute in things, like the world has just taken in a deep breath.

It seemed as though every boat Poppa built was more beautiful than the last. He never turned out any two hulls alike, the way some people do when they get onto a popular model. Everything he learned on one boat he'd put into the next one, but he added to it and chiseled it out and pared it down, like there was one perfect boat that he had an idea of, somewhere back in his mind, that he was working toward. He wasn't in any hurry, either, like these jerry-builders. You'd think a man with an idea like that would work fast, being afraid he might die or something before he got her done, but Poppa seemed to think these things came slow or not at all. "You trust your eye for the lines, and God for the time," he said. The *Susan Stapleton* had a lot of stuff in her that he'd learned building the *Ariel* for Mr. Clapperton, but he'd gone way beyond that. She had the Clipper bow and the same general sheer line but she was a little fuller amidships, which gave her more of an old-time merchant ship look, and she didn't have a regular cockpit at all. What he'd done was build up a real afterdeck with just a footwell to put your feet in and a teak taffrail running all around the stern. There was a big wheelbox for the helmsman to sit on and an eight-spoked teak wheel with a bronze hub, she looked like she'd come straight in off the China Sea. Up forward she had a long bowsprit, maybe six feet, with a catwalk going out to it and a bow pulpit where you stood to bend on the jib. That was one beautiful place to lie out flat on your stomach when you were under way, soaring up and down between the sky and the sea as though you were riding a long-gaited, flying horse. She had wooden nameplates fore and aft, carved like scrolls, with her name burned in script letters and lined with gold leaf: *Susan Stapleton,* that was a boat to make you dream. I stood there looking at her, wondering how you could stay mad at any man who could make a thing like that.

Poppa climbed aboard, he didn't have to jump down, she was riding so high on the tide he just stepped over the lifelines. We handed him our gear and then Sylvie and Jamed climbed aboard and he said to me, "Aaron, you stay there and cast off." So I unhitched the aft lines from the dock piles and tossed them to Sylvie and then stood by with the bow line till Poppa got the motor started. She had a Perkins diesel in her that started up first crack with a coughing roar like a lion and then settled down to a sweet steady snarl. I jumped aboard and me and Sylvie hauled up the big cork fenders and laid them on the deck. Jamed was standing there with his fingers sort of crimped together looking nervous as hell, he never did know what to do next. Poppa said, "You-all get them vests on." We put on our vests and then Poppa slipped her into gear. There was a little jolt when the screw caught, like that boat was shaking herself awake, opening up her eyes, coming out of her dream. She started slow, ghosting out through the still water like a floating cathedral, drifting through the morning mist with a sweet little ripple under her bow and a shiver running through her decks like she had just caught a whiff of that open bay. We followed the channel buoys out through the harbor where the creek mouth widened into the bay, watching the shop fade away behind us, the tin roof sparkling with dew in the morning sun, the boats all still asleep at their berths and the white gulls sitting on top of the sand stakes, very serious, staring out to sea. Back of the hotel I could see the rows of pea vines standing up on their poles like soldiers in green uniforms and back of there the tobacco fields and the clay road winding up through the pine woods to Offutt's. I looked up to the top of the cliff and saw Momma standing on the front porch in her blue apron holding up her hand to shade her eyes from the sun blaze on the water. If you looked back at the land when you were putting out like that it was like seeing it for the first time, somehow you can't see the land near so well when you're right there on it as you can from sea. When we were almost to open water Poppa said, "All right, let's get them sails up. Screech, I want you and Aaron to bend 'em on. Jamed, you work the winches, it'll give you some muscle." I got on top of the cabin with Sylvie and we peeled the canvas cover off the mainsail and Jamed hauled her up with the winch. He got her up all right but then he had trouble making his halyard tail fast to the cleat, he always put his half-hitch on backwards. I knew he'd do it, I started to help him but Poppa said, "You leave him be. That boy's got to learn to make knots hisself some day." Jamed fiddled with it awhile looking up at me every now and then like a dog before he finally got it. Then Sylvie and me went up onto the catwalk and snapped the jib shackles onto the forestay while Jamed hauled her up. He got the knot right first crack this time. Poppa just grunted. We got the mizzen up then and that boat looked purely wonderful with all her canvas set. It wasn't drawing yet though because we were still in the shelter of the cliffs, there wasn't hardly any wind at all and what there was was offshore. But out on the bay I could see the flat sheen breaking up into ripples, there was wind out there, not a lot, an easy morning breeze, but it was starting early. Once we got the kites up I had a few minutes to look around and I took a good long reading on that sky. It looked pretty good, it was nice and blue, but there was some high stratus spread around making a milky stain in the blue that I'd just as soon wasn't up there. Early morning stratus didn't mean much especially if it was thin and just drifting or standing still, it could just burn away and you wouldn't have any trouble. But if it was a really hot day and that stuff started building up and moving you could really catch it. Jamed saw me reading it and he stood there watching me with that worried look of his so I just grinned at him like everything was apple pie. I don't know why I bothered, I wasn't a big grinner, I had a grin about as convincing as a four-dollar bill that I never fooled anybody with, especially not Jamed. But anyway he could see for himself it was a pretty good-looking sky so he wasn't too bothered. What he was really bothered about was that Poppa might put him on the rudder, Jamed hated that rudder. The first time Poppa ever made him take the helm we were going downwind which is the hardest point to sail in my opinion because if you're not careful as hell you'll jibe her and maybe lose your mast and if you're in a small boat the top of your head along with it. Well, this day Jamed was sitting there hanging onto that tiller and sure enough he started getting sort of dreamy and hypnotized which is easy enough for anybody to do let alone Jamed because when you're going downhill you don't have much feeling of speed or movement, you get the idea that you're just about standing still which is what Jamed did and the first thing he knew he'd let that boom slip over until she caught some wind in the wrong side and came roaring across that cockpit like somebody swinging a ball bat, my God there was a jolt like we'd been rammed with a torpedo and that whole hull shuddered like she was coming apart at the seams. I never saw anybody so scared in my life, he was whiter than that sail and shaking just as much too which I suppose all of us were because it wouldn't have taken a whole lot more to carry that mast. Well I guess he shook all that night, he never *did* stop shaking, that bed was shivering so much I couldn't get to sleep. It took him a year to get over that or anyway to stop shivering practically all night long, I don't know if he ever really got over it, it sure as hell didn't improve his outlook on sailing any. Poppa didn't let up on him though. He took us out again the very next day and gave him the tiller again, he said he followed the theory that the only thing to do when you get throwed by a horse is to get up and climb right back on him again before you have time to figure out how close you come to getting killed. What Poppa didn't seem to realize about Jamed was that he spent most of his life figuring out how close he was to getting killed, it wasn't just something that came up every now and then. It was like the minute that boy was born he sat right down with a pencil and a piece of paper and started figuring out how many breaths and heart-beats he had left, he didn't take nothing for granted. I wished Poppa had taken it easy on him for a while and just let him sort of get the feel of things although I guess that really wouldn't have worked too well either because if you sat around and waited for Jamed to get the feel of things the first thing you knew Judgment Day would have rolled around and Jamed would be saying, "Hey, wait a minute, I think I'm starting to get the feel of this thing."

Anyway it looked like he was safe for the time being because Poppa said, "Jamed, you get back here and handle this sheet winch. Screech, you take the wheel for a while. Me and Aaron is going to loaf." Which was great with everybody because Sylvie loved to steer and I loved to get up there on the catwalk with the jib foot fluttering over me in a stiff wind and ride into those seas with that swift up-ward soar and sprinkle of salt on your face and then that lilt at the crest of the wave that seemed like it would fling you up into the clouds, it felt like your heart was just about tearing loose every time. There wasn't anything cleaner or freer than that in the whole world, I just wished Jamed could have felt it. He could of used it more than any of us and I reckon that's what Poppa was trying to give him all the time, but the trouble was he didn't know how the hell to go about it. Those two, it seemed like what they had to give each other was the whole world which just naturally scared the hell out of both of them, you got to take it easy.

We came out of the shelter of the cliffs and hit the stippled water and right then a little breath of air kissed the sails like we were being welcomed out there, you could feel them go full and lively, woke up by that kiss. We heeled a little bit, just snugging down soft to starboard with the wind coming off our port beam and the rigging slanted over against the sky with that businesslike look it gets, working, which is so fine to see, like a hawk's wings when it's riding on air currents, spread full and sort of strained and shivery and powerful. We headed straight out on an easy beam reach with Sylvie holding her steady, sitting there straddling that wheelbox with her hands clenching the spokes and her eyes narrow and sharp and her hair blowing a little bit, dead serious, I loved to look at that girl when she was sailing. Jamed sat there by his winch waiting for the worst and Poppa leaned back easy on his elbows watching everything with those squinty yellow eyes, he liked that boat. After a minute he lifted one arm and pointed up toward Baltimore and said, "Now we going up toward Tilghman's, Screech. Bring her into the wind a little, maybe four points. Jamed, you trim them sheets lively when she comes about. O.K., now—Ho!"

Sylvie swung the wheel and the *Susan Stapleton* came up into the wind in a long easy sweep, her sails luffing loose for a minute till Jamed got to work on his sheets. Then she tightened up and heeled down farther and water started suckling along the hull as we picked up speed, a great swept-away sound with a bump-bump-bump in it from the wave crests, regular as a heartbeat, that meant we were sure enough under way. We headed up toward Tilghman's, quartering off easy toward the Eastern Shore in a set of long tacks with the sun coming up higher and hotter every minute and the water getting bluer in the sun and sparkling up bucketfuls of light everywhere till you felt you were soaked in it and drunk off it, it was like being soaked with bucketfuls of champagne. With the wind the way we had it our starboard tack was always a beam reach and our port tack a broad beat which made the going easy and Jamed's job on those sheet winches not too much for him to handle. He was doing a real good job, shortening up quick and lively and then trimming down just to the edge of a luff the way Poppa had showed him a million times, it looked like it might be getting through to him at last, I felt real good about it. Sylvie was doing good on the helm too but of course she always did good, there wasn't anything special about that, that girl could have showed a lot of grown men how to sail. I didn't have a lot to do so I headed up to my favorite spot on the catwalk and crawled out there on my belly under the jib. I lay flat on the teak grating and looked down at the water zipping past under me slick and blue as dyed ice and watched where the bow sheared into it like a plow blade, smashing it all into foam and glassy splinters to leeward and tossing up a shining furrow on the windward side that looked as if it was pared out of crystal. There wasn't much pitch so I rode easy out there, swooping over the water like a bird, I purely pitied everybody else in the world right then.

We held that course for I reckon two–three hours, it was sweet dreams, sun and blue sky and water and a little Force Three wind freshening from the west and the clouds standing off nicely. About eleven o'clock we passed Cap'n Weems heading out for The Gooses with a party of day fishers in his old tub *Esther B. Weems* and he gave us a yell and a wave.

"I want three good shad, you get any," Poppa hollered at him.

"I'll save 'em, Joel," Cap'n Weems yelled.

Later in the morning the pleasure boats started working down from Galesville and Oxford and there were sails dotting the whole bay. We passed some beauties, big forty- and fifty-foot luxury machines with their chutes flying, all ballooned out bright red and yellow and blue, every kind of color, checkered and barred and quartered, and those lean hulls slicing the water like knives. They were pretty boats but they all looked the same, they could have come out of a sausage machine, fiberglass decks and cabin tops and aluminum spars and destroyer wheels and roller-reefing booms and all the rest of that crap, there wasn't a nickel's worth of difference between them and not one of them come near the *Susan Stapleton* with that salty look she had with her reefing points flying and that China Clipper taffrail soaring over her wake. Some of them put by so they could get a good look at us and you could see the people roll out and hang on the shrouds to watch us sail past, pointing and admiring, it made you feel proud. They sure were pretty people though, I say that, I did like the way they were got up in white pants and striped boating jackets and commodore's caps and the girls in bikinis with their belly buttons showing and their hair blowing, they looked like pictures in a magazine. And here we were in these beat-up old T-shirts and Sweet-Orrs and Poppa in that oil-stained junk he always wore with his beard like a hooraw's nest and that crazy medal pinned on his chest, they must of thought we were a boatload of lunatics.

After a while I had to spell Sylvie on the wheel, Poppa told me to bring her around downwind, we were making a big circle out there. He didn't want to get too far away, I knew that, because he didn't have any electrics on board yet, no depth sounder or radio or RDF or anything, it wasn't any shakedown we were doing, just a little day sail to smooth her out and give us kids a few tricks but most of all for Poppa to have this long conversation with us, that's what it was really, it was like he'd written a book and was handing it to us to read. We didn't have a chute aboard or even a jenny so we just ran with the working sails flopped out full, getting what we could out of them which was plenty, that boat was a marvel off the wind. I did a long trick on the wheel, I reckon an hour or more, all one long downhill run that got a little skittery near the end because the wind was freshening all the time and I had to keep my eye on that boom. Jamed sat down there under me in the cockpit looking up every now and then with those crinkled-up eyebrows, waiting for the word, but of course there wasn't much to tell him because on a long run there's not a lot for a sheet man to do but just sit back and enjoy the scenery, and you might just as well have told that to a man who was being carted off to the hanging tree. He did relax some, though, he had time to start biting his cheek anyway. He sat there pushing it in with his knuckle and gnawing away at the inside of it like a rat, staring over the bow like he saw ghosts out there in the sun. Sylvie went off to the catwalk on the bowsprit and sat there with her legs crossed singing all these corny songs like *Down Mexico Way* and *Perfidia* and *The Isle of Capri*, she was the world's worst singer, she couldn't carry a tune in a bushel basket but she knew every damn word of every damn song that ever was written.

Somewhere around noon I started getting hungrier than hell so I asked Poppa couldn't we have something to eat so he said why hell yes and hollered at Sylvie to come back and rustle the grub. She yelled back she didn't know why *she* had to do everything and Poppa yelled, "Because I say so, is why, and there ain't but one captain on a boat. Now come on and get us some grub, Miss Screech. These men is hungry." He was sort of grinning when he said it, he wasn't mad, no matter how smart Sylvie got with him he didn't take it mean. He'd dress her down once in a while if she got too sassy, but not a whole lot. And yet the funny thing was he didn't take it easy on her because he was all that crazy about her, it was really because he didn't give too much of a damn, it was something you could feel. Right after that fire and for a long time afterwards you could tell that the only thing he wanted her to do was say one nice thing to him, just one time, just crawl up in his lap again or kiss him on the cheek or ask him to take us up to Offutt's for ice cream, but she wasn't about to. Every time he took us out on the boats he built afterwards, the *Hyacinth* and the *Star of Bethlehem*, you could see he was hoping that that'd be the time, that maybe she'd finally figure out what he was all about, maybe she'd smile at him before she even thought about it, maybe it'd just slip out and she'd say, Wow, what a beautiful boat, Poppa. But she never did, she never let herself, even if she felt it, and you could see he'd just about figured out that she never would, not as long as she lived. And he wasn't about to beg her, not that man, he was a boatwright not a beggar. So when she got fresh with him or acted mean which she did practically every damn minute of her life he'd just grin about it, it didn't matter too much to him any more. He'd just about give up on Sylvie.

But the funniest thing was that Sylvie could sass him and spit at him pretty near and he wouldn't do anything but grin, and here was Jamed hanging on the man like honeysuckle on a fence, worshipping every damn move he made and every word he said and Poppa spent most of his time deviling him, driving him, beating the hell out of him, it was crazy. Now why couldn't he take it easy on Jamed? There was something in Jamed that scared him, I knew that. Something Jamed gave him was so fine he was almost afraid to own it, he was afraid of losing it, the way a man is afraid to walk around Baltimore Saturday night with too much money in his pockets, afraid to get drunk, afraid of getting careless, afraid of forgetting one time just how much he was worth, it was a burden on him. Sylvie might have thought she could weigh Poppa down by treating him mean, and she tried, and I reckon she did, some, but she couldn't weigh that man down with ten thousand of her sneers like Jamed could with just one of his smiles.

She finally came back to the cockpit and got the sandwiches broke out and poured some milk into Dixie cups for all of us, her lips pressed together all the time and a look on her face like she was cleaning up cat shit or something. Poppa took over the wheel because he could manage it better one-handed than I could, and swung her around into a soft starboard reach so we would just loaf along without too much fuss while we ate. We had tunafish and peanut butter-and-jelly and hard-boiled eggs and then some oatmeal cookies for dessert, it was all stuff Jamed liked but he didn't break any records getting it down, all he wanted to do was get home and start building sand castles on the beach.

"You eat your lunch, boy," Poppa said.

"I ain't real hungry, Poppa," Jamed said.

"I ain't asked you if you was hungry, I said eat."

"O.K., I will, Poppa," Jamed said. He sat there chewing it up and gulping it down like it was sawdust. The sun was up in the middle of the sky now and it was hotter than hell. Away off in the west you could see a little bit of purple cloud down low on the horizon and up above us the cumulus was building up tall and starting to coast along steady like a big fleet of schooners in a fresh wind. Poppa kept his eye on it while he ate and every now and then he'd lift his head a little and sniff the wind, you could smell it if a storm was coming, I knew that much already, it was a sort of cool ferny smell like you get in a greenhouse when you step in out of the sun. He didn't seem real worried though, he just sat there with his elbow hooked around a wheelspoke and munched away and every now and then stuck his little finger in his mouth and ran it along his gums.

"Hey, Aaron, you know what Birdie Fisher did one time?" Sylvie said.

"Uh uh, what?" I said.

"She put two whole packs of chewing gum in her mouth at once. That girl has got the biggest mouth in the whole United States."

"She's crazy, anyway," I said. "She told me one time she'd been to Toledo, Ohio, so I asked her brother about it and he said she'd never been anywheres near it. She's always doing stuff like that."

"Who's Birdie Fisher?" Poppa said.

"She's not anybody *you* know," Sylvie said. She'd be damned if he was going to horn in on *her* conversation.

"She got a mole up side of her mouth?" Poppa said.

"No, she hasn't got any *mole*," Sylvie said.

"There's a little girl comes up to Offutt's all the time has got a mole up side of her mouth," Poppa said.

"Well, it's not Birdie *Fisher*," Sylvie said. "You've never even *seen* Birdie Fisher."

Poppa crumpled up a piece of waxed paper from his sandwich and shoved it into his pocket.

"You know what they say about anybody has got a mole up side of their mouth?" he said. Sylvie didn't want to know, she just looked away, disgusted, and I had my mouth full so I couldn't say anything.

"What do they say, Poppa?" Jamed said. He couldn't 've cared less right then but he didn't want Poppa to feel bad.

"Say they been kissed by a witch," Poppa said. "That's a fact. I heard it many a time."

"Wow, no kidding," Jamed said.

"There's not any such things as witches, for crumb's sake," Sylvie said. "Boy, Jamed, if you fall for *that*."

"There could be," Jamed said. "You don't know everything, Sylvie."

"Well, I know that much," Sylvie said. "And so does everybody else in the world. I guess there's goblins, too, and elves, and fairies and all the rest of that crap."

"There's a play by Shakespeare," Poppa said, "that has

got a whole scene in it about witches. They sit right there and cook up a big pot of stew. He even tells what they put in it: frogs and snakes and mummies and dog's eyes, all that sort of stuff. Now who knows more about it, you or Shakespeare?"

"That's a play, for God's sake," Sylvie said. "It's made *up*. Anybody can make up anything in a play. My gosh, as if he wasn't nervous enough already, you got to go making him *more* nervous?"

"I ain't nervous," Jamed said.

"That a boy, Jamie," Poppa said. He winked at me and said, "Me and Jamie, we take this witch situation real serious, don't we, Jamie? Old Screech, she's going to keep on ducking it till she wakes up some morning with a great big mole up one side of her mouth."

"Yeah, well I'll know who did it, if I do," Sylvie said.

Poppa stuck a couple of oatmeal cookies in his mouth and wiped his hands on his pants and then stood up in the cockpit and looked back toward the west. That cloud was building up all right, piling way up into the cirrus and then spreading out ragged at the top like it might be getting ready to flatten out into an anvil head, which was not a good sign, when you got an anvil head up there it was time to haul ass. He wasn't getting very excited though, he just squinted up at the sky, munching on his cookies, and then took his pipe and a can of Prince Albert out of his shirt pocket and started filling up, tapping the can to spill the tobacco into the bowl and then tamping it down with the ball of his finger and winking at me again when he got done.

"Well, I reckon we'll get her on back," he said. "They might be a little blow out here after a while, and that'd take the fun out of it. Momma'd get to fussing back there, and all." He sat back down on the wheelbox and fished a match out of his pocket and flicked it lit with his thumbnail and then sucked at the flame till he got his pipe going. "O.K.,

Jamie," he said, "get back on your winch, boy. Aaron, you and Screech go below and break that trysail out of the locker. We might just want that sucker."

I didn't like the sound of that much, I knew Poppa wouldn't use a trysail except in a blow, but still, the stuff wasn't coming up that fast and we weren't all that far out, it looked to me like we had plenty of time to get in. Sylvie didn't seem any too sure of it though, she stuck out her jaw and squinched up her eyes like she was saying, Oh boy, you dumb jerk, I knew you'd get us into some kind of a mess, so I started shoving her toward the companionway before she could say anything. We went below and up through the cabin to the forward stateroom and I climbed up on the V-bunks and tugged the sailbag that was stenciled TRY out of the locker and tumbled it down onto the cabin sole. We felt the *Susan Stapleton* come about, swinging into the wind and heeling over pretty steep. Jamed was going to have his hands full with those sheets, I thought, that wind was getting up to around Force Five, we were going to be sailing on our ear all the way in. Sylvie lurched up against the bunk and banged her shoulder pretty smart on the bunkboard. She said, "Son of a bitch."

"She might get rough," I said.

"How come we're on the wind, going home?" she said. "That wind has backed around, you know that?"

It was the truth. It had backed around to northeast, which is what it does right before a blow, it'll swing around a hundred and eighty degrees and start blowing in toward the cloud mass instead of from behind it, it'll shoot right up those thunderheads like the draft up a chimney. It had happened mighty damn fast, that was all I knew, I'd seen many a storm blow up out there but nothing half as fast as that in my whole life, I didn't like the look of it.

"It ain't nothing," I said. "Just a puff. That stuff is miles off. We got all day."

"The hell we do," Sylvie said. "Not when she backs like that. We're going to get some weather, boy."

"Well, we might," I said. "But anyway, don't start hollering about it up there or Jamed'll blow his top."

"Don't start telling *me* what to do," Sylvie said. "I got enough people telling me what to do. Sons of bitches."

I don't guess we were down there more than five–ten minutes but by the time we dragged that bag up through the companionway there were whitecaps starting on the water and that cloud had built up fantastic, what we had now was a real old ring-tailed snorter, a gigantic cumulonimbus mountain rising up west-northwest of us with roll cloud rumbling in low ahead of it over the water and a great purple heart, a mile high or more, like a bruise. The water had gone gray in the cloud shadow and all of a sudden it was chilly and gusty and you could smell stone in the air. Poppa had her hauled in as close as she would go, we were heeled over till we were damn near taking green water over the gunwales and that canvas was stretched tight as a drumhead and snarling in the wind. He wasn't loafing any more, boy, he was down to work, holding her full-and-by with his arms gone hard as oak wood on the wheel and his beard soaked and his baseball cap tugged down to guard his eyes from the spray, that stuff was blowing back over the bow like buckshot, it stung your face when it hit. Jamed was sitting there hanging onto his winch handle and staring at those sail luffs till you would have thought his eyes would fall out, he was scared stiff. Poppa saw us come up through the hatch and grinned like a fool.

"Hee-oo!" he said. "We got us some fun. You kids get your foul-weather gear on. Aaron, you take them sheets till Jamed gets his slicker on. Step to it, now."

So I took Jamed's place by the winch till he got his slicker on which took quite awhile because he always had a lot of trouble with armholes, he usually put things on inside-out before he got them figured out, on top of which the boat was beginning to pitch considerably now so it wasn't easy even for somebody who had a pretty good idea of where his arms were. Sylvie had to finally tie his sou'wester under his chin for him because he had just barely learned to make a bow in his shoelaces, even while he was looking, if he couldn't see what he was doing he was sunk. She did it without too much fuss, just a sort of quick sour look, because she knew Poppa was going to reach over and smack Jamed on the side of the head in a minute if he didn't get straightened out. When he finally got everything on he had just about disappeared, he looked like that kid on the Morton's salt box, just a couple of eyes and a pair of feet was about all you could see of him but even with just that little bit of him showing you could see he was in pure misery, he didn't want to go back on those sheets. He said, "Poppa, you reckon Aaron could spell me for a while? I'm kindly getting sick."

"Well the only cure for that is keeping busy," Poppa said. "Now you got a job to do, boy. You get back on them sheets." Then he nodded at Jamed and said kind of quiet and solemn, as near to a compliment as I ever known him to give Jamed, "You doing real good, boy."

I slid over and gave Jamed his place back and then got my own gear on and started breaking the trysail out of the sail bag.

"Let it be," Poppa said. "We ain't got time to fool with it. We going to drop the mainsail and go on just the jib and mizzen. Aaron, you and Screech go up there and get her down."

I raised the lid of the gear locker in the cockpit and got out a batch of elastic stops to lash the sail down with and then worked up forward to the mainmast along the windward side, hanging onto the grab rails with my free hand. Sylvie was up there already, she had the main halyard freed and was waiting for the word from me. I said, "Let her go," and she did, but that sail was too tight with wind, she wouldn't budge in the track. I yelled back at Poppa, "You got to bring her into the wind. It's stuck."

"O.K.," Poppa said. "Hang on." He swung up into the eye of the wind and the sail went loose, all of them, luffing with a wild flapping like sheets in a gale. Sylvie and me were draped in snapping sailcloth from the jib, we had to fend it off with our elbows.

"Let her go," I said, and this time with the tension eased she came tumbling down. I worked my way back from the mainmast, bundling up the mainsail and lashing it tight to the boom with the elastic stops until I had her made fast right out to the clew. I'd of been just as happy if we'd doused that jib too, and run the trysail up, I didn't like all that canvas up there, but I could see Poppa wasn't about to, he wanted all the knots he could get out of her.

We were hung up in irons now and losing time, with that mountain of cloud bearing down and the wind rising every minute, we had to get some way on.

"Aaron, grab that jib by the clew and hold her to weather," Poppa said. I skittled over there fast and grabbed the bottom corner of the jib and hauled her out over the weather rail as far as I could reach. She bellied out full, tugging and jerking in my hands like a bull on a leash, I knew I couldn't hold her long but I hung on till the bow came about and we picked up a little way. It didn't take long, she came about as pretty as pie and started nudging toward the coast, enough for Poppa to get some grip with the rudder so he could take over. I eased the jib over, it was flapping in my hands like I had ahold of a goose by the wing, and she filled up on the lee side real sweet, the mizzen did too, you could feel the life come back into the *Susan Stapleton* and she started taking off. We started getting a regular whomp, whomp, whomp from the bow waves, faster all the time as we picked up way. We heeled over deep, beating as close to the wind as she would take and then the spray started flying back again over the cockpit and we were off and gone. I liked driving a boat, it could scare the hell out of you, especially if you had somebody at the helm that didn't know what he was doing, but by golly there was nothing like it for excitement, sitting there on your beam ends damn near with your face soaked and salt on your lips and your scalp prickling, listening to that rigging sing like a harp in the wind, every inch of stay and shroud stretched tight as a bowstring and the boat plunging like a racehorse with the bit in his teeth, waiting for just that one puff too many that would knock you down or carry your mast, every bit of nerve and muscle you had primed to answer true and fast, to bring her up another point closer and ease off so you'd live to sail another day, you felt like your veins were full of cherry wine. Some people did, not everybody. Kids up at school that came off the tobacco farms would have pissed in their pants if they'd gone through a blow with Poppa and of course you couldn't blame them, they weren't used to it. I figured it was like liquor, you had to get a taste for it. Some people never would of course, maybe you could get whatever you needed in that line from horses or guns or women or sand castles even, like Jamed. I guess that's how he got it, he sure as hell wasn't getting it right now anyway, I could see that, that boy was ossified. You could see he had it figured out that this was his last sail in this world but by God he was giving it all he had, he kept one eye on Poppa and one eye on his sails and every now and then he'd take his hand off the winch and wipe the spray off his face and then take a deep gulp like he had a fish bone stuck in his throat and turn his head so he was looking right up at Poppa on that wheelbox with those big scared squirrel eyes like he was saying, Poppa, don't make me do this no more, I can't hang on much longer. You'd have thought he was standing on the edge of a cliff just waiting for Poppa to push him right off the edge of the world but by God he wasn't going to move.

I don't know how long we held that course, it seemed like five minutes but it had to be forty-five anyway because all of a sudden the shore had reared up so close you could see people out on the end of the dock waving and ladies out back of the cottages snatching their washing off the line, shoving it into big wicker hampers on the grass with their skirts snapping around their legs and the clotheslines plunging in the wind and the dust blowing along the clay road through the pines and birds sailing like blown leaves over the cliffs. Up there on the front porch with her hand raised up to shade her eyes like she hadn't moved an inch since we put out that morning Momma was standing watching like a statue.

I looked back out over our wake and I could see we'd beat it. The wind was shifting into the east and the cloud mountain had moved on north and east of us. You could see the rainfall coming down in a big purple column out of its heart, way out on the bay, and the water out there all mist and murk where the squall was breaking. What we were getting was wind and a little spatter of fringe rain, hard as hail, that smacked the sails like shot, and some groundswell too, because there was surf running in under the pier pilings and booming on the shore, but that wasn't anything to what they were getting out there, if there was anybody dumb enough or unlucky enough to still be out there, they were getting the works. Poppa was standing up now, working the wheel with just the tips of his fingers, steering for the creek mouth. His beard and eyebrows were dripping and he had his lips pared back in a kind of dog grin so you could see his big brown teeth clenched around his pipe stem, the briar was wet and blood-colored, he looked like a wolf with a fresh bone between his teeth. I thought, Well old man, you got us out of there all right but I hope you had a good time because it looks to me like you scared Jamed out of six years' growth. I hadn't hardly thought it when we got one hell of a puff from almost dead off our weather beam, it hit that rigging like a bull running into a barn wall. You could feel that boat shudder and groan, she pitched over onto her lee side and took a ton of green water over the rail that came pouring down the decks like a river, rattling the anchor in its chocks, spouting up around the throats of the dorades, flushing out flemished line like spaghetti and swarming over us waist-deep in the cockpit, an ice-cold flood out of nowhere that stopped your heart. I just knew we were gone. Poppa crouched down and grabbed those wheelspokes with both hands, swinging her into the wind to spill the sails, yelling at Jamed to cut his sheets loose. Jamed didn't know what the hell was going on, he grabbed the winch handle and started cranking like a crazy man, he couldn't think good. Of course he shouldn't have done it, he should have eased them or just let them fly like Poppa told him but the fact was it didn't make a hell of a lot of difference what he did, you get smacked with a puff like that and you'll get knocked down nine times out of ten no matter what you do, there's just not time to do anything, and anyway if that winch had been any good it would have stood it. It wasn't though, the purl on it broke with a snap like a pistol shot and then there was a crazy singing whine as the winch ran out backward with the pull of the jib, the handle spinning loose like the hand on a clock gone wild, back toward the beginning of the world. It broke Jamed's wrist, you could see his arm sort of turn into rubber, he gave a scream and fell over sideways right on top of that Goddamned spinning handle and then there was another sound, the most terrible sound I'd ever heard in my life, a meaty hollow thump like a hammer smacking into a watermelon and Jamed jerked over backward like a shot squirrel. His head fell right across my thigh, he didn't move, his eyes were wide open and there was a kind of puckered dent in the crown of his sou'wester, it was driven into his forehead an inch deep. All I could think was My God, I never even got to tell him goodbye. I put my arms around him and hugged him tight.

The jib had bellied out loose and was flapping in the water but Poppa didn't dare leave that wheel. He took one look down there at Jamed and his eyes flared up bright and then went out, the way a coal does when it dies, like somebody had opened the door to hell and he'd taken a quick look through and burned his eyes out, then he turned his head and yelled at Sylvie, "Grab that sheet, girl, and hand-haul her. Get that jib in." I couldn't help her, I didn't dare let go of Jamed or he'd 've rolled out of the cockpit and overboard, we were heeled so steep. I just hugged him tight in my lap and hung my head over him, I didn't give much of a damn what happened anyhow. I felt Sylvie scuttle across beside me and grab that loose sheet and start hauling, I don't know how the hell she did it, she never would have if we hadn't come into the wind by now and lost a lot of way, but she got it in somehow, all the time sobbing like she'd lost her mind.

"Now cleat her," Poppa yelled, so Sylvie did, she made the tail fast to a cleat, then she dropped down and huddled back against the taffrail, her hands clenched around two of the spindles and her face raised up with her eyes closed, letting that wind and spray drive into her like she was taking some kind of a terrible bath that scoured her clean to her backbone.

I didn't see a whole lot of what happened after that, I wasn't watching too close. Mostly I was looking down at Jamed, watching to see would he move or blink his eyes or groan or anything at all, which didn't seem very likely with a hole like that in his head but I didn't dare quit hoping.

He wasn't bleeding too much, just a little bit of slow oozy blood leaking down under the brim of his sou'wester, so I figured he might still be alive. It seemed to me that if I quit hoping it would be just like walking off and leaving him there all alone, so I kept talking to him, telling him all sorts of crazy stuff. "Hey, Jamie," I said. "We're almost in now, buddy. You better come on and get up, or Poppa'll be mad. Hey, guess what we're going to have for dessert tonight, Jamie. I saw it in the icebox. Watermelon, boy." I was getting pretty nutty there.

Poppa didn't say another word all the time he was getting us through the gut, not till he yelled at Sylvie to go forward and drop the sails. He just stood there hunched over, working that wheel, water dripping off his nose and eyebrows, grunting to himself now and then like he did when he was asleep sometimes. When Sylvie got the sails lowered he reached down and switched on the motor and put it in reverse and I could feel us easing in through the quiet water of the harbor. I looked up at him then because I figured he'd need me to fend off and throw line but he shook his head at me and said, "Set still. Hold that boy good," so Sylvie did the fending and threw the dock lines. That girl was doing a man's job, I want to tell you. There were a lot of people on the slip, Reuben Taylor the shop foreman and a bunch of other workmen and Mabel Offutt and a couple of other ladies and Momma. I was hoping to God Momma wouldn't be there, but I knew she would. She saw Jamed lying there with his head in my lap and she pressed her hands together in front of her and held them tight against her chest like she was praying. The wind was flapping her shawl around pretty wild so she reached up and grabbed the end of it and put it in her mouth to hold it and then left her hand up there, pressed against her jaw like she had a toothache.

As soon as Sylvie cut loose with those dock lines Poppa

gave the motor one good burst in reverse and then cut it dead and swung his leg from around the wheelbox and got down beside me in the cockpit fast as a cat. He picked up Jamed off my lap and stood there holding him in his arms in a terrible proud fierce way, like a dog holding a rabbit in its mouth that it won't let anybody get near, that it wouldn't give up if you killed it. He looked up at all those people on the slip and blinked his eyes a couple of times, slow and hot, like a cornered hound and then looked back down at Jamed and said, "All right, little boy." Reuben Taylor had ahold of the dock line, he hauled us up alongside and made it fast to a bollard. The minute we touched, Poppa seemed to come awake, he stepped over the lifelines onto the slip and stood there for a minute right in front of Momma holding Jamed up for her to look at. Momma reached out and touched Jamed's arm that was dangling down broke, and then that awful dent in his skull, and then his mouth, and then she pulled back her hand and laid it against her face and said, "Oh my God, Oh my boy, Oh my God." I had got ashore by this time and I was standing there yanking at her dress and saying, "He's all right, Momma, he just got a little bump on his head, he did a real good job on the sheets, he's O.K., Momma," I don't know who the hell I thought I was fooling. Sylvie was gone, she just took off. The minute her feet hit that pier she started running, up toward the house or somewhere, I don't know. Poppa stood there in front of Momma for a minute and then he turned around and started across the yard to where the pickup was parked by the office door, gathering up Jamed's broke arm while he walked and yelling at Reuben Taylor, "Get that truck started, man." He never looked back at Momma nor anybody, it seemed to me like he was walking away with Jamed forever, taking him off to some secret place he knew about, where he'd be safe forever.

Embarkation

THE MOON HAD GONE DOWN NOW AND IT WAS CHILLY IN THE woods. Also the seat of my pants was getting pretty damp and the Jack Daniel's didn't seem to be working quite right because things didn't have the general air of hilarity I felt I had a right to expect by this time. I had a feeling we ought to be getting home, but Sylvie wasn't about to pull in her horns just yet, she wanted to get the whole story about Cindy. Actually I was glad, I guess, I wanted to talk to her about it, I suppose I had for a long time, really. Somehow talking to Sylvie about my life's adventures gave them a kind of pattern or congruity or something, you could sense a kind of theme running through there that I sure as hell could never discover in the events themselves. I don't mean nobility or glamour or any particular distinction of any kind, but just a sense of continuousness, of sanity, of some modest degree of comeliness; in being laid before her they seemed to fall into a shape that could be recognized as a genuine human existence and not the witless, frenzied, scandalous improvisation it usually seemed to be while things were going on. I guess what I had come to realize was that Sylvie was my life's chief witness and every now and then I needed to furnish her with an account of it in order to believe in its reality myself. I certainly didn't feel any perfervid joy at the opportunity because when Sylvie served as witness to the congruity of anybody's existence there were so many snorts and expostulations and ironic silences involved in the experience that you had to think it over very carefully before you got going, but after all that was Sylvie's dialectical method, outrage, just as Plato's was a kind of placid patience, it was the acid she sprayed over everything like an engraver, to get the picture developed. I was used to it.

"So what happened to your little doll face?" she asked. "She came crawling home, I guess, and you forgave her."

"Well, she didn't exactly crawl," I said. "She called up in the middle of the night from some guest villa down in Bournemouth, where she'd been abandoned by this Derek character. It seems he was disappointed in her performance, or maybe in his own, anyway they had a hell of a row, in the course of which he announced that he didn't have any intention in the world of installing her as a model in the fashion department, as a matter of fact he didn't even intend to pay the hotel bill. He pulled out about two o'clock in the morning leaving Cindy there as a hostage to the landlady, who wouldn't let her go until she'd laid down six pounds ten for services rendered. So she called me up about three o'clock in the morning and asked if I could wire her the money. Well, what the hell could I do? You wouldn't let your *mother* spend the rest of her life locked up in a tourist home in Bournemouth."

"Oh, sure," Sylvie said. "Old half-witted Linthicum, the hustlers' friend."

"Listen, Cindy wasn't any hustler," I said. "She was just dumb. Is that such a crime, to be dumb? She was too dumb to *hustle*, for God's sake. It just about broke her heart."

It was the truth, I got her into bed and gave her a glass of wine after she got home, and she sat there sobbing into it and saying, 'I mean, if a girl can't act, or clerk, or ride an elephant, or even *whore* properly, just what is she to do? I'll tell you what I'm going to do, and I mean it. I'm going to jump off the Waterloo Bridge.'

I told her I didn't think that was the answer and she said, 'No, I am, I mean it. The minute I finish this wine I'm going to go right down there and jump off the Waterloo Bridge. Could you let me have a shilling for the fare, Aaron?'

'I don't have a shilling left to my name,' I said. 'And anyway, I've got a better idea.'

So I talked her out of it, or maneuvered her out of it I

guess would be the best way of putting it, all those tears and professions of remorse had had a very aphrodisiac effect on me, and after an astonishingly strenuous homecoming rite she folded herself up in my arms like an ironing board and tucked her head under my chin and started telling me all the things she liked most in the world. What she liked most in the world was hot cider with a stick of cinnamon in it, rag dolls, raisin toast, rainy Sunday afternoons, Jamaican sailors, Steve McQueen, Mary Quant frocks, wine-colored Jaguars, and a lot of other things I can't remember because I fell asleep before she got to the end of the list. She had the loveliest smell I ever smelled.

After that, though, she fell into a sort of steady decline, the chief symptoms of which were chronic indigence, chronic bronchitis, chronic misty-eyed daydreams, and an occasional binge of shoplifting. She lost her job at Swan & Edgar's, apparently old Dastardly Derek had a hand in that, and after about ten days of trudging around in the rain looking for something else to do she came down with a terrible cold, which settled in her bronchial tubes and kept her coughing like Camille for a month or so. We had a pretty rough time of it. With just my G.I. Bill for income and Cindy needing quarts of penicillin and Coca-Cola to keep her going, I had to take a job of some kind, which was not easy to do because if you were in England on a student visa you weren't allowed to work, you had to find some kind of odd-job handyman stuff or something frankly clandestine such as a night-clerk job in a fleabag hotel in Soho, which is where I wound up. They didn't ask to see any work permits and they didn't file any embarrassing reports with the Labour Ministry or the Aliens Office, they offered me five pounds ten a week for signing in their guests between eight and one every night and presiding over the revels. It was a job that would have brought joy to the heart of Krafft-Ebing but it was no place for anybody who is trying to cram his head full of iambic pentameter which he has got to get up on a stage and deliver at eight o'clock in the morning in a clear and ringing voice. I suppose it was a priceless experience for an actor in one sense, I was learning plenty about what Yeats called "the foul rag-and-bone shop of the heart," but at the moment I'll tell you it was playing hell with my life in art. I would go staggering in to GLAD in the morning after about five hours of sleep with my eyes swollen and full of salt and my mind full of cobwebs and an awful paralytic lassitude loosening all my joints and after I had been rolling around the stage in that condition for half an hour or so I would start hearing these groans from out front where Mr. Bernhalter, who was the most unpleasant director we ever had, would be issuing ironic invitations to God to bear witness to this travesty. My stock wasn't any too high around there anyway since the Bosola affair, and with Finals coming up I could see that the situation was getting pretty damn critical. If I got kicked out of the academy I would lose my student status and my G.I. Bill, and without a visa or any visible means of support I would get ushered out of the country by the Aliens Office quicker than you could bat your eyes.

So that's what happened, finally. I knew it would. I think I knew I'd get kicked out of that place from the first minute I ever walked into it, how do you know those things? I guess it's a tribute to your sense of justice, really. I mean, if you know damn well you're second rate, that you're just not cut out for glory, then it's sort of satisfying to your sense of justice, of cosmic order or whatever you want to call it, when your application gets turned down. I mean, suppose some guy like me *does* happen to stumble or con his way into fame and fortune somehow? It must be puzzling as hell to him. If you've got some crummy politician or somebody up there living high on the hog, you're never really sure whether he deserves it or not, he might have some hidden merits known only to God. But in your own case, you're only too damn sure about it, you *know* it doesn't make sense. It must be offensive as hell to your basic sense of justice, of the fitness of things. I don't think I'd want any part of a world that would set me up as a celebrity, God, I couldn't sleep nights. It's something like that thing Groucho Marx said, about not wanting to belong to any club that would accept him as a member. Only not quite, I mean I'd be a member of the thing, I just wouldn't want any medals or anything.

"Is that how you feel?" Sylvie said.

"I do, really. I wouldn't know what to do with a medal in this kind of a world. Would you?"

"Oh boy," she said. "Do you know what the word demoralized means?"

"It means you've lost your morals, I guess. But it seems to me if you feel like that, your morals are still in pretty good shape."

"You think so? Well, you've lost your *marbles*, that's what you've lost. Give me another drink."

I handed her the bottle and she put away another couple of fingers, we were down to just below the label by this time.

"So what did you do, stand up and cheer or something, when they threw you out? Thank them for humiliating you? What did this Dame What's-Her-Name have to say, anyway? How do they put it, exactly, when they decide you've got too much balls to ever play it their way?"

"She was very nice about it, actually. It was a shock, of course, you still can't believe it's happening, even though you know it's got to, it's like dying, I guess. But she made it as easy as she could. As I remember, she talked mostly about ghosts."

"Ghosts?" Sylvie said. "What the hell have ghosts got to do with it?"

"Well, she had this theory that there are ghosts around,

and that artists are more interested in them than they are in the real world. What actors are supposed to do, she said, is to give birth to these ghosts up there on the stage. It was all pretty eerie stuff, but I think I know what she meant. Then she talked about all the rough stuff that goes on in the theater, all the politics and vanity and eye-gouging and so on, and she said it was a pretty dreary life for anybody who wasn't particularly interested in ghosts. 'And most sensible people, you know, will have nothing to do with them,' she said, I remember that exactly. 'They'd much rather give birth to real, living people.' She was a very smart woman, actually."

Sylvie didn't say anything for quite a while, she sat there staring off into the woods with a drowsy look of pain, like somebody with a terrible headache.

"And you let them do that to you," she said finally. "You let that shiftless little *bitch* do that to you. Oh Jesus, Aaron. You had a great talent, you know that? You shouldn't have let anything in the world stand in the way of it. *Anything*. Or *anybody*. It's a sin."

It gave me a really weird feeling to hear her say that, bloodless and chilly, something pretty close to horror.

"Oh boy, Sylvie, you are really something," I said. "You know that? You are really something."

My God, it never stops, I thought. It just goes on and on like this, forever.

Sylvie and I got off the school bus at the end of Route 59 and stood there waiting for Howie Suggs, who drove the thing, to get it in gear again and the door shut tight, nothing worked too well on that bus. This guy Boone Armitage had been giving Sylvie a hard time on the bus and she was madder than hell. About the time Howie got under way she reared back with her foot and slammed a kick into the metal side that sounded like a sledge coming down on a washtub. She spilled her school books all over the road. There was a lot of whooping and yakking inside the bus and Boone leaned his head out the window and yelled, "Hey, Silly, raise up that foot again, will you? I thought I seen something green."

"You'll see stars next time, you son of a bitch!" Sylvie yelled. They went off cackling down the road like a cageful of hyenas. I got down and helped Sylvie pick up the books.

"You ought to take it easy," I said. "That baboon is not worth getting riled up about."

"I'm going to kill that bastard," she said. "Every time I see him he starts that crap about the Linthicum Loony Bin. He's the one started everybody calling me Silly."

"Well, my God, why don't you just ignore him?" I said. "The guy's a pain in the ass, everybody knows that."

"They're all pains in the ass," Sylvie said. "I hate every one of those bastards. Boy, I'm going to get out of this place so damn fast, you wait and see."

I handed her the books back, one of them had got its cover just about knocked off.

"This one's sort of beat up," I said.

"Well, who gives a Goddamn? Everything's beat up in this place. They ought to name it Beat Up, Maryland."

We crossed the highway and started down the dirt road toward Port Federation. It was cool in the shadow of the trees and we could hear the red sand grinding under our feet. Sylvie hugged her books against her chest and every now and then blew the sweat off her upper lip. You could smell the bay at the end of the road.

"I've got some cigarettes," Sylvie said. "Oma Pearl gave me two. You want to smoke?"

"O.K.," I said.

We left the road and walked into the woods a ways and

sat down on a log. Sylvie set her books on the ground and got the cigarettes out of her skirt pocket, they were pretty badly crunkled.

"Even the Goddamned cigarettes are beat up," she said. She lit a match and got one of them going and handed it to me and then lit the other one. We took a few deep drags and blew the purple smoke out into the still air. There was a cardinal calling in the woods: boogety–boogety–boogety–boogety–choop–choop–choop–choop–choop–choop–choop–choop.

"Listen to that," Sylvie said. "What do you reckon he finds to sing about in this place?"

"It's not all that bad," I said. "I don't mind it so bad."

"No? Well, you can have it. You can have my share, too. I'm getting out of here, boy."

"When do you figure on getting out?" I said.

"Just the minute I get out of high school. Which is two years and eighteen days from this very minute. Boy, you won't see me for dust."

"Where do you figure on going?" I said.

"I'm going to College Park. I'm going to the University of Maryland, and get me an education, and associate with civilized people for a change. I'm going to dances and concerts and plays, and after I graduate I'm going in to Washington or Baltimore and get me a good job with an advertising company and have a private air-conditioned office. And if that son of a bitch Boone Armitage shows up looking for a job I'm going to have him scrubbing out toilets."

"That sounds O.K.," I said. "I bet you can do it, too." She could, she didn't get anything but A's.

"You bet your ass I can do it," Sylvie said. "You can stay here and marry one of these rednecks if you like, and spend your life drinking beer and gunk-holing around this bay, but I'm getting out, boy. I've got a lot of living to catch up on."

"Well, I hope you make it," I said. "I got a feeling you will."

"Don't worry about me," Sylvie said. "You worry about yourself for a change. My God, it's time you did. You'll be out of school the end of next year, and what are you going to do then? I'll bet you haven't even thought about applying for college."

"Poppa wants me to work in the shop," I said. "You know that."

"Oh, sure. Building those Goddamned tubs so the rich guys can come down from Washington and show their girl friends a good time on weekends. Boy, if you do that you're crazy, you know it? You ought to be shot."

"Well, Poppa wants to keep the business going," I said. "You know how he feels about it."

"I know how he feels about one thing," Sylvie said. "And that's Poppa. That's the only thing he gives a damn about in this world."

'No, it isn't."

"Don't tell me, boy. I haven't lived in that house all my life for nothing."

"I live there too," I said.

Sylvie took a drag and blew out a stream of smoke and then started spitting. She spit between her knees onto the ground and then tamped the wet places with the toe of her shoe.

"You are stupid, Aaron, you know that?" she said. "You are really stupid."

"Well, maybe so," I said. I didn't want her to get too riled up, she might take off for Washington in the middle of the night or something if she got really riled up, I wouldn't have put it past her.

"You are going to let that guy kill you," she said. "You're going to let him do something to you just exactly like he did to Jamed. That's the truth, Aaron. Boy, you are so dumb." She spit a couple more times and made a face. "These cigarettes taste like garbage."

"You inhale yet?" I said.

"No. I did, twice, and I had to vomit both times." She dropped the cigarette and stamped on it and sat there looking sadder than hell. "I don't know why it is, but I seem to vomit awful easy lately. You reckon I could have some kind of a disease?"

"You seem pretty healthy to me," I said. "When else did you vomit?"

"As a matter of fact I feel like vomiting most of the damned *time*. I don't know, I think there's something the matter with my stomach. I told Oma Pearl that and she said maybe I was pregnant, how do you like that son of a bitch? Boy, if there's one thing I'm not, it's pregnant. I'm *never* going to be pregnant."

"You're just a very sensitive type," I said. "A lot of sensitive people have trouble with their stomachs."

"I don't know," she said. "I just wish I felt really good once in a while." She reached down and picked up the squashed cigarette stub and broke it apart and spilled the tobacco out into her hand and started sifting it around in her palm with her fingertip. "You know the only time I've felt really good all this week?"

"Uh uh, when?"

"Tuesday afternoon, when I came in there in the auditorium and watched you rehearsing that play. Did you see me come in there?"

"No. Did you sure enough?"

"Yeah. I had a study period, so I came in there and watched you for a while. What's the name of that play?"

"*The Valiant.*"

"You know something, you're really good, Aaron. You really are. I sat there and listened for I reckon ten minutes, anyway. I liked it. You know that part where you say the

Shakespeare? You did that real good. It made me feel great, listening to you."

"No kidding?" I felt prouder than hell.

"It really did. The girl is his sister, right?"

"That's right. But he doesn't want her to know he's her brother, because he's committed this murder and they've got him in jail there, waiting to be executed, so he pretends he doesn't know her."

"So why doesn't she recognize him, right off?"

"Well, it's a long time since they've seen each other, so she wouldn't know him just by sight."

She sat there thinking about it, blowing little puffs of breath at the tobacco, scattering it around in her palm.

"That's a real good play," she said. "I felt really good watching you up there. You know, Aaron, I bet you could be a famous actor if you wanted."

"Oh yeah, sure," I said.

"No, I mean it. You've got a way of talking that makes people listen to you and look at you. Most guys, when they talk, you just want to vomit. Like that Boone Armitage bastard. You know something else about him? I bet he's the guy that gave Jamed that Feen-a-Mint chewing gum that time."

"What makes you think that?" I said.

"Because I heard him telling a bunch of guys up at school about it. He was saying Jamed was the world's champion gum chewer and sprinter. They were laughing their fool heads off."

"I'd sure like to be sure of that," I said.

"Yeah, what would you do? You'd just say, 'That's not nice, Boone. You oughtn't to do things like that.' You wouldn't hurt a fly."

"That's what you say."

"That's what I know. That's the only thing wrong with you in that play, how would a guy like you ever commit a murder? You wouldn't hurt a fly."

"If I find out who gave Jamed that gum, I'll make him wish he hadn't, you can bet on that."

"Well, if you don't, I will," Sylvie said. She blew the tobacco out of her hand and scrubbed her palm against her skirt. "Boy, people are really something, you know that? People are really something. You know what, Aaron? You are the only man I really like. That's the truth. I don't think I could ever really like any man in the world except my brother. I don't want any of these sons of bitches clawing at *me*. I don't know how girls can stand it."

"Yeah, wait'll you fall in love with some guy," I said.

"I'm not going to fall in love with *any*body," Sylvie said. "I'd rather be dead, boy. If any son of a bitch falls in love with me, I'll crack him in the head."

"That's what you say now."

"That's what I say *period*. I really hate men's guts. But a brother is not really like a man, you know? I mean, you can *relax* with your brother, for God's sake."

"Well, I know what you mean," I said.

"That's a funny thing. You're the only person in the world I can really relax with."

I took a couple more drags on the cigarette and then started rubbing it out on the log.

"We better go," I said. "Poppa wants me to come down to the shop."

"You know what you ought to do?" Sylvie said. "You ought to go up to the university and study drama. You know you can get a degree in drama? You could go on the stage and be a famous actor, Aaron. I bet you could be in the movies. I mean it."

"Yeah, sure," I said.

"I'll bet you've got just as much talent as any of those famous actors had when *they* were in high school. You sit around this dump and build boats all your life, you ought to get your head examined."

"Well, I didn't say that's what I *wanted* to do," I said.

"But my God, you can't do everything you *want* to do in this world."

"Why not?" Sylvie said. "*He* does. You can be damned sure of that. *He* does what he wants to do, and the hell with everybody else."

I sat there grinding up the cigarette against the log, I was feeling sort of miserable because Sylvie was upset but also very pleased because she had liked me in the play. That play was my sand castle.

"You know, I really like acting," I said. "That's the only time I can really get free for a while, you know that, Sylvie? When I'm up there on that stage. My gosh, it's really great. It's sort of like sailing."

"Yeah, well you can stick the sailing up your ass," Sylvie said. "I don't want to hear about sailing."

"No, but I mean you feel just as free and easy. You know what I mean, *you* love to sail."

"I sure as hell do *not*," she said. "I hate boats and water and wind and every Goddamned thing to do with it. If there's one thing in this world that *really* makes me vomit, it's sailing. I wish I could never see a boat again in my whole life." She got up and raked her hair around with her fingertips and stared off into the woods. There wasn't anything special in there to see but she stared anyway, she reminded me of Jamed, we were getting to be a great bunch of starers. A little breeze came whiffling in through the trees and started blowing the collar of her blouse against her cheek so she put up her hand and laid her fingers on it to hold it down. Her wrist was bent in a pretty way like a heron's neck when he is drinking, with her fingers lying curved asleep against her shoulder, nestled there like a bird, she seemed to have a special affection for her hands, she welcomed them and allowed them to touch her, her hair or shoulders or the buttons of her blouse, with a sort of experimental delicacy and shyness as if they were attached to somebody else, some invisible person made out of air or gauze maybe, nobody real, that was surer than hell, because if anybody real ever came close to her or moved his hands toward her she would flinch and draw herself away quickly as if she felt pain. She was prettier than hell, I never thought any other girl I knew was really pretty compared to Sylvie, she made them all look like cows. She was also madder than hell most of the time, which you'd think would have spoiled it but it didn't, somehow it made her prettiness all the more exciting and valuable because she didn't put any price on it, she refused to profit by it, she refused to accept flattery or congratulations for it, she seemed almost to resent it, only her own hands were allowed to court her, it made men jealous and mean, even old men, you could see it every time they came near her down on the pier or up at Offutt's or anywhere and tried to say something smart or appreciative or just to smile at her, woozy as hell just from looking at her, and then felt her spite pinch them like claws. I guess the truth was she was going a little bit crazy, and what was also the truth was that I was beginning to discover that I liked crazy people, and wounded people and scared people better than I did happy or prosperous or confident ones because it seemed to me that they paid in some way for the happiness and prosperity of the others. And what seemed to me particularly noble about Sylvie was that although she had been given one of those graces like happiness or prosperity or confidence, which in her case was her prettiness, she refused to rejoice in it, she refused to let the stupid, awkward, ugly girls of the world pay for it with their humility and envy, she was sort of throwing it back into God's teeth saying, "Oh no, Boy, I'm not having any, I know how this thing works, I've had a taste of it myself, me and Jamed and Momma, we've paid plenty so Poppa could have his boats and his whisky and his women, I'm not taking it out on Oma Pearl or Paisley or any of those poor cows, You can have it." Which of course was a pretty arrogant or ungrateful or maybe even blasphemous attitude if you wanted to look at it that way, but on the other hand it had something bitterly scrupulous and sacrificial about it that thrilled me, the truth was everything about Sylvie thrilled me, sometimes I'd wake up in the middle of the night scared weak as a kitten and say to myself, Jesus Christ, what's the matter with me? What the hell am I doing any-way, am I falling in love with my sister or something? God, don't let me fall in love with my sister, please. Send some girl my way that has got ten-inch boobs and will make me fall flat on my face, will You please? I don't want to be in love with my sister, I've got enough problems already.

But I never really looked at any other girl, I almost never even got a hard on, that was another thing that bothered me. By the time you're seventeen you're supposed to have a hard on a good part of the time but I was lucky if I got up one a month. I looked at these dirty comic books and everything that the guys passed around, and they would be sort of mildly interesting, some of them were even pretty funny, but they never really got to me. I decided it was because I worried too much, I've noticed that if you're worried about something it's practically impossible to get a hard on, I mean if Jamed disappeared for example and I went looking for him up the beach I could have seen Marilyn Monroe come walking toward me stark naked and all I probably would have done is thrown her a hiball and said, "Hi, Marilyn. You haven't seen Jamed around anywhere, have you?" Then of course the more you worry about not getting a hard on the less chance you have of getting one on, so after a while you might as well forget about it. But you can't really forget it of course, you worry like hell, you get to thinking you were born a Goddamned eunuch or something, which is another one of the ways in which I sure as hell didn't take after Poppa.

Sylvie stood there staring off into the woods and I sat

on the log admiring the way her hand was lying curled up against her shoulder and after a while she said, "Anyway, I'm getting out, I mean it, Aaron. I'm going up to College Park to the university just the minute I graduate. So you've got a year to think about it."

"Yeah, O.K." I didn't know what she meant by that but I said, "Listen, Sylvie, I've got to get down to the shop. Poppa said he wanted me to help him with some planking because the workmen all went down to Solomons to do that salvage job."

"O.K., sucker," she said. "You go and help Poppa build his Goddamned boat. See what you get for it."

She picked up her books and we walked back through the woods and on down the road past Offutt's toward the shop. There was a bend in the road in front of Offutt's where all of a sudden you could see the bay, a cool dark blue in the sun, and the sky above it, a lighter, robin's egg blue, those two blues, flat but deep, so deep they turned into time, not distance any more but an endless summertime of blue. I know what Sylvie's talking about, I thought, but I don't think I can ever get away from this place.

"You know something, Syl?" I said. "Any road in the world, if you follow it long enough, will lead you to that very same sight. Because there isn't a road in the world that after a while doesn't wind up at the sea. Did you ever think about that?"

"Sure, I thought about it," she said. "But it doesn't curl my hair none. What I like to think about is what's on the other side."

That surprised me because I never did that, I never wanted it to end, just the sea was all I wanted there to be, reaching on forever.

"Hey, would you take my books up to the house?" I said. "I better get on down to the shop, I'm late already."

"O.K.," Sylvie said. I only had two, a math book and a

civics book, I put them on top of hers and she went on up the hill past the hotel, I heard her call out, "Afternoon, Miz Peabody," and Mrs. Peabody say, "Afternoon, Sylvie. My, but it's hot," and Sylvie say, "Yes, ma'am, it is." I went across the road and in through the gate and along the slipway to the shop, the heat was boiling up off the tin roof in waves like off a stove top, it made the tulip trees behind the shop writhe and shudder like you were looking at them through water. That's the way I see things, I thought, I don't see things right, I see everything through water. I had a mysterious feeling, I didn't want that summer to ever end. Jesus, I'm scared, I thought.

I opened the screen door and went into the office. It was empty and the big floor fan was blowing with the ribbons streaming out and fluttering in the wind. I unbuttoned my shirt and stood there and let it blow on my chest for a while and then went out into the shop. Poppa was working on a tonguer that somebody had ordered for the oyster fleet, a rough little roustabout with a wheelhouse like a tool shed and a turn of bilge like a watermelon, he liked to build those things sometimes, you could relax. He was up on a scaffold drilling her planks for fastening, all the time talking to Jamed, who was sitting on the floor underneath with a pile of sawed-off stringer ends that he was building a block castle with. They didn't either one of them see me, I stood there and listened to Poppa, purely fascinated.

"This here wood is called Philippine mahogany," he said, "because it comes from a place way off in the Pacific Ocean which is called the Philippine Islands. That is one fine place, Jamed. You know what they got there? They got coconut palm trees, which is what coconuts grow on. You know when Momma makes a coconut cake? Well, that is where that stuff comes from, all them little white wiggly pieces that is sprinkled on top, comes right from the Philippine Islands. You know what them trees look like? Look just like a feather duster that is stood up on its end. Now that's the truth. And when a elephant walks by one of them trees it tickles him all back of the ears, and he sits right down and laughs and laughs. Sometimes you'll see fifteen–twenty elephants sitting around laughing theirselves sick, I tell you it is a funny sight."

Jamed giggled and started banging his blocks around, it knocked him out.

"You remember what a elephant looks like?" Poppa said.

"Yeah. They got a big nose," Jamed said.

"That's right," Poppa said. He moved along the scaffold raising the electric drill to push a pair of holes through the plank at each rib, the sawdust flew out and made a golden pollen on the hair of his forearms and his beard. "Got a nose ten–twelve feet long. And sometimes when them coconut trees tickles their noses they get to sneezing. Now can't you imagine what kind of a sneeze that is, with a nose that size? Why, my God, it sounds like a cannon going off. Sometimes you'll be walking along there in the woods and you'll hear this noise go Boom! Boo-whoo-*whoom!* Boom, bam, *barroom!* Why, my God, you'd think there was mountains falling over. Then next thing you know, you'll see trees and houses and chickens flying by, with every daggone one of their feathers blowed off, and cats with knots blowed in their tails, and fishes blowed up like balloons, just *every* kind of junk flying by, and you go on a little piece and sure enough you'll see this poor old elephant sitting there sneezing hisself silly, and all on account of them trees."

Jamed whooped and started flinging blocks all over the place.

"Boom, boom, boom!" he yelled. "Listen at the elephant! Hey, Poppa, listen how I do a tickly elephant. Boom, boom, boom!"

"That's it," Poppa said. "You got it just exactly right. Why, I do believe you must be part elephant, you sound just like one." He held the drill at shoulder level and pushed hard on the handle, squinting his eyes against the dust, his elbows trembling with the vibration. "Yes, sir, this boy has done turned into a elephant. Going to have to feed him peanuts, from now on."

"I want some peanuts!" Jamed yelled. He got up on his hands and knees and started swinging his head around, being an elephant, it was weird, he was almost as big as I was. The sunken place in his skull was a dark tender-looking blue and his bad eye was running, he kept wiping at it with the back of his hand.

Poppa looked down and said, "Now you settle down, there, old elephant. Don't wipe at your eye like that, Jamie, it don't do it good."

"Ka-choo!" Jamed yelled. "I run into a coconut tree." He looked up and saw me and said, "Hey, Aaron, I'm an elephant."

"I figured that's what you were," I said. I went over and sat down beside him. He had a funny smell, a milky, sour, little-kid smell, he had wet his pants. I put my hand on his head, he liked that. He always had a dewy, moist feel on his forehead, like a baby. When I put my hand on his head he put his hand on top of mine and smiled.

"Where you been, Aaron?" he said.

"I been at school, buddy."

"You see Paisley?"

"Uh huh, yeah."

"I never do see Paisley no more," he said. "I think she got my turtle. Somebody did."

"No, I think he crawled off somewhere, Jamie," I said. "He's probably sitting in the woods somewhere right now, just as happy as can be."

"I sure hope so," Jamed said.

"That's just about what he's doing," Poppa said. "Them old turtles, they take real good care of theirself."

"I sure do miss him," Jamed said. "He used to write me all them letters. You remember how he used to write me all them letters, Aaron?"

"Yeah, I remember," I said. Every night Poppa used to write a little note and fasten it onto the terrapin's shell with a piece of Scotch tape so Jamed would find it in the morning. It would say something like, "Jamed, I want a tomato for lunch today," or "Jamed, I had a funny dream last night. I dreamed I had wings and could fly." Momma and me used to read them to him, Sylvie wouldn't have anything to do with it. Jamed thought it was the greatest thing that ever happened, he couldn't wait to get up in the morning and hear the letter from his turtle.

"I bet you that's the only turtle there ever was that could write," he said.

"Yeah, I reckon he was," Poppa said. "Well, maybe you'll hear from him one of these days. I just bet you one of these days you'll get a real long letter from him, Jamie, telling you-all what he's been doing."

"I sure hope so," Jamed said. "I sure do miss that old turtle."

Poppa set his drill down on the scaffold and wiped the sweat off his forehead, bending his head into the crook of his elbow.

"You going to work in them clothes?" he said to me.

"Yeah, I'm not going to hurt them any," I said.

"Well, as long as you can make your Momma believe that." He nodded at a keg under the scaffold. "Yonder is the roves. Get yourself an apronful and the roving tools and we'll fasten this plank. I got to go in the office for a minute. Fetch another plank over here while I'm gone, will you?"

"O.K.," I said.

"Paisley was always fooling with him," Jamed said. "I bet she got him."

"No, no, she don't have him," Poppa said. "I done checked

on that." He sat down on the scaffold and then heaved himself off onto the floor.

"Wow, you shook this whole floor, you know that?" Jamed said.

"Yeah, them big old feet of mine," Poppa said. He reached down and wiggled Jamed's ear and went on across the shop to the office. I went over to my locker and opened the door and took my apron off the hook and put it on over my head and started tying the strings behind my back.

"You put your apron on, didn't you?" Jamed said.

"Yeah, that's right."

"You look like Momma when she's in the kitchen," he said. "You going to bake a cake?"

"Yes sir, going to bake a cake."

He giggled and started shoving his blocks around the floor going, "Moom, moom, moom, moom, moom, moom." I took a pair of roving pliers and a ball-peen hammer out of the tool rack and slid them into their straps on my apron and then came back to the scaffold and dug a handful of copper roves out of the keg. They were cool and heavy, I liked the feel of everything you built boats with, bronze and warm wood and slick dacron sailcloth, the funny thing was I didn't like building boats, I didn't like the way Poppa would put his glasses on and peer at a piece of work I'd done and then say, "Yeah, uh huh, that ain't bad. Now let me show you something." I knew no matter how much he showed me I'd never be able to do it as well as he did, not in a million years, I wanted to do my own stuff. What I liked was reading books out loud, pretending to be somebody in the book, I'd already decided I'd rather be almost anybody in the world than me, I'd had plenty of me, this nut that looked like a wet dog and got all those D's on his report card and couldn't drive a nail straight or get a hard on and was probably in love with his sister or some crazy thing, seventeen years of that was just about enough.

I dropped the roves in my apron and went across to the lumber bin where the mahogany was stored and slid out a one-by-eight plank and had a look at it, Poppa was always telling me what to look for in timber, it had got to be a habit to size up a piece of wood every time I got my hands on it. For hull work, where it would be painted over and not seen, you wanted straight-grained stuff, close-grained, strong, seasoned stuff, "Color and pretty surface don't mean a damn down there," he said, "You want something that will last, flexible enough so's you can work with it and tough enough so's it'll take grounding and rough water, something that don't taste too good, you got worms to worry about, worms and rot, that's what you got to fight with hull timber. Up top, for trim and cabinetry and joinerwork you want pretty stuff, you know, pretty color and fancy grain, for show, but unless it's sitting on a sound hull they ain't nobody going to see it but the fishes. I'm a white oak man, myself." He built the bones of his ships out of white oak always, frames and skegs and keel posts and sternposts, and would have used it for planking too, if the buyers would have stood the bill, but they mostly wanted something cheap and serviceable they could soak in Cuprinol and not have to worry about for maybe three or four years. "They don't see beyond ten years no more," he said. "They just worried about looking good today, and then trading it in about two-three years, while she can still stand a survey. They pick boats just like they pick women." He hated Philippine mahogany, he used the stuff when they demanded it, it made the estimates look good, but he told them what they were getting and didn't give any phony guarantees, when he got ahold of a rich guy who could stand the price, like Mr. Clapperton, he used apple and white oak and teak, real Burma teak, not African stuff, and weather-seasoned, too, not kiln-dried, you put kiln-dried timber in a boat and you were *asking* for trouble. He had a whole gospel about wood, he sounded like a preacher when he got to talking about it, which I couldn't help but regard with a certain amount of irony since it seemed to me that he was the worst-qualified man in Maryland to make noises like a preacher.

I yanked the plank out of the bin and carried it over and set it against the edge of the scaffold and then climbed up beside the hull and picked up Poppa's drill and finished making holes for the fastenings in the top plank. It was hot and still in there, just the sound of Jamed mooming away down underneath and the drill whining, I started saying over my lines in the play, which we had to put on next Friday night, and after a while I started feeling very peaceful. I felt like I had a secret possession, a diamond hid under my mattress or a secret love affair with Eva Marie Saint or like I knew the location of the world's most fantastic vein of gold, all the feeling of being scared clean down to my wishbone, of seeing things wrongly, crazily, gradually melted away, that play worked for me like a dose of Epsom salts. It was a weird thing how pretending to be some poor bastard who was just about to get executed for murder could make me feel a hundred percent better than just being myself, I never could figure that out.

I'd just finished drilling the plank when Poppa came back out of the office carrying Jamed's pill in one hand and a paper cup full of water from the cooler in the other, he brought them over by the scaffold and said, "Hey, looky here, Jamie, here's one of them little yeller candies you like so much."

"I don't like 'em," Jamed said.

"Oh, yeah, you're going to like this one, because you know why? Because just as soon as you get it down you going to get a piece of bubble gum. Now ain't that something?"

Poppa was the only one who could get him to take those pills, he'd spit them out if anybody else gave them to him,

I think Poppa could have given him a toad and he'd have swallowed it down. He put the pill in his mouth and chewed it up, all the time looking up at Poppa with those big sorry eyes, and then made a face like he had a mouthful of mud. He grabbed the paper cup and glugged at it, slopping water all over himself, and then started yelling, "I want my bubble gum."

"O.K., come on," Poppa said. "You want to put the penny in?"

"Yeah," Jamed yelled. "I get to put the penny in." He got up and went clumping over to the bubble gum machine beside Poppa, his feet seemed too big for him, like a puppy's, and his hands were flying all over the place. Poppa dug a penny out of his pocket and gave it to Jamed and Jamed put it in the slot and twisted away at the knob, his face all scrunched up like he was trying to get a tight cap off of a jar, he was all out of whack generally. He finally got it turned and the gumball came clicking down into the chute, it was a green one, which really knocked him out. "Hey, it's a *green* one!" he yelled. "*Boy*, I like them best of *all!*"

"Well, ain't you lucky," Poppa said. "There ain't many green ones in there."

"I know," Jamed said. "Hey, Aaron, I got a *green* one."

"Wow, that's great," I said.

Poppa climbed back up on the scaffold and had a look at my drill holes and nodded.

"O.K., good," he said. "Now get around inside, Aaron, and we'll fasten her."

I climbed over the hull and stood on a plank that was rigged inside with block-and-tackle. We started at the stern end, Poppa would drive a copper Everdur nail through the hole and when it came through I'd slip a rove over the tip of it and hold it flush to the rib with the hollow-nosed pliers. Then I'd take my ball-peen hammer and hold it hard against the tip while Poppa hammered the head home outside. The tip would mushroom back and flatten into a rivet, smearing the rove back dead flush to the timber in a fastening that would rip through the wood before it would give. I liked lap-strake boats, I liked that old-time salty look of the shingled planks and the sound they made in a harbor at night with the water rippling against the strakes. They were hell to repair though, you had to rip them to pieces to get a plank out.

"Aaron was just now saying lots of funny stuff," Jamed said.

"Yeah? What sort of stuff?" Poppa said.

"I was doing my lines," I said. "I'm in a play up at school."

"Is that a fact?" Poppa said. "What sort of a play?"

"It's called *The Valiant*," I said. "It's about this guy that commits a murder and is waiting to get electrocuted."

"That sounds like real exciting stuff," Poppa said. "Who are you going to be? The murderer?"

"Yeah," I said. "I'm not much good, but I like it."

"I don't know that one," Poppa said. "But now there's a Shakespeare play about a murderer. You ever read that *Macbeth?*"

"Yes, sir, we had it last year."

"That's a real good play, ain't it? That's fine stuff to say. You ought to 've heard Grandpap read them things, he used to scare me and Uncle Abner to death." He paused to hammer a nail home. "You going to be out of there, end of next year, ain't you, Aaron?"

"Yes, sir," I said.

"Well, what you figuring on doing? You be ready to go to work then?"

"I don't know. I guess so, Poppa." He raised his eyes and looked at me over the top of the plank that separated us.

"You'd be earning good money," he said. "You'll go right on the payroll the minute you come into the shop. Why, hell, you'll be top man around here inside three–four years,

Aaron. Ready to take over when I give out." He winked at me and nodded.

"That would be great," I said. "But to tell you the truth, Poppa, I'd sort of like to go to college for a while first. I mean, if I had some education, like business training or something, I'd probably be a lot more use around here."

"Business training," he said. "Yeah, that wouldn't do you no harm." He hooked the claw of his hammer over the plank and took off his cap and wiped his forehead in the bend of his elbow. "How long would it take you to learn all that stuff?"

"Well, you can get a degree in four years," I said.

"Four years. That's a hell of a long time, ain't it? That's a real chunk out of a man's life."

"Of course if I wasn't going to college I'd probably get drafted, anyway, as soon as I got out of high school. I'd have to put in two years in the army."

"Yeah, that's the truth. But you got that to do anyway, ain't you? College or not."

"Yeah," I said. "But I'd get a student deferment if I went to college, just about everybody does. And I'd have summers off all those four years. I could be home here, working, all summer. I could learn a lot that way."

"Yeah, that's true," Poppa said. "That's the heavy time, of course, the summer."

"I mean if I was studying business administration or something, I could maybe start working on the books here, in the summertime. I guess that's a pretty important part of any business."

"Yeah, you can say that again," Poppa said. "They's many a time I wished to hell I knew something about bookkeeping, I can tell you." He put his cap on and picked his hammer off the plank. "Well, we got plenty of time to think about it," he said. "They ain't no need to get all excited, is there? Slow and steady is the way to do things in this world."

Jamed came up and stood under the scaffold, tugging on Poppa's pants' leg. "You know what I bet?" he said. "Hey, Poppa, you know what I bet?"

"No, what, Jamie?" Poppa said.

"I bet you old Boodle has got run over by a car. I seen one up there in the road the other day that was all squashed flat. I bet you that was Boodle."

"No, no, that wasn't old Boodle," Poppa said. "He took real good care of hisself. He was a smart turtle." He looked at me over the plank and winked. "Hey, Aaron, did you bring that letter in there?"

"What letter?" I said.

"That letter I just got off the desk in there." He winked at me again. "I thought you might 've stopped at the post office."

"Oh, yeah, that letter on the desk," I said. "Yeah, I got that at the post office when I got off the bus."

"Yeah, that's what I figured," Poppa said. He pulled an envelope out of his shirt pocket and handed it to me across the plank. "Read that to me, will you, Aaron? I ain't got my glasses."

"O.K.," I said. I opened the envelope and took out a sheet of paper that had Poppa's handwriting on it and started reading it aloud. " 'Dear Jamed.' "

"Hey, that letter's for Jamed," Poppa said. "I didn't know that."

"I didn't either," I said. "I didn't look at it real good."

"Hey, read it, read it!" Jamed shouted. "Hey, I got a letter!" He started pounding on the scaffold with his fists, excited as hell.

"O.K.," I said. "It says, 'Dear Jamed. I'm having a real good time. I'm out here in the woods visiting some other turtles I met. We have lots of fun, but I sure do miss you. I think about you all the time and all those good tomatoes you used to feed me. I'll be back soon and tell you all about what I've been doing. You might not recognize me though, because I've growed a good bit. I guess you have too. Your friend, Boodle.' "

"Hey, yay! That's from old Boodle!" Jamed yelled. "Hey, Poppa, I got a letter from Boodle. Did you hear what Aaron read? He's going to come back real soon, he said. Boy, I sure am glad he's all right."

"Well now, what do you know about that?" Poppa said. "I told you you'd get a letter from that old turtle before long. Now ain't that a wonderful thing."

"He said he's staying with some friends of his, out there in the woods," Jamed said. "He's having a fine time!"

"Why, sure he is," Poppa said. "He sounded like he missed you, though. I bet that old turtle's real lonesome for you, Jamie."

"Yeah, I know," Jamed said. "He wants some more tomatoes. Boy, I'm going to give him lots when he comes back." He stood there under the scaffold grinning up at me, chomping away on his bubble gum, happy as a clam, pee in his pants, goo all over his mouth, big shallow eyes like a fish's. Well, he got out, one way or another, I thought. Or maybe he's so far *in* he can't tell the difference. Maybe there isn't any difference, who knows.

"I DON'T SEE IT WAS SUCH A TRAGEDY, ANYWAY," SYLVIE SAID. "Is there anything that says you've got to have a piece of paper from an academy before you can call yourself an actor? Did Burbage have one? Or Kean? It wasn't the end of the world, for God's sake."

"Well, it wasn't only that," I said. "It was having to leave London, too. The whole business. I really got to love that town."

"I should think you'd have been glad to leave the place,"

Sylvie said. "All those dead cats. Jesus."

"No, it's a wonderful town. It's the only city I've ever liked. And somehow it seemed a lot closer to here than New York does. New York is about a million miles from any other place on earth, but London is just up the road a piece. It's like a river, that city, you feel like it's been flowing just about forever and it always will be. And even if you drown in it, you'll go down in old, warm, wonderful water full of the bones of great people and all kinds of sunken treasure glinting down under there."

"Well, why didn't you stay, if you were so nutty about the place?" Sylvie said. "Couldn't you apply for citizenship or something?"

"I could have applied," I said. "But if you don't have a nickel to your name, or a trade or profession of any kind, they're not too enthusiastic about your prospects for becoming a solid citizen. They don't just let anybody immigrate, they're pretty damn selective about it. Of course if you marry somebody, a British subject, I mean, they let you stay, then."

"But that's what you couldn't do," Sylvie said.

"No, that's what I couldn't do."

"Well, hell, it's not such a big deal," Sylvie said. "Some people just aren't made to marry, you said so yourself. Is that any crime?"

"It's not the *marrying*," I said. "I mean it's not the actual ceremony, or sacrament, or whatever you want to call it, that's not what I'm talking about. It's just the idea of two people *committing* themselves to each other. I mean, my God, Sylvie, how long are you responsible for somebody you're supposed to love? A week? Six months? Five years? Just until you get sick of the whole damn thing and start thinking about how much nicer it would be in Bora Bora. Just until it starts really getting *hard*, for God's sake? What kind of a world are you going to make that way? That's what bothered me. I could never go the whole distance with anybody."

"Don't be too sure of it," Sylvie said.

"No, I mean it." I laced my fingers together and dropped my hands between my thighs and stared at them. "You see, I've got what seems to me to be the real sickness, Sylvie. I can never finish anything."

"You don't know yet," Sylvie said. "You can't love *everybody*."

"I know, but I'd sort of like to. All the nuts, anyway. I've got this funny thing where I'd like to love about a million people for about ten minutes each, instead of just one person for about fifty years. Maybe it works out just about the same, if you cross-multiply. Maybe you get the same number of love hours per lifetime. That's what I'm counting on, anyhow."

We sat there without saying anything for quite a while. A mockingbird began to sing, the way they do in the dark sometimes, warbling away like a nightingale.

"So what did you tell her?" Sylvie said finally.

"Oh boy, it was awful. I got drunk, in the first place, and didn't get home till about two o'clock in the morning, because the first thing I did after I got the word from Dame Demeter was to go out and get bombed."

"No kidding," Sylvie said. "I wouldn't have believed it."

Well, believe it or not, that's what I did. Then when I got home Cindy was waiting up for me in this ratty-looking Cinderella-type bed jacket, which didn't improve the situation any, and then she insisted on putting together this concoction which she said was a sure cure for a hangover, four aspirin tablets dissolved in a cup of hot Bovril, it just about peeled the lining off the inside of my cheeks. I took one gulp of the stuff and let out a gasp and said, 'Holy God, what are you trying to do to me?'

'I might ask you the same,' she said.

'What does that mean?' I said.

'Well, it's not a lot of fun, you know, being stuck here all hours of the night while you're out romping round Bloomsbury with your chums.'

'Well, my God,' I said. 'I should think you'd be the last person in the world to make a remark like that. *Me* out all hours of the night? What about *you?*' I thought I'd try being indignant, sometimes you can get a certain charge of energy out of a sense of indignation, I had a feeling I was going to need plenty.

'Well, what about me, then? Are *you* going to start on me next?' She was feeling pretty bitchy herself, which wasn't usual with Cindy, an odd, proud kind of bitchiness, after all things hadn't been going any too well around there lately, she acted something like a man who wants to preserve his dignity by resigning before you get a chance to fire him. She gave me a kind of bitter haughty stare that made it very hard to keep my indignation at full boil and said, 'A girl's entitled to a bit of nonsense now and again, you know. That hadn't occurred to you, I don't suppose.'

As a matter of fact it had, I always had suspected that there are certain people who are just naturally entitled to a certain amount of indiscretion in the course of their lives by virtue of the way they're put together, in the way that ducks, by virtue of the way they're put together, are entitled to enjoy a certain amount of water, they're built for it, they need it, they pine without it. And if ever in my life I had met a person who was carefully, meticulously, mathematically designed for indiscretion it was Cindy, she had been put together by a master craftsman, boy, she had been given every known faculty for the full enjoyment of it, just as a duck is given webbed feet, built-in flotation, etc., for getting the most out of water, there would have been a kind of natural injustice in denying her an occasional dip into it.

'Well, I don't know why you limit the privilege to girls,' I said. 'How about us men?'

'You bloody men have got privileges enough. God, don't we spend our lives polishing them up for you.'

'Listen, I don't know what all the fuss is about,' I said. 'Once in a blue moon I go out and get myself quietly stoned with the boys and you go all to pieces about it.'

She picked up the spoon she had been stirring the Bovril-and-aspirin concoction with and pointed it at the lopsided old Victorian armoire across the room.

'Have you had a look inside that wardrobe lately?'

'What do you mean?' I said. 'I look inside it every day.'

'Well, I don't think you take much notice. Look again.'

It wasn't necessary to get up and open it because the door gaped open about a foot, it was impossible to close the damned thing, all I had to do was crane my neck a little to see the four sad, soot-stained pieces of her wardrobe hanging there in the shadows liked smoked haddocks and one of her two pairs of shoes peeking out at me from the floor, not so much peeking, really, as bleakly regarding, it gave me a twinge.

'That's my life, in there,' Cindy said. 'That's what I own in this world. That and my "privileges," as you call them. Where the hell will I be if I give them up? That's all there is of me, my "privileges." ' She bit her lip, her face started getting rubbery, then she banged the spoon down on the table. 'And I'll tell you something else, I don't like the way you screw, if you want to know the truth. I mean it's so bloody mournful or something. I feel as if you're going to break into plainsong every time you get through. If there's *anything* one ought to be a bit cheerful about, it's screwing.'

'How about if I whistle?' I said.

'No, you needn't smirk, either, it's the truth.' She dug around in the pocket of her bedjacket for a Kleenex but there wasn't any of course, she never had a Kleenex, so I took out my handkerchief and tossed it across the table to her. She wiped her nose on it and said, 'Would you mind telling me something? Seriously? Why do you take all this bloody care of me? Why do you fuss around like an old hen, when five years from now you won't be able to remember the color of my eyes? Don't you think it's a bit daft?'

I felt pretty chastened by that, I decided I'd better abandon the indignation bit, it wasn't working too well anyway, it seemed to me that if anything was needed around there at the moment it was a certain amount of humility, so I leaned across the table and tied together the ribbons of her bedjacket in a bow, Cindy's bows didn't hold up too well in this world, and said, 'Well, maybe it's daft, but I'll remember the color of your eyes in five years. You can bet on it.' I started to say, 'You ask me and see,' but just the process of forming the words in my mind gave me a twinge like a cold knife blade laid across my belly, I couldn't get them out.

She sat there staring at me dead levelly, she wasn't going to let me off the hook, I could see that.

'No, tell me the truth,' she said. 'Wouldn't it better not even to try, than to get people's hopes all up, for nothing?' I didn't know the answer to that one so I didn't say a word. 'People go around like millionaires, handing out these bank-notes with Love written all over them, and then they find they can't redeem them. It's like counterfeit money. Well, in future, if anyone wants a screw from me, a good honest five-pound note'll do.'

I was properly humbled by *that*, boy, I can tell you, more than humbled, racked up, I felt as if I were quietly disintegrating, physically as well as every other damned way because that Bovril-and-aspirin solution seemed to be dissolving all the mucous membrane inside my mouth, I nibbled at a few shreds of my cheek that were hanging loose and swallowed them down, I'm going to pieces, I thought, I'd never been rocked like that in my whole life. I sat there trying to pull myself together, feeling as if I'd been stripped and tied to a lamp post for dogs to have their little joke on, to show you the kind of shape I was in, I decided right then to extort a little sympathy from her, shift the burden of guilt or something, any damn thing I could think of, I was hurting.

'Listen, why don't you calm down a little?' I said. 'I'll tell you why I got drunk, if you want to know. I got the sack at GLAD.'

'Oh, Jesus,' Cindy whispered. 'Oh, love, no.'

'Yep. I had my Little Talk with Dame Demeter, so naturally I wasn't feeling so hot.' Cindy reached across the table to lay her hands on mine and dropped her head. 'So I went over to The Rising Sun with Graham and we had a few. One over the eight, I guess.'

She raised her head and peeked at me for a minute with her eyes swimming, then she gave her head a sort of pained, hopeless shake, like a dog with an earache, and said, 'Oh, God, it's all my fault, love. You've been working so bloody hard to take care of me, you were bound to muck it up.'

'It isn't anybody's *fault*,' I said, magnanimity, boy, 'I just couldn't cut the mustard, that's all. It had to happen sooner or later.'

'What did she say, that bloody woman?'

'Oh, she was very nice about it. She talked about ghosts, mostly. She said artists were supposed to give birth to ghosts, or something. Then she gave me a glass of sherry and told me that what I ought to do was to go out and beget some real live children. No ghosts. It was pretty sound advice, actually.'

'She's a bloody fool. She doesn't know talent when she sees it.'

'Yes, she does,' I said. 'The trouble is, I wouldn't be much better as a father than as an actor. I don't know what the hell I would be good at. Peddling stuff, I guess, like everybody else.'

'Don't you believe it,' Cindy said. 'You'd be a bloody great genius at both.' She squeezed my hands and gave a sort of shy, inspirational smile. 'I mean with a bit of help, of course. That's all any of us needs, isn't it?'

That really made me feel like a bastard. I started to nod because I knew that was what she wanted but then I thought, Oh no, you don't, you don't go that far, you bastard. Let's not have any of those quiet ceremonial nods in confirmation of your undying faith, it may be a pretty shabby bundle of goods you've got to deliver but you'd better lay it on the table. I decided maybe a brief sorrowful smile wouldn't compromise anybody's dignity too much so I tried that but it came out one of those movie-type smiles, which wasn't really a hell of a lot of improvement. Cindy seemed to be satisfied with it, however, as a matter of fact she broke out in a rosy glow the minute I sprang it on her, which surprised me very greatly, maybe I *should* stick with this acting business, I thought, if I can get away with a smile like that I'd make a million dollars.

'Listen, love,' she said. 'I've got a lovely tin of veal-and-kidney pie that Mum sent down from Stratford last week. Why don't I pop it in a pan and we'll have a bite of something hot. You've not had any dinner, I don't suppose?'

'No, I haven't, as a matter of fact,' I said. 'That would be great, Cindy, I'm kind of hungry.'

'I'll just put the Hovis and marge on,' she said. 'Will you butter it for me, love?'

I managed to nod this time, I could get one off for small occasions if not for lifetime commitments of my immortal soul, if somebody said to me, "War is hell, don't you think?" I could come up with a really beautiful nod, just as solemn as hell, no problem there, boy, but if somebody said, "Will you love me, Aaron, in all my deformity and folly?" what they got was the old Valentino smile, that said, flickering acknowledgment of tribute that splits the sweet face of man like a ghastly crack in marble.

She set the loaf of Hovis and the margarine on the table in front of me and I started buttering away while she went over and put a pan of water on the stove and dropped in the tin of veal-and-kidney pie and got the burner going, she was humming away there under her breath, all full of the redeeming magic of womanhood, boy, it was pretty agonizing to watch.

'This'll be good, a night like this,' she said. 'You're going to have ulcers, the first thing you know, boozing on an empty belly.' She raked her hair back of her ears and spread herself out in one of her fashion-model seduction poses and started wobbling her head at me, I couldn't figure out what she had in mind.

'What's going on?' I said.

'Haven't you noticed anything?' I had a closer look at her and then with a nasty start discovered that she was wearing a pair of very expensive French enamel earrings that had not been in her possession when I left that morning.

'Oh, for God's sakes, Cindy, when are you going to cut that out?' I said. 'Where did you get them?'

'Harrod's. Right off the counter. Aren't they super?'

This girl is hopeless, I thought, I won't get across the gangplank before they have her locked up in Wormwood Scrubbs. I've got to get her back there to Stratford before I leave, and let Mum take over. She'll go down the drain like a wet noodle if I leave her here in London.

'What are you trying to do, anyway, get yourself locked up?' I said.

'There was no one within a mile, it was an absolute snap. I had to do something to cheer myself up, I was in such a bloody funk. I'd been tramping round the West End the whole bloody morning, getting turned down in one place after another, so I stopped off at Harrod's and went in the jewelry department to have a look round, and here were these gorgeous earrings lying there with absolutely no one about, the girl had forgot to put them back in the case, I suppose. So I said, why not? I mean I owed it to myself in a way.'

'Do you know what happens when you get caught shop-lifting?' I said.

'Well, I didn't get caught, did I? Look, love, I've got to have a bit of something special now and again, honestly. I shall die if I don't.'

'I don't know,' I said. 'I don't know, I'll be damned if I do. What's going to happen to you when—'

'When what?'

'When you get *caught* some time, Goddamn it. You're going to wind up in jail, you know that? With a record. Try and get a job then. *Any* kind of a job.'

'Oh, don't go on about it, love. 'Tisn't as if I did it every day. I mean try and look at it my way.'

I decided I'd better shut up and just butter bread, I didn't like the way the conversation was going, I didn't like the way anything was going, the inside of my mouth for example was one holy mess, my gums were beginning to soften like warm wax, and things weren't any too good from there on down, or up. Cindy fished the tin of kidney pie out of the boiling water and brought it over to the table with a couple of plates and started spooning it out.

'So what will you do now, then, love?' she said. She sounded very hesitant and humble. 'I mean will you have to leave, or what?'

Jesus, I thought, here it comes. Well, as well now as later, I guess, but I would have liked to get through the kidney pie first.

'I guess so,' I said. 'I'll lose my student visa, and I haven't got a work permit or a bankroll. I sure as hell can't immigrate, I'm not sure I'd want to, anyway.'

'Oh,' Cindy said, with that agonizing, craven hesitancy. She spooned a big dollop of veal-and-kidney pie onto a plate and set it in front of me. 'There's no way at all, then. That you can stay, I mean.'

'Well, of course, we could get married,' I said. 'They let you stay if you're married to a British subject. They figure you've got to earn them a living, I guess.'

She said, 'Oh,' again in that spine-chilling way and started stirring her kidney pie around, poking holes in the crust to let the steam out. 'Well, but that's out of the question, of course. People don't get married any more, do they? I mean in our circumstances.'

'Not if they can help it,' I said. 'That's a *really* rough scene. I wouldn't want to let *anybody* in for that.'

"No. No, of course not,' she said. 'Well, I guess that means you'll have to go back, then, doesn't it?' Her lips were starting to get rubbery again but she made a hell of an effort to keep control of them, pressing them together until they went white while she stared at that plateful of slop.

All of a sudden I said to myself, Look, I just can't do this. I just can't sit here and tear this girl to pieces with the truth. I've got to lie, that's all there is to it. I've got to tell her some kind of a fancy lie, and then just pack up and sneak out some day while she's out shoplifting. I had never really tried lying, in a serious way, but I could see that the time had come. It was supposed to be absolutely marvelous for the prevention of pain. It sure as hell can't be any worse than aspirin-and-Bovril, I thought.

So what I did was to take a huge spoonful of steak-and-kidney pie to fortify myself and sit there munching it up and gulping it down, along with about half the raw material of my oral cavity, while I prepared myself for the loss of my virginity. I was working on my lie, getting the lines just right, straightening up my necktie so to speak, flipping the dust off my lapels, getting myself all spruced up for my debut, although maybe my debut had taken place a long time ago, really, but because there wasn't any ceremony at the time I hadn't noticed it.

'Well, maybe,' I said finally, flower in the buttonhole, smile back in place, hat in hand, I stepped right out there on the stage, hello folks. 'But actually it might be the best idea, Cindy. Suppose I was to go back and work for a little while, two or three months, something like that, and save up enough money to send for you? That might be the best way to handle it. Because, you know, you can make a hell of a lot more money over there than you can here. I mean if we got married over here, it would take us *forever* to save up anything. And this way we could get to the States a lot sooner. As a matter of fact, they could be doing us a favor. You'd love it over there, you really would.'

I had to lower my eyes after I said it, modesty having been offended wholesale, the place seemed to shriek with indignation, ratty carpet, lopsided wardrobe, soupstained bedspread, everything seemed to gather itself together with outrage, Listen, it seemed to say, I may be a crummy bed-sitter in the heart of darkest Notting Hill Gate, but that doesn't mean stuff like *this* can take place in here, I have got *some* dignity left, you know, I didn't take you in out of the cold to witness *this* kind of spectacle. Cindy didn't seem to notice it, however, she was sitting there looking across the table at me with the ultimate offering softening those blue seal's eyes, there it was, what every actor is supposed to dream about, the supreme tribute to his craft, Willing Suspension of Disbelief, it came flowing in over the footlights like a stream of pure gold, she was my perfect audience, boy, you don't get any more than that from anybody, that's when you know you've really got them in the palm of your hand, when they settle into that hushed idolatry, they don't even think about the fact that after a while the curtain will come down and they'll have to get up and put on their overcoats and walk back down Piccadilly in the rain. Well, Cindy girl, you're really making sure that I have faith in myself as an actor, I thought. You've really gone all the way to give me what I need. Holy God, will I ever be able to do the same for anyone?

'Oh, love,' she whispered. 'Wouldn't that be wonderful?

Oh, golly. Oh, wouldn't that be gorgeous!' She sat there spilling over, she reached across the table to touch the tips of my fingers humbly with her own, she couldn't say anything else, she was too overcome, both of us were, we were both dripping with tears by this time although for very different reasons of course, this kills pain all right, I thought, it kills damn near everything.

'You mean in just a couple of *months, actually?*' Cindy said after she'd got herself under control a little. 'You could really save up enough money so that I could come over? To New *York?*'

'Well, maybe three or four. But not any longer than that. It depends on how soon I can get a job. Even if I can't get work in the theater, I'll have to do *something*. I mean, I'll be saving up, no matter what I'm doing.'

'Oh no, but you've got to do *acting*, love. That's what you're made for. There'll be something going over there, surely, I mean for someone as good as you.'

'Well, I'll try it, of course,' I said. 'Even if I could do dinner theaters or T.V. stuff, there's a lot of that now. And you can make money, I mean compared to over here. I think Equity minimum is about a hundred and twenty-five a week now. Well, living at the Y or something, I could save half of that.' You know, a funny thing happened, I actually started believing it. Not really believing it maybe, but sort of developing a respect for the idea, an interest in inventing it, in cooking the whole damn thing up, I started feeling a craftsman's pleasure in working out all the details, it was really a pretty good idea, it could be done, why not? I mean by somebody with a genuine, factory-fresh, sealed-in-the-carton soul, why the hell not? I decided I'd proceed as if I were that fortunate guy, manufacture the whole happy scheme, right down to the last detail, there would be plenty of time later to admit it was all garbage. But all the time I kept hearing this hollow brassy laughter clanging away inside of me like somebody banging on a boiler and this snotty disc jockey voice yapping away: 'So if you're going to take care of her all her life anyway, why don't you just marry her, old buddy? What's your answer to that, old buddy?' I couldn't think of the answer so I just kept talking, I talked about student travel rates, steamship fares, the advantages of an ocean voyage, getting there is half the fun, the availability of coldwater flats in Greenwich Village, the joy of marketing on Bleecker Street, Edna St. Vincent Millay, the fact that everybody wants an English secretary on Madison Avenue, I had a whole life planned in fifteen minutes, she was galvanized.

'I never dreamed it would really happen,' she kept saying, we were on the bed by this time and she had her nose nuzzled into my neck, 'I mean, do you remember when I said to you once about meeting your parents? Well, I never dreamed I would, ever.'

I kissed her on the back of the neck and got her pretty well soaked in the process because I was spouting tears again all of a sudden, I decided I must be totally dissolving inside, the old aspirin was working its magic everywhere.

'Ah, no, don't cry, love,' she said. 'I know how you feel, though. Can I get you something?'

'No, thanks,' I said. 'Nothing else, please. Listen, are you sure that was aspirin you gave me before?'

'Well, of course it was. It's right on the bottle. At least I think so.' She wrinkled up her eyebrows. 'Golly, I'm not sure, now. Just a minute, love, I'll see.' She got up and went over to the table and picked up the bottle, peering at it for a minute while her jaw dropped down lower and lower, it looked like bad news. 'Oh, lord, Aaron, you're right, it isn't aspirin, at all. It's that stuff you got me for ringworm. Do you remember when I had that touch of ringworm, last fall?'

So I sighed and closed my eyes and folded my arms across my chest, I thought it was Divine Intervention, I really did.

Well, there you go, I thought, you didn't really expect to get away with it, did you? How much did you think He would put up with, anyway? Of course, in a way, He was doing me a favor, I figured. I was getting out of it with a *little* dignity left, at least, I mean she'd never find out what a son-of-a-bitch I was, anyway. It was really the only solution, a pretty damned expensive one of course, but after all you expect to find a pretty heavy price tage on Revelation. I was surprised as hell when I recovered.

"Are you sure you have?" Sylvie said.

"Well, not really," I said. "But I mean I have got a life of my own, of *some* kind, anyway. I work regularly, I have people to take care of. Not the same people, of course, they change every couple of years or so. But if it's really pain you're interested in, I mean more than people, then I guess it doesn't matter too much what their names are."

"It matters to me," Sylvie said. "I'm interested as hell in people's names."

"Well, I am too, of course," I said. "I mean, why the hell do you think I've been telling you all this stuff about Cindy? I'll tell you something, as a matter of fact, I have this damned nightmare about her all the time, that I can't get rid of. Just about every time I lie down on a bed and close my eyes, I see it all over again."

It wasn't really a nightmare, it was all too damned true, and I didn't have to be asleep to see it. It was a replay or something, of what had actually happened the last time I saw her, on the station platform at Waterloo. I was standing behind the black iron gates that shut off the friends and relatives from the departing travelers, putting my hands through the bars to touch her face for the last time although she didn't realize that, of course, although maybe she did, because that little crick had come back into the corner of her mouth, that little touch of irony, the salt on the melon. She was going back home to her parents to wait until I sent for her, she had decided to leave a day before I did because she couldn't stand the thought of being there alone in our room in Stanley Crescent after I had gone, and anyway who knew what the hell would happen to her if I left her alone there in the middle of London? I wanted to get her back home to Stratford before I left, get out with a clear conscience, boy, all accounts settled. She had her cardboard suitcase at her feet and her stack of movie magazines tied up with a piece of twine and a shopping bag full of odd junk, playbills of shows we had seen together and the philodendron from the windowsill, which had developed leaves the color of saffron, and a music box I had given her at Christmas, with a china ballerina on top of it who pirouetted slowly to the tune of *I Believe in Yesterday*, which was what the carrousel used to play on Hampstead Heath. As a matter of fact the damn thing started tinkling at that very moment, it had tipped over in the bag or something, so we stood there holding hands through the bars grinning at each other and listening to those little tinny notes sprinkling out into the hollow booming roar of the station, it was not very damned auspicious. I had a bar of Drostë Dutch chocolate in my pocket that I'd bought for her, it was something she was nutty about, so I took it out and gave it to her and said, 'That's for you to eat on the train. Not all at once, though, or you'll get sick.'

'Oh, golly,' she said. 'Thanks, Aaron. You're too good to me.'

'Listen, nobody could be too good to you,' I said. 'You remember that.'

'You'll write every week, won't you, love?'

'More than that,' I said. 'Twice a week anyway.'

'Well, just once a week will do, you're going to be busy, I know, finding a job and a place to stay and all. But once a week at least, please.'

'O.K.'

'I'm going to work too. There's lots of jobs I can get in Stratford. I mean it's not like London, where you don't know anybody. I know almost everybody there. And living at home, I can save almost everything I make. I'll bet I can save twenty pounds a month.'

'That'll be great. We'll live in a penthouse.'

She reached through the bars and held me tight, pressing herself as close to me as she could, with the bars between us I could just feel the curve of her forehead against my breast like the nuzzle of the new moon, I laid my cheek down on the top of her head, her hair was as cool as nighttime grass, and cupped my hand around the back of her skull, knowing I had the jewel of the world there in my grasp, in my crippled fingers that could not contain it.

The guy at the turnstile yanked his whistle out of his vest pocket and started tooting on it, everybody broke away from the iron gate, there was a sudden outcry of goodbyes and a flutter of hands and handkerchiefs and blown kisses and then they were all galloping away through the clouds of dream-white steam that came billowing out from under the locomotive wheels, running away to the most distant land there is, where they would never die and from which they could never be retrieved. Cindy lifted her head off my breast and raised her face to be kissed and I could see the marks of two bars branded vertically on her forehead like the shadows of masts. After we kissed she whispered something that I couldn't hear, so I said, 'What?' but she shook her head and bent down and gathered up her junk and started plunging off along the platform through the steam. She hadn't got very far, of course, before the handle of her suitcase broke and the Goddamned thing went tumbling down on the concrete with the bottom corners crumpling in a couple more inches like a collapsing accordion, fortunately I had strapped it up with an old belt so it didn't split apart completely although the next time she unbuckled it would probably be the last. She stood there with her hands full of movie magazines and shopping bag handles not knowing what the hell to do and of course everybody was in such a Goddamned hurry to get a seat on the train that they just went galloping on past her bumping into her elbows and adding to her confusion, she'll never make it, I thought, never in this world, that girl was born to miss trains. I felt furious, I felt as though I were in shackles, I never felt such a fury in my life, I hated everything, the train, the bars, the heartless people, myself, the shabby suitcase she was condemned to carry her belongings in, the whole Goddamned show. I started yelling, 'Listen, you sons of bitches, that's a lady out there, why don't you help her? That's a lady in distress out there in front of you, why don't some of you for God's sake lend her a hand? Can't you see I can't help her any more?'

Nobody seemed to pay any particular attention, they were all hurrying home to find out why the plumbing broke or the wife ran away with the milkman, they had problems enough of their own I guess, you couldn't blame them, who the hell can you blame? I thought of crawling under the turnstile and forcing my way past the guard and going to her rescue one more time, but then I lost sight of her in a great cloud of steam as pure as mountain mist that came flooding over the platform tenderly, mercifully, as if to cloak her ignominy or to shelter her or maybe to snatch her away to a better world or at least one where the handles don't break and where you can smile at the timetables, because, anyway, I never saw her again. When the cloud dissolved she was gone as if by magic, either back to glory or back to Stratford, whichever one it was they had me to thank, so I had one mark on the right side of the ledger anyway, even if it was written in lefthanded.

"Did you write to her, after you got back?" Sylvie said.

"For a while. A couple of months, maybe. The funny thing is, *she* stopped writing so much after a while, herself. She didn't even answer my last letter. I guess maybe she was trying to make it easier for me. I guess she knew what was happening."

"I guess so," Sylvie said. "People seem to understand those things. Some people do, anyway."

"I know," I said. "They do, don't they? And you know, sometimes it seems to me that you can explain yourself best just by being absent. Not to everybody, of course, but certain people. The people who care about you most, maybe. You feel almost closer to them than if you were really there."

Sylvie didn't answer me, she was sitting there huddled up on the log, clutching her elbows and leaning forward as if she might possibly throw up.

"Are you O.K.?" I said.

"Not especially," she said. "Come on, let's go. I think I'm going to be sick."

"Well, you better sit here for a while if you're going to be sick," I said. "You don't want to be sick all over the house."

"Oh, don't I, though?" Sylvie said. "That's what you think."

She got up and went stumbling through the woods to the road, hobbling over the twigs and stubble and bumping into tree trunks occasionally, she seemed to be in quite a hurry.

"Hey, take it easy," I said. "You're not in too good a shape."

"I'm in great shape," she said. She tossed her head like a wild horse somebody is trying to slip a halter over, proud and frightened. "And I'm going to stay that way, too. Just look who's talking."

I LEFT JAMED DOWN ON THE BEACH PLAYING WITH HIS DUMP trucks in the sand, he'd forgotten it was his birthday by that time, he was about halfway to China and had a hole there you could have dropped a mule into, I told him not to go off anywhere, I'd be back in just a minute, and then went on back to the shop. Poppa was bent over fishing around in the desk drawer for his Jack Daniel's when I came in, he kicked the drawer closed and stood up with the bottle in his hand and said, "He down there on the beach?"

"Yeah," I said. "He's digging away."

"O.K., let's get this thing up to the house so's he don't see it. It's got to be a big surprise, you know." He took a quick slug of the Jack Daniel's and then chuckled and said, "Aaron, come out here take a look at this thing. Damn if this thing ain't turned out real good."

I was just about chewed up with curiosity to find out what it was, he hadn't ever told me, and nobody in the world had had a look at it but Poppa because ever since he'd started working on it, about six weeks before Jamed's birthday, he'd kept it covered up with tarpaulin in a pen he'd fenced off in one corner of the shop with chicken wire and a couple of stud posts. He'd hung a screen door on the stud posts and kept it locked up with a padlock so Jamed or anybody else couldn't get in there and every night after dinner he'd go down and work on the thing, he'd be hammering away in there till after midnight. I knew damn well it wasn't a boat, he wasn't *about* to make any boat for Jamed, but that didn't tell me what it *was*, and being draped in tarpaulin like that you couldn't tell much about the shape of the thing, all I knew was it got a little bit taller and a little bit wider every day and right now it looked sort of like a dentist's chair, with all those jointed arms for drills and x rays and air hoses and all that junk, with a sheet slung over it.

He stuck the bottle in his hip pocket and went out into the shop and started unlocking the screen door of this cage he'd made for it.

"One thing damn sure," he said. "They ain't nobody else going to have one like it. Momma got the cake ready?"

"Yeah, she made a chocolate marble one," I said. "That's what he likes best."

"How many candles she put on it?"

"Nine."

"Uh huh."

Jamed was fourteen now but ever since he'd got slugged with the winch handle, which was five years ago, Poppa wouldn't let Momma put any more than nine candles on his cake. Of course it didn't make a lot of difference to Jamed, he didn't know how old he was anyway, he probably thought he was still nine years old, but it bothered Momma, you could tell. For a couple of years there she tried to sneak on the right number of candles but Poppa would always count them before she took the cake in to Jamed and if there were too many he'd yank the extra ones out and throw them in the trash. He wouldn't say anything about it, Momma wouldn't either, but she knew damn well she wasn't going to get away with more than nine. After those first couple of tries she gave up but every year when she stuck the candles in the cake you could see her mouth get thin and her nostrils sort of pinch together. It made Sylvie madder than hell, she would sit there just boiling at the table while Jamed puffed up his cheeks to blow the candles out, and all the time he was hollering and yelping about how the fairies were going to make his wish come true she'd double her fists up and stare down at the tablecloth like she was going to explode. Those were great birthday parties, boy.

Poppa got the padlock undone and hooked it over the hasp and then went into the cage and got hold of one edge of the tarpaulin, ready to toss it off.

"Now what you going to see," he said, "is a genuine patented whompfoddler, only one like it in the world." He flung off the tarpaulin and nodded his head solemnly at the contraption underneath. "Aaron, that there is a work of genius, I just want you to appreciate that fact."

It was the only one like it in the world, all right; even if he had been stoned, Rube Goldberg couldn't have dreamed up anything like it, it was this crazy sort of scaffold-work mechanical nightmare like the insides of some gigantic alarm clock, balance arms and blade wheels and big wooden-toothed gears and drop-weight pendulums and God knows what-all, made out of two-by-two's and fiberboard and light-gauge cable and lead weights, it looked like somebody had sent off for a powerboat kit and got the wrong instruction book with it, one for making a hydroelectric station or something.

"Wow," I said. "Hey, that's really something. What is it, Poppa?"

"I done told you what it was," Poppa said. "A whomp-foddler. Only one like it in the world."

"Yeah, but I mean what does it do?"

"Well, now, I'm going to show you what it does," Poppa said. There was a bucket of sand sitting beside it which Poppa picked up and dumped into a metal box on the end of a fulcrum arm up near the top of the thing. "Now just watch this here. This here is purely amazing." The arm tipped down until the sand spilled out of the box onto the blades of a mill wheel that started revolving slowly, engaging a set of wooden gears with the pinion of a revolving axle around which a length of rope was coiled, which unwound slowly, lowering a gimbaled pail into which the sand fell off the mill-wheel blades until the weight of it tipped over the pail and dumped the sand out into a long chute from where it poured past the fins of a turbine that were colored red-white-and-blue and connected to a pulley system that kept raising and lowering a little flag. It finally wound up in a scoop at the bottom that had a sign on it saying: MAGIC POWDER. There was a rack beside the scoop with a row of empty Bull Durham sacks hanging by their drawstrings.

"Judas *Priest,*" I said. "That is some kind of a contraption. Boy, Jamed'll flip over that."

"You reckon he will?" Poppa said. "Much as he loves fooling around with sand, I figured he'd get a kick out of it."

"Wow, will he!" I said. "I'd like to have one of them myself."

"You see, you can take this scoop out," Poppa said, "and fill up these here little sacks. I'm going to tell him this thing makes magic powder out of just plain sand, makes anybody's dreams come true. He can go around selling it to everybody for a nickel a sack or something. He'll get a bang out of that."

"He sure will," I said. "Boy, how did you ever dream that up?"

"Well, I just set down and figured it out on paper," Poppa said. " 'Course, some of it I sort of made up while I was going along." He pulled the bottle out of his pocket and unscrewed the cap, chuckling like a rooster. "I tell you, I had me one hell of a time. I might even wind up in the business. I figure these things'd sell."

"I'll bet you they would," I said. "I'll bet you people would stay home from the movies to work one of those things." I wasn't so sure of that but I thought I'd give him a shot in the arm, he always worried about Jamed having a good time on his birthday, and he'd worked harder than hell on that thing. I just hoped it didn't scare the pants off of Jamed, you couldn't ever tell how he was going to react to things.

"Well, let's get it on up to the house," Poppa said. "What I want to do is set it up in the back yard. Then you go get him and bring him up the front way so's he don't see it. We'll tell him we heard the fairies out there working away on something all night, and why don't we go out and see what it was?"

"O.K.," I said. "Wow, that looks like it's going to take some hauling."

"Oh, it ain't too bad," Poppa said. "It's good and strong,

though, I'll say that. I made it so's he wouldn't tear it up the first time he used it. He don't realize he's getting pretty strong."

"Yeah, it looks like it'll take plenty of wear," I said.

"Oh, yeah. Now you grab her by the top end there and tilt her over slow, and I'll hoist up on the bottom. We'll take her out the boat door." He took another slug of whisky and then capped the bottle and shoved it back in his hip pocket. "O.K., get set now. Heave."

I grabbed the outside frames up near the top and tugged them back until the contraption was rocked back on one of its bottom edges. Poppa bent down and got hold of the uplifted edge and heaved up on it, he wasn't any too spry about it, that thing must have weighed as much as a piano and he had most of the weight.

"O.K., let's go," he said.

I started backing out toward the boat door taking little two-inch steps and moving mighty damn slow because one false step and I'd have had that thing on top of me, I'd have been a bucket of Magic Powder. We hadn't got more than a couple of feet when a car came roaring down the dirt road outside the shop with somebody leaning on the horn like a riverboat whistle, I damn near dropped that thing on my foot.

"Now what in the hell kind of a crazyman is that?" Poppa said. He set down the bottom edge of the whompfoddler and went over and looked out the window but he couldn't see anybody out there, they'd gone roaring right on by the shop toward the pier, he came back shaking his head. "Some crazy Goddamn kid, full of beer, I reckon." He hoisted up his edge of the thing again and we went on hobbling across the floor to the door. We got it outside and down the stone ramp to the grass and then set it down and stood there puffing for a minute, it was going to be a long Goddamned haul up that hill.

"O.K., come on," Poppa said. "We got to get her on up

there." We picked it up again and hauled it across the yard between the boat cradles, it was a little easier going this time because we'd figured out by now that if we hauled it sideways we wouldn't bang our shins on the bottom edges. We got it across the yard to the fence and then set it down again so Poppa could get the gate open. I pulled out my shirttail and bunched it up under the bottom rail so the edges wouldn't cut into my hand so bad, then I got a good grip on the thing and we carried it across the road and started up the hill behind the hotel. We got about halfway up before I gave out and had to set it down for a minute to get my wind back, I was bushed.

"Yeah, get a little breather," Poppa said. "We just about got it licked, now."

I leaned up against the thing and looked back down the hill, I figured I'd better go back and shut the gate, and right then I saw this car that had gone roaring past the shop. It was parked down at the edge of the sand in front of the pier, an old blue 1954 Ford with the front fenders ripped off and orange flames painted along the door panels, I recognized it right away, it belonged to Boone Armitage, this mean bastard who was always riding Sylvie and me, he hated our guts. I never had figured out why unless it was because Sylvie wouldn't give him the time of day but he sure as hell hated us, he never missed a chance to make some dirty crack about Jamed or sometimes the whole family in general, he referred to us as the Linthicum Loonies. I also had to admit that I hated *his* guts, which was pretty unusual because there were very few people that I really hated and most of them I didn't even know. Most of the people I hated were very important public figures like senators or mayors of big cities or especially generals, guys whose chief business was telling other people what to do and who were so Goddamned impressed with the solemnity of it that they couldn't afford to smile or if they did they looked like somebody was twisting their balls to make them, and also guys who read commercials on the T.V., who were just plain crumbs. But I couldn't think of more than two or three people I actually knew that I really hated, I always found that the better you knew somebody the harder it was to hate him, but Boone Armitage was an exception, he was one guy that if you knew him it didn't get in the way of your hating him at all, as a matter of fact it made it a good deal easier, he gave me the creeps. The minute I saw this car of his parked down there by the pier I got a sort of sick, scary feeling like you get when you're walking along the sidewalk and all of a sudden you spot a big gob of gunk that some guy has hacked up and spit on the sidewalk right in everybody's path, grinning most likely while he did it, those guys always grin when they spit on the world.

"Hey, Poppa, you see that car down there?" I said. "That's Boone Armitage's car."

"Who's Boone Armitage?" Poppa said.

"He's this real mean bastard that's always needling Sylvie and me and making dirty cracks about Jamie. Listen, you mind if I go down there on the beach and see if Jamed's O.K.? I won't be but a minute."

"Why wouldn't he be O.K.?" Poppa said. "You mean that bastard's liable to mess with him?"

"Well, you can't tell," I said. "I'd feel a lot better if I went down there and made sure."

"Come on, we'll both go," Poppa said. I was kind of glad he said it because Boone Armitage was six feet tall and weighed about 190 pounds and he usually had a couple of dim-witted pals with him that thought he was King Shit, they spent most of their time roaring around the county in that car throwing beer cans out the window and yelling at women.

We left the whompfoddler sitting under the willow tree out back of the hotel and took off down the hill toward the beach, making mighty good time although we didn't actually break into a run, that would have looked sort of desperate or something, I guess we didn't either one of us want to appear that way. We swung around back of the hotel and then turned left when we hit the sand and started up the beach toward the cliffs. They were up there all right, there were three of them and they were talking to Jamed, squatting in front of him with their arms on their knees, but they didn't look like they were bothering him too much. He was sitting there beside this big mound of sand that he'd dug looking at something he was holding in his hands, a magazine it looked like, because one of the guys reached out and flipped the page over for him, you would have thought they were being real friendly if you didn't know who they were.

"They don't look like they're bothering him," I said.

"Well, I'd just as soon they left him clean alone," Poppa said. We kept on walking through the sand toward them, when we got about fifty yards away one of them spotted us and said something to the others. Boone snatched the magazine out of Jamed's hand and they all three stood up. They stood there watching us while we walked up to them, nobody said anything but Jamed, he looked up and said, "Hi, Poppa. Hi, Aaron."

"Hey, Jamie," Poppa said. "You got a big old castle there."

"I'm going to dig to China," Jamed said. "I guess I'm pretty near there by now, you reckon?"

"Hey, Aaron," Boone said. He stuck the magazine in his hip pocket, he didn't look too comfortable.

"What's that you was reading, Jamie?" Poppa said.

"A book," Jamed said. "It had ladies in it and all."

"Let me see that book, son," Poppa said. He held out his hand toward Boone.

"I don't know where he got it from," Boone said. "I reckon he found it on the beach somewheres, I was trying to get it away from him." He pulled the magazine out of his hip pocket, he was mighty slow about it, and handed it to Poppa.

"That so, Jamie?" Poppa said.

"Uh uh, I didn't find it," Jamed said. "They gave it to me. You reckon I'm almost to China, Poppa?"

"Yeah, pretty near," Poppa said. He opened the magazine and flipped the pages over with his thumb, I didn't get a real good look at it, I was standing a little bit in front of him and I didn't want to appear too curious, but I could see plenty just out of the corner of my eye, they were some of the dirtiest damn pictures I ever saw, women and men, women and women, women and dogs, it was real raw stuff. Poppa rolled up the magazine and stuck it in his hip pocket. Boone and the other guys started edging away a little.

"Aaron, you take Jamie on up to the house," Poppa said. "I'll be up in a little bit. You take him up the front way, now, you know what I mean?"

"O.K.," I said. "Come on, Jamie."

"I got to dig to China," Jamed said.

"Well, you can do that later on," I said. "Right now we got to go to the birthday party."

"Hey, *boy!* I forgot all about that!" Jamed said. "Oh, *boy!* You coming, Poppa?"

"Yeah, I'll be up in just a minute," Poppa said. "You go up and get your hands washed, now, get all ready."

"O.K.," Jamed said. "Come on, Aaron." He got up and started running along the beach toward the pier, he ran like a St. Bernard dog, stopping to look back and yell at me to hurry up every couple of minutes. I caught up with him and took hold of his hand, I didn't want him running back of the hotel and spotting that contraption Poppa had built for him. When we got to the road I looked back and saw Boone and the other two guys backing up against the cliff and Poppa moving toward them very slow, he had on his blue denim jacket and he was buttoning up the buttons for some reason. I tell you, I was scared. When we got up in front of the hotel veranda I said to Jamed, "Wash your hands off under the spring pipe there, Jamie." He said, "O.K.," and stuck his hands under the spring water that was splashing out on the bricks and while he was scrubbing at them I edged over and took a look down the cliff, it was like switching on the T.V. in the middle of a Western. One of Boone's pals was limping up the beach toward the pier, bent over double and hugging his ribs. The other one was crawling along the sand like a dog that has got hit by a car. It looked like Poppa had saved Boone for last because he was still on his feet, backing away till he was almost flat up against the cliff. He reached down real quick and picked up a piece of driftwood that was lying there, a chunk of bleached log as big around as a ball bat. Poppa snatched it out of his hand and broke it in half across his knee and dropped the pieces in the sand. Then he reached out and grabbed Boone by the hair and started shaking his head, I thought he would yank that boy's head clean off of his neck, he jerked him back and forth like he was shaking apples off a tree limb. Boone swung at him a little bit at first, banging away at Poppa's arm and chest with his fists, but after a minute he went sort of soggy and started flopping around like a rag doll, I was scared Poppa would break his neck. I think he must have passed out because his knees went limp and he dropped down from Poppa's hand twitching around like a puppet on a string, it didn't look like there was any life left in him. After a minute Poppa let him drop, he fell face down in the sand and didn't even budge. He was out for sure, you could see that, but Poppa wasn't satisfied, he reared back with his foot and started kicking him in the ass, I could hear it all the way up the cliff, it sounded like somebody whacking a sack of flour with a club. It looked like he'd gone clean crazy, he reached down and picked up a chunk of the driftwood and raised it up like he was going to crack Boone's skull with it, he wanted to kill that boy. I yelled, "Poppa!" and he heard me because he stopped and looked up all of a sudden, twisting his head around till he spotted me up there at the top of the cliff. He roared at me like a bull, "What the hell you doing up there? I told you to take that boy up to the house."

"O.K., I am," I said. "You better come up too, Poppa."

You could see him sort of pulling himself together, he lowered his hand and had a look at the piece of driftwood he was holding in it and then dropped it in the sand, then he took off his baseball cap and looked inside of it like he expected to find a bird's egg in there or something and finally he raised up his head and yelled at the other two guys, both of them were on their feet by now and headed up the beach toward the car, "Come back here and haul this bastard off. I mean quick, too."

Jamed had finished with his hands by now, he came over to the edge of the cliff wiping them on his shirt.

"What's Poppa doing?" he said. "Isn't Poppa coming to the party?"

"Yeah, he's coming," I said. "Come on, let's get up there. I bet you there's ice cream and cake up there." I hustled him on up the path to the house and we went up the front steps to the porch.

Momma said, "Where you-all been? We got something here that's going to melt, don't you know that?"

"We been coming," I said. She had the table all set with her linen cloth and little favors at everybody's place, paper hats and horns and a bowl of candy corn and balloons hanging down from the ceiling and a couple of presents for Jamed wrapped up in blue paper. He ran across the porch to the table and stood there flapping his hands and yelling, "Oh, *boy!* Hey, Aaron, look at all the *stuff!*"

I said to Momma, "Me and Poppa have been bringing up something special from the shop. I've got to go back and help him. We won't be but a minute, if you want to let Jamie open one of his presents."

"Well, you hustle. This stuff is not going to last."

"O.K., we'll be right back."

Sylvie was sitting in the rocker reading a book, she never stopped reading books any more, she didn't seem to have much faith in anything that was going on outside of a book, you got the impression that she had crawled back into a cave and if you wanted to get her attention you had to stand in front of it and yell your Goddamned head off.

"Hey, will you make sure Jamed stays in the house here till we get back?" I said. She didn't even look at me, she just turned a page over and went on reading, twisting a strand of hair around her finger.

"Hey, Sylvie, did you hear me?" I said.

"O.K., O.K. But you better get back here pretty fast. Momma's been waiting for half an hour."

"We'll be right back," I said. I went out of the house and back down the hill toward the beach. Halfway down the path I saw Boone's car pull out and go tearing up the dirt road toward Offutt's, those guys weren't doing any hollering this time. A couple of minutes later Poppa came around the corner of the hotel veranda and up the hill toward me, he looked cold, his face was white and his nose was as blue as a plum, he kept chafing his arms like it was December, not an eighty-five-degree day in the middle of June. He waved for me to come around back of the hotel so I did, I waited for him under the willow tree by the whompfoddler. When he got up close I could see that one of them must have landed a pretty good whack on him because there was a lump at the corner of his eye that was getting about the same color as his nose.

"You O.K., Poppa?" I said.

"Yeah. Why the hell wouldn't I be? Them little piss-ants."

"Jamie's O.K.," I said. "They didn't hurt him any." Poppa

stood there staring, rubbing his arms. "He didn't even know what the hell it was all about," I said. "He won't remember anything about it by tomorrow."

"Yeah, that's right," Poppa said. "Let's get this thing up there now."

We leaned down and got hold of the bottom rail and heaved it up waist high and carried it on up the hill. Up by the pigeon loft Poppa told me to set it down, there was a big pile of beach sand there that he'd hauled up for Jamed to play in. He got a bucket out of the tool shed and filled it up with sand, then he fished a note out of his shirt pocket that he must have written out down at the office and stuck it on the whompfoddler with a thumb tack, it said: *Built by fairies for Jamed Linthicum. Happy Birthday to a good little boy.*

"O.K., let's go on in," he said. "We best go in the front door so's he won't think we seen it." He didn't sound happy about it any more, he just sounded worn out.

"Boy, he's going to be crazy about it, Poppa," I said.

"Yeah, well, let's go on in."

We went around to the front porch and up the steps into the house. Jamed had unwrapped one of his presents, it was a dump truck with rubber tires, he had it loaded up with corn candy and was pushing it around on the table going, "Rroom, rroom, rroom."

"Hey, Aaron, look what I got!" he yelled.

"Hey, wow, a dump truck," I said. "Boy, that's great, Jamie."

"You can work it with a crank," he said. "Watch how it does." He turned the crank and tilted up the truck bed, spilling corn candy on the tablecloth.

"That's a real fine truck," Poppa said. "You be able to haul a lot of sand in that."

"I know it," Jamed said. "I'm going to haul a whole *lot* of sand."

"What's the matter with your eye?" Momma said.

"Me and Aaron had some trouble with some work we was doing," Poppa said. "It ain't nothing." He went out into the kitchen.

"Well now, everybody sit down at the table," Momma said. "It's wishing time." She got Jamed into a chair and tied his napkin around his neck, he had a lot of trouble with ice cream. Sylvie and I sat down and put our paper hats on, Sylvie pulled hers down to her nose and stuck her tongue out, Jamed thought that was great, he started laughing and kicking at his chair legs.

"Come on now, Poppa," Momma said. "We're waiting."

"O.K.," Poppa said, he was out in the kitchen checking on those candles, I figured, and maybe having a little refreshment too because when he came out I saw him slipping that Jack Daniel's bottle back in his hip pocket. He picked his paper hat up from the table and put it on, it was a tall one with a silver crescent moon on it, with his beard and bushy eyebrows he looked like a magician in a fairy story, he came around behind Jamed's chair and tied a napkin around Jamed's eyes to blindfold him, he did that every year, it was a ritual we had. As soon as he got it on Momma slipped out into the kitchen, then Poppa said, "Now then, the birthday boy has got to make a wish. Let's see does it come true." Jamed giggled and kicked at his chair legs, he was so excited he couldn't sit still.

"I wished it was a cake, right there in front of me," he said. "With little bells on it, and candles a-burning."

"Well, that's a pretty fancy wish," Poppa said. "I don't know about that."

Momma was coming back out of the kitchen by this time carrying the cake on a tin tray, there were nine candles burning in the pink frosting and a row of little silver bells she put on it every year, Jamed loved those bells, he'd have had a fit if they weren't on it. She set the cake down on the table in front of him and Poppa said, "O.K., now: Wagic

Pedagic, here come the magic!" He whisked the napkin off Jamed's eyes and when he saw that pink cake sitting right there in front of him with the candle flames shining in the silver bells Jamed let out a squeal that just about split your skull, he pounded on the table with his hands and yelled, "Hey, it come true! I known it would! Hey look, Poppa, I got my wish!"

"By golly if you didn't!" Poppa said. "You must be the champeen wisher in the world. That is some kind of a cake. Now let's see can you blow out all them candles to once. You might get another wish if you do."

"I bet I can!" Jamed yelled. He puffed up his cheeks and leaned over the table and blew like a tornado, there wasn't anything the matter with his *lungs* anyway, the wax went all over the place and a couple of the candles tilted over like fence posts in the wind and then all nine of them sent up threads of dark smoke like little chimneys and Jamed started plucking them out, kicking on his chair legs and hollering, "Hey, I done it! I get my other wish, Poppa!"

He had to cut the cake then, Poppa held his hand and helped him push the knife through, then Momma served the pieces onto plates and brought out the ice cream which was getting pretty soupy by this time, but Jamed didn't care, he always mashed it up with his spoon anyway. We got down to eating and after a minute Jamed said, "You didn't say the part about the cooking, Poppa." He had the whole damn party memorized, it went the same way every year, word for word, he got all worked up if anything was left out.

"Yeah, I know," Poppa said. "I ain't got to that yet. Just give me a minute." He picked up another piece of cake with his fork and chewed on it for a minute with a faraway look, blinking his eyes like he was doing some important thinking, then he nodded and smacked his lips and said, "By golly, I think that is the best piece of cake I ever did taste. What we ought to do is leave a note and ask that fairy if he wouldn't like to come and cook for us regular, then we could have a cake every day."

"That's right!" Jamed yelled. "That's the real funny part." He laughed and pounded on the table with the handle of his spoon. Sylvie stared into her plate eating little nibbles off the tip of her fork, you could see she wished she was a hundred miles away, she hated that house. I didn't know how Momma felt, she had her party smile on for Jamed and you couldn't tell what was going on by her eyes, Momma's eyes had sort of dusted over, years ago, like a dirty window in an old house, you can't tell whether anybody lives there any more or whether they do and just don't want people to see inside, or what's going on. Those first couple of parties after Jamed got hurt she used to cry, when she brought the cake out from the kitchen her eyes would be all red and puffy-looking, but she didn't cry any more, she just put that party smile on and went through the whole rigmarole, every year, the way Poppa and Jamed wanted. My God, I hated those parties, everybody did but Poppa and Jamed, they had a great time.

Poppa finished his ice cream and cake and wiped his mouth off with his napkin. "Well, thank the Lord for that little bit," he said. "Many a man had made a meal off of that." He fished his pipe and tobacco out of his shirt pocket and started filling the bowl up. "You know, last night I heard something funny going on out there in the back yard. All sorts of hammering and stuff. Anybody else hear it?"

"I didn't hear nothing," Jamed said.

"I did," I said. "It woke me up a couple of times."

"Is that a fact?" Poppa said. "I didn't know whether I dreamed it or not. Maybe we ought to go out there and see what it was."

"I believe I did, too," Momma said. "Maybe we all ought to go out there."

"I want to play with my truck," Jamed said.

"Well, you can play with that later," Poppa said. "Let's go out there right now and see what all that racket was about."

We all got up from the table and followed Poppa out through the kitchen and the screen door to the back stoop. When Jamed saw that whompfoddler thing sitting out there by the pigeon loft I thought he'd have fits, he started screaming and jumping up and down and tugging at it and wanting to know what it was.

"*I* don't know," Poppa said. "It looks like it's got a note of some kind on it, there. Aaron, see what it says there, will you?" So I read the note and Jamed went wild, he figured this was the biggest day in the history of the world, we couldn't get him away from that thing. Poppa and I pretended to figure out how it worked, we let Jamed dump the sand in, and when he saw all those gears and levers and turbines start to crank and wobble and spin he was in pure heaven. He had to fill up sacks with Magic Powder for everybody and hand them around and then load up his dump truck with a batch of it, he turned out three or four buckets of that stuff and started sprinkling it all over the grass and the flower beds and the apple trees, we were in for a long spell of magic around there. You could see Poppa was pleased it went over so well, it gave him a real shot in the arm, his face was getting to be the right color again and he chuckled some, just moderate though, he didn't do any real belly-laughing like he usually did, it was different from Jamed's other parties. After a while he ruffled up Jamed's hair and said, "Well, boy, I'm going to leave you to her, I reckon you got that thing figured out pretty good," and then he went down the hill to the shop, he was going to work on that bottle for a while, I could tell. Momma and Sylvie went in to clean up the dishes and I sat out there and played with Jamed for a while. It was getting to be evening, the whompfoddler was creaking away and the doves were making bubbling sounds like boiling silver in the loft and every now and then an apple would fall from one of the trees at the edge of the orchard with a sound like a footfall in the grass. Jamed would raise his head and listen.

"Maybe it's that fairy creeping around to see whether you liked your present," I said.

"No it ain't," Jamed said. He started filling up another sack with Magic Powder. "I'm going to make a whole big batch of this stuff," he said. "I'm going to sprinkle it all over the whole world."

"Well, you got a good start on it already," I said.

"I'm going to do the whole world," he said. "I'm going to sprinkle it in the bay, too, and all the drowned people will wake up."

I left him out there after a while and went in to tell Sylvie I was leaving so she'd keep her eye on him, I wanted to go down to the shop and check on Poppa, I figured if somebody was down there talking to him he might not hit that bottle quite so hard. They'd finished with the dishes and Sylvie was sitting in the glider on the front porch with her book. I read the title on the cover, *An Introduction to Psychology*, by Baker and Whitcomb, she loved that psychology stuff although she seemed to regard it largely as crap because every now and then she would give a sort of sardonic cackle while she was reading and take the pen from back of her ear and make a couple of very sarcastic-looking exclamation marks in the margin, she read books faster and with less reverence than anybody I ever saw, sometimes she would hoot right out loud and fling the thing across the room, most of her books were in pretty bad shape. She'd already read about ten of them that summer although she'd been working up at Blood's in Marlboro ever since she came home in the spring so she could save up money to pay for her apartment when she went back to College Park in the fall, they weren't about to get that girl into a dormitory. She never had forgiven me for not moving in with her and it didn't look like she was going to because her attitude toward me had become something like a princess's toward some scroungy character who's just spilled soup all over her at a banquet.

"Hey, Sylvie, will you keep your eye on Jamed?" I said. "I'm going to go down and talk to Poppa for a while."

"Where is he?" she said.

"He's out back playing with his machine."

"What's the matter with Poppa?" She looked up at me from the book.

"I don't know. Why?"

"Don't act dumb."

"I'm not acting dumb." She dropped her eyes back to the page and started reading again. "Well, I'll see you after a while," I said, I went over to the screen door.

"Hey, wait a minute, I want to ask you something." She was still reading, twiddling her hair around her finger.

"Yeah, what?"

"Ron's coming down this weekend and taking me over to Annapolis for dinner and dancing. You want to double date with us?"

"You mean you're dating that *faculty* guy?" I said. "In the summer, even? Boy, you better watch it, Sylvie. You can get in trouble doing that."

"What trouble?" she said. "You mean you think that never happened before? What kind of a nerd are you?"

"Well, for God's sake, he's old enough to be your father, anyway," I said. "Dating a *freshman*. What's the matter with that guy?"

"There's a whole lot the matter with him," she said. "But it's not his *age*. He's only twenty-seven, for God's sake, and I'm nineteen. What's the matter with that?"

"I thought you weren't going to go out with any guys, *ever*," I said. "Oh boy, you and all your big talk. You're a real phony, Sylvie, you know that?" It was a pretty dangerous thing to say to Sylvie, any time you started calling her a phony you'd better be ready to duck because you were liable to get a pie in your face, nobody knew that better than I did, I guess I must have been pretty worked up. She let it pass though, as a matter of fact she even gave a little grin, just the shadow of one, and then gave her hair a couple more twiddles and said, "Well, are you going to go with us or not?"

"What do you think I am, crazy?" I said. "Me out on a double date with a Goddamned English professor. What do you think I'd say to the guy, anyway?"

"Just whatever's on your mind," she said. "He's a real cool guy. *We* never have any trouble communicating."

"Yeah, well you go ahead and communicate with him all you want," I said. "You're going to get yourself *ex*communicated, right out of that school, if you're not careful."

"What's the matter?" she said. "You afraid you can't get a date?"

"What do you mean, can't get a date? I can get all the dates I want. I just happen to be dating Becky Stirnweiss, that's all."

"Becky *Stirn*weiss," Sylvie said. "Oh, wow. The Elizabeth Barrett of Prince George's County. What do you do, sit there and count each other's eyelashes all night or something?"

"That's pretty funny," I said. "You're a real riot, Sylvie. You ought to be on the stage."

"Yeah, well, so should *you*," she said, hard as a fist all of a sudden. She snapped the book shut and stuck out her chin at me. "Studying all that bookkeeping crap to keep Poppa happy because you haven't got guts enough to find out who you are. You know what's happening to you, Aaron? You want to know why you don't date anybody but that Stirnweiss creep? I'll tell you sometime, if you think you can take it."

I didn't especially want to hear it, I felt sort of sick, the whole Goddamned day was turning out to be a mess as far as I was concerned, I wanted to get out of there. I let the screen door bang behind me and started down the hill toward the shop staring down at the toes of my shoes, it seemed like my line of vision had been getting lower by inches ever since I got out of bed that morning, I figured that by nightfall my head would be lodged right down between my legs. Jamed's birthdays had a tendency to raise hell with your posture anyway and this was the grandaddy of them all. When I got down to the catalpa tree I stopped for a minute and leaned up against it and raised my head up finally to look out at the bay.

It was a pure miracle out there. There must have been a hundred boats on that rose-colored sunset water, strung out a half mile offshore as far as you could see, from way north of the Calvert Cliffs southward as far as Solomons, all of them steep-heeled, beating to windward, their bows nestled in a swatch of snowy foam, their Genoas blown full like the breasts of swans, silent as white shadows, sweeping southward over the evening sea. It was a big race of some kind, the Annapolis-to-Newport I figured, being that time of year, and because they were all S.O.R.C. class, ocean-going vessels of thirty-two feet or better. I don't think I ever saw anything as beautiful. I stood there and watched them and damned if my eyes didn't get wet and my heart start fluttering and the first thing I knew I was smiling like a fool. Oh Jesus, I thought, men do *beautiful* things too, you just can't say they don't, I don't know how and I sure as hell don't know why, but just look out there, will you? And best of all, not a sound, they're so quiet about it when they do it, not one Goddamned advertisement anywhere. I must have stood there for ten minutes, I didn't ever want to go away, I didn't ever want that sight to end. I watched the sea get darker, the sunset side of the waves turned from rose to scarlet and their night sides were polished purple like wet grapes and the big Genoa sails were tinted with the sunset now, rouged softly like the breasts of mourning doves, and the thin-throated hulls thrust over the black and scarlet water like wild geese, all bathed in clouds of wine-stained foam, I was ready to start singing any minute. Especially when right smack in the middle of the whole fleet, like the prize painting in an exhibition, I spotted one of Poppa's boats, *The Queen of Sheba,* a long slim black-hulled forty-footer that he'd built for a guy named Nunnally up at Gibson's Island. I recognized her in a second, she couldn't have been anybody's handiwork but Poppa's, those raked masts and the Clipper bow with the long steeved bowsprit and the dolphin-striker and a length of Martingale chain shearing the purple water as she rose and fell. I felt my heart swell up like a pigeon's breast, I got cool and quiet inside all in a second with a quietness I thought would surely last me forever no matter what the hell ever happened, I knew that was my father out there on the water, I'd never seen him so clear before.

When I got down to the shop I could tell it was empty, I didn't even have to look inside, it just *felt* empty, so I turned away and started walking up the beach, I felt like I could use a long walk all by myself, I sort of wanted to soak in that feeling I had inside of me, that quietness, the way you want to soak yourself in good music sometimes, or sunshine on a spring day. I passed the pile of sand Jamed had dug up that afternoon and even *that* didn't bother me, I just reached down and picked up a tin shovel he'd left there and stuck it in my pocket, I figured some kid or other would run off with it if I didn't and he'd be all up tight about it. I got up to where the dead tree was stuck in the sand and when I climbed over the top of it I could see Poppa up the beach a ways sitting on a big chunk of mud-rock that had tumbled down from a cliff side. He was looking through a pair of binoculars out at the bay, watching the racing fleet go by. I walked up to where he was, when he heard my feet in the sand he turned his head and said, "Hey, Aaron."

"Hi, Poppa." I went over to the boulder and leaned up

against it beside him. "What is it? The Annapolis-to-Newport?"

"Yeah. That's one of my hulls out there, *Sheba.*"

"I know," I said. "I saw her, up top."

"You did, sure enough?" He lowered the binoculars and grinned at me. "Well, looks like you're getting an eye for a boat. You want to look?"

"No, not especially," I said. "I already saw them."

He raised the glasses again and watched for a minute.

"She's bearing down," he said. "That boat'll go to windward like nothing in this world. That guy don't know how to sail her, though. I wish to hell I was out there."

"You ever win that race, Poppa?" I said.

"You mean one of my hulls? Oh, yeah. Two of them, forty-six and fifty-two. *Skyfire* and *Harmony*. *Harmony*'s called *Witch Hazel* now, they sold her to some guy up at Marblehead." He put the glasses down and picked up the bottle which was sitting on the boulder beside him, there weren't more than a couple of good shots left in it. He tossed back one of them and held the bottle out toward me.

"No, thanks," I said. "I don't like that hard stuff."

"No? What are you, beer drinkers, up there at Maryland? I thought you boys raised all kinds of hell up there."

"Well, some of them do," I said. "I get along fine with just wine or beer."

"That a fact?" Poppa said, he was grinning. "Well, some people is born one drink ahead of the rest of the world, I heard. I reckon that's you, huh?" He sounded a lot better than he had up at the house, I guess the sight of those boats had perked him up. "Red wine, huh?" he said. "That what you drink, Aaron?"

"Yeah," I said. "I figure it's all I need."

"Really get your pecker up when you get lit on that stuff, what I heard. Is that right?"

"Well, I don't know," I said. "If it's the right girl, I guess."

"Yeah? Well, any one that's hot and hollow is the right one, when a fellow's your age, ain't that so?" He smacked me on the shoulder with his fist, I thought it would break my back. "How you getting along up there, anyhow, Aaron? We ain't had a real good talk about it." We hadn't had a real good talk about it because I'd managed to avoid it ever since I'd been home, I wasn't getting along any too well up there and I wasn't particularly anxious to talk about it. Poppa was putting up a lot of money for my education and I didn't want him to get the impression that it was going down the drain. Of course he didn't have to pay tuition for me because I was a state resident but he still had to come up with my dormitory and dining hall fees and my textbooks and clothes and all the rest of it which must have come to a couple of thousand dollars a year anyway, it wasn't anything to sneeze at. And on top of that of course Sylvie was up there too now, even though she paid most of her apartment rent it was still a lot of extra expense for Poppa, he had his hands full, that was for damned sure, I didn't want to give him any more trouble than he needed. I didn't know whether I was going to be any good to him in the business or not, and there were plenty of times when it seemed like the worst mistake I could possibly make in my life would be even to try, but this wasn't one of them, not with all those boats strung out there across that water in front of me. After the kind of day I'd had, it seemed to me that just to have driven one nail into one of those hulls would make a man's life worth living, would give him something to be proud of, in this kind of a world. I figured I'd better just keep my mouth shut and try a little harder.

"Oh, I'm getting along pretty good, I guess," I said. "I'm not too hot at math, but I guess I'll catch on to it after a while."

"Oh, yeah, you'll catch on to it, you ain't got going good yet. You'll know a hell of a lot more about it than I did when

I started, that's for damn sure. If I'd of knowed something about bookkeeping I figure I'd be a millionaire by this time."

"Well, I'm not going to be any millionaire," I said. "I couldn't even *count* to a million. I just want to be able to do a job of work of some kind."

"That's right," Poppa said. "Now that is right." He looked at me and smiled in a way he had of smiling when he approved completely of something you had done or said, an almost mystified smile of unexpected pleasure and secret joy, it didn't happen very damned often, it had happened maybe five or six times in my whole life, but when it did you felt so contented you didn't care if you never got to heaven, things were good enough right here on earth, you felt like a bird in a nest with its belly full and its flesh warm, dozing in the sunlight, for a little while you couldn't even imagine what it was like to be hungry or scared. You could live on one of those smiles for ten years, I thought, where am I ever going to get that from if I leave this place?

Poppa picked up the bottle again and finished it off, there wasn't more than one good swallow in there, then he held it out in his hand studying it for a minute and said, "Yeah, I tell you, Aaron, money is like tail. Or chow, either one. You can't do a damn thing if you ain't getting it regular, but that ain't a man's *business*, for God's sake." He tilted his head back and raised up the bottle again, jiggling and shaking it till the last drop had trickled down through the neck into his open mouth, then he lowered it down and smacked his lips and winked at me. "The closer to the bone, the sweeter the meat," he said. "I don't reckon you'd feel like running back to the shop and getting some reinforcements for your poor old daddy? I kindly want to keep my eye on this *Sheba* here for a minute."

"O.K.," I said. "Where is it?"

"Oh, it's down there in that bottom drawer. That'd be real good, Aaron, then we can have us a real good talk."

"All right," I said. "Will you give me the key, Poppa? I don't have the key."

"Oh, yeah." He reached into his pocket and dug out his key ring, he kept all his keys on an iron ring shaped like a Jew's-harp with a black shark's tooth charm on it the size of an arrowhead. He held out the ring to me and then drew his hand back and unfastened it and took off the shop key and put it in my hand. It was a big old-fashioned iron skeleton key, three inches long, it looked like the key to a castle or something. "I tell you what," he said. "You take that key and keep it. I got another one. You ought to have your own key to that place by now."

"Well, I don't know about keeping it," I said. "This was Granpa's own key, wasn't it? I wouldn't want to lose it."

"Oh, you ain't going to lose it."

"Well, I could get one cut down there at the dime store, it wouldn't make any difference if I lost that."

"Yeah, I reckon you could." After a minute I decided that was all he was going to say because he raised the binoculars again and looked back out at the boats, it seemed to me every question I ever tried to ask him ended that way.

I took the key and walked down the beach to the shop and unlocked the door and went into the office. It was quiet and warm in there, full of a kind of captured twilight, a kind of bottled twilight, like a rare old bonded bourbon, everything in that shop seemed to be soaked in it. I opened the bottom drawer and looked around for the bottle but I didn't see it right away, he had it hidden, laid down flat under a bunch of papers, he bought all his whisky in half pints so he could stick it in his hip pocket or under a newspaper or a mattress, it was better adapted to emergencies that way. I had to rustle around with my fingers before I found it, I flipped a bunch of papers over and one of them fell open right in front of my eyes, I saw the words *importance to your child cannot be overestimated*, now what in the hell would that be about? I wondered. I looked down at the bottom of the page and saw it was signed by a doctor, Sherrold M. Patterson, M.D., he was a guy Poppa had built a boat for a couple of years back. I lifted the letter out of the drawer and read it right through, it said:

Dear Mr. Linthicum:

We took the *Princess Pat* out from Fisher's Island on her shakedown last weekend, and she exceeded our fondest expectations. I took your advice about the 180% Genoa and found she worked much better in light airs than I had dreamed possible, especially to windward. You have designed and built me a beautiful boat, and I'll never be able to thank you sufficiently for the pride and delight I take in her.

Mr. Linthicum, I've taken the liberty of communicating personally with Dr. Massey about the possibility of placing Jamed in Hilltop House, and he assures me that he will make room for your son if you should decide to send him there. As I've pointed out to you in our conversations, it's the very finest institution for retarded children in America, and probably the world. I do urge you to reconsider your decision; I know it would mean a considerable financial sacrifice, but one which I'm sure you would never regret and whose importance to your child cannot be overestimated. Even if Dr. Massey decided the operation I spoke of would not be advisable, I feel certain—just from my brief examination of Jamed—that the course of therapy and reorientation training would be invaluable to him. Of course there's a long waiting list for admission to Hilltop, so this opportunity of his immediate acceptance for treatment is one you ought to give your full consideration. Please let me know your final thoughts on the matter and I'll convey them to Dr. Massey so that he can arrange the details of Jamed's examination and admission. If you decide to place him there, I think this should be done immediately.

Best regards to your family, and again, my eternal thanks for the inspired job you did on the *Princess Pat*.

Cordially,
Sherrold M. Patterson

I looked up at the top of the page and saw it was dated July 23, 1960, which was two years ago.

Oh boy, I thought. Oh boy, oh boy. What in the hell are you going to do about a man like that? I really felt sick, I felt like I'd opened the wrong door in somebody's house and seen something I wouldn't be able to forget for the rest of my life. I wish to hell I'd never come back here this summer, I thought. I wish to hell I'd got hit by a truck or something up there in College Park and never had to find out about this. I don't want to *know* about this kind of stuff, I don't give a damn whether it happens or not, I just don't want to *know* about it.

Here I was not fifteen minutes ago thinking about what a big sacrifice he'd made sending me off to college and now I come to find out that that money I was spending would have gone toward making Jamed well. Or maybe not well, but better, anyway. Or that money and some more, maybe. Maybe a lot more, but what the hell did that matter? What did it matter if he spent every last penny he had to his name to make Jamed better? I wouldn't have believed any man in the world could be that tightfisted, or mean. Maybe he figured he'd lose his business, I thought, that Goddamned precious Linthicum business that he just now gave me the key to. We'd all have been a Goddamned sight better off in this family if he'd never owned that business, if he'd never learned how to make a boat. Maybe the rest of the world wouldn't have been, I don't know about that, but *we* sure as hell would have. I'd rather he'd picked beans all his life, or shucked oysters in some Goddamned lunchroom, maybe we'd have had some peace around here then, maybe we could look each other in the eye up in that house. I tell you I didn't know what to do, I sat down in that swivel chair with that letter in my hand and started crying, I don't know for how long but it must have been a good while, a quarter of an hour anyway, because after a while I noticed that that whisky-colored light was fading, things didn't glow in it any more, there was no more direct light coming through the office windows or the big louvers up in the gable ends, it was getting shadowy in the shop and the furniture was starting to tick as it cooled in the shadows. The fading of the light got me to thinking about the whisky so I reached in the drawer and pulled out the bottle and held it up to my eyes and looked through it, it was like looking through a pair of amber-colored sunglasses, the golden tint was restored to things sort of magically, a kind of artificial light fell all over everything.

I thought, well I've been using blood money to buy my beer with all semester, I might as well have a shot of this stuff, a hair of the dog. I broke the seal and twisted the cap off and poured a slug into my mouth, it was good, I'll say that, although I hadn't tasted whisky since the day Poppa had forced me to drink with him and I had got sicker than a dog, all of a sudden I discovered that I liked the stuff, it was like liquid gold, my tastes must have been changing, I thought, I'm developing a taste for blood here all of a sudden, and no Goddamned wonder. I had another slug and then set the bottle on the desk and stared at it, feeling the juice start to ooze in my cheeks.

Money is like tail, I thought, oh yeah, boy. Tail and whisky too, huh? Well, I guess you like your tail and your whisky better than you do Jamed. You make such a big Goddamned show about beating up a bunch of punks because of what they did to him but what do you do when it comes to the showdown, when it comes down to hard cash, when it comes down to losing your Goddamned shop maybe? If that's all you care about Jamed, what do you care about any of the rest of us, what do you care about me? I guess Sylvie's had your number all along, I guess she knew where she stood with you and she was dead right about it, she wasn't taking any crap, but I was too Goddamned dumb to know, or to admit it anyway, well I've got it figured out now, I'm just a little slow, it just took me twenty years.

I had another shot of the Jack Daniel's and by that time I was pretty well stoned, I had the feeling I was sitting in a tub full of warm water in the middle of a kind of mild tornado, I felt saturated and relaxed from the neck down and everything was spinning slowly around my head like a lot of wrist watches and cufflinks and stuff on one of those revolving exhibition trays in a jewelry store window. I watched the bookcase sail by a couple of times and the big framed photograph of the *Winifred Bascomb* on the wall and the third time it came around I thought, O.K., I'll buy that, how much are you asking for that, old man, how much are you asking for any of this stuff? More than I can afford, I guess, it cost us our house already, it cost us Jamed's good sense and the way Sylvie used to laugh and the way Momma used to hum in the kitchen, we've put down a pretty good down payment and we still haven't got it away from you, this stuff is too Goddamned expensive. I had a couple more drinks and then I yanked one of the meerschaums out of his pipe rack on the desk and stuck it in my mouth, there was a little charred tobacco left in the bowl so I lit it up, I thought, well I might as well try some of this stuff too, there's no telling how many of his tastes I've acquired by this time. I got the thing going and then put my feet up on the desk, it took me quite awhile to locate it, and then tilted myself back in the chair and sat there puffing away, a chip off the old block, boy. Right about then I heard the office door open and I looked around and saw Poppa standing there with his hand on the knob, he looked pretty damn surprised, he had a right to. I was sitting there in this big purple cloud of smoke with the bottle in my hand, half empty, and this goofy grin on my face, I was primed, boy. I took the pipe out of my mouth and said, "Come on in, we're open for business."

He gave a big froggy chuckle and said, "Boy, you are *in* business. You got it made, how it looks from here." He came across to the desk and set down his binoculars and when he did he caught sight of the letter that was lying there open in front of me, he never batted an eye.

"I tell you what, Aaron," he said. "I'm going to have a little shot of that stuff too, before you clean me out."

I set the bottle down on the desk, I didn't hand it to him, he picked it up and cocked his eye at it and said, "Judas *Priest*," then he knocked back a healthy slug and blew out a long whistling breath like a mule sigh and held out the bottle toward me.

"No, thanks, Poppa," I said.

"What's the matter, you had enough?"

"I guess so." I took my feet down off the desk and started to get up but then I sat down again fast, it was going to take some pretty careful engineering. Poppa sat down on the edge of the desk with the bottle in his lap and stuck his thumb in the top of it and popped it out a couple of times, it made a thonking sound like a cork.

"You mean you ain't drinking with *me*, is that it?" he said.

"I guess I had enough, Poppa." I didn't dare look at him, I didn't want to talk to him, I wished I was anywhere else in the world, if I'd thought I could have made it out of there without falling down I'd have made my break, but the last thing I wanted in the world was to fall on my face and need him to help me get up, I didn't want him hauling me up that hill or holding my head if I got sick, I didn't want to have to depend on him for anything, ever again in the world.

"I want to tell you something about that place he wanted to send Jamie to," he said. "That place was way up in Pennsylvania."

"You don't need to tell me about it, Poppa."

"Yeah, I do. I asked around about that place. I done a lot of inquiring. That place wasn't all that good, what I heard."

I didn't say anything, I took a deep breath and tried to get myself together, I was going to make a break for that door.

"The way I figured, Jamie was a whole lot better off right here at home. Right here with his family, where he known folks give a damn about him. You send a little kid off to one of them places, he gets scared and lonely, you know that."

"Well, maybe he wouldn't have been a little kid forever," I said. "Maybe he would have got better, Poppa."

He popped his thumb out of the bottle top a couple of times and shook his head. "Jamie ain't going to get no better," he said. "Aw, they might teach him to seal envelopes or shine his own shoes or something, but what the hell good is that going to do him? I reckon he's better off building sand castles. That's what he always did want to do most."

"Yeah, why do you reckon that was, Poppa?" I said. I felt my face go all to pieces and all of a sudden I had to drop my head and start crying, I bawled like a baby, I had about twenty years' worth to get out. He sat there watching me for a minute, then he leaned toward me as if he was going to put his hand on my head or maybe lay his arm across my shoulders or something, I couldn't stand it, I felt ashamed and sick, I felt like I was falling into a sort of warm pink hole, the next thing I knew I'd be lying on my back gurgling and sucking at my thumb, I might spend the rest of my life doing that, like Jamed. I pulled myself together and heaved myself up out of the chair like a bull coming out of a barn door, the chair went over backward and I banged into the desk and sort of bounced off it and went staggering across the floor to the door and slammed up against the sill. It took me quite awhile to get the door open, I couldn't find the God-damned knob, when I finally did I turned around to face Poppa and said, "Poppa, I'm not going to go back to school. I'm going to sign up for the army and get my hitch done, then when I get out I'll have some G.I. Bill time, and I can go to school on that. I won't have to take any more money off of you."

He sat there on the edge of the desk fiddling with his

beard, I waited for a minute, I wanted him to say something, I don't know what, I thought he might have some final piece of magic he'd pull on me, something that would clean up all the mess around us and make me all of a sudden start smiling, like the stories he used to tell us when we were sitting up in the apple tree.

"You go on, then," he said. "I got work to do."

I went out the door and down those steps like a runaway coal car that has jumped the tracks, those steps came flying up at me like railroad ties, I damn near broke my neck but I kept going somehow, bumping across the yard and through the gate and halfway up the hill before I'd lost my momentum and slowed down a little bit. I'd got out there in the pea field back of the hotel somehow, it had gone wild since the picking and my pants were wet up to the knees with dew from the wild vines, it was near dark, I stood there and looked around. Out across the black water the sky was all splashed with rose-copper and blood colors like rotten-ripe persimmons and there were black masts burned across it and a duck blind way out on the tidal flats, lonesome as a country church, with its roof afire. I don't know why the hell they keep that show going all the time, I thought, it never quits, sunsets, sunrises, thunder and lightning, hailstorms, rainbows, the works, boy, who needs it? How about half as much fireworks and just a good night's sleep once in a while? They're running away with themselves out there, they're putting it on a little too heavy for my money, who gives a damn about all that jazz if he can't get to sleep at night? Some day they're going to figure out there's nobody in the audience any more, you're putting yourself out of work, boy.

I heard Sylvie yelling, she'd come down to the corner of the hotel veranda and was yelling down the hill, "Poppa! Aaron! Momma says to come on, now, dinner's ready."

Well, I better go on back, I thought. Momma's up there with her skillets and her gravy ladles and grease blisters on the backs of her hands and those haunted-house windows for eyes, worrying about the pork chops getting cold, there'll be a sight of pork chops go cold and hearts too before he gets his dream boat set out there against that sunset, I'd rather Jamed could tie his own shoes, Good God Almighty, my little brother drowned in your luxuries, I say that's enough.

I THOUGHT SYLVIE WAS HEADED FOR THE HOUSE BUT WHEN SHE got down to the end of the road she seemed to change her mind, she stood there staring across at the dark shop for a minute and then out at the bay, she lifted her head and sniffed at the salt air and then started climbing through the poles of the fence, she wasn't any too nimble about it, her coordination was pretty well shot by now.

"Hey, what are you doing?" I said. "I thought you wanted to go back to the house."

"Come on," she said. "I want to see what that water feels like, one more time."

"You better get some sack time," I said. "If you're going down to Solomons with me in the morning you're going to have to get up pretty early."

"Come on, Aaron, let's wade a little. I want to get my feet wet."

She managed to get herself between the poles, squeezing and wriggling like a lizard, she was pretty rusty but you could see there was still an indestructible technique at work there, that girl had been through many a fence in her time. I climbed through after her, I wasn't much better at it than she was, having the makings of a pretty substantial bay window under my belt, and followed her down across the sand to where the water ran up lipping at the polished flat sand.

It was full of dark sparkling, as if there were jewels under there, agates and eyeballs, rolling and burnishing forever. She clutched the hem of her skirt and stepped out to her ankles in the dark water, making a hissing sound of affliction through her teeth.

"What's the matter?" I said. "Is it cold?"

She didn't say anything, she stood there waiting for me so I leaned down and pulled my trouser legs up above my knees and came out after her, the velvet laving of that water over my feet was almost unbearable, it made my heart flutter and plunge around inside of me like a scalded moth in a lampshade.

"How does it feel?" I said.

"Let's go out farther."

We waded out to the middle of our calves and then the bottom sloped up gently to the first sandbar, we could feel the coarse sand under our feet stippled like a palate. We stood there surrounded by the bay, the shore had disappeared into the darkness behind us and the light at the end of the pier was buried in the mist like a pearl, we could have been in mid-ocean, for the loneliness of it.

"I wonder what he's doing out there?" Sylvie said. "Rolling around with some mermaid, most likely."

"Why don't you leave him alone, Sylvie?" I said. "Don't you reckon you'll ever get tired of being loved like that, and just want to die in peace?"

"He's not going to die," Sylvie said. "Not while I'm alive." She sounded magnificent, that hushed insatiable fury in her voice, the starlight silvering her hair and brow and making her eyes burn in their wells of shadow like pitch, there was nothing in the world I had ever seen as voluptuous as my sister's sorrow. I reached down and dipped my hand in the water and moistened my forehead with it, it felt as cool as space.

"Do me, too," Sylvie said. So I dipped up some more

water and freshened her face with it and she shivered and pressed her cheek against my hand.

"Come on, baby, let's go home," I said.

We waded back to the shore and climbed through the fence again and went up the hill along the cliff to the house. Sylvie stretched out on the glider and I went into the house to get her a blanket. When I came out she was already asleep, lying on her side with her cheek resting on the back of one of her clasped hands like a child. I threw the blanket over her and went in and got undressed in the dark, sitting in the rush-bottomed chair in my old room across from the big double bed where Jamed was sleeping. After I got my pajamas on I lifted the sheet and crawled in beside him, it was ten thousand years since we'd lain there together in the dark and listened to the apples thump against the side of the house in the autumn gales. He stirred a little and said, "Aaron? Hey, Aaron, is Poppa out there?"

"Yeah, he's out there," I said. "But he's not in any trouble. He's all right now, Jamed."

"I sure am glad," Jamed said. He rolled over until his cheek touched my shoulder and went back to sleep. I lay there listening to his breathing grow soft and regular, feeling warmed by the mysterious and holy strength of him that even through his idiocy shone like the sun. The sound of his breath was like the whisper of a censer swinging, scattering incense on our sins, showering forgiveness on us all.

I THREW MY BAG IN THE TRUNK OF THE CAR AND SLAMMED down the lid and walked over to the kitchen steps where Momma was standing with Sylvie and the Professor.

"Well, I'll be down on the Fourth of July, Momma," I

said. "And I'm going to take you back with me, now you remember. You better be ready."

"She'll be ready," Sylvie said. "I'm going to make sure of that. There's no reason why I can't come down and take care of Jamie for a few days, so she can have a nice trip. You'll have a wonderful time in New York, Momma."

"Well, we'll see," Momma said. "Now you want to get more sleep, Aaron. You're not getting enough, I can see that by your eyes."

"I get about six hours a night," I said. "I get plenty, Momma."

"Well, I don't know about that," Momma said. "I'd feel a lot better if you were married. A man your age." I reached out and took her hands and she folded them over mine.

"I'm glad you're keeping the shop," I said.

"Well, I think it's the thing to do. Because it's where he did his work, you know. And if I should ever have to explain."

"I know. If there are any problems, now, about the insurance or anything, you just write. Or phone me. You've got the number."

"Yes."

"I don't think there will be. It all seems to be in good order."

"I'm grateful for that," she said.

"I wish you'd have Mrs. Cryer come up and stay with you. Just for a while, anyway."

"Now we've been through that. I'm going to be just fine. Did you say goodbye to Jamed?"

"Yes. He won't come out. You sure you don't want me to tell him about Poppa?"

"Well, now, what could you tell him? He knows where Poppa is, better than any of us."

"I guess so," I said. "He takes care of the doves all right?"

"Oh my, yes, I don't have to tell him about that. He never misses a time, feeding them."

The Professor had walked down to my Hertz Thrashomobile or whatever it was and was peeking in the windows, puffing on his pipe. He looked up toward me and said, "This the new fuel injection?"

"I don't know what it is," I said. "The guy told me, but I don't remember. It goes O.K."

"Why don't you write us a letter once in a while?" Sylvie said.

"I write to Momma every week," I said.

"Oh, I see. Well, screw you, too."

"Now, here," Momma said. "It seems to me the more educated you get, the more vulgar you talk. You just leave that kind of talk up there at College Park when you come home. I'll be very obliged."

"Good luck on the dissertation, Syl," I said. "You'll get it published, I'll bet."

"Oh, sure. What the world needs most right now is the message of John Skelton."

Everything was dew-wet and nude-looking in the morning light, the bay was all addled silver under the breeze. One of the doves popped out of the loft onto the door perch and stood there murmuring at the morning, fresh-minted and shining with birth like peeled birch, like a baby.

"Well, goodbye, Momma," I said. I put my arms around her and pressed my face against her hair, she smelled clean and dry like a scoured plate.

"You sure you don't want the Shakespeare book?" she said.

"No, ma'am, I don't think so."

"Well, if there's anything you want."

"Yes, ma'am." I kissed her and she laid her hand against my cheek. I held it there for a minute and then turned and walked down to the car. The Professor was standing there inspecting it with his arms folded, puffing away.

"These Chrysler people make a good product," he said.

"I guess so. Take care of Sylvie."

"I'll do my best," he said. He opened the door for me

and when I had got in, banged it closed. "She'll have her dissertation finished by spring," he said. "She'll be set, then. It's a brilliant piece of work. Nobody's ever touched Skelton that way before."

"She's a pretty smart girl," I said.

He nodded. "I'm sure she didn't tell you, but she got the highest average in her Comps of anybody who's been through the program in years."

"I can believe that. Well, so long, Professor." I shook hands with him through the window.

"Goodbye, Aaron. You've got a nice morning for flying."

I nodded and started the motor, turning to take one more look at them as I eased down the hill. Sylvie was standing with her arm around Momma, fussing at the collar of Momma's dress with her free hand. Only the Professor waved. I eased down onto the dirt road and drove without stopping up as far as the bend in front of Offutt's store, then I stopped and looked back through the window, I could see the masts of Poppa's boats tilting above the eaves of the shop and out in the middle of the creek one of his racing sloops moored to a yellow buoy, her prow pointing out toward the water of the bay. The pickup was standing in front of the shop where he had parked it for the last time, and I could almost hear the cold metal ticking as the sun touched it and the springs creaking like carnival music as we went walloping up the dirt road to Offutt's for ice cream cones on an August afternoon.

Goodbye, Poppa, I said. Let me go now, please. While you dream about our poor lives out there, have mercy on them. Let us be worthy masters of the beautiful boats you set upon the waters. Let us find in your silence the right to love in peace. Let us sail out free to found a republic of love with your blessing, under the wings of your doves, in the ships you built for our faring-forth.

A NOTE ON THE TYPE

The text of this book was set on the Linotype in Janson, a recutting made direct from type cast from matrices long thought to have been made by the Dutchman Anton Janson, who was a practicing type founder in Leipzig during the years 1668–87. However, it has been conclusively demonstrated that these types are actually the work of Nicholas Kis (1650–1702), a Hungarian, who most probably learned his trade from the master Dutch type founder Dirk Voskens. The type is an excellent example of the influential and sturdy Dutch types that prevailed in England up to the time William Caslon developed his own incomparable designs from them.

This book was composed, printed, and bound by Kingsport Press, Inc., Kinsgport, Tennessee.
Typography and binding design by Carole Lowenstein.